**Praise for *New York Times* bestselling author
Lindsay McKenna**

"McKenna provides heartbreakingly tender romantic
development that will move readers to tears. Her military
background lends authenticity to this outstanding tale,
and readers will fall in love with the upstanding hero and
his fierce determination to save the woman he loves."
—*Publishers Weekly* on *Never Surrender*

"Talented Lindsay McKenna delivers excitement and
romance in equal measure."
—*RT Book Reviews* on *Protecting His Own*

"Lindsay McKenna will have you flying with the daring
and deadly women pilots who risk their lives... Buckle in
for the ride of your life."
—*Writers Unlimited* on *Heart of Stone*

NEW YORK TIMES BESTSELLING AUTHOR

LINDSAY McKENNA

&

USA TODAY BESTSELLING AUTHOR

STELLA BAGWELL

TAMING THE RANCHER

2 Heartfelt Stories
Stallion Tamer & Home to Blue Stallion Ranch

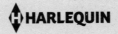 HARLEQUIN

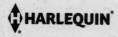

ISBN-13: 978-1-335-50837-9

Taming the Rancher

Copyright © 2023 by Harlequin Enterprises ULC

Stallion Tamer
First published in 1998. This edition published in 2023.
Copyright © 1998 by Lindsay McKenna

Home to Blue Stallion Ranch
First published in 2019. This edition published in 2023.
Copyright © 2019 by Stella Bagwell

Recycling programs for this product may not exist in your area.

For questions and comments about the quality of this book, please contact us at CustomerService@Harlequin.com.

Harlequin Enterprises ULC
22 Adelaide St. West, 41st Floor
Toronto, Ontario M5H 4E3, Canada
www.Harlequin.com

Printed in U.S.A.

CONTENTS

Lindsay McKenna is proud to have served her country in the US Navy as an aerographer's mate third class—also known as a weather forecaster. She was a pioneer in the military romance subgenre and loves to combine heart-pounding action with soulful and poignant romance. True to her military roots, she is the originator of the long-running and reader-favorite Morgan's Mercenaries series. She does extensive hands-on research, including flying in aircraft such as a P3-B Orion sub-hunter and a B-52 bomber. She was the first romance writer to sign her books in the Pentagon bookstore. Visit her online at lindsaymckenna.com.

Books by Lindsay McKenna

Shadow Warriors

The Wyoming Series

Visit the Author Profile page at Harlequin.com for more titles.

STALLION TAMER

Lindsay McKenna

To Dan York,
who's way ahead of his time, and a good friend.

Chapter 1

No! The cry careened through Jessica Donovan's head. She tossed and turned on her old brass bed, one of the few items taken from her life on the Donovan Ranch before she'd fled at age eighteen. Her blond hair swirled across her shoulders as she moved from her back to her side. The dark cloud was pursuing her again. Only this time it was even more malevolent. More threatening. She began to whimper. Her small, thin fingers spasmodically opened and closed in terror.

That black cloud reminded her of one of the torrential thunderstorms that every summer rolled across the Mogollon Rim and then across the expanse of the Donovan Ranch. Those terrifying downpours of her Arizona childhood were every bit as devastating and unrelenting as the monsoons of Southeast Asia and India, or so she'd been told. As lightning and thunder now careened and rolled through the black cloud in her dream, Jessica's breathing became shallow. Faster. Her hands curled into fists as she saw the black cloud begin to take shape.

For whatever reason, the normally lethal, roiling cloud that often chased her was now, for the first time in a year, beginning to take form. Jessica saw herself on the mesa, on the Rim, watching the bubbling cauldron of a storm racing toward her. The wind was tearing at her clothes, punching and pulling at her. Her blond hair streamed out behind her shoulders. As scared as she was, she lifted her chin and directly faced the oncoming, savage storm.

Her mother, Odula, an Eastern Cherokee medicine woman from the Wolf Clan, had not taught her to be meek or mild in the face of fear. No, Odula had always counseled Jessica to face her fears. Not to run away from them, but to work through them and stand her ground no matter what.

Jessica moaned and rolled onto her back. The storm cloud was taking on the appearance of something. An animal? A man? She expected it to be her abusive ex-husband, Carl Roman. Her heartbeat sped up as she saw the lightning stitch and lance through the black-and-green clouds. The winds began to screech like a banshee. An old memory surfaced…old and wonderful. Exhilaration momentarily wiped away the fear she could taste in her mouth. And then it slipped away from her, blotted out by the savagely moving storm.

Jessica felt as if she were going to die. It was a feeling she'd felt often in real life, while married to Carl. Was she remembering the time he'd sent her to the hospital? Tears trickled out of the corners of her eyes as she faced the storm. This time, she knew, it was going to consume her. Kill her. Oh, she'd been near death too many times already! She was tired of being afraid. Her soul was dying. She knew that. Somehow, even while caught in this nightmare, which haunted her several times each week, Jessica knew her soul was withering, dying like a beautiful flower not given enough care, love or nurturance.

The wind picked up, pummeling her bodily. Jessica's turquoise eyes widened as she watched the black clouds take shape.

It was a horse! A black horse. Her breath hitched in her throat as she watched the beautiful, threatening animal form midway up that spiraling, anvil-shaped mass towering forty thousand feet above the Mogollon Rim.

For an instant, her fear turned to awe. She saw the finely dished head of an Arabian stallion—ebony colored, his nostrils red and flaring. His eyes were black and wild. White and red foam trailed from the sides of his mouth. As the front half of his magnificent body formed out of the clouds, Jessica gave a cry of recognition. It was Gan! The Donovan Ranch Arabian stallion! Gan was the horse that her father, Kelly, had repeatedly abused, trying to beat him into submission. During one of his frequent drunken rages, Kelly had even used a whip.

Jessica sobbed. She watched as the figure of Gan developed fully in the writhing, roiling clouds. The stallion was at once beautiful and terrifying as he seemed to gallop, free at last, across the darkening sky. Jessica's hands flew to her mouth as she watched Gan's savage, primal beauty. He was big boned for an Arabian, his raw power evident in the taut muscles that rippled with each long stride he took. His black mane and raised tail flew like banners, proclaiming his freedom from man's hands—or more to the point, from Kelly Donovan's cruel hands.

Jessica felt tears streaming down her face. She began to sob harder as she watched the powerful celestial vision. Gan had wanted nothing more than to roam freely with his herd of purebred Arabian mares. Her father had always kept him in a small, eight-foot-high corral where he couldn't stretch his long limbs or truly exercise. And a stallion servicing a hundred mares a year needed exercise. Kelly had been so cruel to the stud.

During one of his drunken bouts, Kelly had won Gan in a high-stakes poker game in Reno, Nevada. Gan was brought home by Kelly to procreate black Arabian offspring. Black was a rare color and in high demand in the equine world, for there were few true black Arabians. Gan was able to throw that color eighty percent of the time. Often Kelly had lost mammoth sums with his gambling ways, but this time he'd walked away with a prize.

But what he'd won, Jessica thought as the stallion and the thunderstorm began to fade away in her dream, was trouble with a capital *T*. Kelly had expected a submissive stallion, not the fighter that Gan turned out to be. In some ways, Gan was like her—badly beaten. And like the stallion, she was bloody, but unbowed. Thanks to her mother's spirit, her nurturing, Jessica had managed to hold her head up through her disastrous marriage and successfully carry on.

It was Jessica's own sobbing that awakened her. In the early morning grayness, she opened her eyes and slowly pushed herself up into a sitting position. As she leaned forward and brought her knees up beneath the downy quilt, she placed her hands against her face and felt the wetness of spent tears on her cheeks. Her silky hair fell around her face, covering it like a curtain as she took in a deep, unsteady breath.

That dream, that nightmare...why did it haunt her still? It had since she'd gotten the call that her father had died unexpectedly in an auto accident. Lifting her chin, Jessica sniffed and reached for a tissue on the nightstand. Blowing her nose and wiping away the remnants of her tears, she gazed out the window near her bed. Her mother had been a medicine woman, and she was Odula's daughter. She had the mystery, the magic of her mother's blood running through her veins. She knew dreams were not sent without a reason. Jessica knew she had to try and understand the context of the nightmare.

Shafts of grayish dawn penetrated the Victorian lace curtains at her bedroom window. Jessica lived north of Vancouver, British Columbia. How she loved the area, having been here since age eighteen. The pristine big Douglas fir forest that surrounded her home provided a wall of safety for her. She loved the scent of the pines, and unconsciously breathed in deeply now. Even in the coldest of winters, Jessica kept her window slightly cracked to let in just a little fresh, outside air. Odula had had the same habit.

A soft smile played on Jessica's lips. In so many ways, she was the image of Odula—at least inwardly. As far as outward looks went, she wasn't. Kate and Rachel, her older sisters, had gotten her mother's black hair. Where Jessica's blond hair had come from was beyond her! It certainly wasn't in Odula's Eastern Cherokee lineage. At least her large, expressive blue eyes were her mother's gift to her. The Cherokee people were lighter skinned than other Native American tribes, and some had blue, green or hazel eyes. The Cherokee people also had brown and reddish brown hair in their genetic background, too. Odula had had ebony hair, shiny like a raven's wing in early morning light. And while Kate had Odula's dark hair, Rachel's strands had a decided reddish gold cast to them.

Jessica had to get up. Today was the day. The day she would leave Vancouver to start her long drive home. Fear struck her as she eased her slender legs from beneath the covers. The white, knee-length flannel gown she wore kept her warm against the chill of her room. Even in early May, Canadian weather was cool. In her hometown of Sedona, Arizona, it would already be in the nineties on some days, with lots of brilliant blue skies and unrelenting sunshine—unlike Vancouver, which had days of grayness interspersed with shafts of rare sunlight.

Jessica would miss her little cabin, surrounded by its massive tree guardians. Her lovely fir trees had acted as a barrier against the world. Hurriedly, she got dressed in a pair of well-worn jeans and a pale pink, long-sleeved, jersey shirt. With a colorful scarf she tied up her hair in a ponytail before heading for the warmth of her tiny kitchen to make herself some scrambled eggs and coffee.

On the maple table stood one of her favorite orchids. Spontaneously, Jessica went over and stroked one long, oval leaf, which felt like leather.

"You didn't have any nightmares, did you, Stone

Pinto?" She smiled admiringly at the lovely Phalaenopsis orchid's first blossom. Phals were known as moth orchids, their blooms looking like the outstretched wings of a very huge moth—only the orchid's colors were far more spectacular than any moth! Stone Pinto was a white Phal with violet-colored dots all over her large petals. Although it emitted no fragrance, Jessica admired the plant's incredible beauty as it graced her table. How could anyone live without an orchid in each room of the house? It was beyond Jessica, who was sensitive to the energies not only of people, but of animals and plants as well, and knew how much certain plants improved the atmosphere.

Hurrying back to the stove, she added some sprinkles of shredded cheddar cheese to her scrambled eggs and placed the lid over the skillet for a moment. She looked sadly around her small cabin. She'd lived here since her divorce, two years ago, and loved this place. So had her orchids and the other flowers she'd raised for her company, Mother Earth Flower Essences. Yes, the dream her mother had had for her daughters had really taken root in Jessica. Of the three sisters, Jessica walked most directly in her mother's medicine footsteps—but in her own unique way.

At ten o'clock she would be leaving her place of safety and moving home—back to the Donovan Ranch. It would be different this time, Jessica told herself sternly as she dished up the eggs onto a stoneware plate covered with a bright, pretty wildflower design. Very different.

A knock on her door interrupted her thoughts.

"Come in," Jessica called breathlessly. She quickly brought down another plate from the cabinet as the door opened. A young woman about five foot ten, with long black, shining hair and lively forest green eyes, entered.

"You're just in time, Moyra," Jessica said in greeting. She placed half her eggs on the other plate and beckoned her best friend to come and join her for breakfast.

"Oh," Moyra whispered, waving her long, ballerinalike hand, "you go ahead and eat, Jessica! I'll just grab a cup of coffee." She took the percolator off the stove and reached for two cups decorated in a flower design.

Jessica eyed her. "Have you *had* breakfast?"

"Well..." Moyra said in her low, purring voice, "not really, but—"

"Then sit," Jessica demanded with a flourish. "Here you are, helping me pack my orchid girls for the trip, and what kind of hostess would I be if I didn't feed my help first?"

Moyra grinned broadly and placed the steaming cups of coffee on the table. She sat down and graciously accepted a plate with half the scrambled eggs on it. "I'm going to miss you terribly," she said, picking up the fork and knife.

"I know...." Jessica felt a terrible sadness. Moyra had entered her life unexpectedly two years ago when Jessica had been in the middle of a messy and life-threatening divorce. A young woman in her thirties, Moyra had come from South America. In Jessica's eyes, she was an incredibly gifted person with a wild beauty to match her mysterious lineage. Because Moyra had been raised in the jungle of Peru, she was quite knowledgeable about orchids. She had helped the

Mother Earth company grow and become financially solvent, assisting Jessica in expanding the distribution of the healing orchid essences around the world.

"Well," Moyra prompted between bites, "you'll get on well back home. I just feel it, here in my heart."

Jessica tried to smile. "I hope you're right…." She had tried to talk Moyra into coming south with her to Arizona, but her friend had refused, saying the hot, dry weather wasn't for her. She was used to the warm, humid Amazon jungle and loved the rain, which Vancouver had a lot of. Now Jessica would be without help. She would have to train someone down at the ranch. But who? It was a real problem, because orchids needed unique care and sensitivity on the part of those who worked with them. And most people didn't have the level of sensitivity that Jessica desired.

"Besides," Moyra continued, wrinkling her long, chiseled nose, "leaving Vancouver and getting away from Carl stalking you is the best thing that has happened to you."

Glumly, Jessica nodded as she sipped her coffee. Normally, she loved this time of day, the talking and sharing that went on between her and Moyra. Each morning, Moyra would come and they'd talk over what had to be done during the day: what orders needed to be filled, which essence was to be made or what orchids carefully tended, watered or fertilized. But today Jessica felt her heart breaking.

"I had that nightmare again," she finally confided.

Moyra's eyes narrowed. "Again?"

"Yes." Jessica finished off her eggs and put the plate aside. She wrapped her slender fingers around the warm mug of coffee. "Only this time it was different...." She shared the frightening vision with Moyra.

Tossing her head, her black, long hair thick and curled with the humidity, Moyra nodded thoughtfully. "Where I come from, my people—my grandmother, who was a jaguar priestess—would say that your nightmare is telling you something. The threat of the clouds turned into a stallion. What does that mean to you?"

"Isn't that the sixty-four-thousand-dollar question?" Jessica asked with a chuckle. She sipped her coffee, wanting to prolong her last morning with Moyra as much as she could. She would miss her wisdom. Perhaps they were so close because Moyra's background paralleled her own. Her Peruvian friend came from a mixture of Indian and Castilian Spanish aristocracy. Her mother's side of the family were known to be members of the powerful and mysterious Jaguar Clan. Legend had it that those who carried the blood, the memory of once having been a deadly, powerful jaguar, could, when they wanted, go from a human form into a jaguar form in times of threat or emergency. It was called shape shifting. Jessica had only seen Moyra turn into a jaguar once, but she felt her friend's incredible energy—an energy that was very different from any other person she'd ever met. At times, Moyra's green, almond-shaped eyes, would turn a distinct yellow color when she was angry, and Jessica would almost swear she could see a jaguar overcome Moyra's human shape, could see the face of a jaguar staring back at her.

Nonsense? Maybe. Moyra had been Jessica's right hand since the divorce. And on more than one occasion, Moyra had stood up to Carl, who'd come to stalk Jessica, to harass her and hurt her. In this way, Moyra truly was a jaguar who had guarded and kept her safe. Now, where Jessica was going, there was no safety. Carl had threatened to find her and kill her— that hadn't changed. But perhaps it was time for this chapter of her life to close. A new one was certainly beginning for her. Would Carl try to follow her to Arizona? A shiver of dread wound through Jessica.

"Are you glad to be leaving? Going home?" Moyra asked as she finished off her eggs with relish.

Shrugging, Jessica sighed. "I don't know. Part of me is. I've missed my family terribly. It's like a hole in my heart that never got fixed."

"Family wounds are the worst," Moyra murmured, buttering her toast and adding orange marmalade. And then, with a husky laugh, she said, "Not that I'm one to talk!"

Jessica nodded. The air of mystery around Moyra was always intact. After two years Jessica still knew very little about why Moyra had moved to Canada. Family meant everything to her. So why didn't she go home?

Home was several places to Moyra, though. She had family in the jungle of Peru as well as in Lima, its capital. Jessica did not pry, however. Like a typical Native American, she figured if Moyra wanted to tell her something, she would share it. Otherwise, it was not on the table as a topic to be discussed.

"The only thing I've got to do this morning is put my orchids in my pickup, and then I'll be ready to go." Once Jessica had made arrangements to bring the plants across the Canadian border, she had rented a large trailer to bring the rest of her supplies—the beautiful one-ounce, cobalt blue bottles, the eyedroppers, labels and other office items that were needed. Her computer, printer and files were already packed. She had fifty orchids of different varieties and types from around the world, and they would need careful temperature and humidity control. To expose them to chilly Canadian temperatures could kill them, as most orchids could not survive below fifty-five degrees Fahrenheit. Only her truck with the cap on it would be able to transport them properly. Moyra had fixed the heater in the truck so that the warm air would flow back into the bed where the orchids would be packed.

The Peruvian woman stood up, tall, lean and graceful. She even moved like a jaguar, Jessica thought, smiling to herself. Moyra was, indeed, more jaguar than human most of the time. Maybe that's why they got along so well, hidden out in the forest, absorbing the peace and quiet of their natural paradise. But then, Jessica knew her own Cherokee blood had given her a need for such surroundings rather than the craziness and the stress of city living. She could never survive in a city! Nor could her orchids, which were quite sensitive to air pollution.

"I'll start up the truck and get the heater going," Moyra said. "We need to warm that bed area for them. I'll make sure there are no leaks so that colder air can't get back there. I've got the temperature gauge set so you can just turn your head, glance at it and know that it's in the right range for your girls." Moyra leaned over and delicately touched the Phal. "How I'm going to miss Stone Pinto. She's so lovely!"

"I know." Jessica rose and put the plates in the sink. "Worse, I'm going to miss you...."

Moyra hugged her. "I'll be around in spirit. You know that. Once a jaguar priestess adopts you into her family, you are one of us, and you come under the protection of the jaguar goddess herself." She frowned, her thin brows knitted. "And I hope Carl has the good sense not to follow you to Arizona."

"He wouldn't dare," Jessica whispered, her throat automatically closing with fear.

Moyra threw back her head and chuckled. "Ha! That poor excuse of a man would do anything! He's capable of anything." The smile disappeared from Moyra's full mouth and she studied Jessica, who was inches shorter than her. "And you, my fine, delicate wisp of a friend, need to embrace the power of your Wolf Clan. You've run from your own power all your life. You're so much your mother, and yet you're afraid of the power of the wolf." She gripped Jessica's shoulders, deadly serious now. "I ran from the Jaguar Clan for years, but don't do as I've done. Our life path is part animal, part human. We are here in this lifetime to learn to integrate both halves into ourselves so that we are whole."

"I know you're speaking the truth. I feel it here, in my heart," Jessica admitted.

"Well," Moyra growled, sounding exactly like a jaguar in that moment, "you are going home to complete the first circle of your life. Claim the Wolf Clan power that is rightfully yours. Don't keep running from it." Allowing her hands to slip from Jessica's shoulders, Moyra added primly, "That dream of Gan, the Arabian stallion, has something to do with this. I know it."

Jessica felt lost suddenly. "What am I going to do without you?"

Moyra smiled enigmatically. "My jaguar sight tells me there is a man in black who will be near you soon. He will be someone you can trust, so run to him."

Jessica eyed her jadedly. "Oh, sure, a man. My track record with men is horrible and you know it. Besides, I don't trust them anymore...."

"Carl was a mistake." Moyra closed her eyes and took a deep breath. "This man who is coming into your life is dangerous—not to you, but to himself." She continued in a low voice "I see him...swathed in black. Covered in darkness. But it's not a dangerous darkness like Carl has around him." Opening her eyes, she smiled down at Jessica. "And don't ask me any more questions because we both know that discovering the truth on your own is the only way to do it. I've said enough! I'm off to the truck. Meet me when you're ready and I'll help you load your orchid girls."

Jessica felt a heaviness in her chest and knew it was sadness at leaving Vancouver, Moyra and the many other friends she'd made here. Canada had been good for her—a home away from home. How she loved this beautiful country and its wonderfully friendly inhabitants!

Jessica's heart ached. And yet, as she finished washing, drying and packing the last of the kitchen supplies into one final box, another part of her was very excited about seeing Kate again. Their sister Rachel could not come home for a while because she had to fulfill her teaching contract at a college in England. But by December, Rachel would be moving back, too, and then what was left of the Donovan family would truly be home for the first time since their chaotic childhood.

As she carried the box outdoors, Jessica saw that the dawn had brightened, revealing a pale blue sky. She smiled. Even Canadian weather was going to bless her travels—blue sky and sunshine in early May was wonderful!

At least she wouldn't have to struggle through snow, sleet or rain on her southward journey back to the States...back to Sedona, Arizona.

Moyra had the pickup backed up to the small, glass greenhouse that housed most of her orchids. Going to the trailer, which would be hitched on afterward, Jessica packed away the final boxes. One of them contained her goose-down quilt, her most precious possession, made by her mother when Jessica was fifteen. Odula's energy, her love, her heart, was in this quilt and no matter how alone or bereft Jessica felt, even in the darkest days with Carl, she could wrap that quilt around her and feel the love and healing energy of her mother being absorbed into her battered spirit.

Closing up the trailer, her breath white and wispy, Jessica hurried to the greenhouse. Opening the door and quickly shutting it, Jessica saw that Moyra had carefully packed the orchids in plenty of newspaper and then moved them into cardboard boxes so that they wouldn't tip or fall over during the three-day trip down to Arizona. Jessica appreciated Moyra's attention to detail. Many of the orchids were just coming into bloom, their long, thin green spikes about to yield inflorescences or buds.

"Ready?" Moyra asked, looking up from the last box she'd packed with larger orchids already in bloom.

"I think so," Jessica whispered. She looked around the greenhouse. Kate had made her one exactly like this back at the ranch and it stood waiting and ready for her orchids—for her new life.

Moyra smiled gently. "Little Jessica is once again closing one chapter in her life and opening up a new one. You have to be excited."

"And scared," Jessica admitted softly, easing her arms around the first box of orchids.

Laughing, Moyra took another box and followed her out to the pickup. "Be scared, but stand in the storm of fear and walk through it, my friend."

"Spoken like a true jaguar priestess," Jessica teased, smiling over her shoulder at Moyra. The woman positively glowed with life, her green eyes sparkling mischievously. Jessica knew that Moyra was psychic. In the past, she had used her abilities to warn her when Carl was in the vicinity. Jessica had been able to call the police and avert Carl's stalking each time. She shuddered now. She didn't know what Carl would do if he got his hands on her again. For two years, ever since Moyra had magically walked into her life to become a big, cosmic guard dog of sorts, Carl had not been able to fulfill his threat that he would hunt her down and kill her if she divorced him.

They put the first boxes in the pickup, the warmth satisfactory for Jessica's orchid girls. Hurrying back and forth, both women finally got all the boxes in place and the cap closed to protect the orchids from the chill of the Vancouver morning. Then Moyra maneuvered the pickup to the trailer and they quickly hitched it up.

"There," Moyra said, rubbing her hands and grinning. "Don't look so sad, little sister. I'll be with you in spirit, looking over your shoulder. You know that."

Tears filled Jessica's eyes as she looked up at Moyra. "You've been a true sister to me. I don't know what I'd have done without you, Moyra. Really, I don't feel like it's been a fair exchange. You've given me so much and been such a wonderful role model for me—"

"Hush, sister. You are going home to reclaim your power.

"You know, a shaman is always most powerful where she was born. You are a long way from your source of empowerment. Go home. Don't be afraid." Moyra moved closer and placed her hands on Jessica's small, slumped shoulders. "Listen carefully, Jessica. I see much." Her fingers dug more deeply into Jessica's shoulders. "You are in great danger. You will be tested once you reach home. In order to survive this test, you *must* embrace your power. If you don't…" Moyra looked upward, tears in her eyes. "But I know you will. You are a frightened little shadow of your true self. There is a man clothed in black who will help you, guide you, if you allow him to."

"I don't *trust* men!"

"I know that. Carl has hurt you so deeply, he's wounded your spirit, Jessica…but this man, whoever he is, can help you heal at a soul level." She gave Jessica a gentle shake, her voice turning raw with emotion. "Your test is twofold, my sister. You must face your fear head-on and you must learn to trust men again. Neither is an easy task, but you are the daughter of a medicine woman. You must learn to embrace your inherited power from her, and become it. If you do this, your life will be spared. But you will be in danger.

Just embrace your wolf senses—your exquisite hearing, your sense of smell—and remain on guard...."

"Sometimes I wish you wouldn't speak symbolically," Jessica said with a little laugh, taking Moyra's hands into hers. "Sometimes I wish you'd just spit it out."

Moyra grinned. Her laugh was a husky purr. "I was raised by my grandmother, an old jaguar priestess. I was taught at an early age to discern and not say too much. Life is a process of discovery, little sister, and it's not my right to take that way from you." She hugged her fiercely and then released her. "Go, Jessica. Drive toward your new life. Trust this man in black. Open your heart to him. See what happens."

Jessica nodded and climbed slowly into the pickup. The sun was just edging the tops of the spruce, making the sky look like a crown of pure, white light surrounding the small meadow where they stood. "And you? What of you? Where will you be?"

Moyra smiled sadly. "I must go home to Peru now, little sister. My people have called me home."

"Which ones? The Jaguar Clan or your family?" She started the engine, her heart already crying for the loss of her friend. Jessica knew that she'd probably never see Moyra again—except in her dreams, where the jaguar ruled night journeys of all kinds.

With a laugh, Moyra said, "One and the same."

"Stay in touch?"

"I will see you on the Other Side."

Jessica blinked back her tears. "Okay.... I love you, Moyra. You're like a fourth sister to me. You know that."

"Yes, and you've helped heal my heart, you know."

Moyra's voice became choked. "You gave me a place to heal, Jessica, whether you knew it or not. You taught me about the goodness, the positiveness of family once again. I needed that. In your own way, you are a great healer." Moyra motioned to the orchids in back of the vehicle. "And look what you do for thousands of people around the world who buy your orchid essences. Look how many you heal in that way. Go, my little sister. Drive toward your destiny. I must go to mine now. I promise, I'll be in touch...."

The driveway blurred in front of Jessica as she put the truck in gear and drove away, leaving behind her cloistered, safe existence. The sunlight glared brightly down on the rutted dirt road. She drove slowly and carefully, not wanting to jar her orchid girls. Sniffing, she wiped her eyes on the sleeve of her shirt. Fumbling for her dark glasses, she put them on. In the rearview mirror, she saw Moyra standing so proud and tall. And then she saw her form change—suddenly a jaguar with a gold coat covered with black spots stood in her place. Blinking the tears away, Jessica almost slammed on the brakes. Blinking once more, she saw Moyra again in human form.

Jessica was grateful that her mother had called Moyra from South America to be her guardian for these past two years, since her divorce from Carl. Jessica knew her mother could use her power from the Other Side. Odula had embraced her Wolf Clan power, but she herself was afraid of it.

And what about this man in black? Jessica shook her head and paid attention to the winding road. The greenhouse and the log cabin disappeared one final time as she drove around the curve that would take her to the asphalt highway—that would take her home. Her real home.

Fear warred with expectation and joy. Jessica had felt little joy in her life—except when she worked with her orchid girls and made the essences. There she was free—like Gan, the black Arabian stallion—to run wildly without fear. She examined her dream of the night before. A man in black...who was that?

Suddenly, Jessica felt a trickle of hope—something she'd not felt in a decade. Hope had been torn from her the day she'd fled from the Donovan Ranch. Now, miraculously, she felt it coming back—a small tendril of flame, so tiny and weak—yet it was there. Yes! Taking in a deep, shaky breath, Jessica absorbed that wonderful feeling. Just thinking about this mysterious "man in black" lifted her wounded spirits. Maybe, just maybe, as Moyra had said, she was going home to face her old fears, to try to work through them and walk out the other side, healed—finally. With the help of this man in black....

Chapter 2

The darkness gripped Dan Black's belly, twisting his fear into pain. Sweat trickled down from his furrowed brow, running into his eyes and making them sting. The low, husky voice of Ai Gvhdi Waya, Walks with Wolves, trembled through the darkness of the sweat lodge where Dan sat. Ai Gvhdi Waya was an Eastern Cherokee medicine woman who lived up on the Navajo reservation where he'd been born, thirty years ago. She wasn't Navajo, but she was known to be one of the most powerful healers on the res. He focused on her now as she poured ladle after ladle of cooling water on the red-hot lava rocks making them glow eerily through the steam. Why the hell had he come here? Why had he thought this would help?

The pain knotted in his stomach. The heat was building. Her voice was low, powerful and searching. His fear heightened. Squeezing his eyes shut, he tried to control the fear. Wasn't that why he'd come? To walk through his fear, not control it? He'd been taught that fear was not to be ignored or denied. By walking through it, feeling it, allowing it to consume him, he would be healed.

He felt anything but healed. He was scared to death. Death...yes, how many times had he faced that horrible possibility? It hurt to admit he had a fear of dying. Dan hadn't realized the depth of his fear until he'd gone over with his marine reconnaissance unit during the swift-moving Gulf War. Desert Storm had been a living, fiery hell for him—externally as well as internally. *No!* He shook his head, moving his long, roughened fingers along the hard curves and lines of his sweaty face. He tried to wipe away the bubbling fear that was snaking up his gullet.

The medicine woman stopped singing. Dan opened his eyes. He could not see her in the sweat lodge, the darkness was so complete. So terrifying. All he saw was the vague outline and shape of glowing red rocks. He centered all his attention on them. He had to or he was going to scream. And then what would she think of him?

"You are frightened, Dan Black."

Her voice sounded like a bullhorn over his head. Dan instantly jerked upright. It was as if Ai Gvhdi Waya was leaning over him, talking directly into his right ear. Automatically, he moved his right arm outward, but the space was empty. Though he was sitting opposite the door she sat next to, he could not see her at all.

"Tell me of your fear."

His throat closed. He felt the penetrating heat of the steam burning the back of his shoulders and neck. His flesh prickled and he cried out, feeling another type of pain.

"Fear is walking around you. I see you clothed in black. Are you going to become your namesake?"

"No..." Though Black was an honored name on the Navajo reservation and there were many branches of the family, Dan's mother had done the unthinkable—she'd wed an Anglo schoolteacher. Dan was a half-breed, and he'd been mercilessly teased about it as he'd gone through the school system on the res. He'd regained his honor among his family by becoming a tamer of horses. Horses were still a powerful, moving force on this reservation today.

"Sometimes we take on a name to walk through it. How far into your journey are you?"

Dan closed his eyes. "It's so dark I can't see daylight at either end," he rasped, forcing the words between his thinned lips.

She threw more water onto the rocks. The hissing and spitting threw up more billowing, steamy clouds into the closed, confined space. "There are people who have a black heart. You are not one of those. I see your heart in pieces, but it is not dark. It is bleeding. You do not have a black spirit, but I see your spirit clothed in darkness, instead."

Was there any good news? Dan felt his heart pumping wildly in his chest. The heat scored his flesh. The sweat ran in rivulets from his head down across his naked body to the white towel he wore around his waist. He dug his fingers into the earthen floor he sat upon. There was something soothing about the red sand. He'd been born on this red desert, in a hogan in Monument Valley, a hundred miles from the nearest hospital. It was one of the most sacred places on the res. The medicine woman in attendance at his birth had proclaimed him a light among his people.

Some light. His last name was Black. And he was clothed in darkness. His spirit sagged. He felt so damned alone, so afraid and unable to help himself. Maybe part of it was his own fault. He never reached out and asked for help because of his childhood on the res as a half-breed. The Navajo children had tortured him daily at school because of his lighter skin and gray eyes. He had black hair like they did, but that was where similarities ended. They said his eyes looked colorless, like those of a predatory owl. And owls were not looked upon kindly in Navajo cosmology. No, they were the symbol of death.

"I'm dying…." he managed to say, his voice low and terribly off-key.

"Sometimes, in order to move forward, a part of us must die. Cut out the old. Let it go and die. And then you will have space for something new, something better, to take its place."

He wished she wouldn't speak in such riddles. But then, all medicine people did. His head was swimming with terror, with trying to control the pain in his stomach. He was overcome with the same fear he'd felt over in the Gulf War when— Instantly, Dan slammed his mind shut, obliterating that scene.

"Look into the stones. The stone people talk to us in many ways," she directed in a low voice.

Eagerly, Dan focused his smarting eyes on the red-colored rocks in the fire pit. Any attempt to take the focus off his terror and pain was worth doing. The clouds of steam came and went. For a moment, he thought he saw the shape of a face in the glowing rocks. And then it vanished. Was he seeing things? His Anglo side pooh-poohed this stuff. His Navajo side was starved for it. Which to believe? Was he hallucinating or did he truly see a woman's face in those rocks?

"There is a woman coming."

Dan's breath hitched. He snapped a look across the blackness to where Ai Gvhdi Waya was sitting. She saw it too? Then he wasn't delusional? Holding his breath, he waited and prayed that the medicine woman would say more.

"Look again."

Disappointed, he shifted his gaze back to the rocks. She poured more water on them. It was so hot now, so strangling with humidity that Dan thought he was going to die for lack of cool, clean oxygen. Everything was becoming claustrophobic to him—again. A new fear, the fear of being in too tight a place, raced through him.

Concentrate!

He had to concentrate or he would begin sobbing.

His gaze fell to the red rocks, where clouds of mist swirled and moved. He blinked, trying to get the stinging sweat out of his eyes in order to see the rocks better. Would he see the woman's face more clearly this time? It had been so vague before.

There!

He gasped.

Yes! It was her—again. Only this time, the face was far more distinct. Its outline wavered in the clouds and heat rising off the rocks. An oval face. He saw huge blue eyes staring back at him—blue like the turquoise color of the endless sky that blanketed his beloved Southwest. The expression in them tugged directly at his heart. He felt a strange spasm there and the sensation was so real that he automatically rubbed his chest. The feeling continued. There was more pain as he felt something opening inside him like a rusted door that had never been opened before.

Gasping, Dan felt his breath leaving him. He clung to the vision of her face, wavering inches above the heated stones in thick, misty clouds of steam. Pain surged outward, like ripples from a pebble thrown into a quiet pond, each one a wavelet of more intense agony. The sensation continued inside his heart and tripled as it moved outward, expanding rapidly across his chest.

"Release it!"

Ai Gvhdi Waya's order came as a physical blow, her voice low and snarling. His hand fell from his chest and he straightened up and tipped his head back, gulping for air as the knifelike sting continued to ripple outward across his chest. He was having a heart attack. Dan was sure he was going to die.

"Lie down!"

It didn't take much for him to do that. He practically fell over, feeling the warmth of the sand on the side of his face, arm and lower body. Air! There was cooler air near the bottom of the sweat lodge. He gulped it greedily, his breath ragged.

"Let the pain continue."

He couldn't have stopped it if he'd tried. Rolling helplessly onto his back, he dug his fingers deep into the red sand on either side of him. The pain deepened and felt like a red-hot brand now, centered in his heart region. Oh, no, he *was* going to die! The air in his lungs was shallow and he was unable to get enough oxygen because it hurt so much to breathe.

Suddenly, Dan felt a swirling sensation around his head, and then it moved down, inch by inch, across his body. The more he became enveloped in this cloud, the less of a coherent hold he had on reality. Somewhere in the distance, he heard Ai Gvhdi Waya beginning another song. He tried to hold on to her voice, to where he was, but found it was impossible.

There was a deep, snapping, cracking feeling emanating from within him. He not only felt it, but distinctly heard it. It sounded like good crystal being smashed with a hammer. Almost instantly, he closed his eyes and he felt himself become featherlight. He was drifting in the darkness, but he had no idea where. The need for breath no longer mattered. He wasn't breathing, he realized, but he was still alive. Or was he? Dan was no longer sure. Miraculously, he no longer felt the fear from the Gulf War. No, he felt an incredible sense of peace—and love.

Shaken by the experience, he allowed himself to move. At times, he felt like a leaf that had fallen off a tree and was gently wafting on an invisible breeze. There was a rocking motion to his weightlessness, reminiscent of a cradle. It was nurturing. Supportive. How wonderful it felt not to be pursued by the demons from hell that had lived within him twenty-four hours a day since the war. He breathed in a sigh of absolute relief.

And then he realized that this was what death must feel like—a warm, embracing cocoon that made him feel like an infant swaddled in a blanket, lovingly held. Held by what, he wasn't sure, and his mind wasn't functioning all that well to ask or to care. Little by little, he thought he saw a grayness somewhere above him. It seemed as if he were moving upward, slowly but surely, toward that emanation of light.

Dan watched in awe as the blackness changed to gray, and then transformed into an incredible gold-and-white light that surrounded him. He should have been blinded by it, but wasn't. Instead, it embraced him, cradled him and held him in a loving security he'd never known before. How he liked being in this place! There was no fear, only an incredible sense of being loved for who he was—faults and all. There were no judgments in this place, only an incredible sense of nurturance. Perhaps this was what white man's heaven was all about.

Out of the light, colors began to congeal. Sometimes they would disappear, but they'd always return, more vibrant than before, eventually taking the shape of a blossom. He had no idea what kind of flower he was looking at. It was white with purple spots all over it.

The apparition danced and moved slowly in front of him, and then it faded. In its place he saw the most beautiful turquoise blue he'd ever seen. In this reality, wherever it was, colors were more vibrant, more dramatic and pure than what he saw with his physical eyes.

The blue color began to take the shape of a set of large, wide eyes. Beautiful eyes, Dan thought as he clung to the gentle love that seemed to emanate from them. And then he began to see the rest of a face fill in around those eyes—the same face he'd seen in the fire. Only this time the vision—of a lovely woman about his own age—was very clear and unmistakable. She had long, straight blond hair that shone like precious gold in sunlight. Her face was oval, her lips full and delicate. Dan didn't know which of her features he liked better. She was smiling, and the fact sent his heart skittering with unaccustomed joy.

He watched as she raised her small, stubborn chin and laughed, her pink lips curving deliciously. The sound of her laughter reminded him of angels singing. It was soft, low, and held such love and nurturing that it brought tears to his eyes. He felt the heat of his tears mingling with the sweat that ran across his face and body in rivulets.

And then her face began to fade. *No!* He tried to call out to her, but he had no voice. His chest region was throbbing with warmth now, not pain. The light began to fade and he felt himself being pulled rapidly back into the cloistered blackness once again. This time he didn't fight it. He surrendered totally to it because he knew he was safe and loved.

The spinning began again, sharp and violent. Within seconds, he felt heaviness. He was in his body once more. He could feel the sand he still gripped beneath his fingers, could hear the ending of the song Ai Gvhdi Waya sang, could feel the prickling heat against his taut flesh and the endless streams of sweat washing off of him.

"You have returned."

He lay there in awe. Dan had no idea how long his journey into the other world had taken. He'd never had such an experience before—ever. But then, he had never sought out the help of a medicine person, either. He'd always gone the Anglo route when it came to medicine, rather than rely on his Navajo heritage. Maybe he should have come long ago, he thought wearily. He moved his hand across his chest where an intense, branding warmth still throbbed. There was no pain, just a wonderful feeling of joy. What had happened? What had the medicine woman done? And who was the woman he'd seen in his vision?

"Come out when you want," Ai Gvhdi Waya instructed as she threw open the blanketed door. "Go to the hot springs down the path, wash off and dress. Then come see me at my hogan."

Dan felt incredibly tired, as if his body weighed twice what it should, and he was thirsty, too. It was probably dehydration, the loss of water during the hour-long sweat lodge ceremony. As his mind slowly began to function again, he felt the grit of the sand on his naked back. It felt familiar, comforting. He watched as the medicine woman, who was dressed in a faded cotton shift, crawled out of the sweat lodge and then got to her feet. Outside the door, the sun was shining brightly, the shafts of light piercing the darkness of the lodge.

Closing his eyes, Dan gasped for the cooling air moving into the heated, humid confines. Air! Fresh air. All he could do was lie there and allow his weakened body to recuperate. His mind spun with questions and no answers. Emotionally he felt lighter. The fear was less. Why? What had the medicine woman done to make it so? The questions drove him to sit up and then weakly crawl out on his hands and knees.

The midafternoon May heat moved across the red desert as he stood up on unsteady legs. Rewrapping the white towel low on his hips, Dan picked up his clothing and cowboy boots and headed down a well-worn path toward the hot springs behind Ai Gvhdi Wa-ya's hogan. In the distance, he heard the familiar and soothing sounds of bleating sheep. Right now, he just concentrated on putting one step in front of the other.

At the springs, a natural well of hot water surrounded by smooth red sandstone guardians, Dan lay with his head on a stone that served as a pillow and felt the healing effects of the water on his body. His mother would be proud of him—going to see a medicine person. His father would have told him to see a psychotherapist—which Dan had many times.

Oddly, his fear remained at a distance from him. Before, he'd anesthetized the fear with alcohol. That had gotten him into a lot of trouble, too. When he was drunk, he was violent. He'd spent some time in the Coconino jail in Flagstaff. He'd recently gotten fired from his job on a ranch, where he'd been the head horse wrangler. Alcohol had made his fear lessen, so that he could continue to function in the world. His mother cried and begged him to seek help of her medicine people.

A tired half smile tugged at Dan's mouth. He lifted his head and knew it was time to climb out, dry off and get dressed. Well, he hadn't been much of a prize to his family, had he? He'd shamed them repeatedly. Now his name was mud. Any honor he'd gained for being one of the best horse wranglers they'd ever seen was now destroyed. It had hurt to see his mother cry when she visited him in that damned jail. It made him angry when his father did nothing but castigate him and tell him to go to a shrink to get cured.

Dan had disappointed them. Shamed them in front of the rest of his large, extended family. Gossip was one of the worst habits Navajos had, and there was plenty about Dan Black, the "black sheep" of the family, and his crazy ways. He was shunned by his own people. Well, why not? Since returning from the Gulf War six years ago, he'd pretty much made a disaster of his life.

Before going into the marines, he'd had a good job on a ranch near Flag. He'd joined the marines because his father had been one. Dan had wanted his dad to be proud of him. And he was, until Dan was sent to the Gulf, where all hell broke loose. He'd come back broken not only in body, but in spirit. His mother had pleaded with him to walk the Navajo way and get his spirit healed. His father had said that in time his fear would go away and that he didn't need help from some medicine person.

Why the hell didn't he listen more to his mother? Dan thought as he got out of the spring and quickly dried off in the ninety-degree, midday heat. He donned his light blue, short-sleeved shirt, his faded jeans, and settled a dusty, black felt Stetson on his head. Sitting down, he pulled on his socks and badly scuffed cowboy boots. The boots looked like how he'd felt before coming to this incredibly powerful medicine woman.

Standing, he stretched his arms toward Father Sky. The blueness of the sky reminded him of this unknown woman's turquoise eyes filled with such loving warmth. Just remembering the vision of those eyes caused his heart to expand with joy. It took him off guard. What was going on? What was happening to him? Maybe the medicine woman could tell him. Dan hurried up the slope, looking for answers that would explain his vision.

As he rounded her hogan, Dan saw Ai Gvhdi Waya with a white man. Word had gotten around that she was living with an Anglo named Dain Phillips. Gossip had it that he was very, very rich. If he was, Dan didn't see it. The tall, intense-looking man stood near a beat-up old blue pickup that looked a lot like his own—in dire need of a paint job and some bodywork. He saw Ai Gvhdi Waya reach up and kiss him quickly on the mouth. She was once again dressed in familiar Navajo clothes: a long-sleeved red velvet blouse and a dark blue cotton skirt that hung to her ankles. Her hair was in two thick braids, tied at the ends with feathers and red yarn.

Dan stood near the door to the hogan, his eyes averted. But he hadn't missed the love for Ai Gvhdi Waya shining in the Anglo's eyes. Dan wondered if he'd ever find a woman who made him feel that way. So far, his luck with life in general, not to mention women, was pretty bad. He supposed it had something to do with that curse of darkness that surrounded him. When he was growing up on the res, the children had always teased him that his skin was lighter because the copper color had faded away due to the blanket of darkness wrapped around him since birth. And because of this owl darkness, his skin seemed lighter to those who looked at him. Dan hated that explanation. He'd fought repeatedly to defend his honor throughout the twelve years of schooling here. Fighting didn't come naturally to him. No, he'd rather work with horses, to feel in tune with their wild, free spirits, than take on the school bully.

"You feel lighter."

Dan lifted his head, suddenly realizing he was staring down at his dusty, booted feet. Ai Gvhdi Waya stood directly in front of him, no more than six feet away. He looked past her and saw that the Anglo had driven away in the pickup, down the rutted dirt road. Shaking his head, Dan rasped; "I don't know what's happening."

"Come in. You need to drink water."

Her hand felt comforting on his arm. He liked this woman, her quiet power, her ability to soothe him and make him feel decent and not ashamed. "Thanks," he mumbled, and followed her into the cooling comfort of her hogan.

He always felt at home in the hogan, an eight-sided structure made of mud and logs. The door faced east, to welcome Father Sun as he rose each morning. The odor of sage filled his nostrils and he saw that some was burning slowly in an abalone shell on top of the old pine table. She gestured for him to sit down at the table while she went to the kitchen counter and poured two large glasses of water.

"Thanks," he said sincerely as she handed him the glass. Dan drank the contents quickly, his body eager to replace what he'd lost in the sweat. She placed a pitcher of water between them and he poured himself a second and third glass before he was satiated. When he was finished, he sat opposite her at the table, the tendrils of sage smoke drifting upward and spreading out across the hogan. Sage, for the Navajo, was purifying and healing. Whenever he got a cold or flu, Dan would make sage tea and drink quarts of it to flush and cleanse his body. It always worked.

"Tell me what you saw in your journey," Ai Gvhdi Waya urged softly.

He took off his hat and set it on the table. "You'll probably think I'm crazy." He tried to smile, but failed miserably. "Everyone else thinks I am, anyway...."

She smiled gently. "One person's craziness is another's sanity. So who is sane and who is really crazy?"

He laughed a little and tried not to feel so uncomfortable. "Listen, this is my first time with a medicine person. I didn't know what to expect."

"Expect nothing. Receive everything."

He stared at her, more of the tension draining from him.

"You've been called crazy by many, but you are not. Your spirit is sensitive. Things that wouldn't wound others wound you. The road you walk, Dan Black, is a hard one." She closed her eyes and gestured with her hands. "I see a man walking with one foot on one road, an asphalt one. And then I see him walking with the other foot on the good red road of our people." She opened her eyes and smiled a little. "You carry the blood of two worlds in your body. You are *heyoka,* a contrary. You must learn to blend these two paths you walk into one road and then make it your road."

"Easier said than done," he muttered.

"One path is that of a warrior, the other of a healer. A warrior healer. You have tasted and done both. But neither is comfortable with the other. Your spirit hungers for the touch of our mother, the earth. And for her living things. Today I saw horses surrounding you. I knew of your reputation before you came here—of being one of our best horse wranglers. Horses are important to you. They are part of your healing. Stay with them."

He nodded. "Yeah, I just got a job down at the Donovan Ranch. The ranch foreman gave me a chance. He knew I was a—that I drank too much...."

"Yes." She nodded. "I know him. Sam McGuire is a good man. He will give you the chance you deserve."

Earnestly, Dan met and held her sympathetic gaze. "Look, I came to you to try and stop this fear. That's why I drank. I had to make it go away somehow...it was the only way."

"Not the right way and you know that, Dan."

Grudgingly, he nodded. "My father calls me an alcoholic. My mother cries for me all the time. I had to do something."

Reaching out, the medicine woman closed her workworn hand over his. "Listen carefully, stallion tamer. You drink to run from the pain you received while being a warrior. There is only one way out of this and that is to walk through it. Alcohol will not cure you. Only your heart's desire to do this for yourself will cure you." She lifted her hand, all the while her gaze holding his.

"I know... I agree," Dan rasped.

"The path you walk is a hard one. There is no disagreement on that. The Great Spirit gives you the strength you need to walk it. All you have to do is surrender to a power higher than yourself and trust what you know instinctively. You use it to tame the mustangs. Why not use it on yourself?"

Dan watched her smile. It reminded him of the coyote, the trickster. He smiled a little, too. "I'm going to try. I've got to save my family's reputation. This is tearing my mother apart. I don't mean to hurt her—I really don't...."

"I understand," Ai Gvhdi Waya soothed. Tilting her head slightly, she asked, "What else did you see in your vision?"

Shaken, he stared at her. "You saw it, too?"

"Yes, but I want to hear in your words what you saw and experienced."

Dan took a deep breath, and, risking everything, told her the details of the vision. She nodded wisely now and then, as if to corroborate his story. Little by little, he didn't feel so foolish. By the time he finished, Dan felt oddly comfortable. He wondered if everyone had such visions in a sweat lodge, but didn't ask.

"What do you make of it?" he asked instead.

She shrugged. "It's more important what you make of it."

Quirking his mouth, he leaned back and tilted the chair onto its rear legs. "I knew you were going to say that."

Ai Gvhdi Waya laughed deeply. "It is your life, your interpretation of events, that counts. What I think about it is unimportant compared to how you feel, how you respond to what you saw."

Nodding, Dan looked up at the earthen ceiling. His voice dropped. "I feel lighter, almost happy...expectant that something good is coming my way—finally. I don't know this woman I saw. I've never seen eyes like hers. She's so beautiful...like a dream I might have. And the flower...it was white and purple. I've never seen anything like it, either." He shifted his gaze to her. "Do you know this flower?"

"No. I've never seen one like that."

Shrugging, Dan eased the chair downward. He placed his hands on the table and folded them. "A woman and a flower. Got me."

"And what did you feel when you saw this woman's face?"

He gave a shy grin. "A lot of things."

The medicine woman smiled back. "Your heart opened. By just seeing her face, some of your injured heart was healed. It is no longer as fragmented. Do you have the feeling that she could heal your heart?"

Dan felt telltale heat creep into his face. That was one of his flaws—blushing. "Yeah... I think she could—"

"No," Ai Gvhdi Waya admonished, "stop saying 'I think' and switch to saying 'I feel'. You must disconnect from that Anglo head of yours and move down to the true center of your being, which is your Navajo heart. There you feel and you *know*. You can know without knowing why you know." She smiled enigmatically. "Your father is Anglo. Anglos think too much. They think only their brain has answers. That is not true. Our heart is our only true voice. You use your heart when you break and train horses. Why not use it *all the time* with regard to yourself? Switch off your thinking. Not all of life is logical. And reality?" She laughed deeply once again. "The Anglo mind sees only what it can weigh, measure or perceive with these two things we call eyes." She pointed to her own eyes. "There are many other realities. When you're with a wild horse, you move into his or her reality, don't you? You are no longer a human, a two-legged. You become like a four-legged, a shape-shifter. You become the horse to feel him, his fears or whatever, don't you?"

Dan had never thought of what he did in those terms, but looking at it her way, he had to nod his head. "Yes," he said slowly, "something does happen, but I couldn't tell you what, or how it happens."

"That," Ai Gvhdi Waya said firmly, "is your skill, your power. That is what you need to embrace twenty-four hours a day. I call it your flow. It is a flow of life. If you can get into it and stay in it, life becomes one unfolding miracle after another. If you will try to stay in your flow, this woman with the flower will come into your life."

He chuckled. "I wish. I'd be happy just to see her now and then in my dreams." Instead of his terrifying nightmares, he thought, but didn't say it.

The medicine woman rose. "Become more aware of what feelings and sensations you have when you work with the wild horses. And then start to feel them in other situations. Watch what happens."

Dan stood and placed the black cowboy hat on his head. He'd brought fifty dollars' worth of groceries to the medicine woman in exchange for her help. He wished he had more, but he was broke—as usual. "I don't know how to thank you...."

"You can thank me by getting into your flow." She led him out of the hogan and walked him to his rusty white pickup. In the back was all his horse-training equipment and other meager belongings. He would head down to the Donovan Ranch and be there by sunset.

Entering the pickup, Dan tipped his hat in her direction. She stood six feet away, with a white wolf now at her side. There was an ethereal presence to this medicine woman; an inner beauty and power resonated from her person. Dan was in awe of her, and he was grateful. As he drove away from the hogan, the woman's face, the one with the incredible turquoise eyes, seemed to hover like a mist in front of him. He shook his head. He had to concentrate on his driving or he'd end up stuck in one of these sandy washes.

Today, he thought, *is the first day of my life. My new life.* In a sense, he felt reborn by the experience in the sweat lodge. He also knew Ai Gvhdi Waya saw a lot more than she was telling him, but then, she was right: his personal discovery of his own process was far more empowering to him than her just telling him. He understood her reasoning.

Dan knew this was his last chance at a good job—a way to salvage his family's name. The foreman at the Donovan Ranch was giving him a break when he deserved none. His first order of business was to tame a black Arabian stallion known as Gan. *Gan* was an Apache word for devil. From what the foreman had said, Gan hated humans, and had been badly abused by his alcoholic owner. Dan's fingers tightened momentarily on the steering wheel. In front of him rose the red sandstone buttes that were scattered over the red desert of the Navajo res. It was a beautiful sight, one that Dan never got tired of looking at.

Hadn't he been abused daily by his schoolmates when he was growing up? Been called names? Been shunned? He'd always had to defend himself. And how many fights had he lost? How many times had he come home with a black eye or a bloody face? Or worse, a broken hand or nose? Navajo children were not kind to one who did not fit their concepts. Dan wasn't a fighter. All he wanted was peace. So why the hell had he joined the marines and gone into the warrior branch, the Recon Marines? He knew now that he'd been trying to make his father accept him. It hadn't been the right choice.

No, Ai Gvhdi Waya was right—he had to stand in his power as a horse trainer and not always be apologizing for not being a teacher, as his father wanted to be, or the marine Dan had once tried to be for his father's sake. He had to find himself and like himself for what he was. Or else the man clothed in darkness would become a homeless person on some cold street of Flagstaff, looking for handouts, for money to go buy his next bottle of whiskey.

The alternative was no alternative at all to Dan. Somehow, he *had* to save his own life. This was his last chance and he knew it. And the woman with the flower was part of his healing. Did she exist? Would he be blessed by getting to meet her in physical reality? He fervently prayed that it would be so.

Chapter 3

"Welcome home!" Kate cried as Jessica parked her truck in front of the main ranch house and got out. The midday sun beat down as her older sister took the steps two at a time to get to her. Though she was tired and stressed out, Jessica rallied and gave Kate a big smile in return.

"Oh!" she cried, throwing her arms around her tall, lean sister. "It's so good to see you, Katie!" She basked in the love that emanated from Kate, before she finally stepped away.

"I don't mean to be in a hurry here, Katie, but my girls, my orchids..." She pointed to the rear of her pickup. "They've got to have a cooler temperature or they're going to die!"

Sam McGuire, the foreman, came out of the house. He grinned and tipped his hat respectfully to Jessica.

"Did I hear a call for help? Welcome home, Jessica. Kate couldn't sleep at all last night because she was so excited about your coming home today."

"Hi, Sam," Jessica whispered, and hugged the tall, strapping Arizona cowboy. "It's great to be home. Where did you put the greenhouse you and Kate built for my girls? I have to get them into it pronto or they're going to die of heat prostration." Jessica quickly pushed a wisp of blond hair away from her brow. She saw the love in Sam's eyes when he and Kate shared a warm look. If only she could someday find a man like Sam—who loved her, warts and all.

Sam put his arm around Kate's shoulder and pointed to the house that stood to the left of the main ranch house. "That's your new home, Jessica, over there. I'll drive your truck around and back it up to the greenhouse door. Kate put on the humidifier, and the temperature was reading eighty-five just about half an hour ago."

Relieved, Jessica nodded. "That's wonderful. Thanks so much, Sam."

He brushed past her and drove the pickup around to the other side of the cottonwood-enclosed main house.

Jessica gazed up at her sister. "You look so happy, Katie. Love really does work, doesn't it?"

Kate nodded and said softly, "Sam is wonderful. I'm afraid that it's all a dream and that I'll wake up someday and be without him," she confided as she put her arm around Jessica's shoulders and guided her toward her new home.

"Pshaw. Sam isn't some dream. Judging by the way he was looking at you, he's never going to leave under any circumstances," Jessica responded. It felt so good to have Kate's tall, lean body against hers. "Boy, to tell you the truth, Katie, I'd sure like to find a guy like Sam, but my record isn't so good in that department."

Kate touched Jessica's flyaway blond hair. The ninety-degree weather in early May was sending waves of heat across the canyon floor, where the ranch headquarters sat. "Give yourself time. Carl was a real bastard. Not all men are that way."

"I'm worried, Kate. Carl might try to follow me here. He threatened to hunt me down and kill me. I seem to have a curse. All I pick are abusive types."

"Is it any wonder? Kelly was abusive to us. That's all we know." Kate sighed. "And as for Carl following you here, if he has any brains at all, he won't."

Jessica looked up into Kate's face, which was darkly tanned despite the fact that she wore a straw cowboy hat today to protect her skin and shade her eyes. "Then tell me how you ended up with Sam. He's certainly not an 'abuser' type."

Mystified, Kate shrugged her shoulders. "I don't know, Jessica. I really don't." And then she grinned down at her. "You tell me. You're our little spiritual sister out here in the desert wilderness."

Jessica chuckled as they rounded the corner of the ranch house. About three hundred feet away was a beautiful cream-colored, Santa Fe adobe home. It was one of three houses that Odula had insisted be built for her daughters. Kelly had built them, but he'd been angry about doing so. In Odula's world, children not only were raised together, they lived in close proximity to one another even after they were grown. Jessica remembered how Kelly had railed at spending what little money they had on building these homes. Sadly she recalled how their mother had wanted her daughters to stay on after high school, but it had been impossible with Kelly's continual drinking and abusive behavior toward them.

"The house..." Jessica said with a sigh. "You've given it a new coat of paint!" A thrill went through her. Home! She was really home—and it felt so good! A bubbling joy kept moving up through her and expanding her heart until she was breathless from it. Not until this moment had Jessica realized just how much she'd missed her family.

"Actually," Kate murmured, releasing Jessica and opening the gate in the white picket fence, "our new wrangler, Dan Black, just finished painting it."

"Oh, you've got help finally."

Kate grimaced. "We're not in any financial shape to be paying anyone yet, Jessica. Sam knows Dan Black. He's part Navajo and part Anglo. Got a real chip on his shoulder, but Sam said he was good at breaking and training horses. And he's going to be working at taming Gan." Kate moved to the front door and opened it for Jessica with a flourish. "Welcome home, little sis."

Jessica stepped into the much cooler environment of the house. It was empty, but the colorful flower-print curtains on the windows made tears come to her eyes. "Oh, Katie, it's beautiful. I'd forgotten how much I'd come to love this house after Kelly built it." She wiped tears from her eyes as she looked around. Happiness deluged her.

"Grudgingly built," Kate reminded her grimly. "Why don't you go unload your Mother Earth Flower Essence stuff from the back of your pickup into your new greenhouse? I'll get Dan to help unpack your trailer, and he and Sam can move the contents into here."

Jessica sighed, relishing the cool interior of her home. "Which of the two guys would be more sensitive to my orchids?"

Chuckling, Kate moved to the door. "Sam is all thumbs. If you need help unloading the orchids, I'll call Dan over from Gan's corral to help. Okay?"

"But you said he's got a chip on his shoulder."

"Ah, he's shy and doesn't say much. Like most Navajos, he won't look you in the eye. He looks up, down or to the side, but not straight into your eyes. They think it's rude to stare at a person. Sam says the only time he ever got ugly was when he hit the bottle after coming back from Desert Storm. Dan hasn't touched alcohol since that time, so I think it's in the past. He's been here for a week, and so far, so good. Dan's really wonderful with animals, Jessica. Far more sensitive than Sam. He'll be okay. He takes orders well. I'll go get him and he can help you unload your orchids. Sam and I will move your furniture into the house in the meantime."

Nonplussed, Jessica nodded and hurried out the back door. It was so hard to concentrate on the care the orchids demanded at a time like this. All Jessica really wanted to do was settle into her new home, spend time with Kate and simply reacquaint herself with the place where she'd grown up. With a sigh, she opened the side door to the hothouse. Checking the thermometer and humidity gauge, she noticed the rows and rows of lattice type, wrought-iron shelves that had been set up for the bulk of her orchids to sit on. The environment within the greenhouse felt wonderful compared to the

much drier, hotter air outside. The swamp cooler kept
the greenhouse at a reasonable seventy-five degrees.

"I hear Dan's going to help unload your orchids with
you?" Sam called from the front door.

"Yes," Jessica said, hurrying to where Sam had
parked her pickup near the door. "Thanks for helping, Sam."

He nodded. "Dan will be better at this than I am.
I'm all thumbs."

She smiled up into Sam's rugged face. "Okay,
thanks. I think Katie wants you to help her move my
furniture into my house." Sensitive to the needs of others, Jessica could feel that he was trying his best to
be warm and welcoming to her. She knew Sam was a
strong, silent type, and for him to be putting out this
much for her meant a lot. She appreciated his trying to
make her feel comfortable about coming home.

"Yep, that's where we'll be. When you're done here,
come back to your house. Kate's got some nonalcoholic
grape bubbly to toast your coming home."

Touched, Jessica nodded. "I will! Thanks for everything, Sam. It means so much…."

Nodding in turn, Sam left.

A few minutes later, Jessica heard a slight, hesitant
knock at the side entrance to the greenhouse. It must
be the wrangler, the one with a chip on his shoulder,
she thought. Jessica chided herself for thinking of the
man in that way. It wasn't right. She hurried to the
door and swung it open.

For a split second, Jessica froze before the open
door. A man, tall and lean, his skin a dark golden
brown, and his eyes gray and intelligent, stared back
at her. Her heart pounded in her breast. She felt her

breath torn from her. It was as if time had halted and
frozen around them. She studied the man before her
more closely. He wore a dusty, black felt Stetson hat
low across his broad forehead. His prominent nose was
crooked, as if it had been broken a number of times. A
scar along his left cheek scored his hard flesh. His face
was narrow, and the lines at the corners of his pale,
almost colorless eyes showed he squinted or laughed
a lot. On closer inspection, Jessica surmised that he
probably squinted more than laughed. This was a man
who wore sadness like a huge blanket around himself.

Because of her sensitivity to people, to the feelings
surrounding them, she felt an incredible weight settle
within her, the weight of his absolute sadness. And yet
he stood lean and tall, his shoulders strong and thrown
back with an unconscious pride. She saw the Navajo in
him, from his shining, short black hair to the leanness
of his body to the golden color of his skin. She liked
the warmth she saw banked in his gray eyes, eyes that
seemed to change color slightly as he stared down at
her. He seemed surprised—shocked—at seeing her.
Why on earth would he be shocked?

Almost unconsciously, Jessica touched her hair.
She was sure it was in disarray and needed a good
combing. Why was he looking at her like that? Had
she spilled something on her skirt or blouse when she
ate that veggie burger on the road? Nervously, Jessica
touched her lacy cotton blouse. No, no ketchup there.
How about her skirt? She quickly flattened her hands
and brushed them over the dark green print decorated
with various shades of pink and lavender morning glo-
ries. She found no damage to her skirt, either.

Lifting her chin, she frowned as she felt his shock

deepen. He was staring at her as if he'd seen a ghost! His gray eyes had widened considerably. Those black pupils had enlarged and she saw an almost predatory intent in his gaze, as if he were an eagle checking out a possible prey. Laughing at herself, Jessica quirked her lips.

"Hi, I'm Jessica Donovan. You must be Dan Black. Come on in." She stepped aside and he slowly entered, still continuing to appraise her sharply. Closing the door, Jessica offered him her small, slender hand. "You can call me Jessica...."

Dan stared at that very white, delicate-looking hand with such slender, artistic fingers. This was the woman he'd seen in his sweat lodge vision! His heart was pounding like a sledgehammer in his chest. An internal trembling began deep within him and he felt outwardly shaky. Unable to tear his gaze from her beautiful turquoise eyes, Dan stood there, looking like a gaping fool, he was sure. How could he tell this beautiful woman of the sky that she'd been in his vision? Automatically, he felt a strange, warm tendril curling around his heart.

"Do you shake hands?" Jessica demanded a little more briskly. "Because if you don't, we have to get to work. My orchids must be cooled down quickly or they'll die."

Rousing himself, Dan jerked his hat off his head and quickly raised his hand, swallowing hers up in his. Her fingers were so soft and firm compared to his dirty, range-worn and callused ones. "Sorry," he mumbled. "I'm Dan Black. Most folks call me Dan unless they don't like me."

Jessica felt the warm strength in Dan's hand. It was

a hand that had known hard, even brutal physical labor.
Suddenly she felt a new sensation and she didn't want
to release his hand. Though she could feel energy and
emotions around people, if she touched them she got a
far more intimate portrait of them. Dan's strength was
there, quiet and deep, like the cold Canadian lake near
Vancouver that she loved to sit beside, watching the
wildlife. The sadness she'd felt melted away, and instead she discovered the man who was hidden within
it. Yes, he was terribly shy, and unlike the typical Navajo, he *was* staring at her. As if she were a specimen
or something.

Laughing softly, she reluctantly released his hand.
"Am I a ghost to you, Dan Black?"

Shaken, Dan placed the hat back on his head. How
pretty Jessica Donovan was in person. The blouse she
wore had Victorian lace around the throat. The skirt
was full, brightly colored with flowers, and fell to her
thin ankles. She wore some kind of sandals on her
small, perfectly formed feet. As his gaze moved up
again, he noticed how her mussed golden hair fell in a
tumble around her shoulders. She reminded him of the
clouds that moved along the Mogollon Rim above the
ranch, fleeting, ethereal and transparent with beauty.
But in the sunlight, those clouds disappeared. Dan
wondered if she was an apparition. He hoped not.

"No, ma'am...you're not a ghost. You, uh, remind
me of someone I saw one time, that's all. I'm sorry for
staring. It's not polite."

Jessica felt heat rise in her cheeks as he averted
his gaze. "Oh, that's okay. I hope I reminded you of
someone who was good and not bad." She chuckled,
gesturing for him to follow her. A new thrill moved

through her. How handsome he was! Twice in the span of a short while, Jessica found herself detoured from the care of her orchids. On a feminine level, she found herself helplessly drawn to Dan Black. There was an air of mystery around him and it drew her effortlessly.

Even the way she moved reminded Dan of a wispy cloud. It was as if Jessica's feet weren't really touching the gravel of the greenhouse floor at all. He shook his head. What was going on? Was he hallucinating? How could this woman be real? Yet his fingers tingled wildly where he'd touched her hand. If she was a ghost, a vision, she certainly felt real. His entire body was resonating with her presence, her impish smile and the kind warmth that danced in her eloquent eyes—eyes that were a window into her sweet, vulnerable soul.

As he followed her to the door where the truck was parked, Dan realized that as closed up and guarded as he was, Jessica was just the opposite: she was open, available, trusting and sweet. So very, very sweet. How did she survive in this harsh world? Early in his life, he'd been a lot like her, but the meanness of the schoolchildren had forced him to close up and protect himself against such attacks.

Looking at Jessica's flyaway, spun-sunshine hair, the almost ethereal way she walked, he realized life hadn't treated her in the same way. Halting, he watched her pull a box out of the pickup, and he opened his arms to receive it. All he saw were a lot of lumps of newspaper in it.

"These are orchids, Dan," she said a little breathlessly. As she slid the cardboard box into his waiting arms, she found herself *wanting* to make physical contact with him again. Jessica felt such hesitancy around him, such excruciating shyness and...what else? As her arms brushed his darkly haired forearms, bared because he'd rolled up the sleeves of his dark red cowboy shirt, she felt something else. It was so hidden and elusive...and yet, as she slid the box into his arms, it was there. What was it?

"Treat them gently. Just start putting the boxes over there, on the metal table." Jessica found herself wanting to touch him again. How strange! After her experience with Carl, she had learned to distrust men, yet here she was, wanting more contact with Dan. Her emotions were like a roller coaster and she simply couldn't stop the blazing joy that curled through her heart every time she looked at Dan Black.

For the next twenty minutes, Dan helped her bring in box after box. He'd heard of orchids, but he'd never seen one, so he was curious. When Jessica finally shut the door to the greenhouse, her cheeks were flushed a bright red and her gold hair was growing slightly curly in the humidity, framing her oval face beautifully. Dan tried not to gawk at her. He tried not to rudely stare into those beautiful, bottomless eyes that shone with such life.

"Now, watch what I do," she directed softly as she brought the first box over to where he stood.

Dan moved closer. He liked how he felt around her. Remembering Ai Gvhdi Waya's instructions about opening himself up to that mystical flow he always had with horses, he allowed that to consciously happen now. Jessica felt safe to him. In fact, he'd never felt more safe with a person than her. There was nothing dark, manipulative or abusive about her. She was like an incredible rainbow of color to him, and just as

otherworldly. He still wasn't sure he wasn't hallucinating. But each time he got to brush her hand or her
fingertips, he knew she was very human.

In his world, the Navajo world, he had heard tales
of gods and goddesses who turned from animal form
into human form. Sometimes, they became human in
order to instruct the Navajo people. That was how he
saw Jessica—as a goddess from the Other Side, come
to instruct him. She couldn't really be human. She was
too beautiful. Too loving and open to be like him or
the people he knew.

Jessica gently began to unfold the newspaper from
one of the orchids she had taken from the cardboard
box and set on the metal table in front of her. "Have
you ever seen an orchid, Dan?" She thrilled to his
nearness. There was such raw, barely controlled power
around him. He was a stallion tamer, a man who could
handle a thousand-pound horse and not be afraid. Admiration for him spiraled through her and a hundred
questions about him sat on the tip of her tongue.

He shook his head. "No, ma'am, I haven't."

She glanced at him out of the corner of her eye.
"Please call me Jessica. Ma'am sounds *so* formal. I'm
afraid I'm not a very formal person." The warmth in
his eyes melted her and she saw one corner of his
mouth gently curl. It was a slight response, but she felt
the feathery, invisible touch of it upon her.

Out of habit, he tipped the brim of his cowboy hat
in her direction. "Yes, ma'am! I mean… Jessica." Her
name rolled off his tongue like honey. He liked the
sound of it. In his world, names had meanings. Someday he'd like to ask her what her name meant.

Smiling warmly, Jessica met his shy gaze. She saw

color rising in his cheeks. Dan was blushing! What a delightful discovery. This hard-bitten man, whose face was carved with sadness, could blush. Jessica felt her pulse speed up as his gray gaze met hers for a fleeting moment. She saw again the hint of thawing in his eyes and felt a shy smile emanating from him. But it never appeared on his hard, thinned mouth. She wondered if Dan's lips would seem fuller if he didn't keep them so tightly compressed, as if to protect himself from what she might say. She sensed that he was like a beaten animal—a beaten, wary animal that didn't quite trust her.

As much as she wanted to be nosy and ask him more, Jessica had grown up with Navajo people and knew they did not like to be asked direct questions about themselves. Perhaps with time and careful watching, Dan Black would be like one of her mysterious orchids. As he blossomed and began to trust her more, she would understand more of these feelings she picked up around him.

"Watch me carefully," she said, and unfolded the newspapers one by one and set them aside. "Orchids are very sensitive plants. They must have a certain range of temperature in order to survive. For instance, many of my orchid girls like the temperature no lower than fifty-five degrees at night and no higher than eighty-five during the day. And—" she pointed to the two temperature gauges hung on a redwood spar "—humidity is an absolute must or they won't bloom or flourish. The humidity has to be set around eighty to ninety percent to create the best environmental conditions for them."

He watched, mesmerized as her hands flew know-

ingly around the packed orchid. Although Dan wanted
to see what one of these plants looked like, her long,
beautiful fingers were worth watching. There was
nothing but grace to Jessica Donovan. No move she
made was jerky or hurried. Everything she did flowed
from one gesture directly into another, making it seem
as if she were always in motion. He smiled to himself,
absorbing the warm, sunny energy that emanated from
her. Getting to stand only inches from her, looking
over her shoulder as she worked quickly, was pure,
unadulterated pleasure for Dan.

"See?" Jessica said excitedly as she pulled the last
remaining newspaper away. "This is Stone Pinto!" Her
voice softened with excitement as she turned the orchid in the red clay pot around so that Dan could see
the spike with twelve blossoms on it. "Isn't she lovely?
Oh, I love this orchid so much. She's one of my personal favorites. Here, look at her. Carefully touch her
leaves and her flower."

Jessica was delighted to see real interest in Dan's
eyes as he moved closer, much closer to her. She unconsciously absorbed Dan's nearness; it was a powerful sensation, but one that did not put her on edge.
Ordinarily, if any man got this close to her, she would
shy away. But she wasn't afraid of him. Although she
was puzzled as to why, Jessica had enough intuitive
sense to allow the exchange of energy to take place.
In some ways, she was like a starving animal and Dan
was giving her what she needed. But when she remembered he was a man, wariness invaded her. Yet her
heart whispered that he could be trusted. Could he?

Dan stared at the orchid. "The flower…" he began,
choking up. Without thinking, he reached forward and

delicately touched the white blossom with the field of purple dots across it. "I've seen this flower before—" He felt his throat close up completely. When he touched the orchid blossom, he felt the strength of it, as well as the velvety softness of the petals.

Jessica saw so many different emotions cross his once hard, unreadable face. She was amazed at his response to Stone Pinto. She'd seen similar responses to other orchids when she'd allowed friends and customers to come in and see the plants from which she'd created the flower essences that cured them.

"You like her?" she whispered, touched by his emotional reaction to the orchid. As he leaned over and carefully examined the orchid, he grazed her arm with his. Being with him, Jessica realized, was wonderful! She'd never felt this way around any man. Ever. Absorbing his profile, she felt confused and exhilarated all at once. "When I did tests with Stone Pinto, I found out her essence was for people who carried too much responsibility on their shoulders or worked too hard. People who saw life as just one big responsibility and had lost their ability to play, to laugh or even smile...."

She reached out and stroked the long, leathery leaf of the orchid. "Stone Pinto is for people who usually have had a very hard, rigid life, Dan. If you took her essence, it would help you unbend, allow you to feel more vulnerable and to be able to laugh or smile again." She shared a soft smile with him as he turned and looked down at her. The predatory look was gone from his eyes now; instead, they appeared to be a soft dove gray, showing his emotions.

"Already," Jessica whispered, "she heals you as you touch her...."

Dan stood there, mystified. He withdrew his hand and stood looking at the orchid on the workbench. "But how... I saw this flower in my vision...." And then he stopped. Most people would never understand. He didn't trust that Jessica would. And when he saw her eyes change, and tears swim in them, he felt his heart opening like that orchid bloom. He was helpless to stop the reaction as their gazes met and locked. There was such an incredible sense of love moving from her to him in that moment that it made his breath hitch in response.

Stepping back, he looked away, unable to understand or digest all that was happening. Embarrassed, Dan moved the hat around on his head. It was a nervous gesture, something he did when he was afraid he'd humiliated himself once more in front of a stranger.

Jessica reached out, wrapping her fingers around his arm and drawing him back to the bench. "Let me show you something. You're part Navajo. You're close to the land, the plants and animals, like we are. My mother was a medicine woman and she passed on much of her skills to all of us." Jessica didn't want to release his hard, muscled arm, but she forced herself to do it. How strong and capable Dan was. Her hands tingled wildly from contact with him. Sliding her fingers around the six-inch clay pot, she drew the Stone Pinto forward.

"You understand that all living things have a spirit, don't you?" Her gaze dug into his widening eyes.

"Yes." He took the clay pot she placed in his hands. The spike on the Stone Pinto arched close to his face, like a bower full of beautiful blossoms.

"All right, then take what you know about plant spirits. They are just like people, aren't they? There're grumpy ones, happy ones, shy ones and everything else in between." Jessica moved her fingers along the leaves in a loving, caressing motion. "They have an aura around them, just as we do. Like people, not all plants are created equal. We know from our belief systems that there are young souls and old souls down here on Mother Earth."

Jessica became very serious as she placed her hands around his. "Dan, when I share this with you, I know you'll understand what I'm saying. I don't normally tell people this because they'd think I was crazy, but orchids are the most evolved plants on the face of Mother Earth. They are the pinnacle, the most spiritual of all the species of flowers that grow down here. Why? Because—" she slid her hands off his and tapped the bottom of the pot "—orchids do not live in soil like every other plant we know. No, they are air plants. They require absolutely no soil to grow. All they need to not only survive, but flourish, is humid air and the right temperatures. They absorb all the water they need right out of the air."

Jessica sighed and held his awed gaze. "Isn't that something? I'm so amazed by these plants. I feel like a child among very old, learned teachers when I work with my orchids."

He nodded, slowly turning the clay pot in his hand. "So, they are like the stone nation. Stones are millions of years old and hold much knowledge, too."

Jessica clapped her hands delightedly. "Exactly! Yes, you've got it!" She saw the redness in his cheeks and realized she'd embarrassed him. "I'm sorry, I didn't mean to seem to make fun of you, Dan. Just the opposite. Do you know how few people I can talk to about orchids and their spiritual qualities and evolution?" She held up one hand and spread her fingers wide. "Not even five people for the five fingers on my hand!" She laughed.

A hint of a smile tugged at the corners of his mouth as he gently placed the orchid back on the workbench. Jessica's childlike joy was infectious. She made him want to return her sunny smile, her uninhibited joy. "I see. They are flower teachers to us because they are so advanced on their own path of learning?"

With a sigh, Jessica whispered, "Yes. Oh, yes. You've got it, Dan. I'm *so* glad you're working here at the ranch. You really understand. And I need someone to help me. Would you like to do that? I can teach you so much about them, but in the long run, they will teach you ten times more. Just to get to work with orchids is like being in the most wonderful school of life you've ever experienced. I love it! I love working out here most of the day with them. They are so loving, so warm and giving to us." As she gazed at him, she realized the woman part of her wanted him around for other reasons. She savored his maleness because it did not threaten her, rather, it made her wildly aware of herself and her femininity. Each time he looked at her, she felt as if her heart would explode with raw joy.

Stunned, he muttered, "I don't know anything about them, though. I'm afraid I'd hurt them."

"Pshaw!" Jessica handed him another orchid clothed in protective newspaper. "Unwrap this one. Let's see which one she is! I don't believe for a second that you'd hurt a fly, Dan Black." And then she became serious. "Maybe you've been hurt, like Gan out there, but you're not mean and neither is that stallion."

Shaken, Dan stared at her, the silence building. "How—no, never mind...."

"I'm pretty psychic," Jessica said, quickly going about the business of freeing up the orchid in front of her. "It was a gift from my mother, Odula. She had the Sight, as we call it. Kate has good gut feelings and intuition. Rachel has the same thing, but I got gifted with more than them in some ways. I can feel people, and sometimes I'll know something about them without ever having been told beforehand. Don't let it shake you up. If you want to work in here with me and my orchid girls, you'll just have to get used to it."

As he unwrapped the orchid, a beautiful yellow one with a spicy scent, Dan nodded. "I know a medicine woman who sees like you."

"Will it bother you?" Jessica demanded primly. But from his expression, she knew it wouldn't. As she watched Dan carefully unwrap the orchid, she almost smiled. Despite his long, large-knuckled hands toughened with calluses, he had been ultracautious unwrapping that orchid. Yes, he was the perfect helper for her. Even if he was a man, he had that wonderful gentleness that many Navajo men possessed. She sent a prayer of thanks upward to the Great Spirit for sending such a person to her. Jessica had been very worried about not having help, since Moyra was no longer at her side. And she certainly couldn't ask Kate or Sam to help. They were already working sixteen hours a day to keep the Donovan Ranch afloat. She could not expect help from them.

"You know," Jessica whispered as she set the orchid on an upper shelf, "you are an answer to my prayers, Dan."

His head snapped up and he momentarily froze, the orchid in his hand. "What?"

"I said you're an answer to my prayers. Is that so awful? Judging from the look on your face, it is. Do you not want to help out in the greenhouse? Maybe Sam's given you other duties that I don't know about?"

"Oh...no," he muttered, placing his orchid next to hers on the wrought-iron shelf. "It's not that—"

"What then?" Jessica removed two more pots from the cardboard box. Her heart broke a little at the thought that Dan didn't want to work out here with her and her orchid girls. He seemed so perfect for it. Besides, if she was really honest, she had to admit she liked having him around, shyness and all. He was terribly handsome in a rugged, western kind of way. Maybe he was married, she thought as her gaze went to his left hand. There was no wedding ring on it, but a lot of Navajos never wore much jewelry on their fingers—just on their wrists and around their necks.

"No... I'd like to work out here," he admitted in a low voice. "I'll have to have Sam okay it. He's my boss. My other duty is to try and tame Gan and get him under saddle."

"Big order," Jessica said, relieved that Dan wanted to work in the greenhouse.

For the first time, Dan chuckled. He began unpacking another orchid. The pleasure of having Jessica less than a foot away from him was all he needed. "Gan is wary and he hates men. I've got to get him to trust me even if I am one. That's the first order of business."

"When my father drank," Jessica said in a low voice filled with pain, "he used to beat Gan with a rubber hose." She slid Dan a pained look.

Dan's hands stilled around the orchid. "What did he do to you when you tried to stop him?" He saw her face go pale and those glorious turquoise eyes of hers veil with deep grief and sadness. In that moment, he wanted to reach out and cup her small face protectively.

"I don't want to talk about it," she managed to answer, hurriedly unpacking the next orchid.

Dan felt her anguish and heard it in her strained voice. He'd heard a lot about Kelly Donovan; he knew he had been a mean bastard when he hit the bottle. Frowning, Dan returned his attention to the orchid he was unwrapping. It wasn't the Navajo way to ask personal questions or intrude into someone's life. He'd already overstepped the bounds with Jessica. It was so easy to do, he was discovering, because she was accessible and vulnerable.

Sighing, he realized his vision had been real. And the woman he'd seen in it was Jessica Donovan—a woman completely out of his reach. She was the owner of this ranch. She was rich and had land. He was nothing but a horse wrangler with no money, no savings. Pain racked his chest. Life was cruel, he decided. Cruel and hard and merciless. Here was the woman in his vision—unreachable. Untouchable. In a different class from him. In a different world from him.

His hands trembled slightly as he picked up another orchid. Great Spirit help him, but he wanted Jessica. He wanted her breathless laughter against his mouth, the warm touch of her hands exploring his hard body. He longed to discover every inch of her and love her until he died, knowing he'd given her every ounce of his passion.

Dan was even more unsure about life now than ever before. It had thrown him a curve he could never have imagined. Not ever. What was he going to do? How was he going to handle this hotbed of bubbling emotions in his chest that refused to be stilled or denied? Could Jessica feel it? Feel how he *really* felt toward her? He lived in fear of her finding out because he was afraid she'd misinterpret his feelings. Yet just watching her hurry back and forth, like a fluttering, beautiful butterfly, Dan felt his fortitude dissolve like honey in hot sunlight. He ached to remain in Jessica's presence. And somehow he was going to have to control himself, his emotions and his desires in order to keep his job on this ranch. How was he going to do it?

Chapter 4

Jessica awoke suddenly. She sat up in her old brass bed, the quilt falling away from her. Sleepily, she pushed her blond hair away from her face and looked toward the open window. Outside, she heard wonderful, familiar sounds from her childhood. The soft lowing of the cattle, the call of the rooster and the snort of horses were a welcoming balm to her. Inhaling, she could smell the scent of juniper in the cool, damp dawn air that flowed through the window into the small room.

Looking at her watch, she discovered it was only five a.m. She never got up this early in Vancouver. As Jessica sat there, Dan Black's face seemed to waver in front of her. Her heart tugged, gently stirring her sleep-filled thoughts. A soft smile pulled at her mouth as she eased from bed. Her feet touched the shining cedar floor, which had been waxed to perfection days earlier. Bless Kate and Sam for their help. Jessica knew that Dan had helped prepare her home, too. That made her feel inexorably good.

Quickly taking a hot shower, she pulled on a short-sleeved white blouse, a pair of jeans and very old but comfortable cowboy boots. She smiled as she stood up. She hadn't worn these since she'd left the ranch. Noticing that the leather was cracked and worn, she ran her fingers across the roughened texture of one of the toes. Despite their condition, the boots were steel toed and would protect her if a horse or steer accidentally sidestepped and came down on her foot. Cowboy boots were an important part of the uniform of the day here at the Donovan Ranch.

Humming softly, Jessica moved to the small kitchen and made some hot, fresh coffee. The odor filled her nostrils as she stood leaning against the beige tile counter decorated with the Cherokee colors of the four directions—red, yellow, black and blue.

As her gaze moved around the silent room, she saw many places for some of her hardier orchids, which would love to live here part-time and bring more color and life into the adobe house. Again Dan crossed her mind. How much fun she'd had yesterday unpacking the orchids with him! He was so gentle. So sensitive. Many times during the day she'd watched him carefully unpack one of her girls, enjoying the sight of a man with work-worn hands using a delicacy she'd rarely seen. She hoped Sam would allow Dan to continue to help her set up her business. She needed to get back on line with her company as soon as possible to take care of her back orders.

Pouring coffee into a dark red mug, Jessica moved out to the roughened log porch that enclosed her home. As she gently sat down in the swing, her ears picked up music—a Native American flute being played, she realized. The rasping, husky notes seemed to waft on the coming dawn. The sky in front of her was turning from gray to a pale pink color. High above the ranch a few wisps of cirrus, which reminded Jessica of a galloping horse's mane flying outward, turned a darker pink. Sighing because she'd missed the intrinsic beauty of the Southwest, Jessica stood and followed the sound of the flute.

As she rounded the large, freshly painted red barn, which housed thousands of bales of hay for the horses and cattle during leaner times, Jessica saw that both ends of the structure were open to allow maximum flow of fresh air to the broodmare stalls that lined the aisle. A few of the mares near foaling nickered as she walked by, probably thinking she was bringing them their oats for the day. But their meal would come later, when Dan made his rounds.

Behind the barn were several huge, rectangular corrals. All of the barbed wire had been replaced either with heavy wooden poles or, in the case of the Arabian horse corral, with solid and safe pipe fencing. Jessica was glad to see the wicked, scarring barbed wire finally replaced. Kelly had never wanted to spend any money on suitable fencing.

The Arabians in the corral all pricked up their ears as she approached, and a few of them nickered in welcome. Jessica smiled and continued to follow the flute music, which was coming from farther north. Who was playing it? She hadn't had time yesterday to explore the ranch and get a feel for it.

In front of her was a huge, enclosed wooden arena. As she headed toward it, she realized it was the place where horses were broken and training was begun. The walls were ten feet high so that the horse could not look anywhere but at the trainer and the animal's attention would be focused one hundred percent.

Moving around the training area, Jessica halted. Her breath hitched momentarily. There was Gan, the black Arabian stallion. And Dan Black. Neither saw her, and she remained perfectly still, gazing at the unbelievable sight. Though Gan was now twenty years old and middle-aged, the proud stallion looked larger than life. Gan's size had come from Raffles, a stallion of English lineage and one of the most profoundly influential bloodlines in North America. Gan wasn't more than fourteen hands three, but what he didn't have in height he made up for in muscle and power.

The stud had been a year old when he'd come to Donovan Ranch. Because of Kelly's abuse, the stallion hated all people, and men especially. The only person who'd ever gotten close to Gan was Odula.

Now Jessica's gaze moved from the stallion, which stood frozen, his wide nostrils flaring, his full attention on the opposite side of the corral, to Dan. He was sitting outside the pipe fence, his back to a post, playing his flute. The soft, plaintive notes filled the air, bringing tears to Jessica's eyes.

The music was subduing Gan, she realized. She watched with fascination as the stallion snorted and pawed the ground angrily, the dirt and red sand flying from beneath his sharpened hoof. And then he'd stop, fling his magnificent head upward and listen. At no time did Dan pause to see what the stallion was doing. Luckily, he was in a protected place, where Gan was unable to charge and bite him.

The sky turned a darker pink. Jessica heard the familiar call of quail families, which lived around the ranch. She saw a flock of mallards skimming northward, heading toward the Rim and Oak Creek. Slowly, she lifted the cup of steaming coffee to her lips and took a sip. Enthralled by Gan's attention to the stallion tamer, she smiled. Sam had said Dan was the best horse wrangler in the state of Arizona. Well, his methods were certainly surprising. As the last notes of the mournful flute song ended, she watched Gan.

The stallion shook his head from side to side. He pawed the ground again, a wary look in his eyes as Dan slowly eased away from the post and stood up. It was at that moment that Jessica saw Dan raise his head, take his attention off the stallion and look directly at her. Her pulse skittered. Her heart opened like an unfolding orchid bloom. His gray eyes were dark, the pupils huge and black. For the first time, she saw relaxation in his features—not that hard, guarded look that had been on his face yesterday. Jessica realized Dan was happy. Even more, his mouth, which was usually tightly compressed into a thin line, was now full, the corners tilted upward. She realized she was seeing the real Dan Black now—the man without the mask in place.

Suddenly she felt like an interloper; heat swiftly moved up from her neck, warming her cheeks. She gripped the coffee mug a little more tightly and an apology came to her lips.

As if sensing her embarrassment, Dan pushed his black Stetson off his forehead with his thumb and gave her an uneven smile of welcome.

"May I come closer?" Jessica asked in a low voice. She knew that horse trainers liked to work alone, without interference from other people. They needed one hundred percent of the animal's attention at all times or training didn't occur.

Dan nodded. "Walk very slowly," he told her in a low voice. "No fast movements."

"Right...." Jessica said. She paid attention to the uneven red clay and sand beneath her feet as she walked carefully toward the corral. Gan started, snorted and leaped from the center of the corral to the opposite side, away from her. Her heart sank. She hadn't meant to scare the stallion.

Her pulse skipped erratically as she approached Dan. He stood completely at ease, one foot hitched up on the bottom rail, the flute in his left hand resting across his thigh. How terribly handsome he looked today, Jessica thought, despite the fact that the long-sleeved, white shirt he wore had seen better days. She saw a number of places where the material had been torn and sewn carefully together again. Still, she couldn't help but admire the broad shoulders and powerfully sprung chest beneath that shirt. His blue jeans outlined his lean, hard lower body to perfection and a red bandanna was wrapped loosely around his neck. His cowboy boots were in just as bad a condition as hers, worn and cracked by years of use.

Dan's eyes narrowed as he watched Jessica approach. Had the Great Spirit ever made a woman more beautiful, more untouchable than her? As she closed the distance to him, he thought not. Her gold hair was drawn back into a ponytail that moved with her graceful movements. Her white blouse was feminine and enhanced the blush staining her cheeks. Yesterday she had worn a skirt, but today, he noticed with more than a little interest, she wore snug-fitting jeans and cowboy boots. She was small and delicate. Dan wondered if she had been sick as a child, because she seemed so fragile compared to Kate, who was more solidly built and much taller.

When Jessica lifted those lashes and revealed her turquoise eyes, Dan felt heat gather in his lower body. And when her pink lips drew into a hesitant, almost apologetic smile, his heart opened wide. Again that same warmth he'd experienced during his vision in the sweat lodge avalanched through him. How beautiful she was! How untouchable! Pain moved through him and doused the joy he'd felt. His fingers closed more firmly on the flute as she halted about four feet away from him.

"Your music was beautiful," she whispered with a sigh. "I woke up early for some reason and made coffee. When I came out on the front porch, I heard your song. It was so incredibly beautiful, Dan." Jessica closed her eyes and sighed again. "You should record what you play. It's as good as any other recording I've heard of Native American flute music."

He felt heat tunneling up his neck. With a shy laugh, he pulled his hat back down on his brow, unable to accept the look of admiration in Jessica's eyes. "I'm afraid, ma'am—I mean, Jessica—that my playing is pretty basic. I learned from my uncle, who died when I was a kid and passed on his flute to me."

"So what if you're mostly self-taught?" Jessica said, some indignation in her voice. "You have a natural, raw talent for it. Don't apologize."

With a shrug, he lifted up the flute for her to take a look. "My uncle made it out of cedar. He carved it himself. I remember he used to play it for us kids when we'd get in bed at night. I always liked his music." Sadness moved through him at the memory. "He died of liver cancer. I was real sorry to see him go. He's the one who brought laughter to us."

Jessica set her coffee cup down on the ground and gently took the nearly three-foot-long flute in her hands. The wood was a warm color, a mixture of red and yellow. There was a beaded band of red, blue, green and black around one end of it, and several red-tailed hawk feathers hung beneath the rust color of the feathers matching the reddish hue of the wood.

"This flute feels so warm. So alive...."

Dan studied her widening eyes. "You feel it, too? Why should I be surprised? You're sensitive like your mother."

Shrugging, Jessica moved her fingertips lightly over the wood. "Wood has spirit. So do these hawk feathers. You have a tree and a hawk spirit who work with you when you play this flute."

"Yes." He smiled inwardly, liking her understanding that all things were connected and that all things had spirit. Even though Jessica looked more Anglo than Cherokee, she still had the powerful blood of her mother moving through her, as Kate did. "I guess I have to get used to the fact you've got blond hair, but you're still Native American."

Jessica chuckled as she continued to examine the

flute. "I'm the renegade in the family. Mom said she had no idea where my blond hair came from. It sure wasn't from her side of the family."

He enjoyed watching her, studying how she stroked the wooden flute. How would it feel if she touched him the same wonderful way? Dan surprised himself with the thought. Generally, he didn't pay much attention to women, because he'd never had any luck with them. Who wanted a drunken Navajo cowboy for company? Not many, that was for sure. But he couldn't help wondering what Jessica's light touch would do to him. His skin tightened in response. Deep down he knew, but he didn't dare follow that line of thinking. She was part owner of a large ranch. And him—he was just a tumbleweed cowboy without money or property. She would never be interested in him.

"On your father's side, I thought they were all red-haired like he was."

"No, looking back in family photos, I can see that many of our descendants from the Bay of Donovan had black hair or reddish blond hair." She reluctantly handed the flute back to him. Their fingers met briefly and Jessica absorbed Dan's warmth. She withdrew her hand quickly because her heart sped up again, as if to underscore how much she enjoyed his touch.

Dan felt his hand tingle wildly as a result of their contact, and the heat in the lower part of his body flared for an instant. Would she sense how much he liked touching her? He hoped not, or his shame would be complete. Shaken, he unhitched his boot from the rail, leaning down to pick up the carefully folded leather flute case.

"How long have you been working to tame Gan?" Jessica asked.

"Sam and Kate hired me less than two weeks ago. I've been working with Gan about a half hour a day. That's all he'll put up with for now." Dan lovingly slid the cedar flute back into the case and then hitched his boot up on the rail again. Balancing the flute across his thigh, he tied the leather strings at the top so that the instrument would not slide out.

Jessica studied the stallion, which was watching them from across the corral with large, intelligent brown eyes. He was switching his black tail from side to side, as if peeved with their continued presence. His fine, small ears kept moving back and forth.

"I never thought anyone could tame him," she admitted.

"I may not be able to. I'll try. But I'm not going to get killed in the process of trying." Dan placed the flute against the pipe fence and rested both his arms on the rail in front of him.

Jessica moved closer to Dan. She liked his lean, masculine grace. There was never a wasted motion with Dan. She sensed an underlying steadiness in him and knew that he would be someone to rely on in a time of emergency. He was someone she could trust. Moving to the fence, she placed her hands on the rail and watched Gan. The stallion's coat gleamed in the dawn light.

"He's so terrifyingly beautiful," she whispered.

"Well, he wouldn't be so terrifying if people hadn't made him that way," Dan said, absorbing her closeness hungrily. "I sometimes wonder what he would be like if your father had not beaten him into hating two-leggeds. In my mind, when I play my flute for him, I see him coming over to me." He pulled a carrot from his back pocket. "Coming to take this from me."

Jessica shared a brief smile of understanding with him. "Gan, if I remember correctly, loves apples and carrots. That is how my mother got him to trust her. She always brought him an apple or carrot a day. He always waited for her right over there, next to the gate."

"Did Gan ever try to charge her or bite her?"

"No, he was a gentleman with her, like he was to the mares he was bred with." Jessica shook her head. "Gan is a paradox in some ways. He'll bluster and charge you, and I've seen him take a pound of flesh out of Kelly two different times. And he charges with the intent to hurt you bad. But if you turn a mare ready to be bred into his corral, he's such a gentleman. He's never hurt a mare."

"There are some stallions that hurt their mares. But Sam said this stud's gentle with them. He never bites or scares them."

"Then there's hope," Jessica said, "that you can tame him and get his trust. Gan is not completely bad. No animal or human ever is."

Dan grimaced. "I don't know," he muttered, "some of us two-leggeds have pretty bad reputations that we aren't ever going to live down. People's memories are too long."

She looked at him and felt his inner pain and deep sadness. Jessica almost asked him if he was referring to himself, but something cautioned her not to be too nosy about Dan Black. He was a lot like that stallion in the corral—wary of people and not all that trusting. She felt him wanting to reach out, to trust her, and she hoped she could be there for him when he did. She liked his easygoing nature when his mask wasn't in place. Out here on the desert with his untamed stallion, she was privileged to see the real Dan Black.

"I know what you mean," Jessica said. She shrugged painfully. "My track record isn't one I'm proud of, either. Thank goodness it's in Canada, not here. But I know what you mean about gossip and people never forgetting. If you're bad, you're always bad in their eyes. There's no way to reclaim yourself or try to better yourself. People hold on to what's bad about us, not what's good or decent."

He held her sad, blue-eyed gaze. "Somehow I don't believe that you are bad."

Sighing, Jessica said, "I married a guy, Carl, up in Canada. I'd just arrived there after leaving this ranch. I didn't want to leave, but Kelly was driving us all out. He didn't want women running his ranch. Me and my sisters each left at age eighteen, as soon as we graduated from high school." Her fingers tightened around the coolness of the pipe railing.

"I didn't want to leave Mama. I was the baby of the family, the last to go. She wanted me to stay, but I just couldn't stand what Kelly was doing to her, to the ranch and to himself."

"Or," Dan said gently, "to you?" He knew he shouldn't ask, but something drove him to. He wanted to know more about Jessica, about how life had treated her. In his heart he knew without a doubt that Jessica had the goodness he'd searched for and never found in himself, much less anyone else. It anguished him to think that Kelly might have struck her, for the rancher had been known to be violent and abusive to friends, neighbors, strangers and family alike. Dan could hardly stand to think Jessica might have been hurt by him.

She closed her eyes. "Let's just say that my growing-up years followed me to Canada, Dan." Opening her eyes, she stared sightlessly into the corral, no longer seeing Gan, but her past. "My marriage to Carl Roman was like my life with my father. I spent eight years in a hell with him. *Hell*." The word came out bitter and hard.

Dan watched her closely. He fought the desire to ask more personal questions. His Navajo heritage told him not to—that if she wanted to, she would divulge what she felt he should know. He tightened his mouth and stared down at the ground in front of him.

"Hell comes in many forms," he said. "It sounds as if you were not at fault, but you walked into a bad situation with a person with a dark heart."

Jessica took in a deep, shaky breath. "What was it my mother called a person who was a liar? Who chose to use only their bad traits instead of their good ones? A two-heart? Yes, that's what Carl was. He had two hearts, not one good heart. I was too young, too naive and blind to see the real him."

"That is the past now. You're home and you are loved here. Kate has done nothing but talk of you, of your arrival. Sam cares for you as a brother." Dan gestured toward the rising sun in front of them. "Here you are wanted and cared for."

"But I'm not safe here," Jessica muttered, unable to meet his eyes. She felt wave after wave of concern coming from Dan. How protective he was of her! His care was like a warm blanket that could assuage her pain, fear and worry all at the same time.

His black brows knitted and he blurted, "Safe? What do you mean?" Damn! He hadn't meant to probe! Inwardly, Dan chaffed over his rudeness.

Jessica looked up at him, searching his intense features. She was discovering that when Dan was upset, that mask came down across his face. No longer was he relaxed or at ease. Every line in his body had gone rigid with tension. His face was hard now and his eyes nearly colorless. It reminded her of a hawk ready to strike its unsuspecting prey. A shiver ran through her and for a moment Jessica had to remind herself that Dan's demeanor was not aimed *at* her, but rather was a protective response to what she'd just said. Shaken, she managed to whisper, "Carl had always told me that if I divorced him, he'd hunt me down and kill me. He said he couldn't live without me. That if he couldn't have me, no one would."

Dan's nostrils flared and he released a held breath. "The man's crazy, then."

"No kidding. I divorced him two years ago and the most wonderful and strange thing happened. I know if I tell you, you won't think it's bizarre. I was in the middle of divorcing Carl, and I was hiding out in an apartment in Vancouver under an assumed name so he couldn't stalk me. At the time, I ran my flower essence company from my apartment. I was trying to keep my business afloat and stay hidden. I desperately needed help, someone who could assist me with my orchids, fill orders and answer mail.

"One day, I went out in disguise to the grocery store. I was so scared that I dropped a bottle of orange juice in one of the aisles. It broke all over the floor. I was so ashamed, I just stood there looking down at the mess at my feet and burst into tears. I was sobbing almost hysterically when this tall, dark-haired woman came out of—I swear—nowhere. She took me by the shoulders and moved me away from the mess in the aisle, talking soothingly. She just kept patting my shoulder and telling me that it was all right, that I was safe.

"When I looked up through my tears, I saw not this woman's face, but the face of a jaguar! And then the jaguar disappeared and I saw her human face. I was so stunned by it, I stopped crying. I saw her smile and she offered me a handkerchief for my tears. She said her name was Moyra and she was from South America. She told me in a low voice, as an employee from the grocery store cleaned up the mess I'd made, that she had been sent not only to protect me, but to help me for the next two years."

With a nod, Dan said, "She was a shape-shifter."

"Yes," Jessica admitted. "She's a jaguar priestess from South America. She came from an unbroken lineage of the Jaguar Clan."

"The Great Spirit sent her to protect you, then."

"And she did, too. I could never have survived and flourished in these last two years without her help, Dan. Moyra had a jaguar's senses, and she was completely clairvoyant. She knew exactly where Carl was at all times. She helped me find a beautiful cabin out in a meadow north of Vancouver. We moved everything out there and she helped me build a greenhouse for my orchid girls. And if Carl got too close, she always knew it and would tell me."

"You avoided your ex-husband for two years, then?"

"Yes, thank goodness." Jessica shuddered. "I don't

know what I'd have done if Carl had found me. I—I'm still afraid. I talked it over with Kate and Sam, and they said for me to come home, that I'd be safe here." She looked beseechingly up at Dan. "I don't know that for sure. I have bad feelings about it. I feel pretty naked and alone without Moyra around. She said she had to go home, that her family was calling her back to Peru, that she was needed there."

"You're feeling vulnerable," Dan said.

"Yes, unprotected. Moyra was a real friend."

Dan saw Jessica's eyes swim with tears and he laid his hand gently on her shoulder. How badly he wanted to say "come here," to open his arms to her and embrace her until she no longer felt so alone and unprotected against her predatory ex-husband.

Dan's hand felt firm and stabilizing to Jessica. She closed her eyes and absorbed his care and concern. "I shouldn't be telling you all of this. You barely know me...."

"What are friends for if you can't unload what worries you?" he asked huskily, and removed his hand reluctantly. "I'm not Moyra. I'm not a medicine man, but if you want, I can be like a big guard dog for you. I'll protect you, Jessica. If you want...." Never had he wanted to do anything more. Dan suddenly realized that he *could* help protect Jessica. He hadn't been trained as a Recon Marine for nothing. No, he was very good at such things. Far better than most men ever would be. Besides, his Navajo side, the man in him, would automatically protect the woman he felt so strongly about. Maybe it was a knee-jerk reaction, but it felt right to offer her his protection.

Reaching out, Jessica briefly touched his arm, feeling the hard, lean muscle beneath her fingertips. There was a dangerous quality to Dan that she'd never encountered until now. She saw it in the wild look in his almost colorless eyes, and she heard it in the grate of his voice. This side of Dan surprised her for a moment, because he'd shown her only his softer, more sensitive side. Now she saw the warrior unveiled. She allowed her hand to drop back to her side.

"No... I couldn't put you or my family at risk if Carl decided to get even with me, Dan. I don't want to put anyone else in danger. He's—he's horrible and he's insane at times...just like Kelly was when he got drunk. Only," she said, her voice dropping with terror, "Carl was never drunk. He was that way all the time. And I never realized it until it was too late, until after we were married. He hid the real person inside of him until it was too late for me to back out and run from him."

"Listen," Dan said, cupping her shoulders and turning her toward him, "you don't have any say in this matter. There are things you don't know about me, either—good and bad. One thing I can do is help you, protect you, should he ever come here to the ranch." He saw her open her lips to protest. "No," he ordered tightly, "this is not up for more discussion, Jessica. I now know why the Great Spirit sent me here—to help protect you. Because this man is coming here. I don't possess the Sight like you or Moyra do, but I feel it here, in my gut. And I've been in enough situations to trust my gut completely. It's never been wrong."

Trembling, Jessica tried to breathe, but she felt suffocated by the possibility of Carl stalking her once again. Her intuition told her it was only a matter of time. Only Dan's reassuring, strong hands on her shoulders gave her any sense of hope or stability. "Oh, no… I hope you're wrong. Leaving Vancouver, I tried to cover my tracks completely, so he'd never find out…."

Her terror avalanched over him, catching Dan completely off guard. As he felt the depth of her fright, he realized just how much danger she was really in. He wasn't expecting to be that open, that vulnerable to another human's pain or emotions, but it was happening. He felt this exchange of feelings when he worked with horses, but never with humans. Not until now. He remembered Ai Gvhdi Waya's words about allowing himself to shift into that flow, and he did everything in his power to keep his heart and mind open to Jessica.

"You're going to be all right," he said, giving her a small shake. "Look at me, Jessica. Please…." Her eyes opened and he drowned in the blueness of them. "The Great Spirit didn't leave you defenseless by coming here. You traded Moyra for me. I'm just a poor tumbleweed of a horse wrangler, but I have abilities and skills that can protect you. Do you believe me?"

The confidence in his speech cut through her terror. She stared up into his rugged features and absorbed the toughness of his rasping voice. His hands were firm and protective at the same time. "Dan, I can't ask you to do this. Carl is insane and he's manipulative. He was in prison for second-degree murder, but just escaped. The police are after him, but he's smart. They still haven't caught him. He's already killed one human being. I—I couldn't ask you to do this for me, don't you see?"

"Shi shaa, I am not much of a warrior, but I will be

like a shield in front of you when Carl comes here, and he will. I know that now. That is my promise to you. Your jaguar priestess may have left, but in her place you find the spirit of the cougar, instead. My spirit guide is just as powerful in some ways as that of my jaguar sister. Trust me. I will be your eyes and ears from now on. You will be able to live here safely...."

Chapter 5

"Hey, how are you doing?" Kate called from the door to the greenhouse.

Jessica jumped at the noise. She whirled around, a plastic sack filled with redwood chips in her hands. "Oh! You scared me, Kate."

Kate grinned and closed the door behind her. Wiping her brow, she took a deep breath. "Whew, it's a lot cooler and nicer in here. Must be close to a hundred degrees outside." Moving over to the workbench, she perused the four orchids in clay pots sitting there. "I dropped by to see how things were going. Sam and I just came off the north range, moving some pregnant cows to a greener pasture." She wrinkled her nose. Untying her dark blue bandanna from around her slender throat, she wiped her perspiring face with the cloth. "Not that there's much green. This drought is a killer. I've never seen anything like it in all the time I've lived here."

Jessica nodded and placed the wood chips back on the bench. "I know. It's awful. So much is dying. And the money you're having to use up to buy bales of hay…yuk."

Kate grinned a little and retied her bandanna. "Little sis, you do not want to look at the accounting books, believe me. Or you'll spend your nights like I do—tossing and turning and wondering when the bank is going to foreclose on us."

Jessica looked up at her oldest sister. Kate had her dark hair in a ponytail, a straw cowboy hat, stained with dust and perspiration from many hours of work, on her head. Tall and angular, she was a living testament to the rugged Southwest and what hard work did to a body. She looked good in her bright red T-shirt, faded blue jeans and dusty cowboy boots. Jessica had always admired Kate in so many ways, even though her sister had spent time in prison for a crime she'd been unjustly accused of. Now Kate's eyes sparkled with happiness, and Jessica knew it was because she was so in love with Sam. Jessica was so happy for Kate. It was about time her sister had something good happen to her.

"Well, if Sam and you will okay it, I could use Dan's help in here to begin processing orders for Mother Earth Flower Essences and start collecting money for that hay you need."

Kate shook her head and put her arm around Jessica's slim shoulders for a moment. "You're so generous, Jessica. I don't know what possessed you to help out so much, but we're all grateful for it."

Jessica put her own arm around Kate's waist and hugged her in return. "I wouldn't have it any other way. Besides, we're going to get out of this financial nightmare with the ranch someday."

"I hope sooner rather than later," Kate said, her voice strained. She sat on a tall wooden crate next to the workbench and watched Jessica begin to repot the orchids. "Hey, on a happier subject, if you want Dan Black to be your assistant, go for it. Sam would like him to divide his day into working at taming Gan, helping you in the mornings and then helping Sam run the fence and handle the other ranch duties in the afternoon."

Jessica turned the first pot upside down. Old redwood chips fell onto the bench, and she gently drew the orchid's long, white root system to one side. "That's fine." Taking fresh redwood chips, she leaned down, retrieved a new clay pot and put some into it.

"What do you think of him?" Kate asked, watching her sister work quickly and efficiently.

"Who?"

"You know who. Dan Black."

"Oh…" Jessica risked a look at her sister's frowning features. "He's, uh…"

"Aren't you getting along? Did he say something?"

"Now, Katie, don't go jumping off a cliff, okay? No, Dan didn't say anything wrong to me."

"You look…" She searched for the right word. "Uneasy?"

With exasperation, Jessica picked up the orchid, carefully arranged the root system in the larger pot and began to drop small pieces of bark around it. "It's just me and my big mouth, Katie. I barely know the guy, right? What do I do the second day I see him? I blurt out my whole life story."

Grinning, Kate took off her hat and set it on her thighs as she propped her heels up on the box. "What else is new? You always trusted everyone without wondering what their ulterior motives might be. Me? I'm just the opposite of you. I walk in wondering what the son of a bitch wants from me—a pound of flesh?" She chuckled indulgently.

"A little paranoia is good," Jessica admitted, frowning.

"Especially in *your* case," Kate warned heavily. "This thing with Carl isn't over. We both know that."

Jessica shot her a look of anxiety. "I'm worried, Katie."

"The guy is nuts. He's a sick stalker. He killed a guy. He could kill you. He might try it."

"Now you're talking just like Dan."

"Oh," Kate murmured, raising her brows, "you told Dan about Carl, too?"

With a sigh, Jessica placed the newly repotted orchid into a small dish of water so that the clay would absorb some of the moisture for the plant's root system. "That's what I mean—I blurted out everything about my life to Dan this morning."

"And?" Kate asked carefully. "How did Dan react to Carl's potentially showing up here to finish what he started in Vancouver?"

Agitated, Jessica felt fear and consternation roiling within her. She raised her eyes to the ceiling and then back down to Kate. "I was surprised at his reaction, to tell you the truth."

"Tell me about it."

Shrugging, Jessica took another orchid and turned it upside down to loosen the old wood chips around the roots. "He said that he knew now why he was sent here to the ranch." She glanced at Kate. "To protect me...."

"Hmm..."

"That's all you have to say? I mean, I was a little taken back by his passion for wanting to protect me. He doesn't know me! I mean, for all he knows, I could be a murdering thief in disguise."

Kate laughed and shook her head. "No, Jessica, you just don't fit the profile, and Dan knows that." She tapped her fingertip on the workbench. "Dan's a lot like Sam. He's a realist. He's pragmatic, too. He may not value himself as much as he should, but he's good with animals and some people. He's been kicked around enough to know the world isn't a goody-goody place. Unlike you, Miss Idealist."

Jessica grinned a little and set the unrooted orchid aside. "Okay, okay. So I think ill of no one. I don't question people's motives or their reasoning like you do. In most cases, my view of life works."

"That's what got you into trouble with Carl," Kate growled. "You believed the facade he put up for you. You didn't bother to ask what might be behind it."

"Carl's manipulative. It took me a year to know the real man behind the mask. I don't think anyone could have known." Her hands trembled slightly as she put redwood chips into a new pot.

"Listen," Kate whispered gently, "Carl's insane, as far as I'm concerned. And he's dangerous. Sam and I think he'll try and get to you here, at the ranch."

Her heart plunging in terror, Jessica set the pot down and fully faced her sister. "If you honestly believe that, why on earth did you let me come here? Carl could kill *all* of us if he goes off into one of his ballistic rages. He has an arsenal of guns he keeps hidden from the Canadian authorities. He could bring them down here and begin shooting up the ranch."

"Hold on," Kate said, putting up her hands. "Don't get upset, Jessica. First of all, you've got three big, bad guard dogs here at the ranch—Sam, me and Dan. We are being watchful."

Grinning a little, Kate continued, "Besides, Dan Black is a hell of a lot more dangerous than his mannerisms might show. He was a Recon Marine for four years, and according to Sam, he was damned good at what he did. Those men are taught to be invisible until the right moment. Dan got a lot of experience during the Gulf War. He was in the thick of things. And if a worst-case scenario happens and Carl is stupid enough to come down here thinking he can hurt you, well, he'll be in for a few surprises. Dan may not be able to be everywhere with you all the time, but when he is, Sam told him to watch out for you. And if Dan isn't there, Sam will be. Twenty-four-hour protection, Jessica."

"So Dan knew about me already? About Carl?"

"No, Sam told him that you needed to be watched, that was all."

Miffed, Jessica put the repotted orchid aside. Her fingers trembled badly now. "That's why Dan was so intense with me, then. He was all worked up about protecting me."

"He's not getting paid any extra to do this, you know. I don't know where his passion is coming from." And then Kate tilted her head and smiled a little. "Maybe he likes you?"

"Oh, please, Katie! I'm not exactly a great gift, am I? I've got an ex-husband who wants to kill me. Who might be really stupid and drive all the way from Canada to do it. If I were Dan Black, I'd sure stay away from me, with good reason!"

"But you have a lot going for you that any man worth his salt would be interested in. You're pretty, smart and ultrafeminine, just the way a man likes a woman."

"Please...." Jessica begged, truly upset now. She took the third clay pot, forcing her hands to stop shaking so much. "I just wish I had your nerves of steel, Katie. Look at my hands. I'm such a wimp. I think of Carl coming to stalk me, to hurt me, and I feel like I'm falling to pieces all over again. I think about the time he put me in the hospital. The pain. The horrible thought that I had to go back and live with him again. It's as if this nightmare is never going to end." She stopped and forced back the tears that stung her eyes.

"It's not easy," Kate whispered gently, her face soft with sympathy as she got up and walked over to Jessica and hugged her. "It's my fault. I shouldn't have brought this up. You're still tired from your trip. You've got a lot of pressure on you to get your orchid girls taken care of, not to mention a lot of orders that haven't been filled."

Shrugging painfully, Jessica looked up at Kate. "Compared to you, Katie, I've got the spine of a jellyfish. I wish I didn't let day-to-day pressures and stresses get to me like this...."

"It's not every day you realize your life is in danger," Kate answered wryly, releasing her. She settled her cowboy hat more firmly on her head. "Look, you need help here. Let's rearrange the schedule for the next week. I'll talk to Dan. He can still work with Gan in the early morning, but I think I'm going to ask him to work with you the rest of this week full-time, to help you get on your feet with your business. That way, that's one more stress off your shoulders. Okay?"

Jessica's heart pounded briefly and this time it wasn't out of fear, but rather something else she couldn't identify. Whatever it was, it felt good and steadying. When she realized Kate was watching her like a hawk, she said, "Ask Dan. He may not want to do this. I don't even know if he likes working in a greenhouse with orchids. I mean, he's a wrangler, for heaven's sake. He's used to doing a man's work outdoors, not spending time in some hothouse…."

Chuckling, Kate headed for the front door of the greenhouse. "Oh, Jessica, you are so funny! I swear, sometimes you wouldn't see a Mack truck barreling down on you."

"What's that supposed to mean?"

Kate turned, her grin widening considerably. "You really are naive, little sis. When a man brings 'passion' into conversation with a woman, there's something there, you know? Yep, I'd say that horse wrangler likes you just a little bit."

Heat washed across Jessica's face as she stared at Kate. "You mean, personally likes me?"

"*Arrgh,* I give up!" Kate lifted her hand in farewell and left.

Muttering to herself, Jessica returned to her work. Her fear over Carl's possible appearance and her apprehension over Dan's feelings for her warred within her. Yes, she'd felt something when Dan had gripped her by her shoulders early this morning. She'd felt his care, his powerful protection blanketing her, like something warm and good. Oh, why wasn't she wiser about people? Or, better, wiser about men? She supposed the fact that she'd married Carl at age eighteen, shortly after leaving home and moving to Vancouver, was to blame. She really didn't have any experience with men except for Carl.

No, Kate was right—her naiveté was getting her into a lot of hot water. But how did one become wise in that way? Too bad there wasn't a flower essence she could take to give her that wisdom. She laughed out loud at the thought as she repotted the next orchid. She could make millions if that were possible.

Suddenly Jessica heard the door open and close. She looked over her shoulder and her pulse leaped. It was Dan Black. His mask was in place, that unreadable, hard expression, and his eyes were nearly colorless, measuring her.

"Hi, Dan. Did Kate send you?" The corners of her mouth moved upward in greeting. How handsome he looked!

She absorbed his tall, lean frame and the easy way he walked. She saw his expression soften just as soon as she smiled at him. His eyes changed from colorless to a soft dove gray. The tightness around his mouth eased, revealing the fullness of his lower lip.

"Yes, she did." He gazed hungrily at Jessica's petite form as she stood at the workbench. She had on a dark green canvas apron that fitted her body to midthigh. In her hands was a large orchid in a clay pot. "She said you needed help this next week," he continued, taking off his cowboy hat and wiping the sweat from his brow with the back of his arm. "This place is a lot cooler and nicer than out there, anyway."

She brightened. It was so hard not to stare into his large, intelligent eyes, which seemed banked with so many emotions he fought to hide from her. There was a sparkle in them today, and she felt their penetrating power. Shaken by the sensation, she stammered, "W-well, if it's okay with you, I can use some help getting set up the rest of this week. I know you're probably used to being outside and doing ranch work, and this sure isn't anything like that, but—"

"I want to help."

The words, husky and filled with emotion, silenced Jessica. She saw the honest sincerity burning in his eyes, and the roughened quality of his voice was like a cat's tongue licking her flesh, making it tingle deliciously.

"Oh…." she replied, at a loss for words.

"My people honor the plant nation," he said simply, looking around at the hundred or so orchids sitting at various heights on the wrought-iron steps. "My uncle, the one who died of cancer and gave me his flute, knew a lot about plants. He wasn't a medicine man, but he passed on his love of them to me. I know a lot about the plants that live on the res." He shrugged slightly. "Not in a scientific sense, but I know which ones the Navajo people use for medicine purposes."

"That's wonderful! I've been thinking of expanding my business line to include plants from the Southwest now that I've moved my company down here! Maybe you could help me identify some of them and tell me what you know of them?"

Dan felt her unbridled enthusiasm, her childlike awe

and joy. There wasn't anything not to like about Jessica Donovan, he decided. All morning he'd tried to find things to stop himself from liking her so much—from wanting her, man to woman—but he'd found nothing. Now, for better or worse, he was being put to work with her for seven whole days, except for the early morning training sessions with Gan. He frowned. Either this was heaven or his personal hell, he couldn't decide which. It was heaven just to be privileged to be in Jessica's exuberant presence, but it was hell trying to keep his hands off her, to maintain a respectable distance from her and treat her like the owner of the ranch. He had to remember he was only a ranch hand.

"I'd like to learn about your orchids. I know nothing of them."

"And you were so gentle with them," Jessica said. "I would never have thought a man could be like that, but you are."

He held her wide, innocent gaze. "Not all men are like your ex-husband, Jessica. There is a man in Sedona who owns a nursery, Charlie McCoy. He loves his plants like you do. They grow well for him because he cares for them with his heart—like you."

Chastised, Jessica nodded and returned to the workbench. "You're right, of course. I shouldn't be projecting that every man is Carl." And then she laughed sharply. "It's a good thing they aren't!"

Dan followed her over to the workbench. "Show me what you'd like me to do."

For the next hour, Jessica went through everything that Dan would need to know about the care, watering and repotting of orchids. He proved an apt student. Time flew by as she became immersed in her love of the brightly colored orchids that lived in the greenhouse. She enjoyed his nearness, though he seemed somewhat distant compared to earlier this morning, when he'd become impassioned about protecting her.

Finally, she said, "Enough for now. I'm sure your head is spinning with too much information on my girls."

Dan nodded and rested his hands on his narrow hips as he surveyed the many orchids. "There's a lot to them. More than I realized." He noticed a light veil of perspiration across Jessica's furrowed brow. Her blond hair was slightly curly from the high humidity in the greenhouse, and he had an urge to move several strands away from her eyes, but he resisted.

"When you talk about them," he told her, "do you know your eyes light up, your voice becomes excited?"

Laughing, Jessica nodded. "Yes, I've been told that many times before."

"It's your love of them that does it." Dan followed her back to the workbench.

"Don't you think that whenever a person loves, he or she should show it?"

"Maybe," he hedged. "But not many people I know are willing to reveal themselves, their real feelings, like you do all the time."

"Kate's warned me about that. She says I'm too transparent. That I need to put up some barriers until I get to know people better."

"I don't agree," Dan said.

"No?" She looked up and smiled as she washed her hands in bleach and water to keep from spreading potential viruses among the orchids.

"No."

"You hide behind a mask like Kate and Sam do."

"Guilty."

Jessica laughed a little as she dried her hands. She stood aside for him to rinse his hands and dry them off. "But I shouldn't be like the three of you?"

"No." Dan replaced the towel on a hook on the side of the workbench. "I don't pretend to know orchids very well yet, but I think you're a lot like them. You're different. As you said, they don't need soil to survive in, just air and moisture. In my mind, they are plants of Father Sky, not Mother Earth." He turned and held her warm, soft gaze. How badly he wanted to reach out and caress her reddened cheek, touch his mouth to those parted lips that were begging to be kissed. Battling his needs, Dan said, "You are like the sky people. Like the clouds that form and disappear. You respond to sunlight, moonlight and the temperature of things around you, as these orchid people do. You *are* different, Jessica, but that doesn't make you wrong or us right. In some ways you are able to see things better. You don't think badly of anyone."

Maybe he'd said too much. Dan supposed he had. But Jessica's expression changed to one of such sweetness that his hand itched to reach out and stroke her cheek. "Father Sky sees all that goes on down here on his lover, Mother Earth. His eyes are set differently. So are yours. You belong to the cloud people, who see above and beyond what we mere two-leggeds, who are root bound on Mother Earth, can see. So no, do not change. Do not try to become like us." He touched his face momentarily. "Masks are shields. We put them on to protect our soft, inner side. Cloud people do not need masks. They have the safety of Father Sky's embrace to protect them."

Jessica stood there for a long, silent moment, digesting Dan's heartfelt words. His sincerity touched her heart as nothing else ever could. "How you see things is so beautiful," she began in a strained, low tone. "I wish—I wish...well, never mind."

Dan saw her eyes darken. "What is your wish?"

"Oh, it's a stupid one. An idealistic one, as Kate would say." Jessica could not bear to look at the compassion she saw burning in his eyes. For a moment, she wanted to take those two steps forward and simply embrace Dan, lean against him and feel the solid, hard beat of his heart against hers. This man was surprising her on so many levels all at once that she felt flustered emotionally.

"Would you share it with me?" he asked, moving next to her at the workbench.

His closeness was wonderful. Jessica was only beginning to realize how *hungry* she'd been for a positive male presence in her life. Moyra had often teased her that she didn't know how Jessica had survived two years without male companionship. Moyra had a boyfriend who she saw on weekends in Vancouver, and Jessica had wished for something similar for herself, but it had never materialized. Maybe because she lived in abject fear that Carl would unexpectedly show up to hurt her, she supposed.

Jessica also realized she hadn't been ready to reach out and trust a man, either. Until now. Dan was different, very different from any man she'd ever encountered. He was so in tune with nature, with her flowers and most importantly, with her. It was amazing—and scary. Carl had come on to her like that, too, pretending an interest in her flowers, and in the philosophy of life that she lived every day. Her memories of Carl warred with what she saw in Dan. Was he really like Carl? Her heart said no, but her head was screaming at her to be wary, to watch out and to give things time, instead of rushing willy-nilly into some kind of relationship that might turn out similar to her marriage.

Heaving a sigh, Jessica wrestled with her confusion. Who to trust? Who not to trust? Frustrated, she finally said, "It's a stupid wish built on fantasy."

Dan heard the finality in her voice, the strength that came up unexpectedly from deep within her. Her tone implied that he was to drop the subject—completely. He would respect that for now. There were many feelings he was picking up around Jessica, he realized, noticing how her fingers trembled slightly as she removed an orchid from an old clay pot. From the stubborn set of her lower lip and the darkness haunting her glorious turquoise eyes, he knew the beautiful cloud person was gone, at least for now. Somehow their conversation had brought up ghosts from her past that now stood between them. He felt badly about that. All he wanted was to see Jessica remain in the clouds, to be that magical, wondrous, happy creature he'd first met.

For the next fifteen minutes, Jessica concentrated on showing Dan how to repot an orchid. He no longer questioned her, but stood respectfully nearby, just far enough away to keep her from feeling threatened.

When Jessica handed him another orchid to repot, he went through each step perfectly. Just the way he touched the plant made her ache for him to touch her in the same way. It was a ludicrous idea, but her body was responding to him even if her mind whispered warnings to her. Unhappy with how she was feeling, she sat on the wooden crate beside the workbench to watch Dan complete the repotting process.

The silence remained between them for a long time, except for the occasional instructions he needed from her. By noon, Jessica felt her stomach growl. Glancing to the left, she watched Dan's angular profile as he worked. His mouth was relaxed now, not thinned. His black brows were drawn down in concentration as he worked with the fragile orchid, his touch light and careful. A light perspiration made his dark, golden skin gleam beneath the diffused light in the greenhouse. Sweat dampened his white shirt beneath each arm and around his upper chest. She saw the creases and lines at the corners of his mouth and eyes and she wondered how he'd gotten that scar on his left cheek. But, she remembered, there were a lot of things she wanted to know about Dan Black.

"This morning," Jessica began awkwardly, trying to find a diplomatic way of asking what she wanted to know, "you said something to me I didn't understand."

Dan glanced over at her. "Which part of it?"

Knitting her hands nervously, Jessica looked away. In that moment, the brief smile that pulled at the corners of his mouth made him look years younger. Dan had a beguiling face; she knew his rugged features had yet to reveal his every emotion to her. She wondered what it would be like if he really smiled, or laughed fully.

"You said something in Navajo—*sh* something. I didn't know what it meant."

Dan's hands stilled over the orchid. His heart plummeted. "That…" he muttered self-consciously.

"Yes?"

He didn't *dare* let Jessica know what it meant. "It was…nothing. When I get excited, I drop into my own language, that's all."

She watched him closely. His expression had closed up faster than a snapping turtle. It was surprising to her. Her head whispered, *See, he's not to be trusted. He's lying to you. He knows what it means, but he won't tell you.* Jessica tried to ignore her mistrustful thoughts.

"Oh…."

He felt her sadness and looked at her sharply. "It wasn't anything bad, Jessica. I promise you that." And it wasn't. It was a beautiful expression that a man used for the woman he loved. He knew Jessica had grown up with Navajo people, but he was grateful she didn't recognize the wonderful endearment that was only shared between two people who were deeply in love with one another. He had no wish to embarrass her with his slip of the tongue, or the wild way his heart and his passion had galloped away from him in those moments out of time with her. At all costs, he must hold how he felt toward her to himself. She must never know his real feelings, because if she did, he was sure he'd be fired from the job and asked to leave the ranch. And right now, Dan was helpless, unable to walk away. Jessica was like an answer to his lifelong prayers—a woman who could fulfill him on every level. And she could. He knew that as surely as he took each breath of air into his lungs.

Jessica sighed and stood up. "You did a great job

of repotting that orchid. Let's go get some lunch. I'm starving to death."

Relieved that she wasn't going to pursue the topic, Dan nodded. He put the orchid on the bench and, grabbing his hat, followed her out of the humid, moist depths of the greenhouse. He wondered how he was going to handle his unraveling feelings for her in the days to come. Yes, he felt like a man with one foot in heaven and the other in hell. Or maybe he was like that man in the Greek myth, who ached to capture the golden fleece that was guarded by a killer giant, but knew he never could. Not ever...

Chapter 6

Where had the first three weeks of her time at the ranch gone? Jessica stood out on the porch of her house, the hot breeze ruffling her hair. In frustration, she caught the tousled strands and put them up in a ponytail. The sunlight was blindingly bright, the sky an incredibly deep, cobalt blue. It was a beautiful day, she thought as she watched Kate and Sam riding off to the north pasture. A lot of new calves had been born, and she knew they wanted to check on them and the mothers today.

In her hand was a list of things to pick up at the Sedona Hay and Feed Store. Sam had asked her to get veterinary items they were running low on, such as antibiotics, hypodermic needles and thrush ointment. At the clip-clop of horse hooves coming around her house, she turned expectedly. Instantly, her heart rate increased. Dan Black sat tall and proud on a dark bay gelding with four white socks. His face was a sheen of perspiration, and she admired once again his powerful chest outlined by the sweat-damp, dark blue shirt he wore. Oh, how she'd missed his company!

Jessica had become spoiled by Dan's presence that first week at the ranch. He'd worked sixteen hours a day helping her get her business set up and running smoothly once again. The only time she saw him now was for an hour—if that—in the morning. Their time with one another was extremely limited. How often she had gone over to the bunkhouse to invite him to her house to eat, only to learn that he was still out on horseback, doing ranch chores somewhere.

She saw Dan's gray eyes narrow heatedly upon her. That mask he always wore softened considerably as he pulled his dusty, sweaty horse to a halt. Putting his fingers to the brim of his hat, he tipped it in her direction.

"Going somewhere?" he asked. Dan knew he should continue to avoid Jessica all he could, but when he'd seen her step out onto the porch, he couldn't help himself—he'd had to ride over to visit with her. It was a selfish decision on his part. He'd just finished herding some broodmares from the south pasture to the west one and was coming back in to grab a late lunch. Now he was hungry on a much different, more galvanizing level.

"Hi, Dan." Jessica held up the paper in her hand. "Sam wants me to go to the feed store and get some antibiotics for him."

He nodded. "Yes, we're going through them lately. A lot of sepsis with the cows and their babies." He squinted at the dry, yellowed pastures. "Might be the drought doing it. Everything's dying."

She sobered and stepped off the front porch. "I can hardly wait until Rachel gets here. She's got homeopathic remedies that can cure sepsis better than an antibiotic, and it will cost us a lot less, too. She left a few kits here on her last visit, but we've already used them." She paused, then said, "Hey, why don't you come into town with me?"

The idea was tempting. "I can't, I got—"

Jessica pouted prettily. "Dan, I'm going to need some help. Sam wanted me to take the pickup truck and get about eight hundred pounds in feed. I'm going to need a strong body to help lift that stuff into the truck. Sam said Old Man Thomas at the store is in his eighties and he's too stingy to hire help. The poor old gent can't handle hundred-pound sacks of grain, and I can't, either." Flexing her arm, she pointed to the almost nonexistent bulge of her biceps. "I'm a wimp."

He chuckled. The sparkle in her eyes was one of warmth and welcome. Instantly, Dan felt embraced by her bubbly enthusiasm and humor. "Okay, Miss Jessica, let me get my horse unsaddled and cared for. It'll take about ten minutes."

"Great! I'll drive over to the barn in about ten and meet you."

Her heart exploded with happiness as she saw him grin. How little Dan laughed. The more she pried, the less he allowed her entrance into his unknown life. She longed for his companionship again. Kate and Sam had been so busy that Jessica largely left them alone. They worked from dawn to almost midnight every day and then fell exhausted into one another's arms, and slept deeply. The drought was putting a terrible edge on the struggle for life at the ranch, and they were doing everything in their power to save the lives of their stock. She knew Dan was working every bit as hard, but she wished she could spend more time with him.

Jessica couldn't still her excitement as Dan drove the beat-up pickup into town. There was no air-conditioning in the truck, so both windows were down as they pulled slowly into uptown Sedona, the area known to the locals as the "tourist trap."

"Can you imagine, six million people a year visit us?" Jessica asked, looking at the line of tourist shops crowded together along the highway.

Dan grimaced. "I stay away from this place as much as possible."

"Why?" She looked at his chiseled profile, her gaze settling on his mouth. His lips were thinned, which meant he was tense. She wondered if this trip was the reason. Rarely did Jessica see Dan leave the ranch premises. It was as if he were hiding out there.

With a shrug, Dan turned the truck into the hay-and-feed-store parking lot. "Crowds bother me, that's all."

"Oh…" She looked at the storefront. It was badly weathered and in dire need of a coat of paint. The wood was graying and splintering from the heat. A rusted old sign hung at an angle and moved slowly back and forth in the inconstant afternoon breeze, creaking in protest. Dan backed the pickup against the wooden loading dock at the barn portion of the building, where the grain and hay were kept.

Jessica caught sight of an old man sitting beneath

the cottonwood tree near the entrance. He was probably in his seventies, his white hair down to his shoulders, a bright red wrap around his head as he sat with his back against the tree and weaved from side to side. He was drunk, Jessica realized as she stepped from the truck. The clothes he wore were rags, and very dirty looking. She frowned. Instead of going up the stairs into the store, she moved to the man's side.

Jessica had forgotten most of the Navajo she'd learned as a child. She'd been multilingual, knowing English, Eastern Cherokee, some Navajo and Apache. Now she worked to remember Navajo phrases.

The old man opened his bloodshot eyes and looked at her as Jessica knelt down in front of him. *"Ya at eeh,"* she began tenuously. That was Navajo for "hello." She wasn't sure he *was* Navajo, even though the reservation ended where the city of Flagstaff, an hour north of Sedona, began.

The old man's tobacco brown skin crinkled. He gave her a toothless smile, his gums gleaming. *"Ya at eeh..."* he slurred.

Jessica knew there was a mission in West Sedona that helped the homeless. She was distraught by the man's condition. The odor of alcohol assailed her, and she spotted an empty one-gallon wine bottle lying next to him.

"Jessica, leave him alone."

She looked up to see Dan scowling darkly over her.

"No. He needs help."

"You can't help him. That's Tommy Wolf. He's the local drunk here in Sedona."

She heard the embarrassment in Dan's voice. He was edgy and nervous, looking around as if he were ashamed to be seen with her and Tommy. "I'm not leaving him, Dan. Look at him. He's filthy! He needs a bath and some help. Can you speak Navajo to him and tell him we'll take him to the mission? It's only a few blocks from here."

Pulling his black Stetson lower on his sweaty brow, Dan frowned in irritation. "Jessica, you're throwing your care away. Tommy knows where the mission's at. He'll eventually get over there when he wants a decent meal and a bath. Right now, he's drunker than hell. Just leave him alone."

Her jaw became set. "Dan, just go get the feed and antibiotics, okay? I'll take Tommy over while you do it." She moved forward to lift the old man's arm, placing it around her shoulders. Instead, she felt Dan's strong hands on her arms. He lifted her up and away from Tommy.

"Dan!" She stood there, staring up into his angry features.

"I'll do it," he rasped. "Just get the door of the truck open for me."

Jessica's eyes widened as she heard the grating in his deep voice. She watched as Dan easily hefted the old Navajo to his feet and aimed him in the direction of the pickup. Tommy began a slurred conversation in Navajo with Dan as they walked toward the truck. Jessica hurried ahead of them.

The honk of a horn startled her. She halted as a brand-new pickup truck roared into the hay and feed store next to where they were parked. If she hadn't stopped when she did, she would have been sideswiped by the swift-moving vehicle. Her mouth dropped open in shock as she stood there, the truck passing only a foot away from her. Blinking, she realized she knew the two cowboys in the cab—Chet and Bo Cunningham from the neighboring ranch. Old memories flooded her.

Angrily, Jessica moved around the red pickup and quickly opened the passenger door for Dan, who was slowly easing Tommy along on not too steady feet. The old Navajo had no shoes or socks on, and her heart bled for his condition.

"Well, well, another one of the prodigal daughters has returned to the Donovan Ranch. Whad'ya know...."

Snapping her head to the left, Jessica met the dark eyes of Chet Cunningham. A two-day growth of scraggly beard shadowed his narrow, pale features, and his straw cowboy hat was low over his eyes as he swaggered around the front of his red truck toward her.

"Little Jessica Donovan," he crowed, and then laughed. "Out saving the world again?" He slapped his hand on his jean-covered thigh.

To her consternation, she saw the taller, darker brother, Bo, appear around the front of the truck in turn. "Mind your own business, Chet," she said.

Chet snickered and put his hand over hers where she held the door to the pickup open. "Naw, that's too easy. The Cunninghams run Sedona. You're trespassing, missy."

"Get your hand off her."

Jessica jerked her head toward the dark, lethal-sounding voice. She realized belatedly that it was Dan speaking. He stood there, still holding Tommy in his grip, and glared past her to Chet. She'd never heard Dan speak in such a tone, nor had she ever seen the expression his face held now. There was a dangerous quality radiating around him that made the hair on the back of her neck stand up in reaction. His eyes were colorless, his mouth a hard line, his face emotionless.

Chet snickered again and glanced over at Bo, who came and stood at his shoulder. "Go to hell! You got guts coming into Sedona in the first place," he roared, raising his gloved hand and jabbing it at Dan. "You takin' Tommy over to the mission to dry out again? Together?" And both brothers laughed loudly.

Jessica jerked her hand away from Chet's and held it out to Tommy, who weakly grasped her fingers. "Pay no attention to them," she ordered the older man as Dan helped her maneuver the Navajo into her truck. Before she knew it, she felt Dan's hand on her arm. It was a strong, guiding grip, not hurtful, but meant to re-move her from between him and the Cunningham men. She opened her mouth to protest, but it was too late.

"You two sidewinders go about your business," Dan snarled. "And leave off your jawing, too."

"Whooee!" Chet crowed, slapping his brother's shoulder. "Listen to this guy give orders, Bo. Whad'ya think about that?" Chet's eyes narrowed in fury. "Take your bottle and the old Navajo rug your granny made for you and crawl back into your hole, Black. Better yet, crawl off to Flag, where you were the butt of ev-eryone's jokes."

Dan felt the heat creep into his face. He saw the leering anger in both men's expressions. Worse, Jes-sica was hearing what they said about him. His heart pounded in fury and dread. Now she would know the truth about him. A serrating pain scored his heart.

"Get the hell out of here, Chet. Just leave us in peace and we'll do the same for you."

Chet took in a couple of deep breaths and stuck his chest out. He glanced again at Bo, who barely nodded. Pulling his stained leather gloves a little tighter, Chet grinned. "Gonna be the cock of the walk here, Black? Showing off for Miss Goody Two-shoes, who rescues drunks like you?"

Dan heard Jessica's protest. Before he could answer, he saw Chet draw back his arm, his fist cocked. To hell with it. If he was going to go to jail on assault charges, he might as well make Chet Cunningham pay in full for his actions.

Jessica gasped as she watched Chet's fist barrel forward to strike Dan. Suddenly she saw Dan move with the speed of a striking rattlesnake. Only he didn't use his fists, he used his entire body in a karatelike motion. Blinking, Jessica cried out as Chet went flying backward with a grunt, slamming into the dock and letting out a loud *ooooff* sound.

Bo cursed and leaped toward Dan. Jessica put her hands to her lips and cried out a warning. Dan moved with the grace of a ballet artist and swung around, his booted foot arcing out and catching Bo in the stomach. The older brother was slammed into the side of the red truck. Chet, his nose bloody and crooked, scrambled off the ground and leaped at Dan.

Jessica stood there, stunned by Dan's prowess in fighting. All of a sudden the easygoing, mild-mannered cowboy had turned into a lethal warrior she'd never known existed. She watched as Dan's open hand caught Chet just beneath the nose. Cunningham went down like a felled ox, unconscious this time.

"Stop it!"

A shotgun went off.

Jessica leaped and screamed. She saw Old Man Thomas hobbling out onto the dock, the shotgun aimed at the three cowboys below.

"Now, galdarnit, you three young roosters take yore fights elsewhere. You got that? Or you want yore pants full of buckshot?"

Dan eased out of his karate position. Breathing hard, his hands aching, he looked up at Old Man Thomas, who was red-faced and angry as hell. Holding up his hands, Dan said, "We'll leave, Mr. Thomas."

"Damn right you will! Get outta here! All of ya! Chet, Bo, get a move on. I'm a callin' yore daddy and tellin' him yore up to yore same ol' tricks again. Dagnabit, yore nothing but trouble! Now git! The lot of ya!"

Dan moved swiftly over to Jessica, who stood white-faced and frozen, her hands pressed against her stomach and her eyes large and glazed. Damn! "Come on," he rasped, grabbing her by the arm and leading her around the front of the truck. "Let's get Tommy over to the mission. We can pick up the supplies down at Cottonwood Hay and Feed, instead."

He looked over his shoulder just to make sure the Cunningham men weren't foolish enough to try and attack again. He saw Bo holding a hand up to his bloody nose and mouth.

"You drunken bastard," Bo snarled as he got to his feet, "I'm callin' the sheriff. You're going up on assault charges—"

"No, he ain't!" Old Man Thomas roared, glaring down at them from the dock. He aimed the shotgun directly at Bo. "You two started it. I saw it with my own eyes. You two ain't got the sense of a rock. Get the hell outta here! Any sheriff to be called, I'll be doing that, ya hear? And if you put charges against Black, I'll be slappin' them against you. Understand?"

Bo glared over at Dan, wiping his nose with his gloved hand. "Yeah, I hear you, Mr. Thomas."

Chet stood on wobbly feet, his face a mass of blood coming from his nose and the corner of his badly cut mouth. Bo strode over, jerked his younger brother forward and pushed him back into the pickup. He looked up at them.

"Black, you're on my list now. You'd better watch your back, you drunken son of a bitch." His mouth curved into a hard grin. "Yeah, you'll hit the bottle again and I'll come looking for you. Next time, things will be different," he finished, punching his gloved index finger toward Dan.

"Come on," Dan urged tightly, getting Tommy out of the truck in front of the mission. He didn't dare look at Jessica. Now she knew about his sordid past. Damn! Gently moving the old Navajo up the sidewalk to the two-story wooden house that served as a center for the homeless in Sedona, he avoided Jessica's gaze. But he could feel her eyes on him, his skin scorching hotly at her appraisal. She hadn't said a word as he drove the three blocks to the mission.

The ache in his heart widened. Well, he was stupid to hope that Jessica wouldn't find out about his past—his bout with the bottle after the war. He brought Tommy into the cooler depths of the front lobby, sitting him into a chair near the reception desk.

Jessica moved to the desk and talked to the young woman with glasses behind it, while Dan stood back, his hands shoved into the pockets of his jeans. His knuckles hurt, but it was nothing like the pain he felt in his heart or the shame that burned through him. When Jessica turned, he saw her avoid his gaze and stare down at the floor instead. Humiliation avalanched through him. Grimly, Dan opened the door for her. Tommy was in good hands now and the folks who ran this mission would get him a bath, clean clothes, shoes, some hot, nutritious food and a place for him to sober up.

The heat of the sunlight laced across them as they walked to the pickup parked beneath two huge cottonwoods. He opened the door for Jessica.

"Thank you," she whispered. She got in, pressed her hands into her lap and hung her head. She felt Dan get back in and heard the door slam. Closing her eyes, she took a long, shaky breath.

"Jessica," he began awkwardly, "I'm sorry…"

She slowly opened her eyes and lifted her chin. Dan sat tensely beside her, both his bloodied hands gripping the steering wheel. As she met and held his sad, dark gray eyes, tears stung hers. The incredible sadness around him enveloped her and she just stared at him, at a loss for words. Finally, she saw him scowl and push the cowboy hat off his wrinkled, glistening brow.

"Something came over me," he muttered. "I saw Chet trap your hand against that door and something just snapped inside me. That little rattler is no good. He knew what he was doing."

"Y-yes, I think he did," she managed to answer haltingly. Her gaze shifted to his white-knuckled hands.

"At least let me clean up your hands, Dan. They're bleeding pretty badly."

He hadn't even noticed, Dan realized as he watched Jessica lean down and pick up the plastic quart bottle of water she'd brought along for them to drink. From the glove box, she took a clean cloth. Turning in the seat, she eased his right hand off the steering wheel after dampening the cloth. Her touch was incredibly gentle and warm. He felt his heart breaking. It would be the last time she ever touched him this way. The last.

"You don't have to touch me," he muttered, and tried to draw his hand out of hers.

"Stop!" Jessica cried, her voice rising. "I'm upset, Dan. The least you can do is sit still and let me clean you up. Now just relax, will you?"

He heard the strain in her soft voice. Her full mouth was compressed and he knew she was angry—at him. Still, he relished each touch of the cooling cloth against his aching knuckles. He never wanted her to stop. "You make the pain go away," he murmured unsteadily, catching and holding her fleeting blue gaze. "Just your touch...."

Heat swept through Jessica. She closed her other hand over his. Taking a ragged breath, she said brokenly, "Dan, you could've been killed by those two! I've rarely seen evil in this world, but I think Chet and Bo were *born* that way! It's just so upsetting."

Without thinking, Dan tugged his hand from between hers. "Listen to me," he rasped, pulling her into his arms. He felt her trembling like a frightened fawn. Closing his eyes, he buried his face against her soft blond hair. Slowly her trembling ceased and he felt her relax against him. He expected Jessica to fight him, to push away from him in disgust. Instead, he felt her moan softly, her face pressed against his, her arms sliding around his torso.

"It's all right...." he whispered against her ear. She smelled like a meadow full of wildflowers. Her hair was thin and fine, like soft, spun gold against his cheek and nose. All of his barriers dissolved as she sought his protection. "Stop shaking. It's all over, *shi shaa.* You're safe...safe...."

His voice was low and singsong. Jessica felt the strength of Dan's arms around her, holding her protectively. She smelled the odor of hay and horses on his roughened cheek. She felt the powerful thud of his heart against her breasts as he pressed her hard against him. Everywhere she contacted his lean, whipcord strong body, her skin burned with desire.

She heard him speaking low, in the beautiful, rhythmic Navajo language, and she sighed softly and sank more deeply into his arms. She felt his mouth against her hair as he pressed a kiss to her head. How she'd longed for his kiss all these lonely weeks! Summoning all of her courage, all of her driving needs, Jessica turned her face slightly, and this time, as his mouth came down to press another kiss to her hair, his lips met hers instead.

A jolt of heat tore through her as his pliant mouth closed over hers. At first she felt surprise vibrate through Dan, and then, as she moved her lips softly, searchingly against his, she felt the surprise dissolve into a swift, returning pressure against her lips. Suddenly, the world ceased to exist. She was enclosed within his strength, the searching boldness of his mouth. The molten heat of his tongue moved slowly across her lower lip, making her moan with a pleasure she had never before experienced. His roughened hand moved slowly up her bare arm, his touch eliciting fire, yet gentling her at the same time.

This was the Dan Black she had wanted all along, Jessica hazily realized as she sank more deeply into his searching, molding kiss, which stole her breath and bound their aching souls into one. As she ran her hand up across Dan's shoulder, she felt every muscle leap and harden beneath her foray. He felt so good to her! So solid, warm and giving. For an instant, she had thought he would be not only hurt, but killed by the Cunninghams. They were dangerous men. But she'd never realized how dangerous Dan was. To know that the hands that now roved roughly across her arms and shoulders were hands that could hurt as well as protect was shocking to her. He was a man of many surprises. A man wrapped in the darkness of his past.

That realization caused Jessica to pull away unexpectedly. She gazed up into Dan's eyes, which appeared almost silver and black as he studied her. Their breathing was ragged. Their hearts were pounding in unison. Blinking, Jessica realized that Dan was the man Moyra had told her about—the man wrapped in darkness! Her lips tingled wildly from his onslaught. She stared at that mouth, that full lower lip, and then back up into his narrowed eyes. He seemed like a predator right now, and she his willing quarry. Her fingers opened and closed against his broad, powerful shoulders. Her legs felt weak and she didn't want to move. All that existed, all that she'd ever dreamed of having, was here, in Dan Black.

"No...." Jessica whispered faintly.

Chastened, Dan released her. His body was on fire. He ached for her, the pain making him want to bend double. What the hell was he doing? Why had he kissed Jessica? What demon from his darkness had driven him right over the edge to take her? Helping Jessica sit up on her side of the seat, he leaned back, taking off his hat and allowing his head to rest against the rear window. What the hell had he just done? His heart was pounding like a wild horse in his chest. His mouth was warm from her soft, breathless kiss. She tasted like sweet honey and warm sunlight. His skin throbbed wherever she'd touched him with her delicate, hesitant fingertips. Dan cursed himself richly. He could feel shame flooding through him as if a dam had burst. What kind of fool was he? He'd not only overstepped his bounds, he'd probably be getting his walking papers from Sam McGuire tonight when his boss got off the range. Dan had no business kissing the owner of such a huge ranch.

Taking in a deep, ragged breath, he tried to tame his fear and shame. But his desire to make Jessica his, to couple with her not only on the physical level, but to entwine their souls in beautiful lovemaking, overwhelmed him. He ached to take her all the way with him. He wanted to feel her small, firm body against his, to feel their flesh sliding hotly together.

It was all just another broken dream, Dan realized as he opened his eyes and sat up. He risked a look at Jessica. She sat there, hands clasped tightly in her lap, her head tipped back and her eyes closed. Those delicious, pale pink lips were softly parted, and he wondered if he'd hurt her with the power of his kiss. His brows drew downward as he replaced the hat on his head and started the pickup. By tonight, Sam would be asking him to pack his bedroll and leave. By tomorrow morning, the sheriff would probably be out looking for him, to slam him into the county jail on assault charges. Dan couldn't fool himself. Old Man Cunningham ran Coconino and Yavapai Counties, including Sedona.

Dan's hands shook momentarily as he backed the pickup away from the mission. Heaven and hell. He'd just held heaven in his arms and stolen a wild, hot kiss from Jessica. The hell was that he was going to pay for all his indiscretions. Every single last one of them. Worse, he'd never see Jessica again, and he felt his heart crack and begin to break into anguished fragments deep in his chest.

Chapter 7

Dan leaned moodily against the last hundred-pound sack of grain that he'd stored in the barn. The hundred-degree heat was making him sweat profusely. His knuckles ached and he automatically flexed them. Taking his red bandanna from around his neck, he removed his cowboy hat and wiped his perspiring face. Through the large open doors of the red barn, he could see Jessica's house.

Hell and damnation! He might as well pack what few belongings he had into the old carpetbag that he'd inherited from his great-grandmother. It was only a matter of time, Dan concluded, until Sam came to the bunkhouse to give him his walking papers. Especially now that he'd got entangled in a fight—and he'd kissed Jessica.

His lips tingled hotly in memory of her soft, sweet

mouth against his hungry, searching one. Frowning, he settled the black Stetson on his head and walked out to the pickup. Climbing in, he drove it around to the front of the main ranch house where it belonged. His gaze caught a rising cloud of dust from the dirt road that led into the ranch from 89A.

Trouble. He could feel it. Getting out of the truck, he looked toward the greenhouse. It was probably the Coconino County sheriff come to slap him in cuffs and take him to jail on assault and battery charges. Rubbing the back of his neck, Dan felt a storm of emotions roll through him. He needed more time. He *had* to talk to Jessica about their unexpected, shocking kiss. He wanted to apologize. Afterward, she'd retreated into a silent shell, and they'd passed the entire trip to the hay and feed store and back to the ranch in stilted, embarrassed silence.

Dan knew she was sorry. The look on her face— the chagrin written across it and the high, red color in her flushed cheeks—told him everything. She didn't like him. He hadn't asked her permission to touch her, much less kiss her. What the hell was the matter with him? He was acting crazy, like that black Arabian stallion when he got around a mare in heat. No brains, just hormones.

Dan decided to wait for the approaching vehicle. As it crested the top of the hill that led down the winding, narrow dirt road to the canyon below, where he stood, he scowled. It wasn't a white car with lights and sirens. No, it was a red car with antennae sticking out of the trunk area. Someone from the fire department. But why? Stymied, Dan folded his arms against his chest and waited, leaning tensely against the back of the pickup. The shade of an overhead cottonwood cooled him slightly and the off-and-on breeze felt good to him. He was sweating plenty, probably out of fear of being jailed again. He never wanted to return to that hateful place.

As the red car drove up and parked near him, Dan saw a man with black hair and blue eyes at the wheel. When the stranger opened the door and unbuckled the seat belt, Dan got a better look at him. Wearing dark blue, serge pants, highly polished black boots and a light blue, short-sleeved shirt, he had a tall, lanky build, reminding Dan of a cougar's lethal grace. He looked vaguely familiar, but Dan couldn't place him. On his shirt he wore a silver badge and his left sleeve bore a red-and-white insignia that said Emergency Medical Technician. Dan tensed as he caught the nameplate affixed to his left pocket: J. Cunningham.

Slowly uncrossing his arms and spreading his feet slightly for balance, Dan studied the man before him. He was the youngest of the three Cunningham brothers, and from town gossip Dan knew that Jim had recently quit his forestry job as a hotshot firefighter and come home to try and mend fences with his cantankerous father and brothers. Rumor had it that Jim had left years ago during a hellacious family fight, swearing never to return. For ten years, he had remained up in Flagstaff. The only time Dan had heard of him coming home was at Christmas. But he always left shortly after to resume his fire fighting duties around the U.S. Now that he was working for Sedona's fire department, everyone wondered if he'd stay for good.

As he quietly closed the car door, Cunningham's blue eyes were dark and disturbed looking, though he held Dan's gauging look. His full mouth was pursed as he moved in Dan's direction.

Dan didn't know what to expect. Had Jim Cunningham come to finish off the fight? His heart began a slow, hard pounding as adrenaline began to pour into his bloodstream.

"You Dan Black?" Cunningham demanded, halting about six feet away, his hands resting tensely on his narrow hips.

"I am."

"You know who I am?"

"Got an idea."

"My brothers just came over to the fire department to get patched up from the fight they just had." Giving Dan a frosty smile, he continued, "I'm an EMT, on the medical staff of the Sedona Fire Department. I came to apologize to you in person for my brothers' actions and to see if you were okay."

Stunned, Dan stared at him in disbelief. Cunninghams weren't known for apologizing for anything they did—they played by their own twisted rules and their reputation in Sedona was nasty. They never had any compassion for folks they chose to take on and destroy. Dan knew many people Old Man Cunningham had torn apart over the years. The father was a merciless bastard just like his two sons. But as Dan heard it, Jim Cunningham had always been different, set apart from the rest of the family, like a black sheep of sorts. Or rather like a *white* sheep.

When Jim thrust out his hand, Dan swallowed hard. "My knuckles are bruised up a little," he muttered, taking the man's offered hand. Cunningham's grip was firm, and Dan found himself respecting the guy for what he was doing. It was absolutely unheard of that a Cunningham apologized for anything.

Jim nodded and released his grip. "And Miss Jessica Donovan? Is she okay? Chet said she slapped him, but I don't believe my brother. Maybe you can tell me what really happened?"

Dan nodded and told him the entire story. The EMT's oval face and strong chin became tight with anger by the time he'd finished.

"I see," Jim rasped. "Well, both of them have broken noses out of the deal. Just deserts, I'd say." He cocked his head and perused Dan speculatively. "I heard you were in the Corps for four years, or is that just gossip?"

Dan relaxed. He liked Jim Cunningham, even though something about his stance reminded him of a dangerous cougar ready to strike. "Yes, I was."

"What part?"

"Recons."

Cunningham grinned a little. "Thought so."

"Oh?"

"My brothers said they couldn't lay a hand on you. That you'd done all the damage to them. I figured you had some special training to do that."

"I don't like to fight, Mr. Cunningham. It's not in my nature. I'd rather have peace."

He nodded. "I'm with you. Coming back to this family of mine this last month has been hell. I'm going to try and stick it out, but I don't know...." He looked up at the clear blue, cloudless sky for a moment.

"Family troubles are the worst kind," Dan agreed quietly.

Jim looked over at him. "Look, if it's okay with you,

I'd like to meet Jessica Donovan and make my apologies directly to her."

"You shouldn't be cleaning up the messes your brothers make."

"No, but if I'm going to break the patterns of abuse that run through my family, somebody is going to have to take responsibility and start changing things, aren't they? My two brothers don't have a clue yet." His eyes flashing, Cunningham muttered grimly, "They sure as hell will when I get off duty tomorrow morning and we have a friendly little chat over breakfast with Dad about it. That's a promise."

Dan didn't envy Jim's position, but he respected the man. He wanted to say that the Cunninghams were a barrel of rotten apples and that if a good apple like Jim were put in among them, they'd infect him, too. Instead, he said, "I admire your mission."

Jim grinned tightly. "Not a job for the faint of heart, is it?"

"No," he murmured, "it isn't." In that moment, Dan realized Jim knew all the sordid tales of his brothers' and father's escapades in Coconino and Yavapai Counties, and that he was well aware of the hatred many people had toward the Cunninghams. Their greed, stinginess and manipulative, underhanded business dealings were famous in these parts. "Come on, I know where Jessica's at. I think she'll feel better hearing that there's one Cunningham who cares about other people's feelings."

Dan was going to leave once he showed Cunningham to the door of the greenhouse, but the EMT persuaded him to come in and make introductions. It was the last thing Dan wanted to do, but he had no choice.

Opening the door, he felt an immediate drop in temperature inside the structure and the high humidity enveloped him. He saw Jessica perched up on a stool tending to one of her orchids at the workbench. When she turned to see who was coming in, her eyes widened, first with shock and then surprise mixed with some hidden emotion. Probably disgust for him, for his earlier actions, Dan thought.

Getting a grip on his own feelings, Dan led the EMT over to the workbench and made introductions. Then he stepped back, tipped his hat in Jessica's direction and left. He could see that look in her flawless turquoise eyes. She was so heartbreakingly innocent and beautiful—and he'd abused the privilege of being with her. As he shut the door behind him and crossed the yard, he felt suffocated by his own feelings toward Jessica. How could he have fallen so in love with a woman he'd known only three weeks? How? It had never happened to him before. Not ever.

"I wanted to apologize directly to you for my brothers' actions, Miss Donovan," Jim said to her in an apologetic tone. "I drove over here after they came into the firehouse to get some medical treatment from me and my partner. That's when I found out about it. They told me their side of the story, and I just got the truth as to what really happened from Dan Black. I'm sorry. I want to know if there's anything I can do to patch things up between us."

Stunned, Jessica stared up at the tall, well-muscled EMT. "Y-you're *Jim* Cunningham?"

"Yes, ma'am, I am."

"But," Jessica said, putting the orchid aside, "I thought—"

"I just came home a month ago. Permanently, I hope. My father's ill and—"

"Oh, I'm sorry to hear that." Jessica saw the sadness in his narrowed gaze. She immediately liked Jim Cunningham. "This is such a change from normal Cunningham actions."

"I realize that. I'm trying to break the old habit patterns. They die hard, but someone has got to make Chet and Bo straighten out and become better citizens of Sedona and the county, don't you think?"

His easy smile made him look more handsome, and Jessica warmed to him even more. She wondered if he was married. There was no wedding ring on his left finger. "So, you're home for good now?"

"Yes, I am. For better or worse, I'm afraid."

"Gosh, I admire your tenacity, Jim. You don't mind if I call you by your first name, do you?"

He relaxed slightly, his hand on the edge of her workbench. "No, ma'am, I don't. To tell you the truth, my own lack of formality has gotten me into a lot of trouble with superiors all my life." He looked down at his fire-department uniform. "I'm kinda the wild card around here."

She smiled, enjoying his openness toward her. Jessica was the youngest Donovan girl, and she vaguely remembered Jim in school, but they'd been many grades apart. She knew he'd been a very shy young man, a mere shadow, compared to his two brothers, who were always in fights of one kind or another. Shortly after graduation, he'd been hired by the forest service and had taken a job as a hotshot firefighter. It was the last Jessica had seen of him.

"Sometimes it takes a wild card—or a black sheep—to make the changes, you know?" She saw him relax completely, his broad shoulders drawn back proudly.

"Your reputation around here seems to be true," he murmured.

Jessica raised her eyes and laughed. "Oh, dear, Sedona gossip, I suppose?"

"Well," Jim hedged, "you know there's some truth to gossip. Not much, usually, but there's a seed in it somewhere."

"And what's the gossip going around about me? I imagine because you're in the fire department you hear a lot of it."

Jim pushed his long, strong fingers through his short black hair. "Just that you were insightful, that you always thought the best of a person and his behavior, that's all. After what my brothers pulled, you didn't have to see me or be this kind to me. I think that speaks volumes about you, personally. At least, it does to me." He scowled. "I want peace between our families. I know the Donovans and Cunninghams have fought for decades, mostly because of our stubborn, wrongheaded fathers." Spreading his hands open in a gesture of peace, he continued, "I want to bury the hatchet, Jessica. I want to come over here some time and tell Kate and Sam the same thing. I've only been back for a month, however, and my hands are full with my new job, plus trying to help run the ranch on my days off."

She felt his commitment, as well as his incredible

anguish. Noticing the tiny scars on his brow and right cheek and all over his hands and darkly haired arms, she knew without a doubt that Jim Cunningham carried the scars not only of his own life, but those of his family, too. Her heart went out to him.

"I'll tell Katie and Sam that you dropped by to apologize, Jim. I'm sure they'll be relieved to hear this. We don't want to fight, either. We just want to be able to work with your ranch in the event of some crisis or emergency. We're just as tired of the bad blood between us as you are. Kelly's dead now, so most of the problem is gone. Right now Kate's trying to pick up the pieces, and Sam's trying to help her save our home." Jessica sighed and looked at his serious, dark features. She saw the Apache blood of his mother in him, in the set of his high cheekbones, his glossy black hair and the reddish tone to his dark golden skin. "I know Katie will be glad to hear you're back and trying to change things."

"I don't know if I can," Jim admitted heavily, frowning down at his hand resting on the workbench. "But I'm going to give it one heck of a try."

"You're a catalyst," Jessica said. "The lightning bolt your family needs. By you coming home, things must change or else."

He grinned a little recklessly and held out his hand to her. "Thanks for the vote of confidence. It's the only one I've gotten around here so far. Maybe I should come over once a week and get a pep talk from you so I can carry on."

Giggling, Jessica shook his proffered hand. "I'll tell you who's a real cheerleader. My sister Rachel. She's coming home in December from London, England.

Talk about someone cheering people on to strive to be all they can be—that's Rachel!"

"I remember her. She was two grades behind me in high school," Jim said.

Jessica heard a sudden wistful quality in his voice and saw longing in his blue eyes. It occurred to her that maybe Jim had had a crush on Rachel in school. But Rachel hadn't said anything about it back then, so Jessica shrugged off the intuitive hint. "Hang tight until December. I'm sure Rachel is going to be thrilled to death to hear you're home to change the ways of the Cunningham family. Besides, she's going to be setting up a clinic in Sedona to practice homeopathy. You're an EMT, I see. You two will have a lot in common—medicine."

"Sounds good to me, ma'am."

"Call me Jessica. Please."

He smiled a little. "Okay... Jessica."

"You already talk to Dan?" she asked, sliding off the stool and walking out of the greenhouse with him.

"Yes, I did. And I apologized to him, too."

Jessica felt the dry heat strike her as they walked around the main ranch house to his dark red car. "I think he was worried the sheriff was going to come out and arrest him or something. I think he worries too much, sometimes."

"Chet and Bo started it. He was only defending himself, you and Tommy." Jim halted at the car and opened the door. "If you wanted, you two could press charges against them and land them in the county jail."

Jessica shook her head. "Why perpetuate bad feelings, Jim? I'm willing to let bygones be bygones."

He climbed into the car and shut the door, rolling

down the window. "I hope someday my brothers and father have your kind of understanding heart, Jessica. Thanks." He lifted his hand after starting the vehicle. "If you get a chance, drop over to the main fire department and take a look at our emergency medicine facilities. I hope you don't ever need us out here, but if you do, dial 911 and we'll be here."

Jessica lifted her hand. "I'll do that, Jim. I'm sure Rachel would love to see your medical station, too."

"You've got a deal. Next time I see you, I hope it's for happier reasons."

Jessica watched him drive slowly up the winding road that led out of the canyon. With a sigh, she turned to find Dan. It was time to talk. More than time.

Jessica found Dan in the barn, moving hay that had been brought in by truck earlier that morning. Her heart beating rapidly, she stood at the doorway, absorbing his lean, hard body and graceful movements as he lifted the hundred-pound bales as if they weighed next to nothing. He had put his cowboy hat aside, and she saw damp black tendrils clinging to his sweaty brow and neck. It was stifling in the barn, and except for the breeze that blew through the open doors, there was little fresh air.

"Dan?" she called, her voice swallowed up by the barn. At first she didn't think he'd heard her, and she was about to call his name again when she saw his head snap in her direction. Instantly, she watched his stormy gray eyes go colorless. She knew that meant he felt he was in danger. Or at least he didn't feel safe—with her. That hurt more than anything, and fear threaded through Jessica as she stepped forward, her fingers twisted together.

"I know you're busy, but could you take a break so we can talk?" Her throat felt dry, and her heart was pounding relentlessly in her breast. Whether Jessica wanted to or not, her gaze settled on Dan's mouth. Oh, that kiss he'd given her had been so incredibly galvanizing! She felt as if he'd breathed life back into her wounded soul, such was the power he'd shared with her in that exquisite moment.

"Yeah, hold on...." he rasped between breaths.

She stood to one side as he grabbed his hat, wiped his face with his bandanna and moved out into the aisle, where there was at least a breeze now and again. She saw his eyes narrow, making his wariness more than evident. She went over and unscrewed the cap from the jug of water he always kept with him, and taking his beat-up, blue plastic cup she poured him a drink.

"Here," she whispered, "you need this."

In that moment, Dan wished for something a lot stronger to anesthetize the pain he felt in his heart. Alcohol always stopped him from feeling and took the painful knots out of his gut, too. He saw her unsureness; her eyes were shadowed and that soft, delicious mouth was compressed. He knew what was coming. Inside, he cried. Outwardly, he took the glass with his damp, gloved hand.

"Thanks," he said.

Jessica watched as he tipped his head upward, his Adam's apple bobbing with each swallow. Some trickles of water ran down his chin to the strong, gleaming column of his throat. Trying to gird herself emotionally, Jessica sat down beneath his towering form on a bale of hay.

Wiping his mouth with the back of his hand, he placed the blue cup next to the water jug. He saw Jessica hang her head, unable to meet his gaze. She was twisting her fingers nervously in her lap. Crouching down, his hand on the bale behind where she sat, he took a deep breath. "Okay," he rasped in a strained tone, "what do you want to talk about?" He pushed the brim of his hat upward with his thumb.

Jessica tried to smile but couldn't. She risked a very brief glance in his direction. Dan seemed to realize she didn't want him towering over her. Instead, he'd crouched down to be at eye level with her. Her heart mushroomed with strong, powerful feelings toward him. Touching her breast, she managed to say in a strangled voice, "This is so hard for me, Dan. I hope you can forgive me if I bumble through this. I—I just feel so scared and unsure right now. And I feel a lot of other things that I've never felt before."

She gave a helpless little laugh and met and held his gaze. His eyes had gone from colorless to a dove gray and she knew he'd let down some of his guard. Opening her hands artlessly, she said, "Here I am, a woman who was married for eight years. You'd think I'd be a lot less naive than I am. Or I'd know a lot more than most people think I should when it comes to relationships. Or—" her voice shook "—about men and what they want from me…"

Dan shut his eyes tightly for a moment. "Jessica, I never meant to—"

"No," she whispered, twisting toward him. "Please, Dan, let me finish. This is so hard for me to come to terms with, and you more than anyone should know the truth." She watched his eyes open slightly to study her. "Right now, my heart's pounding in my chest. I can taste my fear."

Concerned, Dan reached out and gently grazed her flushed cheek. "Jessica, I swear to God, I *never* meant to make you feel fear...."

Jessica drowned in his darkening, stormy gray eyes, but his gentle touch gave her courage. "Oh, Dan, I was hoping you'd understand, and I believe you do without even realizing it. My heart said you would." She looked away, tears choking her voice. "When you kissed me earlier today, my world just fell apart around my feet. It wasn't your fault. It was my past coming to meet me. I didn't expect it. How could I know?" Jessica opened her hands and gave him a pleading look.

"Your kiss made me feel so clean and good inside, Dan. I would never have thought it was possible to have a man's kiss do that to me instead of...well, making me feel...awful." She avoided his sharpening gaze, hanging her head and staring down at the fingers she'd nervously clasped together. "When I married Carl, I fell in love with the mask he wore, not the man beneath it. I guess if I'd been older, more experienced, or maybe not such an airhead, I'd have realized he was a two-heart underneath that facade. He presented such a wonderful mask to me, Dan. I thought he was the kindest, gentlest, funniest man in the world. I fell for him so hard that I married him three months after meeting him.

"Within a year of being married to him, I realized I'd married an insanely jealous, controlling monster, not a man. He didn't care about me. Over the years, I realized that he just needed someone else to control, to be a slave to his whims and needs, to cook for him and keep house for him. My love, or whatever it was, died over those years. I felt so trapped, like I was in a prison, or a bad nightmare that just got worse and worse with time. It got so I hated his touch. My skin would crawl when he'd touch me…when he'd kiss me. Toward the end, I'd get physically sick to my stomach if he tried to make love to me."

There, the words were out. Jessica took a deep, ragged breath and risked a look at Dan. To her surprise, his face was open and so readable. Gone was his mask; here was the real man beneath. More than anything, she saw anguish in his dark gray eyes, and his lips were parted, as if he wanted to say something to her.

"There's more," Jessica continued in an unsteady whisper. "Only my sisters know about it, and now Sam, because…well, you'll see. I need to tell you all of this, Dan, because it's not fair to you to walk into something without knowing the whole truth. That's why I have to tell you…." She closed her eyes, unable to stand the judgment she knew would be on his face when she was finished.

"Carl would question my every move. If I went to the grocery store, he would accuse me when I returned of seeing another man. He'd accuse me of sleeping with someone else. But he made up everything in his own sick head. I *never* had an affair, Dan. I never could. I'm just not made that way. It got so I had to not only tell Carl where I was going, but what time I expected to be home. If I wasn't home at that time, all hell would break loose. He'd fly into a fury and he'd accuse me again of having an affair. I tried to tell him I would never be with another man…but," Jessica whispered, "he never believed me."

Rubbing her face, she dropped her hands in her lap and stared across the aisle of the barn, her voice losing all trace of emotion. "The last three years of our marriage were pure hell for me. Carl would hit me and knock me down when I denied I was having an affair. At first he'd just shove me around. Then, later, he'd use his fists and hit me in the stomach. He never hit me anywhere a bruise would show. Over time, his attacks escalated. At the end of the third year, he beat me up so badly that I ended up in the emergency room."

Dan whispered, "Jessica—"

"No…please…let me finish this, Dan. You must." Jessica was too ashamed to look at him. She heard the heartbreaking tone of his voice and it drove tears into her eyes. She fought them back and went on, her words coming out stiltedly, in fits and snatches. Caught up in those terrifying times, she could feel the terror eating her up once again.

"That final time, when I was in the emergency room because of what Carl did to me, I lost consciousness. I remember waking up two weeks later in a Vancouver hospital. The nurse told me I'd been in a coma. I was amazed, because when I lost consciousness, I went into the light. I saw my mother, Dan. She held me while I cried. I had needed her so much over those years, but I was afraid to call home, to tell her what I'd done, what I'd gotten myself into. Carl was just like Kelly, only worse. I'd left home and then married someone just like my father. I felt so humiliated, so stupid, that I didn't want my mother to know…but then she died, too, so I was alone. I didn't call Rachel or Kate because of the same reason. I just felt stupid and ashamed.

"When I was with my mother in that beautiful white light, I told her everything. I knew she had gone over the rainbow bridge, and I knew I was talking to her spirit. I thought I'd died, too, and now I could be with her forever, which made me very happy. We had so many wonderful talks and I was able to tell her everything.

"Her love was so great that she told me it was all right, that what I had to do when I got 'back' was to leave Carl. This was a test, she said, to break the bondage of the past with my father, and to move forward, free to soar like the eagle I really could become. My mother said someone would be sent to help me leave Carl and my worthless marriage. She said I would always have protection, from the day I decided to divorce Carl.

"When I regained consciousness, I remembered everything my mother had told me. From my bed, I called an attorney, and then I called the police and got protection. I started divorce proceedings that day. I was so scared, but I was more scared of the hospital releasing me, of going back to that house and Carl. I knew he'd kill me eventually." Her voice broke. "I didn't want to die that way.... I knew life had more to offer than this kind of horrible abuse. I didn't feel I deserved it, but Carl kept telling me how worthless I was, that I was no good, that I was a bad seed. After a while, I bought it. I was brainwashed."

Gently, Dan sat down and put his arms around Jessica. Hot tears stung his eyes as he enclosed her in a light embrace. He felt her tremble, and then she leaned back against him, her head against his shoulder as she surrendered to him completely. The precious gift of her trust sent an incredible joy tunneling through him. Closing his eyes, Dan pressed his face against her hair.

"Listen to me," he whispered unsteadily, "you aren't bad, Jessica. You never were. I—I don't know how you stood eight years of something like that. I couldn't have...." He felt her hands fall over his where he'd clasped them against her torso. "You're a survivor. You know that? Just like that black stallion out there who was beaten within an inch of his life by Kelly."

Jessica relaxed in his arms. She could feel the powerful beat of his heart against her back where she lay against him. His arms were strong and caring. His voice was riddled with emotion—for her. "I don't know how you can hold me, Dan. I really don't...."

He smiled softly and squeezed her momentarily. "I know one thing brings an animal that's been abused out of his pain, and that's love and care."

Jessica wanted to tell him she needed his love, but she didn't dare. It was too soon. Her past had taught her that hurrying into a relationship was not smart or healthy. The other thing she'd discovered was that the fact that she had been raised by an abusive father had led her to marry an abusive man. The clarity of that realization was sinking into her now. But Dan was nothing like her father or Carl.

Then she remembered the fight he'd had that day. "When you protected me against Chet, I was so shocked. I don't know why. When he put his hand over mine to trap me at the door of the truck, I panicked inside. It brought back horrible memories of my abusive marriage."

Jessica stirred in his arms, slowly sitting up and turning to him. Dan's face was filled with sadness, and she saw anger burning in his dark gray eyes now, but she knew it wasn't aimed at her. Placing her hands over his, she whispered, "When you fought them, it just shocked me. I never thought of you as a warrior. And the way you fought…"

"I picked up karate when I was a Recon Marine," he told her. "It comes in handy sometimes."

"Yes…it did. You protected Tommy and me." Looking up at the thick rafters of the barn, Jessica said, "I was so shaken up by it all. I'd escaped Vancouver, the violence, to come here and live in peace."

"And your peace was shattered this morning."

Jessica nodded and knew Dan understood better than anyone else what she'd felt. "Yes," she said simply. "I guess it was stupid and idealistic of me to hope that violence wouldn't follow me. But it has…and will…."

Dan gave her a strange look. "The Cunningham boys and I have tangled before, Jessica. They were after me because of my own past, not because of you."

She held Dan's earnest gaze and felt the powerful blanket of his care enveloping her. "There's something else you need to know, Dan, before this goes any further. You need to know the whole truth."

Dan gave her a puzzled look.

"I already told you about my friend Moyra, how she watched out for me while I was living in Vancouver. When I moved down here because Katie needed me to help try and save our home, Moyra warned me that Carl would come after me. Somehow, he'd find out I'd left Canada and would come and hunt me down. She warned me that he would kill me this time if he got a hold of me." Looking at Dan, she said, "But Moyra also said a man 'clothed in darkness' would be sent to me, to protect me and help me. I believe that's you. The day I first met you, I felt something here, in my heart." She touched her breast with her fingertips. "I don't know what it is, but being around you, Dan, makes me feel clean and pure again, like I felt before I met Carl and married him."

Heat thrummed through Dan—a delicious, warming heat that made his heart open wide like a flower in his chest. Jessica was pale as she spoke now, her face etched with strain and so many emotions. He reached out and captured her hand. Normally, her fingers were warm and dry. Now they were cool and clammy.

"And when you kissed me…" She sighed and closed her eyes, relishing the feel of his roughened fingers wrapping around her cooler hand. "I felt things I'd never felt before in my life." She opened her eyes and held his gaze. Tears slipped down her face. "I felt a joy like I'd never knew existed, Dan. All I had known was one man's kisses… Carl's. Your kiss was like life. His were like death. You were so gentle and coaxing when you kissed me. You didn't take, you shared. I was so stunned by your kiss. Nothing had ever felt so right, so good, to me." Quickly, Jessica looked away, unable to stand the pity she saw in Dan's eyes. "That's why I had to tell you everything," she said hurriedly. "I don't know how you really feel toward me, but I know my feelings for you are growing. I don't want to put you in harm's way. Carl could find me. He's so insanely jealous that—that—if he knew you liked me, just a little, he might kill you, too." Pressing her hands against her face, Jessica cried out brokenly, "And I couldn't stand for that to happen, Dan! I just couldn't!"

Chapter 8

Dan slowly released Jessica and turned her around on the bale of hay they sat on, so that she could look directly at him. It was time to be as completely honest with her as she had been with him. Taking off his sweat-stained leather work gloves, he dropped them to the floor of the barn. Her cheeks glistened with spent tears, and her eyes were red rimmed, filled with sadness, betrayal and fear. And yet as she lifted those thick blond lashes, met and held his intense, burning gaze, he felt his heart lift euphorically in his chest, as if for the first time in his life he was flying.

The sensation was new and startling. Beautiful and filled with hope. Hope wasn't something Dan had ever felt much of. Lifting his hands, he brushed away her tears with trembling fingers. Her skin was soft and warm beneath his touch. He ached to lean forward and kiss her mouth, kiss that trembling lower lip as she clung to him.

"Your life path has been hard," he murmured huskily, allowing his fingers to drop from her cheeks and fold around her hands. "I barely knew any of this. Sam only told me that you would need watching out for when you came here. He didn't say more than that."

"It's pretty sordid, don't you think?" Jessica said. How gentle Dan's face had become. She would never have believed he could be so tender if she hadn't seen it for herself. The harshness of the land he'd been raised on made men hard. All she saw now was his dark, stormy eyes burning with a powerful, intense emotion that caught and held her gently in its embrace. His touch was firm and yet gentling. Perhaps it was the same touch he applied to a scared mustang he was breaking for saddle.

He shook his head. "It's a crime what Carl did to you. You're stronger than I believed." One corner of his mouth hitched upward for just a moment. "If you weren't telling me all of this, I'd never believe it secondhand." Gazing at her face, he touched some tendrils of blond hair and smoothed them across the top of her head. "You don't look scarred, Jessica. You're untouched by the darkness life can wrap us in. Like it did me." He saw the puzzled expression in her eyes. "It's funny how we see other people without really knowing them, or what path they had to endure. I see nothing but the beauty in you—in the way you walk, the way you treat others, the way you lead with your heart, not your head."

Dan's mouth curled into a sarcastic line. "I know

you heard what Chet and Bo said about me today at the hay and feed store."

Sniffing, Jessica pulled a tissue from the pocket of her Levi's. "Yes, I did." She blew her nose, apologizing as she tucked the tissue back into her pocket. "Chet and Bo are well known for lying, so I didn't take it seriously."

Dan held her hands firmly. It took every ounce of his escaping courage to hold her gaze and say, "It wasn't lies this time. They were telling the truth about me."

Jessica stared at him, the silence stretching stiltedly between them.

Dan felt his heart begin to beat hard with fear of her rejection. He saw the question, the shock registering in Jessica's easily read expression. Whatever he'd thought he might have with her was rapidly dissolving. Risking it all, he rasped in a low, pain-filled tone, "I never touched alcohol until I entered the Marine Corps. My father was a Recon Marine. He wanted me to be one. That was always his dream for me—to be like him. He was an officer. I went in enlisted because I didn't have the college education that was needed in order to become an officer.

"I wanted him to be proud of me. When I went into the marines, I didn't like it. But I stuck it out and worked hard, and eventually, I was able to go into Recon training. I became a communications specialist for my team of five Recons. Each of us had a skill. Mine was radios, computers and stuff like that.

"I liked the Marine Corps in one way because it was about teamwork. My team was good. One of the best, at Camp Reed out in California. We worked hard

together, we played together and—we drank together.
It was real easy, after a hard day humping the hills of
Reed, to go over to the enlisted men's club and grab a
few beers. It never got out of hand.

"When Desert Storm wound up, they sent ten
Recon teams over to Iraq. We worked with army special forces and black berets, as well. We were part of
a contingent no one has ever known about to this day.
We were dropped way behind the lines, to cause havoc
among the elite guard units."

"Oh, dear," Jessica whispered. "It must have been
dangerous...."

Dan tightened his hands around hers, staring down
at their soft, white expanse. "Jessica, what I'm going to
share with you, I've never said to another soul. I—I'm
ashamed of it. I see it almost every night in my dreams.
I wake up drenched in sweat, feeling my heart trying
to beat out of my chest, and I want to die."

Murmuring his name softly, Jessica eased her hand
from his and rested it against the side of his face. She
saw the harshness and judgment in his eyes. "Dan,
whatever it is, you can share it with me."

Taking a deep, ragged breath, he rasped, "I ended
up killing five men that night. My team and I para-
chuted into an Iraqi stronghold. We'd gotten bad information. We were surrounded. Once the captain
realized what had happened, we went about our business of causing havoc. The ammo dump was blown
up, and that was the start of the whole thing. Then
we ran out of ammo ourselves. We had no way to get
help or support from either the sky or the land units.
It ended up," Dan continued, scowling heavily, his
voice dropping to a bare whisper, "that the only way

we could get out of there alive was to use our Ka-bar knives as weapons…."

Jessica shut her eyes tightly. "Oh, no…."

Something old and hurting shattered inside of Dan. He felt it, felt the pain drifting from his chest down to his knotted gut. "That night I thought I was going to die. In a way, I wanted to. I had to take five men's lives. Their blood is on my hands to this day. I remember every sound, their cries…. I wonder about their families, their loved ones, and the fact their children no longer have fathers to raise them." He swallowed hard, the lump in his throat making his voice tight. He saw Jessica's eyes widen with such pity that he couldn't handle it.

"Two members of my team were badly wounded. Marines never leave their wounded or dead behind. The other three of us got them out of there, past their lines. Then a rescue team began firing artillery blindly into the night, trying to find us. Well…they did. We were heading down off a sand dune when a shell exploded just behind us. I remember the concussion wave slamming me and the marine I had over my shoulders in a fireman's carry, and that was the last thing I recalled."

Jessica held her breath. "You were hurt, too?"

He shrugged. "The pain I carry inside me every day is much worse than the physical wounds I received."

"How badly were you hurt?"

"I was the only one to survive that blast."

Jessica stared at him, watching his thinned mouth work. He would not look at her, only down at her hand, held so tightly in his own. "Thank the Great Spirit you lived," she breathed softly, leaning over and sliding her fingertips along the hard, unforgiving line of his jaw. She felt the prickles of his beard beneath her flesh.

"I was lucky in one sense. Another returning Recon unit found what was left of us right after dawn. They called in a chopper, which took all of us back to a hospital unit in Kuwait. I didn't wake up until a week later, in some hospital in Germany. I had shrapnel all down my back and both legs. I'd taken a piece of metal into my helmet, which tore it off my head." He grimaced. "I guess the docs thought I was going to die because the shrapnel fractured my skull and caused bleeding underneath. The nurses looked pretty surprised when I woke up. The docs were even more surprised when I didn't seem to suffer any aftereffects of the skull injury. My speech was okay, and so was my memory, unfortunately.

"I got a medical discharge from the Marine Corps after that, and I got transferred to Prescott, Arizona, where they have a Veterans Administration hospital. My wounds were healing up fine on the outside, but inside I was falling apart. I couldn't erase any of what I'd done or seen. As soon as I could, I started drinking hard liquor. It was the only thing that stopped the memories, stopped the sounds careening through my head day and night. By the time I left the VA hospital and headed home to Flagstaff where my parents lived, I was drinking a quart of vodka a day."

Jessica sighed. "Oh, Dan, that's terrible. I can't imagine how much pain you were in, how much you were suffering...."

He held her tear-filled gaze. "I'm not proud of what I had become, Jessica. You realize that?" It hurt him worse to say those words than any others he'd ever said to anyone in his life. "Chet was right. I was a drunk for a while. My parents tried to help me, and asked me to move in with them."

With a little cry, Jessica whispered, "Your pain was so great. You drank because of the pain, not because you craved alcohol."

"That's right," Dan said with a sigh. "But it doesn't matter. I can't handle alcohol. At all." He couldn't believe she was still sitting there with him. People had disdained him for years because of that painful period of his life. "I dishonored myself, and worse, my parents and their good name. I had hit bottom. I decided that the only way to get out of this cycle was to want to do it. My father looked around for a job for me. He knew if he could get me to stop thinking so much about what I'd done, that I could survive it. There was an opening at a Flag ranch for a horse wrangler. I went over there and got the job. I kept it for five years until they let me go. Then Sam asked me to come down here and be the head horse wrangler for your ranch. He couldn't promise much pay up front, but I needed a change. The people up in Flag remember me as a drunk. The stares, the gossip, the looks they always gave me reminded me of my past, my shame...."

Risking everything, Dan looked up. Jessica's face was filled with suffering. When he realized it was for him, that she was not going to judge him harshly as the people of Flagstaff, and those who had heard gossip about him here in Sedona had, his heart took wing like an eagle that had wanted to fly for a long, long time.

"I know Kelly Donovan was a roaring alcoholic," he admitted hoarsely. "But I'm not like your father, Jessica. I would never hurt you or any other woman.

Though I did get into a few brawls, all I wanted to do was go and hide away and—cry. I needed to be alone. The Great Spirit knows, I've hurt and killed enough people already—"

"No!" Jessica said fiercely, grabbing his hands. "You killed to survive, Dan. That's different!"

He shook his head. "It's wrong to take another person's life. I'll never do it again. Not *ever*. I—couldn't. The hell I went through just to get this far away from my past has been the hardest thing I've done in my life. When I finally realized what the alcohol was doing—when I finally got tired of watching my mother grow old because of my choices—I quit." He shook his head. "If I had to kill again, I'd probably go put a bullet in my head afterward because I couldn't handle the pain, the guilt and all the crap that went with it. I'm not that strong. I try and ignore those voices in my head, the faces I see in my nightly dreams."

"Dan, you're an amazing person," Jessica said gently. "You've gone through hell and come out the other side of it. Yes, your spirit was wounded, but you had what it took to pull yourself up by your own bootstraps."

He crooked his mouth a little and looked up at her. "So did you."

"Maybe we don't give ourselves enough credit for our strength and courage," Jessica admitted sadly. "I know I'm horribly ashamed of my past, of my inability to leave Carl before he put me in the hospital."

"Jessica," Dan whispered in a raw tone, "you were like a beaten animal. You came from a family where your father did not respect women. What you have to understand, *shi shaa,* is that when you met Carl, that was the only kind of man you knew. Like draws like. Because you are so intuitive, you, more than most, must realize that. The Navajo have a saying—we attract what we are or we attract what we need. You were young, running away from home, probably homesick, scared and alone in Vancouver. You had no friends, so when Carl saw your beauty, your cleanness, he was like a wolf leaping on an unprotected lamb."

She nodded, amazed by Dan's insight, his understanding of what had really happened up in Vancouver. "You're right—I was scared and alone. I didn't know what I was going to do. I cried all the time because I missed Mama, I missed this ranch...but I didn't miss Kelly. I was so scared of him, Dan. I used to hide under the bed when he was drunk. I remember crawling under it and then rolling into the fetal position, my head buried against my knees. Mama did what she could to protect us, but she couldn't be in three places at once. Kelly usually picked on Kate, not me or Rachel half as much." She shook her head, tears spilling from her eyes. "It's all so sad, Dan. So sad.... Kelly destroyed our family with his drinking binges. And for what?"

"I heard from Sam that Kelly was in the war," Dan murmured. "That he had post-traumatic stress disorder. I'm not making excuses for him, but my gut hunch was that he drank for the same reasons I did— the horror of what we had to do in a wartime situation, or what he saw...."

"Probably," she sniffed. "But it didn't give him the right to abuse us, either."

"No, it didn't," Dan admitted quietly, studying her flushed, glistening face.

She drowned in his dark gray gaze. "You said something in Navajo just a minute ago. I know you've said it to me a couple of times. What does it mean?" She took a clean tissue from her pocket and wiped her face free of tears.

Avoiding her searching look, Dan tightened his mouth. "I have no right to call you what I did. I'm sorry...."

"No!" Jessica slid her hand into his. There were so many white scars across the darkness of his hand. His fingers were calloused and rough, and she ached to feel them once again, moving against her body. What would it be like to love Dan? The thought was exhilarating, scary and appealing to Jessica. She was surprised, because she'd thought she was emotionally dead. She thought Carl had destroyed whatever her heart could feel of desire, need and love. "Please," she begged, "share with me what you said."

Heat crept up into his face and he compressed his lips.

The silence hung between them. Did he dare? Dan knew that once she understood what it was, the utter intimacy of it, that it would reveal far too much of how he really felt about her. Jessica knew Navajo ways. She understood that certain sayings, certain words, such as his endearment for her, were never said unless meant from one's heart.

Yes, she had accepted his sordid, drunken history, but so what? She might see him as the spitting image of her father. Maybe Jessica would never get beyond seeing the overlay of Kelly on him, would never accept him for who he was—a man who was falling helplessly in love with her. Dan wanted to say all of this, but he was afraid to. Right now, he felt raw inside from revealing his dark past. He could see the fragility written across Jessica's sweet face, too.

"I had no right to call you what I did," he repeated. "I'm afraid of what you'll do if I share it with you right now, Jessica. We're both hurting...."

She took a deep breath and straightened her shoulders slightly. "I know we're raw, Dan. Maybe we needed to share our pasts with one another for whatever reason. I'm not sorry we did. Are you?"

He shook his head. "No...."

"And your kiss...?"

He snapped a look at her. "That was a mistake... a stupid reaction on my part, Jessica. I had no right, no—"

"Hush," she whispered, placing her fingertips across his strong mouth. "Don't apologize for that, too," she said, a partial smile on her lips. "I liked it, Dan. And since we're telling the truth here, I think I should share with you how much I liked it...."

He took her fingers in his hand, kissed the center of her soft palm and felt a fine tremble go through her. He couldn't believe what he was hearing. Yet as he ruthlessly searched the depths of her glorious eyes, he saw no lies in them. Only a shining warmth that enveloped him like sunshine on a bitterly cold winter day.

"I never thought," Jessica said in a choking voice, "that I would *ever* want a man to kiss me again. Carl, well, he didn't care what I wanted. Ever. He made me hate his kiss. And soon, I hated him. I guess, in the end, I hated all men because of him. Moyra told me that with time, I'd be able to separate Carl from the rest of the men in my life, but I didn't believe her."

Jessica slid her hand against Dan's cheek and held his widening gaze.

"When I came here and I met you, something happened, Dan. I still don't know what it is, or pretend to understand it all—yet. I just know that with you, I feel safe—and good. I can feel again. You know, real feelings. Before now, I thought Carl had killed my heart, beaten my spirit. The only time I felt good, felt alive and happy, was when I was working with my orchid girls. My heart would open and I would feel such joy, such pure love from them surrounding me. I would love them back in my own, wounded way, I suppose.

"With you," Jessica continued, giving him a shy look, "I began to experience feelings I'd never felt before in my life. I'd never felt them toward Carl. And all you had to do was be with me. It's kind of wonderful—but kind of scary, too."

Capturing her hand, Dan kissed the back of it gently and said, "You're like that stallion out there in many ways. He's coming around because I'm gentle with him. I use a gentle touch and voice. I would never do anything to hurt him or make him want to distrust me." He smiled a little. "Although he watches me like a hawk, I give him no reason to think I'm like the other men who he's grown to hate and be wary of."

"We're a lot alike, Gan and I," Jessica agreed painfully. "Now you're able to put a saddle on him and ride him. I find that amazing, but in another way, I don't."

"Why?" Dan absorbed the softness of her skin as he moved his thumb across her palm. Touching Jessica was like feeling the sun shining down into his dark, scarred heart. She gave him hope, and so much more....

"It tells me about your quality as a person, what you bring to the situation, Dan. That stallion out there is smarter than most human beings. He's got a wild, innate intelligence, a survival drive. He knows who he can really trust and who he can't." She reached over and pressed her hand, palm down, against the center of Dan's chest and felt the pounding beat of his heart. "No matter how much darkness you've been wrapped in, trapped within, Gan saw your purity, your heart's intentions. He *knows* you won't ever hurt him. You would never lay a finger on someone to hurt them. Even I know that."

"Then why doesn't that stud pick up the fact that I killed five men?"

"He knows the same thing I do," Jessica whispered unsteadily. "That you didn't do it out of enjoyment or pleasure. Gan instinctively knows that you, like him, have the ability to survive some awful storms in life. You're a survivor, as he is. As I am. He trusts you. So do I...."

Closing his eyes, Dan felt her move her hand from the center of his chest upward. His skin tightened deliciously beneath her light, hesitant exploration of his chest and shoulder. As her fingers curved around the back of his neck, an ache built in his lower body. He wanted her. Great Spirit help him, but he wanted all of her, from her bright, shining soul, to her wounded heart and beautiful physical body. And yet, his heart cautioned, Jessica was no different from Gan—badly brutalized and beaten by a man. Dan realized fully that he couldn't just sweep her off her feet, carry her to his bed and love her wildly, fully and with all the hunger he felt. She was still too emotionally wounded from her bad marriage to an abusive man. Dan knew that he had to move slowly, gain her trust and let her tell him when and if she was ready for him to love her.

His heart broke over that realization. Nothing bad should ever have happened to Jessica. She was an innocent victim in all of this. Completely innocent. She'd been a child scared into hiding deep within herself, and then to have a monster like Carl come and complete the damage to her spirit by destroying her femininity was almost too much for him to bear. But as Jessica explored him now with her sweet, almost shy, exquisite touch, he understood what she was doing. For some reason unknown to him, she was giving her trust to him, as that stallion had done. For him to reach out and respond in like manner would scare her away, too.

Opening his eyes, Dan held her luminous blue gaze. "Whatever we have," he rasped, "is good and clean and pure, Jessica. You never have to be scared of me. You can keep on trusting me. I won't take your trust and twist it like Carl did. You're too beautiful...too pure of heart, to do that to. No human should be disrespected. No one." He slowly reached up for the hand she had wrapped around his neck and eased it away. "Right now, all I want to do is kiss you and return to you in some way the feelings you're sharing with me, but I won't unless you tell me you want me to."

A sweet hotness moved through Jessica as he took her hand between his own. Dan was more than a stallion tamer; he was taming a wounded, hurting woman—herself. His gentleness was real. Still, it seemed incredible to her that any man could possess such sensitivity. And yet, as she clung to Dan's dark gray eyes, she not only heard his words, she felt them in every dark corner of her scarred spirit. Her lips parted and she shyly leaned toward him.

"Yes," she whispered unsteadily, "kiss me. Again." Closing her eyes, she felt his hands fall away from hers. The seconds seemed so long as she waited to once again feel his strong mouth upon hers. She no longer knew what was happening between them or why. She no longer tried to sort it out, nor did she care to.

As Dan's lips covered hers, the warmth of his breath cascaded down across her cheek. Sighing, she felt his roughened hands move slowly upward, across her exposed flesh, and a delicious prickle began within her. The very motion of his hands massaging the tension away lulled her into a euphoria she'd never felt before. His mouth moved tenderly across hers, giving, not taking. She felt his power, but she also felt him monitoring how much strength he put against her lips, too. His beard was rough and sandpapery against her cheek as she turned her head to more fully press her lips to his. His fingers drifted to her shoulders, then traced the outline of her neck until finally, he gently captured her face between his hands. She felt no fear, only a deep ache throbbing between her legs, longing to have him completely, and in all ways.

With each gliding movement, he rocked her lips open a little more, tasted a little more deeply of her. Jessica sighed, realizing with amazement that she wanted to feel and taste him more deeply, too. For the first time, she felt bold, as if she could risk it all and explore this powerful man wrapped in darkness. Carl had always taken from her, hurt her. Now Dan was asking her to take however much of him she wanted. Pressing herself more surely against him until her breasts barely grazed his chest wall, she embraced his strong, corded neck and felt him tremble. But the sensation didn't frighten her, it excited her.

As she moved her lips in a soft, searching motion across his mouth, she felt desire pouring through her. Each time she kissed him, he returned the kiss with equal strength, but he never did anything more than that. Her hands drifted to his head and she removed his hat. She heard it drop to the floor as she lost herself in the sensation of running her fingers through his thick, short black hair. It was so soft and yet strong, like Dan. Moving her fingers downward, she felt his sculpted brow and then the wrinkles at the corners of his eyes. He trembled again and his hands moved to her face. As she slowly absorbed each line in his skin, each part of his face, he felt hers, too.

It was a delicious, pleasurable exploration, Jessica realized. There was safety here in Dan's arms. *And love,* her heart whispered. At first, she didn't catalog her feelings because she was too caught up in the sensation of Dan's breath against her cheek, the movement of his strong mouth against hers and the thudding beat of his heart against her breasts. Finally, she eased her mouth from his. As she did, she barely opened her eyes before she drowned once again in the burning grayness of his. They slowly drew apart, his hands steadying on her shoulders as she created more space between them. Her world spun out of control and she felt heady, almost dizzy, until Dan's hands tightened around her arms to support her.

Her lips felt lush and full and well kissed. She stared up at him and marveled at what she was feeling. "I…"

she whispered. "I've never been kissed like that before in my life, Dan. It was so wonderful. You are wonderful...."

Chapter 9

The hot August sunlight was scorching the ranch and sucking out the very lifeblood from the drought-ridden land, Jessica noted with growing dismay. She had just finished filling orders for her flower essences when Kate stepped into the doorway of the greenhouse.

"Anything's better than that heat out there," Kate groused, taking off her cowboy hat and wiping the perspiration from her darkly tanned brow. "How are things going? We haven't seen each other in the past couple of days."

Kate joined Jessica as she sat on her workbench, the cobalt blue bottles labeled and set in groups on the table before her. Jessica looked up and smiled at her older sister as Kate placed a hand on her shoulder and said, "You've been looking awfully happy lately. What's going on?"

"Questions, questions, Katie," she said with a laugh. "You won't even let me answer the first one before you fire off one or two more." Placing the order sheets aside, she brushed back a few crinkly tendrils that had escaped from her ponytail as Kate sat down on the wooden crate next to her workbench.

"First, I'm fine. Secondly, there's lots of orders coming in and yes, I'm happy." She grinned. "Now are *you* happy?"

Kate reached for the plastic bottle of water Jessica always had on her bench and took a swig from it. She recapped it and set it between them. "You look happier than usual. And Dan has sure been changing, too," she hinted.

"How has he changed?"

Kate grinned belatedly. "Like he's walking on cloud nine. You know.... Sam and I have been wondering when things were going to gel between you two."

The serious expression on Kate's face was belied by the dancing sparkle in her eyes. Jessica relaxed. "Pretty obvious, huh?"

"A little...but then, when two people are in love, well, it sort of becomes obvious."

"It's not love," Jessica said quickly. "I like him an awful lot, Katie, but—love? No, I don't think so."

Her sister scrutinized her for a long moment without speaking. "It's Carl, isn't it? You're still scared of him finding you. And that's why you can't openly admit you love Dan?"

"No," Jessica said softly as she folded her hands in the lap of her dark pink skirt decorated with bright yellow marigolds, purple irises and pale pink tulips. "It's—I, well, I'm just wary, I guess, Kate. You know how Carl treated me. My stupid head gets in the way when Dan touches me. It triggers a lot of bad memories."

"Yeah." Kate sighed, reaching out and putting her work-worn hand across Jessica's. "I know that one." She squeezed her sister's clasped fingers. "It takes time, Jessica. You have to give yourself that leeway and don't expect miracles."

"Dan has been so patient with me." Jessica pulled her hands from Kate's and gestured with them. "His kisses are wonderful. I've never been kissed like he kisses me." Sighing, she whispered, "And when he touches me, I feel like I'm on fire and I'm so hungry for him...." She laughed, embarrassed by her admission.

With a crooked smile, Kate nodded. "Sam makes me feel the same way."

"I'm just, well, afraid, Katie, that's all. Dan knows it. He's patient with me. And..." She frowned. "And he's afraid you and Sam won't approve of his feelings toward me."

With a laugh, Kate stood up and stuffed her leather gloves into the belt at her waist. "Why not?"

"He's got this thing in his head that he's not good enough for me, Kate. That because he doesn't own land and have money in the bank, he's in a lower class than me. Isn't that stupid?"

With a shake of her head, Kate muttered, "Well, Dan sure as heck isn't getting rich working here. He's got this class thing hammered into his head from the res. There's a lot of Anglos who think they're better than the Navajo people, but that's pure bull. No, Sam and I consider Dan an equal, like you do. So don't worry about it." Her brow wrinkled as she looked around the lush greenhouse where so many of the orchids were in colorful bloom. "If only this damn drought would just end. We've lost so many cattle by having to sell them off because we can't feed them. We've lost money." With a sigh, Kate placed her hand on Jessica's sagging shoulder. "Without your financial input, we'd be waiting for the banker to come down the road to foreclose on the ranch. Damn, I just wish this poverty cycle with the ranch would end."

"I pray for rain every day," Jessica said passionately. "I worry about these hot winds we're having. Lightning could strike one of the tinder-dry pastures and we'd have a ranch fire on our hands. So much could be destroyed."

"This is monsoon season," Kate griped, patting her sister's shoulder one more time, "but whoever heard of *dry* monsoons? Usually, we get four inches of rain in three months. Enough to sustain life around here for the following six months." Her mouth moved into a grim line. "All we have now are incredibly beautiful thunderheads that build around ten in the morning. And when the thunder and lightning start around three p.m., that's when Sam and I begin to worry about forest and range fires."

"Speaking of Sam," Jessica said, trying to dissolve the worried look from Kate's eyes, "have you two decided on *when* you're going to get married?"

She shook her head and settled the hat back on her dark hair. "We're working sixteen hours a day. Who has time to discuss the future? Every day we get up, Jessica, there's a hundred things that need to be done and we divide the list between us. By the time we fall into bed at night, we're so exhausted we can't talk." She pulled the gloves from her belt and jerked them back on her hands. "No, until we become more financially stable, I just don't feel we can take the time and energy to finalize wedding plans."

Sadly, Jessica nodded. "I understand. At least you have one another. Sam loves you so much."

"I know," Kate whispered, tears glimmering in her eyes. "I don't know what I did to deserve him, but Lord help me, I love him with every breath I take into this bruised, beaten body of mine."

"If things start turning for the better, maybe a marriage, say, in December? Rachel's coming home at that time," Jessica hinted.

Kate nodded. "Sam mentioned that time frame, too. We can sell some of the Herefords to meet our expenses. I'm all for it." She grinned and ruffled Jessica's bangs. "And you...when are you going to fess up to doing something more than 'liking' Dan? The guy has cow eyes for you every time he sees you."

"Cow eyes," Jessica protested with a giggle. "He does not!"

"That's what we called boys in junior high, remember? If they got a crush on some girl but never had the guts to go over and tell her because they were too scared?" Kate's smile broadened as she considered Jessica's blazing cheeks. "Sam says that since coming here, Dan has really straightened out. I told him it was your influence. He said it probably was, that Dan wanted to put the past behind him and make a more positive statement with his life. He's done that. He works just as hard as we do and he's getting a pittance of what he should be getting. But—" she winked at Jessica "—he's got something else here at the ranch that's giving him reason to work hard—you."

Touching her hot cheeks, Jessica avoided Kate's laughter-filled eyes. "Oh, Katie, you're reading too much into it. Dan's never said he loved me."

"You said it to him?"

"Well, no… I don't know if I really am in love or not…."

"Silly girl," Kate chided as she walked toward the door, "what's the poor guy to do? If you don't say it, how can he? What's it going to take to get you to see the guy loves you more than life—an act of Congress? I hope your fear goes away soon, or Dan's gonna die of loneliness out there in the bunkhouse."

Squirming inwardly, Jessica watched her big sister open the door to the greenhouse. "Hey, I'm going to leave tomorrow morning and go up near the Rim in the north pasture to try and find some wildflowers to make some new flower essences with."

Kate turned, her gloved hand on the door. "You taking Pete, the packhorse, again? Last time you went out, you made something like ten new essences."

Jessica nodded and slid off the stool. "Yes, Dan's going to get my gelding and the packhorse ready for me tomorrow morning. I hope to scour the Rim itself and see if anything else is up there. I'm taking my wildflower identification books with me and my log and my camera. I'll be up there until about two p.m. I want to be down off the Rim before those lightning bolts start flying."

"Hmm, good idea." Kate patted the redwood frame of the door with her hand. "Okay. But I don't think you're going to find anything alive up on the Rim, especially wildflowers. It's been over a hundred degrees every day and the humidity is so low that the forest service says the pine trees up there are going to start dying off soon because of no rain. I don't know how a wildflower could be alive, much less blooming in those kinds of conditions."

Shrugging, Jessica couldn't disagree. "It's a scouting expedition, is all. I've been wanting to explore that area of the ranch, anyway."

"Probably to get into some cooler air," Kate teased, lifting her hand in a wave. "I'll see you then, tomorrow afternoon sometime? Is Dan going with you? He did last time."

"No, he's at a crucial point in Gan's training."

"Okay, but be careful. There's a lot of rattlers out this time of year."

"I hear you," Jessica said, and watched her sister disappear through the door.

"I wish I were going with you," Dan said as Jessica mounted her small gray Arabian gelding, Jake. Though Jessica wasn't the best of riders, Jake, who was over twenty, was steady and reliable. Dan gazed up into Jessica's face and saw the excitement in her eyes over the daylong adventure ahead of her. She had been working so hard at her business that Dan knew she needed this kind of minivacation from the greenhouse activities.

Jessica reached out and touched his gloved hand, which rested on her thigh. "I wish you were coming, too. Are you sure Gan isn't tractable enough to ride so you could?"

He shook his head. "No, Gan's been backing up on me, testing me. I can ride him in pastures and open areas, but when I try to get him into woods, he starts getting real skittish and hard to handle. He's not given his trust to me fully yet. Until he does, he's a danger to ride anywhere but on the flatlands of the ranch."

Jessica leaned down and quickly brushed his mouth with a kiss, relishing the hot, returning passion of his lips against hers. He gripped her arm, holding her in place to give her a long, thorough goodbye kiss. Her heart pounding, Jessica found herself aching for him again, just as she did every time he kissed her or touched her. "I'll miss you," she said breathlessly, sitting up in the saddle.

"Three p.m. can't come too soon," he rasped, reluctantly releasing her. As he stood there looking up at her, sitting so proudly in the saddle, he wanted to love her so badly he could taste it. He wanted to do more than love Jessica physically. He wanted to speak the words. She wasn't ready for that, he knew, but it didn't help him. Swallowing, he stepped back and smiled up at her. Jessica didn't look like a cowboy, wearing a straw hat with silk flowers affixed to the wide brim. Her white, simple tank top, dark blue jeans and comfortable leather loafers completed the picture. Cowgirl she was not. And he loved her with a fierceness that defied description.

"Hey," Jessica called as she picked up the packhorse's soft cotton lead rope, "do you want to see a movie tonight in Sedona?"

"Sure."

She laughed softly. "Okay, let's make it a date!" Then she clapped her heels and Jake moved off at a steady, slow jog.

Dan watched her form grow small against the towering Rim country that was topped with pine trees thousands of feet above them. The sun was coming up over the canyon wall and he knew it was going to be another blisteringly hot day. He had to get the work done now, while it was still somewhat cool. From one p.m. to seven p.m., he worked indoors because the unrelenting, hundred-degree heat made it nearly impossible to stay outside.

Something bothered him, but he couldn't put a finger on it. Taking off his hat, he rubbed the back of his sunburned neck ruefully before settling the hat back into place. He had an uneasy, gnawing feeling in his gut. The last time he'd had this feeling was when he was dropped behind the lines in Iraq. Why now?

Unable to make heads or tails out of it, Dan moved in long, easy strides back to Gan's pasture to work with the stallion. Right now, he had to concentrate entirely on the stud or he could end up on the ground. That Arabian was smart. Too smart for his own good, Dan thought with a careless grin. But with patience and time, the stallion would reward him with his trust.

Looking over his shoulder one last time, he saw that Jessica had already disappeared behind the ranch buildings. Something niggled at him again. Frowning, he shrugged it off and went to work.

"Dan! Dan!"

Dan was pounding a shoe into place on one of Gan's hooves when he heard Kate's terrified voice. He saw her run into the barn.

"Whoa," he murmured in a low voice to the stallion. "Stand…"

The black Arabian's small ears twitched nervously

as Kate came running down the aisle. Dan quickly finished putting the last nails in the shoe and allowed the stallion to stand on all four legs. Automatically, he put a soothing hand on the stud's arched neck. He could feel the sudden tension in him.

"What's wrong, Kate?" he asked as he removed the thick leather blacksmith's apron from around his waist. He saw that Kate's eyes were wide with terror and his gut shrank as he walked down the aisle to meet her. Gan wasn't too trustful of other human beings yet, and he didn't want the horse starting to rear upward in the cross ties.

"Dan!" she cried, breathless. "Jake's back!"

He frowned as he watched her halt, her breathing harsh. "Jessica's back?" It was three p.m.—time she returned.

"No," Kate rasped, holding up her hand, trying to catch her breath. "Jake just came galloping into the yard. He's covered with sweat! Jessica wasn't on him!"

His eyes narrowed. "Jessica…"

"Yes." Kate leaned over, her hands on her thighs as she took in huge gulps of air. "I'm afraid, Dan. I've had a bad feeling since I woke up this morning. Something's happened to Jessica. Sam's in Flagstaff and I can't reach him. We've got to get out to find Jessica. She said she was going to the north pasture. I'm going to drive out there right now. Maybe Jake just spooked and took off. I don't know, but I'm worried."

So was Dan. Frowning, he hung the leather apron on a nail. "Jake isn't the type of gelding to spook or run off, Kate. He's ground trained." That meant that if anyone dropped the animal's reins, he would halt and not move a muscle until those reins were picked up by the rider once again. Terror began to flood Dan as he stood there, his brain racing with questions and possible answers. "What about Pete, the packhorse?"

"No sign of him."

"Well, even if Jake did startle and take off for some unknown reason, Jessica could ride Pete back to the ranch."

Kate wiped her brow with trembling hands. "I've already thought of that, Dan. Oh, God, I'm afraid it's Carl."

Dan froze. *Carl.* How could he forget about the insanely jealous ex-husband of Jessica's? A steel hand suddenly gripped his heart, the pain excruciating. "No!" he rasped, his eyes narrowing to slits.

"I don't know for sure," Kate whispered brokenly. "Jessica's enough of a rider. She's not the type to get thrown off. I'm going to drive out there and see if I can locate her or Pete." She gulped, her eyes filled with fear. "Dan, if I can't find them, I *know* Carl has kidnapped her. Just like he threatened he would."

"That means we need to call the police. A search will have to be mounted," he rasped.

"Yes. Look, I'll drive out right now. It shouldn't take more than half an hour by truck at high speed. You stay here. I'll call you on the cell phone and let you know if I find her. In the meantime, if I don't find her, you're going to have to try and track her. You're the best tracker in the county. If Carl has kidnapped her, he's got some heavy forest to get through before he can get to 89A and then drive off with her."

"*If* he drives off with her."

Anguished, Kate looked away. "He said he'd kill her. Oh, Lord…"

Gripping Kate's arm, Dan propelled her down the aisle and out of the barn. "Get out to the north pasture as fast as you can. I'm going to saddle Gan and take a rifle, ammunition, food and a cell phone with me. If Jessica isn't out there, I'll call 911 and get the sheriff out here, then hightail it toward you. I'll tell the police your location and then meet you out there."

Kate nodded. "Gan's the only horse that has the stamina this is going to take. That Rim country is rough and dangerous, Dan. He's got nine lives."

"Yeah," he whispered, opening the door to the white pickup truck for Kate, "and he's going to need every single one of them." He saw the paleness on her face, the fear in her eyes. He felt the same. Giving her a pat on the arm, he said, "Remember, I'll have the other cell phone with me. Call me as soon as you know...."

Kate choked back a sob. "Y-yes. I'm so scared, Dan. I thought this was all over. I hope I'm wrong. Maybe I'm jumping to conclusions."

He was helpless to assuage her pain and worry. "Drive carefully out there," he cautioned. "Keep your eyes open, Kate. If Carl's half as dangerous as Jessica says he is, the man could have a rifle and could train his sights on you, too."

Grimly, Kate nodded. "I'll be in touch very soon...."

Dan had just finished saddling Gan, packing the leather sheath with the 30.06 rifle and his knife scabbard and strapping a heavy set of saddlebags in place with more ammunition, when Kate's call came. Grabbing the cell phone, Dan pressed the On button.

"Kate?" His heart was pounding in his chest. He could barely breathe as he waited to hear Kate's report.

"It's horrible, Dan!"

He gripped the phone hard. "What do you mean?"

"Pete's dead! The gelding's been shot through the head," Kate sobbed, trying to speak coherently. "Jessica's nowhere. All her stuff—her bowls, the water and logbook—are scattered around the area. I see some signs of scuffling, but I'm not enough of a tracker to know what the hell it means. Oh, Dan, Carl's got her! Call the sheriff!"

Closing his eyes, his mind whirling, Dan whispered, "Get a hold of yourself, Kate. Tell me exactly where you're located."

"I'm at the most northern part of our pasture, at the gate that leads up the path to the Rim."

"Good. I'll call the sheriff. When's Sam due back?"

"Tonight," Kate cried, sniffling. "Everything is such a mess out here. There's paper that's been torn out of Jessica's sketchbook crumpled up all over the place. She'd never do that. She loved her drawings of plants. He'll kill her, Dan! I know he will! He's an insane bastard. Oh, Lord..."

"Kate, come back. Now. You have to be here when the sheriff arrives. I'm going to mount Gan. I'll take a shortcut to the north gate. Just tell the sheriff I'm tracking them from this end. I'll keep the cell phone in my saddlebags. I'll call you if I see anything, all right?"

"O-okay..." She replied with another sob.

Shutting off the cell phone, Dan carefully placed it in the left saddlebag. Gan, sensing his trepidation, pawed the aisle, snorting and moving his head up and down.

Stay calm, stay calm, Dan harshly ordered himself as he mounted the black stallion. But he couldn't. As he turned Gan out of the barn into the intense afternoon sunlight, he felt like crying. Jessica...sweet, innocent Jessica, had been kidnapped by a man who'd sworn to take her life. No! No! He clapped his heels to the flanks of the stallion and instantly Gan responded. The horse was not large, but he was built like a proverbial bull, heavily muscled in the hind quarters with a wide chest and a long slope to his shoulders, indicating larger than normal lung capacity.

As Dan rode the stallion away from the ranch buildings, he felt the powerful surge of the animal beneath him. What would Gan do in the Rim country? The stallion shied at everything. Gan could throw him, or worse, slam him into a tree to get rid of him. Dan's gloved hands tightened on the leather reins as he leaned low, the horse's black mane whipping into his sweaty face as they sped along the hard, dry road toward the north pasture. He was going to need every ounce of Gan's power, his heart and his spirit. He was going to ask everything of this horse, and he prayed that the stallion trusted him enough to give everything in return. Jessica's life was in the balance. He could feel it. He could taste it.

"You little bitch!"

Jessica shrieked as Carl reached out to grab her by the hair, all because she'd tripped and fallen over some black lava rock hidden by dried pine needles on the forest floor. She felt his hand thrust into her hair, his fingers curl and tighten. Her scalp radiated with pain as he hauled her upward. Hands bound behind her, she had no choice as Carl brought her up hard against him. Staggering to catch her balance, Jessica shut her eyes.

She expected him to slap her. Instead, Carl shoved her ahead of him again.

"Get moving faster!" he snarled, poking the rifle barrel into her back. "We've got to be at 89A before sundown. And if we aren't—" he grinned "—I'll shoot you anyway."

She gasped for breath. She had been pushed into a jog repeatedly for the last two hours. With her hands bound, she often lost her balance on the slippery, dry pine needles. Her knees were skinned and her joints ached. But that was nothing compared to the unadulterated terror she felt in her heart. Carl had found her. He intended to kill her. It was that simple. That terrifyingly simple.

Chapter 10

By six p.m. Dan was still moving the stallion along at a brisk walk, following the trail barely visible in the pine needles up on the Rim. Three hours had seemed like a lifetime. He'd called in his findings to the sheriff. Overhead, he could hear a helicopter hovering around the general area where he was tracking.

The prints he saw were of two people. A number of times, pine needles were scattered helter-skelter. He was sure Jessica had either fallen or been pushed down on the ground. His mind refused to contemplate why she would be shoved down on the dry, hard forest floor.

Gan was snorting and wringing with sweat, his ebony skin reflecting every muscle movement. Luckily, the stallion had expended a great amount of energy on his heroic climb up the Rim so that by the time they got on top of the three-thousand-foot crest, he didn't have much energy left to be shying at every pine tree they passed.

All of Dan's old military training had come back in startling fashion. He felt as if the forest had eyes— that every dark apparition and shadow was potentially Carl Roman. He didn't know what Jessica's ex-husband looked like. She never spoke of him except when necessary. She was trying to put him and their terrible relationship behind her. Dan couldn't blame her, but right now, he wished he knew what the man looked like. He could tell a lot by looking at a person's face. There was no doubt Carl could kill Jessica—and probably would try. But was the man good at hiding in a forest? Was he a true hunter in that sense? Or only a crazed, insanely jealous man who would make mistakes out here—enough for Dan to continue to track him?

Or maybe Carl knew how to throw a tracker off a trail. Was he that good? Dan was unsure. All he could do was lean over the stallion and follow the wisps of evidence in the disturbed pine needles. The sun's rays were long now. Sunset wasn't until around eight p.m., and then Dan would have just enough light until nine p.m., when it grew totally dark. He had a flashlight and he would use it to follow the trail if necessary. But he also knew he would be a target with that light on. It was a risk he was willing to take.

His mind went back to the dead packhorse. Because of his Recon background, Dan could see that Carl had used a high-powered rifle to shoot the innocent horse in one clean shot. Carl knew how to use the rifle, there was no question. Mouth compressed, Dan halted the stallion, took the canteen from the side of the saddle and drank a little water. Luckily, he knew this country well. He'd chased his fair share of cattle that had broken through the barbed wire fence—sometimes chased them for days at a time. Carl was heading due west, probably trying to intercept 89A. What Carl didn't know was that the sheriff was patrolling that area, too.

The cell phone rang. Dan retrieved it from the saddlebag.

"Dan? It's Sam."

"Yeah, I hear you, but you're breaking up a lot." Dan knew the cell phone wouldn't work well as he rode more deeply into the forest. "What's up?"

"The sheriff found a Ford camper with Canadian license plates parked on the berm along 89A. They broke into it and found the registration for the truck—in Carl Roman's name. It's him. And he's got Jessica."

Mouth flattening, Dan glared ahead at the murky depths of the dry pine forest. "Yes…"

"The helicopter is up and searching. They haven't seen anything yet, but that forest is thick."

"They'll be lucky to spot anything," he growled as he continued to look around. Sweat trickled down his temples.

"Have you found anything?"

"Just two sets of tracks. They're heading due west."

"Toward the highway?"

"Yes."

"Well, that bastard will have a real surprise waiting for him. They've called in the Yavapai SWAT team. They'll be in position in an hour near the camper if Carl manages to evade you and make it that far with Jessica. The sheriff said that if they get a clear shot of Roman, they're taking him down. No questions asked.

No negotiations. They got the prison info on this guy and it's not pretty. He murdered a man in cold blood."

A chill ran through Dan. "I understand."

"No, you don't," Sam said harshly. "That means if you find them, Dan, you're to take Carl out if you can. You were a sharpshooter in the Recons. If you find him, take your time, target him and blow him away. He won't let Jessica live. The sheriff thinks, based upon Roman's profile, that he'll more than likely try to rape her first and then kill her. They've got the hospital and police reports from Vancouver. I've seen them. Believe me, this bastard is crazy and he'll kill Jessica."

"Rape?" The word almost strangled him.

"Spousal rape. It's on Roman's rap sheet from the police. Jessica charged him with it after he put her into the hospital and into a coma."

Dan shut his eyes tightly, tasting even more terror. "I—understand."

"I'm going to be riding with the sheriff along 89A. They'll be patrolling it from Flag down to our ranch. I'll be in touch. Just be careful."

"Yeah…"

Taking a ragged breath, Dan put the cell phone back in the saddlebags. Rape. Jessica had been raped repeatedly by the son of a bitch. No wonder she was afraid of *him*. Dan tasted bile in his mouth and he wanted to vomit. Closing his fist over the saddle horn, he tried to get a hold on his unraveling emotions. Jessica had never talked about rape. Oh, she'd skirt around it when pressed, but he'd had no idea. None… Wiping his face with the back of his hand, he grimly swung Gan into a fast walk. Now more than ever he had to find her, before it was too late.

His heart wouldn't stop pounding. His emotions whipsawed. He'd have to kill a man—again. In cold blood. So much of him rebelled at the idea, and yet another part of him *wanted* to kill Carl Roman for what he'd done to Jessica. Guilt rubbed Dan raw, but his cold rage toward the man pushed him onward. Carl Roman was less than animal. Animals never killed except to eat, to survive. Roman killed because he enjoyed it. He didn't have to kill the packhorse, but he had.

The fact that Carl savored killing scared Dan more than anything. Roman had no feelings. He was a dead man walking. And he had Jessica. How much Dan loved her! Wiping his mouth, he stared hard at the tracks in front of them. Why hadn't he *told* her that? Why? Maybe it would have given her hope, a fighting spirit to try and escape Carl. A serrating loneliness cut through Dan—along with terror for Jessica. He couldn't begin to imagine how she was feeling. Pushing Gan faster, he urged the stallion into a slow jog. The prints on the forest floor were fairly obvious now and he had to try and catch up with their makers.

Up ahead, he knew the Rim began to drop down to the canyon floor three thousand feet below, where Oak Creek wound through the sharp, pinnacled red sandstone, the black lava spires. After passing through there, Carl would have to climb up the other side, another two-thousand-foot incline, to finally reach the highway where his truck was parked. Now was the time to push the stallion. Once they got off the Rim and down among the dangerous, sharp rocks, Dan would have to be very careful or risk his and his horse's life.

* * *

"Sit down!" Carl snarled at Jessica.

She collapsed onto the pine needles. Gasping for breath, her mouth dry, she sobbed as Carl strode around her. She winced when his leg brushed against her arm as he passed. She had to *think!* She had to stop panicking. Carl shrugged out of his large backpack and dropped it to the ground, digging in it for a bottle of water.

Jessica lifted her head. Her ex-husband was a large man, densely boned and heavily muscled. He was nearly six foot three and weighed over two hundred pounds. There wasn't an inch of fat on him. He was athletic and powerful. And dangerous. The rifle he'd used to kill Pete stood leaning against the pine tree next to where he was crouched, drinking water to slake his thirst. His red hair was short and plastered wetly against his large skull. Jessica shuddered. If anything, Carl was stronger and more intimidating and dangerous than she'd ever seen him.

How could she escape? He'd tied her wrists tightly with cord behind her back. Looking around, she knew they were heading off the Rim, down to the canyon floor and Oak Creek, though she couldn't see it below. The dusky shadows were deep. Threatening.

And Dan? *Oh, Dan!* Shutting her eyes, Jessica drew up her knees and rested her brow against them. Why hadn't she admitted her love to him? If he knew she was gone, he'd know Carl had her. What was Dan doing? Anguished, Jessica wondered if he was searching for her, though she knew rescue was out of the question. Carl had hunted all his life in the mountains near Calgary where he'd grown up, and was quite re-

sourceful in the woods. Several times he'd gone out
of his way to create sets of tracks to throw off anyone who dared to follow them. He kept his rifle—
one with a high-powered scope on it for long-range
shots—locked and loaded. His green eyes were slits
as he glanced up from drinking the water.

Jessica quickly looked away. The icy glitter in his
eyes made her nauseous. She saw what lay in their
depths. She knew Carl too well, as if she were still attached psychically with an umbilical cord to his sick,
twisted mind. The helicopter overhead told her that
someone was looking for them, so that gave her hope.
Every time the chopper flew over at treetop level,
Carl would haul her against him under a tree until it
left. She knew a helicopter had little chance of locat-
ing them. Still, it gave her hope, and she desperately
needed some to cling to now.

Something told her Dan was following them. Was it
her active imagination? Or some gut instinct? Jessica
couldn't be sure because she was so scared.

"Get up!" Roman snarled as he jammed the water
bottle back into the pack.

Jessica scrambled awkwardly to her feet. "Can't
you untie my hands? We're going down into a canyon,
Carl. The rocks are sharp. If I slip, I could hurt myself."

He grinned savagely and hoisted the heavy pack
back on his thick shoulders. "Pity. No, your hands are
staying tied, little girl." He gestured sharply. "Move
ahead. Down that way. We'll follow this deer trail into
the canyon. They know the easiest ways to get to the
water."

Jessica was sorry she was wearing flat loafers with
no tread on the bottom. The brown pine needles were

like a slippery carpet beneath her feet, which was why she'd fallen so many times earlier. Carl, on the other hand, had leather hiking boots with heavy treads. He wore army camouflage gear and seemed almost to blend into the dusky shadows of the forest.

Trying to concentrate on the thin trail left by deer that traversed this area every day at dawn and dusk to go get water, Jessica tried to steady herself as they began to go down the incline. What was Carl going to do? He hadn't said much. All along, he'd pushed her into a trot or a fast walk, obviously trying to get off the Rim as quickly as possible. He had to have a vehicle stashed along 89A. And then what? Jessica knew he wouldn't try and take her back across the Canadian border. No, he wouldn't even attempt it.

She knew what he'd do: he'd get her to the vehicle, rape her and then shoot her afterward, dumping her body somewhere inaccessible. She remembered what he'd done to the man he'd killed in cold blood—he'd stalked him for weeks, plotted and planned and then, at the right moment, kidnapped him. The police had found forensic evidence in the back of a Ford van where the victim had been tortured and then shot.

They'd found the poor man's body fifty miles away, thrown into a ditch and covered with leaves and branches. Only by luck had another hunter, out during deer season, seen Carl dump the body and cover it up. Otherwise Carl would never have been discovered for the cold-blooded murderer he was.

Dan! As her heart cried out for him, Jessica slipped and skidded, then caught herself. The lava rocks poking up through the brown needles were long, razor sharp and could kill her if she struck her head against one. Breathing hard, her mouth parched, she carefully placed each foot as she descended the long, steep slope. Dusk was coming, the shadows growing deeper and darker. Somewhere in her head, she knew this was her dark night of the soul. Would she live to see the sun rise again? Suddenly, life became even more precious than before.

Jessica desperately wanted to live. She wanted to tell Dan she loved him! She wanted a life where she could marry him, carry the children made out of love they shared, have that family she'd always dreamed of. *Oh, Dan, where are you? Where are you?* she silently cried. Part of her knew it was foolish, but still Jessica prayed that Dan would be on their trail, would find them, would save her. *If only...if only....*

Dan knelt down on a promontory of black lava at dusk, the rifle stock tight against his cheek to steady it. Suddenly, through the rifle's scope, he spotted a big, red-haired man with a huge, awkward backpack working his way down into the canyon. Ahead of him— Dan's heart thudded hard—was Jessica! Yes, he saw her! She was alive! Alive! Worriedly, he gripped the rifle tighter. He could barely see her; he only caught glimpses of her now and then, as she slipped and slid down the steep canyon wall. Her hands were tied behind her, and he could make out a rust-colored patch at each elbow. It had to be blood. She must have fallen a number of times.

Rage tunneled through him as he swung the rifle site back to Carl Roman. It was almost dark. The grayness of the dusk mingled with the dark blue of Roman's pack, and the camouflage clothes he wore made him almost invisible now. It was impossible to get a good, clean shot. Dan couldn't risk it. He knew if he only wounded him, Roman would turn on Jessica and murder her on the spot. Lowering the rifle, the pain in his heart tripling, Dan pulled out the cell phone. Punching in the numbers, he heard nothing but static. Damn! Standing up, he slung the rifle across his shoulder and tried facing several different directions while he dialed again. Nothing. He was too deep in the forest and too low into the canyon for the signal to get out and connect with another phone.

He was alone. Grimly, he put the cell phone away and mounted Gan. The stallion was restive. He hadn't had water to drink all afternoon and had to be thirsty. Dan's mind spun with plans and possibilities. Turning the stallion away from an outcrop of lava, Dan moved him down a well-used elk path, a shortcut to the creek below. Could he get down before Carl did? Would he have time enough to set up a shot that would kill the murdering bastard and save Jessica's life?

Dan wasn't sure. The stallion grunted, throwing out both front feet and sinking down on his haunches as they started the dangerous descent toward the creek. Halfway down the slope, the grayness began to turn to blackness. Dan held his breath, his legs clamped like steel around the stud's barrel as they slipped and slid, trying desperately to avoid the larger boulders and outcroppings that could rip into flesh and shatter bone.

Finally, they reached the creek. Dan dismounted and allowed the stallion to thrust his muzzle deeply into the icy cold water. The snowmelt off Humphreys Peak, which rose above the city of Flagstaff, helped to fill this creek. In some places it was over a man's head, while in others it was shallow enough to cross. Dan knew they were about half a mile downstream from where Roman would come off the canyon wall with Jessica.

It was completely dark now and he realized only belatedly that his rifle didn't have infrared. There was no way he could pick Carl out in the darkness. No, he'd have to stalk him, jump him and pray to the Great Spirit that he could subdue him before Roman killed him first. Moving to the sated stallion, which stood eagerly eating at the lush grass along the bank, Dan took out a pair of sheepskin-lined hobbles and put them on the horse's front legs. The gurgle of the stream sounded so happy and soothing compared to the violence he would be heading toward in a few minutes.

He tried the cell phone again, but to no avail. In a two-thousand-foot-deep canyon, no signal was going to get in or out. The helicopter that had been flying overhead from time to time was gone now, too, probably heading to Flag. Unless the aircraft had night-time capability, such as infrared, more than likely it wouldn't return to the area to search until dawn.

Dan took off the stallion's bridle and hung it from the saddle horn. Patting the Arabian affectionately, he knew the horse would remain at the creek eating and drinking. Hopefully, if everything went right, Gan would be their transportation up and out of here later, carrying them to 89A and safety.

The ifs were huge, Dan realized as he got rid of his cowboy boots, trading them for a pair of soft deerskin moccasins instead. There was no doubt Carl Roman was an expert hunter. Dan had been led off the main trail four different times by him. The fact that Roman wore camos and carried a high-powered rifle told Dan he'd hunted and knew what he was doing. Had Roman been in the Canadian military? As Dan stood up and picked up the rifle, he wished he'd asked Sam about that earlier.

Near the banks of Oak Creek, the grass was tender and the earth soft under his silent moccasins. Dan hurried upstream toward where Roman would emerge off the cliff wall. Maybe they had already made the descent. He wasn't sure. What he hoped to do was find a good place to hide, and then jump Roman, surprise him.

How was Jessica? Sweat trickled down Dan's face as he loped along. Did she know they were hunting for her? Trying to save her? She must. She had to. His love for her vied with his building terror. All the old memories of the war—the stealth, the stalking, the terror, the odor of blood and the grunt of men dying—enveloped Dan. He shook his head savagely. Somehow he had to get clear of all of that and concentrate on the here and now.

For a moment, he crouched near the creek, just listening. Picking up the normal night sounds of crickets chirping and frogs croaking, he waited. Suddenly he thought he heard a woman's cry. Jessica? He almost stood, but harshly ordered himself to remain still.

There! He heard it again. It *was* Jessica! She was screaming. He couldn't hear the words. He only knew it was her voice careening off the walls of the canyon in an eerie echo. It was filled with anger—an emotion he'd not heard from Jessica before.

Rising, he hurried along the creek, being careful where he planted his feet. His night vision was good, and with the slice of moon in the sky, he could make out branches and rocks along the bank just well enough to avoid them. Leaping over a fallen log, he gripped the rifle hard. He heard Carl's voice then and froze. It had a deep, threatening tone.

He had to hurry! Dan's heart began to pound, rattling in his chest. He controlled his breathing—it was important not to be heard. Crouching down, he dropped his cowboy hat aside. He knew the color of his skin would help him hide in the shadows, and he wore a dark blue shirt and dark blue jeans. He looked like darkness itself. Roman wouldn't see him coming—until it was too late.

Jessica screamed again. Carl laughed as he lunged for her. She rolled along the bank of the creek, over and over, trying to avoid him. He had shoved her on her back as she'd knelt at the stream, thirstily sucking up badly needed water.

The moonlight was just bright enough for her to see that crazed, wild look in his eyes that meant he intended to rape her—once again. That look filled her with such terror that as he shoved her down on the ground again, Jessica lashed out in self-defense with both her feet. Her shoe caught him along the jaw and, thrown off balance, he roared like a wounded bull.

Gasping for breath, Jessica scrambled to her feet as she watched Carl fall backward. She had to run! Where? No matter where she went, she knew Carl would get her. And he'd tear the clothes off her body, like he had before, and he'd hurt her and make her scream all over again. No! No, she wasn't going to be a victim this time! She'd fight to her death!

Turning, she leaped into the stream. Oak Creek was barely knee-deep at this point, but the rocks were algae covered and slippery. She lunged forward, all the time tugging at her numbed wrists. She had to get free! Her sweat and blood had been loosening the rawhide cords all along. Water splashed around her now as she waded forward. The creek was about a hundred feet wide and the bank was covered with thick brush on the other side. If only...

"You bitch!" Carl roared, scrambling to his feet. "You're dead!"

Crying out, Jessica jerked her head around. She saw Carl leap into the water after her, his face icy with fury. There! She jerked one hand from its bonds. Free! She was free! Leaping from the water, her feet slipping, Jessica crashed up the far bank. Her hands closed over a pine branch the size of her arm. It would do.

She heard Carl's heavy breathing coming up behind her. Thrusting herself onto her feet, Jessica clenched her teeth. She grabbed the limb with both hands and as she whirled to meet her attacker, swung it as hard as she could.

Roman obviously wasn't prepared for her to fight back, and belatedly threw up his arm to protect himself. *Too late!* The wood smashed into the side of his face, catching his hard, square jaw. Her arms vibrated with the impact and her fingers were ripped opened by splinters as the solid connection was made.

With a groan, Carl staggered backward, his hands flying to his bloody, torn face. Jessica blinked uncertainly. Was she seeing things? There was movement, like a dark shadow, back along the creek. Who? What? She froze, unsure, her legs turning to jelly. Carl was roaring and cursing and flailing around in the middle of the creek.

Dan! A cry almost ripped from Jessica's lips as she saw him materialize out of the darkness. Unable to move, she watched in horrified silence as he dropped the rifle he was carrying and pulled out a knife from the scabbard at his side. His face was carved from darkness and light, his eyes narrowed slits of glittering fury as he lunged into the stream after Carl.

Her heart contracted in terror as Dan made two huge leaps. In seconds, he was behind the unsuspecting Carl. She watched in utter fascination and horror as Dan lunged out with one leg and knocked him completely off his feet. Roman grunted hard, falling with a loud splash. Water flew up in sheets all around them. Dan made one, two, three hard jabs with his fist against Carl's face. In moments, her captor was unconscious, his head sinking below the water.

Jessica trembled, watching as Dan hauled Roman to the other side of the creek, quickly tying his hands and then his feet. Was she dreaming this? Was it all her imagination? No!

"Dan!" Her cry echoed through the canyon as she waded jerkily across the creek toward him.

Throwing the knife aside, Dan whirled at the sound of Jessica's cry. He saw her white face, her eyes huge with horror, her arms outstretched as she slogged against the current toward him. Wordlessly, he jumped into the water. In four strides he was at her side, his arms wrapping tightly around her.

"Jessica...." he rasped brokenly, pulling her hard against him, holding her tightly.

Uttering his name, Jessica felt her knees giving way.

Her arms numb, she fell against him, feeling the dampness of his shirt against her cheek.

"It's all right, all right," Dan breathed savagely, whispering the words against her tangled, dirty hair. "You're safe, Jessica, safe. I love you... I need you... you almost died...." He squeezed his eyes shut and held her fiercely. He could feel the rapid thud of her heart against his pounding one. Her body felt limp against his and he realized that she'd fainted. Was she wounded? Alarmed, Dan picked her up in his arms. Jessica was like a rag doll, her head lolling against his shoulder, her face pressed to his chest as he hurriedly got her out of the stream and onto dry land.

Raising his head, he whistled sharply, twice. He knew Gan would hear the whistle. He had trained the stallion to come to him. Even though the horse had hobbles on, Dan knew Gan would easily make the trip upstream in about fifteen minutes.

"Jessica? Jessica?" he rasped as he gently laid her down on the green slope of the bank. "*Shi shaa,* can you hear me?" He rapidly scanned her arms, legs and head with his hands. Her flesh felt cold. Shakily, he held his fingers against the carotid artery at the base of her neck. She had a strong, rapid pulse. Besides the blood on both her elbows, he detected a scratch along her brow, but that was all.

Gently, he began to move his hands slowly up and down her arms as he straddled her, calling her name. Shortly, he saw her thick lashes begin to flutter and he breathed a sigh of relief. Taking her into his arms, Dan sat down and cuddled Jessica against him to keep her warm. She was in shock, her flesh cool and damp from being in the water.

Jessica felt the thud of Dan's heart against hers, felt the warm moistness of his breath against her face, the soft kisses he was pressing against her brow and cheek. This was real. She wasn't dead or imagining this. Just the way Dan held her in that gentle, cradling embrace made her sob.

"You're safe, safe," he crooned, running his fingers through her mussed blond hair. "It's okay, Jessica. It's all over. Just lie against me. I'll hold you for as long as you want. We're going home, *shi shaa*. Home. I love you.... I'll always love you...."

Chapter 11

"Don't leave me, Dan…." Jessica whispered. Sam and Kate had just brought her home from the Flagstaff hospital where she'd been taken. Luckily, the Yavapai SWAT team had contacted the Sedona Fire Department, and the medical team had met Dan and Jessica along the highway, when they crested the canyon rim on Gan. Jim Cunningham was the EMT who'd cared for her. With a gentle, quiet voice, he had talked to her soothingly as he treated her many scratches and cuts. He'd allowed Dan to ride in the back of the ambulance with her as she sat on the gurney, still in mild shock. Once at the hospital, a doctor had examined her thoroughly and said she could go home and rest.

She saw Dan hesitate at the door. It was dawn now; a bleak grayness was visible on the western horizon outside her window. Sam and Kate had left her once she was settled in, and had gone back to their ranching duties, despite how tired they were. Absolute exhaustion played on Dan's features as well. "Don't go," she said pleadingly. "I—I don't want to be alone right now. Will you hold me? I think I can sleep if you hold me for just a little while…."

Dan's heart was torn at her tearful plea. "Sure," he said, slowly turning around and coming back into the gloom of her bedroom. The nightmare they'd lived through had chiseled away his normal sense of decorum, of what was right and wrong. Now, all he wanted, needed, was Jessica—to remain in physical contact with her. Though her hair had been washed at the hospital, he saw that the strands needed to be brushed away from her pale features. Picking up the brush lying on the dresser, he came over and sat down, facing her.

"First things first. They should have at least combed your hair up there."

The fleeting touch of his hand against her jaw made Jessica close her eyes. A ragged sigh tore from her lips as Dan gently moved the brush through her tangled, damp hair. Just his touch stopped the pain and fear she was still feeling. With each gentle stroke of the brush, her raw state began to dissolve. Dan was close, and he was caring for her. He loved her. Hadn't she heard him say that? Jessica lifted her lashes and drank in the strong, tired planes of his face.

"You saved my life."

The corner of his mouth twisted. "I think you saved your own. When I saw you pick up that branch and use it like a club against Roman, I was surprised."

An unexpected giggle came from her lips, sounding slightly hysterical. "You were surprised? I was surprised! I'd never done anything to defend myself against him. Ever."

Grimly, Dan brushed her hair until it shone like fine, molten gold. "Then it was about time, Jessica. You empowered yourself in that moment. For a little thing, you can sure heft one hell of a wallop when you want to." A slight, tired smile pulled at his mouth as he dropped his gaze and held her tired, luminous one. Putting the brush on the bed stand, Dan framed her face with his hands. His smile fled as he searched her features. Jessica had many scratches here and there, all from falling so many times.

"Did you hear me out there as I carried you out of the stream?" he said finally.

His hands were so warm, so steadying. Jessica felt like the desert after a turbulent thunderstorm had ravaged it for hours. "I hope I did," she whispered fervently, clinging to his dark gray gaze. "Oh, I hope I did, Dan. I wasn't making it up, was I?"

Leaning over, he met her soft, parting lips with his own. Her breath was moist and warm against his cheek and her hands fell automatically against his upper arms, her fingers digging into his muscles as he caressed her mouth. "I said I loved you," he whispered hoarsely. "I'll always love you even if you never love me, *shi shaa....*" As he pressed his mouth more surely against hers, he tasted the warmth of her salty tears trickling down her cheeks. It was a taste of life, of her, of her strong, courageous heart inside that small body she lived within. A body he wanted to love and hold sacred forever.

Easing away, Dan felt hot tears gathering in his own

eyes as he gazed down at her glistening ones. There was such adoring, fierce light in Jessica's eyes, but he didn't trust what he saw there.

"The one thing," she began, sliding her fingers up across his shoulders, "the one thing I regretted after Carl kidnapped me was that I'd never told you how I really felt about you, Dan." Sniffing, she continued, "I was afraid. So afraid. I was like Gan. Me and that stallion are a lot alike, I think...."

Dan smiled tenderly. "You two are like twins in some ways," he agreed. He released her and reached for the box of tissues on the bed stand, pulling a few free and handing them to her. She blew her nose several times and then blotted her eyes. As she sat there in the gloom, his heart opened wide. Here was how he wanted to be with Jessica, sharing the richness of all their feelings with one another. It didn't matter if they were sad, happy, bad or good feelings, it was the simple, beautiful act of sharing them that was important to Dan.

"I recognize myself in Gan. The more you worked with the stallion—the *way* you worked with him, Dan—I found myself wishing you would be like that with me."

He cocked his head and trailed his hand across her smooth, shining hair. "Why didn't you share that with me? I would have." He shook his head and looked at the light spilling through the fragile lace curtains at the window. "I *wanted* to, Jessica. You don't know how many times I wanted to reach out and touch you, kiss you, tell you how beautiful you are to me, how you made a difference in my life, how you made me feel good inside once again...."

"I was scared," she said.

"I realized that after a while." Frowning, he picked up her hand and cradled it between his own. "And after seeing Roman, seeing what he'd done to the horse and what he might do to you, I understood very clearly why you were afraid. That man is a two-heart, like you told me earlier. I've rarely seen a human being like that, but as I looked through the scope of my rifle and I saw his face, I knew why you were afraid of all men." He pressed a soft kiss to the back of her hand. "Even of me."

Sniffing, Jessica took another tissue from the box. She wrapped her fingers more strongly around Dan's hand. "Even knowing the Yavapai SWAT team went down there and got him doesn't make me feel any safer. I know he's up in Flag, in jail under heavy guard, but I'm still scared to death, Dan."

"I know, I know...but listen to me." He gripped her hands and made her focus all her attention on him. "They'll deport him, take him back to Canada. He'll go on trial and this time, he'll be put away for life with no possibility of parole. That's what the captain of the SWAT team told me."

"I'll have to go back to Vancouver to testify," Jessica said with a shudder.

"This time," Dan said grimly, "you won't have to go alone. I'll be there, Jessica. At your side. I'll protect you because I love you."

The words fell softly, soothing her emotional turmoil. "I never told you, did I?" she whispered, reaching up, her fingertips softly brushing his cheek. She felt the prickle of beard beneath her hand. The darkness of his beard made Dan look even more dangerous.

"I guess I didn't realize just how much of a warrior you really were until today. I know better than anyone what it took to ride Gan into the Rim country. He could have refused. He could have bucked you off and tried to kill you. To know that you tracked me all that way…to have seen you come out of the darkness like that and jump Carl…" Jessica inhaled raggedly and shifted her gaze to the ceiling for a moment. "You're a man of surprising facets, Dan Black. I think I'm one of the few people who have ever witnessed you in action like that."

Jessica saw him avoid her eyes. He pressed her hands between his and she felt his warmth and care radiating out to her. "The reluctant warrior," she whispered. "I know how you said you'd never kill again—ever. Yet when I saw that knife in your hands and Carl starting to get up out of that stream, I knew that you'd do what you had to do."

Lifting his head, his eyes narrowing, Dan rasped, "Yes, I'd have killed him to save you. There wasn't any question in my heart in that moment. I didn't want to hurt anyone, but I wasn't going to let him hurt you, Jessica. Not *ever* again."

Whispering his name, Jessica leaned forward and wrapped her arms around Dan's shoulders, embracing him. She rested her head against his neck and jaw. "I—I know. As I crouched there, I watched you stalk him. I saw the look in your eyes, the way you moved toward him. There wasn't a doubt in my mind that only one of you would come out of that creek functional. I was so scared for you, Dan." Her voice wobbled dangerously and she tightened her arms around his neck.

She felt Dan's hands move gently around her torso and draw her fully against his lean, hard frame.

"I knew all the pain, the horror you'd carried for years from the war, Dan. And to be there and see you set aside your own suffering, and possibly add to your nightmares and more pain to yourself to save me… well, it just blew me away. I couldn't believe you'd do that for me. It was then, as I struggled to get out of the water, that I realized you'd come after me because you loved me. It was the only thing that would make you set aside your own values."

Dan turned his head slightly and pressed a kiss against the warmth of Jessica's cheek. Easing away just enough to meet and hold her tear-filled gaze, he felt a self-deprecating smile tug at his mouth. Moving his hand across the crown of her head, he rasped, "Sometimes when you love someone, you do whatever has to be done, Jessica. This was one of those times. And believe me, I'm not sorry about any decisions I made, or what I did or would have done to keep you safe. In my heart, you are my woman. Even if I never told you so, you are. A man keeps his woman safe. He doesn't step back from that line in the sand when her life is in the balance."

It wasn't until today that Dan had come to realize the violence within him wasn't wrong; in every case, he'd acted out of a protective instinct—to defend himself and his team in the Gulf War. And to protect Jessica now. It would be one thing to enjoy killing, but he didn't. In a way, yesterday's event had helped him realize that not only was he a healer instead of a murderer, he was also a good person who was worthy and deserving of Jessica's love.

Looking deeply into his soft, dove gray eyes, Jessica felt the power of his words, the depth of his love for her in those priceless moments. "I don't know when I fell in love with you, darling, and it doesn't matter. What does matter is that I share how I feel with you now. I prayed out there that the Great Spirit would let me live, let me survive Carl, to tell you that."

"Well," Dan whispered, trailing a finger across the high slope of her flushed cheek, "you survived."

Closing her eyes, Jessica rested her head against his strong, broad shoulder. "And now I'm going to live, Dan. With you at my side."

The words sounded good to him and he embraced her tightly for a moment. "Maybe two wounded human beings with dark pasts can walk into the light together, hand in hand?" he teased her huskily.

Jessica moved her head slightly. "Love creates the light for us," she said, feeling safe, warm and so well loved by Dan. She saw the new sense of confidence in him, saw it in the glimmer of his eyes. Somehow this whole nightmarish event had made him realize what she already saw and knew of him—that he was a wonderful man who had many skills and talents to be proud of. No longer would he walk apologetically. Whatever he'd feared before was gone now. She knew love had a lot to do with it. He'd saved her life and that was the gift he'd given her. Life.

"You're tired, *shi shaa*," he whispered, gently untangling her from himself. "You need to sleep." And he eased her back on the bed and drew up the blankets to her breasts, covering the pink cotton, lace-trimmed nightgown that she wore. He saw a soft smile play across Jessica's lips as her lashes drooped downward.

"Yes, I'm tired now, Dan. I can sleep because I've told you how I really feel...."

Getting up off the bed, he watched as Jessica quickly sank into the depths of sleep. Exhaustion shadowed her face, but as he stood there, he was aware of that inner strength that had kept her going, that had given her the courage to protect herself in those last few deadly moments.

Jessica's inner bravery had come out and she had, in reality, saved her own life. Dan was proud of her. He loved her fiercely. Lifting his head, he looked toward the dawn, the pinkness of the horizon heralding a new day. A better day. Because of his Navajo upbringing, he said a silent prayer to Father Sun. The east was the direction of new beginnings, of a new day. A new way of life.

As he quietly moved from the room, he left the door ajar. Right now, all he wanted was a hot shower to rid himself of the stink of fear, of sweat and terror. And then he'd come back to Jessica's house and sleep at her side, where she wanted him. Where he wanted to be....

"Isn't this a beautiful place?" Jessica asked as she leaned against Dan. Her arms moved gracefully around his shoulders and she gazed up at him, up at his strong mouth and those burning gray eyes. She felt his arms move firmly around her, capturing her and pressing her fully against him. It was late fall and the autumn leaves on the Rim had turned a multitude of colors. Jessica loved autumn, and here on the Donovan Ranch it was a spectacular time of year. Where they stood near Oak Creek, picnic basket and blanket at their feet, the reds, yellows and oranges of the cottonwoods and sycamores surrounded them like a beautiful chorus of joy.

He grinned and playfully pressed a quick kiss to her full, smiling mouth. "What I'm looking at pleases me the most." In the months since the kidnapping, Dan had reveled in the love that had poured forth from Jessica toward him. They had not made love to one another— yet. In many ways, he was glad to wait because he understood Jessica had to not only heal from her past abuse, but to work at trusting him completely, too. He wasn't Carl, but he was a man. And trust in men hadn't been high on Jessica's list—just as it hadn't been with Gan. In the ensuing months since the kidnapping incident, though, Jessica had worked to change her perceptions. More than anything, Dan knew she needed time. Just as that black stallion had needed time to learn to trust him, too.

The warm, woody smell of decaying leaves surrounded them as Jessica leaned fully against him. He loved her fiercely, ached to have her, but he was content in allowing her to explore him in ways that felt safe to her. Today her hair was shining, molten gold in the sunlight that danced down between the falling leaves.

"*Shi shaa,*" he whispered as he stroked her hair. "My sunshine…."

"You," Jessica whispered, as she stood up on tiptoe and found his mouth, "are my life…." And he was, in every way.

Today was special, Jessica admitted to herself as she pressed her lips more fully against Dan's. Today, she knew, was the first day of her life with him. She'd awakened this morning knowing it, as surely as she breathed air in and out of her lungs.

Since the kidnapping, Dan had been incredibly gentle and understanding with her. Sam and Kate understood clearly that they'd fallen in love, and offered no comment when she asked Dan, a month after the kidnapping, to come and live in her house instead of staying out at the bunkhouse. Little by little, day by day, Jessica had discovered that living with Dan was like living life in the happiest of ways. Sure, they had their differences, but what two people in love didn't? Dan never allowed bad feelings to stay between them for long. He'd sit her down and they'd talk until they'd talked it out. So many times, Jessica discovered, it was misunderstandings, not anything else, upsetting her. How different it was living with Dan than with Carl!

As Jessica relished the rich splendor of Dan's lips against her own now, she surrendered completely to his hands, his mouth and his hard, strong body pressed fully against her. Over the months, he had shown her the positive way to live in a relationship. Because she had had such a bad relationship with Carl, she hadn't known what a good relationship consisted of. That was why, by living with Dan for so many months, Jessica knew she was ready to share the final gift with him. And she knew it would occur naturally, wonderfully, between them.

Dan never pressed her or made her feel she had to make love with him. No, not ever. He made it clear that she had to initiate, that she had to tell him how far he could go with her, and when to stop. Never once did Dan cross that line of discretion with her. She saw him struggle sometimes, and she felt guilty, but when he saw her reaction, he'd sit and talk it out with her to make her understand a hurt animal or human being couldn't be rushed or forced into giving something he or she didn't want to give.

But now his mouth was hot and wet and inviting. Jessica smiled to herself as she ran her fingers through his thick, black hair. Yes, today was the day. A day of loving Dan fully, completely. A day of freedom for them. And where else should they spend it but here beside Oak Creek, where her life had almost ended and then been reborn on that tragic night? It made symbolic sense to Jessica. And fall was a time for allowing old things to die, to float away, only to be reborn the next spring. Yes, this was the moment....

Dan felt her tugging insistently at the closures on his dark red, long-sleeved shirt. He smiled beneath her lips.

"You in a hurry?"

Giggling, Jessica eased away from his mouth and looked up into his dancing gray eyes. "I guess I am." She proceeded to open his shirt fully, revealing his firm flesh beneath it, and spread her hands against the dark hair of his well-sprung chest. "Mmm, you feel so *good* to me, Dan Black. Today is special, you know."

He drowned in her turquoise gaze, absorbing her searching, exquisite touch. His flesh burned beneath the exploration of her cool, slender fingers and his heart began to pound with need of her. "Oh?"

She stilled her hands against his chest, absorbing the thudding sensation of his heart beneath her palms. "Yes," Jessica whispered more seriously. "I brought you out here for a reason...."

Dan eased his arms around her and held her, rocking her slightly from side to side. The gurgling creek, the soft, intermittent breeze that danced around them, all seemed playful and joyous to him. "Women *always* have reasons," he teased, laughing huskily as he watched her grin. His lower body began to ache, as it always did when Jessica touched him, kissed him and explored him. As badly as he wanted to consummate his relationship with her, he knew it had to be her call, her choice. He wanted her to come willingly, joyfully, to him. He wanted his woman looking forward to his embrace, to his kisses, his adoration of her in all ways. It was the only way.

"What web do you weave today, my spider woman?" he teased, grazing her flushed cheek with a fingertip. Her eyes were so beautiful to him, a haunting mirror of the depths of her priceless soul—a soul he was privileged to see, to share and love fiercely.

Easing the shirt off his shoulders, Jessica stepped back and began to undo the thick leather belt on his jeans. "It's time, darling." Fingers stilling, she lifted her chin and met his flaring gray eyes. "Love me, Dan," she quavered. "Love me fully. In all ways. I'm ready...."

Frowning, he gripped her hands as she tried to push his jeans off his narrow hips. "Are you sure?" Never had he wanted her more than in that moment. The wind played with her hair, which shone like gold and framed her flushed face and sparkling blue eyes. She was a woman of nature, a child to the tree nation and to the flower people. No one was closer to Mother Earth's heartbeat than Jessica, and he loved her for that connection because life flowed so powerfully through her all the time.

Jessica sobered and held his concerned gaze. "I've never been more sure, darling. I love you. I want to share my love with you." She removed his hands and began to slide his jeans downward.

Dan believed her. He saw the change in her eyes, saw a fierce light there, a hunger aimed only at him. Pushing off his boots, then his jeans, he nodded and moved her over to the blanket. Once he'd set the picnic basket aside, he eased her down on the soft, dark blue surface. "Remember," he rasped as she lay down next to him and he began to unbutton her pale green blouse, "you can stop me anytime, Jessica. Just say it or show me...." The blouse opened to reveal her silky camisole. His fingers ached to brush those small breasts beneath it. How would she react to his touch? Suddenly, he was afraid as never before. But he had to push beyond his own fears.

Sighing, Jessica closed her eyes. She took his hand and guided it to the side of her breast. "Touch me, just touch me, Dan. I ache for you. I ache so much...."

Her words fell heatedly over him. Her fingers were so white against his darker hand. He felt the soft, firm roundness of her breast. "You feel so good," he whispered as he leaned down and captured her mouth. "So good...."

The provocative movement of his hand against the swell of her breast, against her camisole and her silken bra, left Jessica wanting more. The sounds of the creek, happy and bubbling, the clatter of the drying leaves moved by the breeze, the far-off call of a blue jay, all blended together in a beautiful song for her. When he tore his mouth from hers, gently removing the soft fabric and settling his lips on the peak of her taut breast, she uttered a cry of absolute pleasure. Her fingers bunched and released on his strong, firm shoulders. A hot, jagged bolt of lightning coursed down through her as he caressed her nipple, suckling it gently. Her body became molten beneath his gentle, exploring touch. A haze of heat throbbed through her, robbing her of any thought processes.

As his lips moved to the other nipple, Jessica arched upward. He slowly removed the rest of her clothing, and when her hip touched his, she realized only belatedly that he was also naked. The movement of his hard, muscular body against her softer one was a mesmerizing experience for her. As his hand grazed her arched spine and he trailed a fiery path of kisses from her throbbing breasts downward, all she could do was gasp raggedly, longing for more of him. The fire between her thighs was hot and burning. She cried out for more of his touch, more of his delicious, dizzying exploration of her. Never had she been touched, kissed, caressed like this.

As she arched more deeply against him, her thighs automatically opened to allow him entrance into her sacred self. Each scorching touch of his lips against her rounded abdomen, moving slowly downward, was a new kind of torture for her. A wild, throbbing ache built and she rolled her head from side to side, frustrated and needing him so badly. As his lips trailed a path of fire to each of her taut thighs and he moved his tongue against her, a moan shattered through her. With each silken movement against her womanhood, she felt the pressure within her build. She reached out, begging him silently to enter her, to consummate their union so that the burning ache within her would be satiated.

Gasping, she felt him move his hand in a languid, caressing motion against that sacred, moist area between her thighs. Consumed in the flames of her need, Jessica lay helplessly in his arms, a prisoner of pleasure to his touches, to kisses that built the fire within her higher and higher, brighter and brighter. Her breath was ragged. Her heart was pounding. How badly she wanted him! She tried to speak, but it was impossible. Just as she sobbed out his name, she felt him move. Within moments, he had opened her thighs even more and she felt the power of his maleness against her, his hard masculine form blanketing her. Jessica barely opened her eyes, her hands coming to rest on his arms. She saw the tender, burning love in his eyes, the way his mouth was twisted in pain as well as pleasure. In that second, she realized he was aching just as much as she was. In the next second, she understood the fierceness of love between a man and a woman.

Without thinking, only responding to the innate knowledge of her body, Jessica lifted her hips upward to allow him entrance into her hot, moist depths. As he surged forward, he bracketed her head with his hands and captured her mouth in a swift, hungry kiss that tore the breath from her. The power of him within her, the rocking motion he established, the cradling of the fire, his hard body pressed surely, provocatively against her—all conspired to dissolve her last coherent senses. In that moment, with that delicious movement tunneling up through her, she understood the mating of moonlight with fierce, hot sunlight that occurs between a woman and a man.

There was such joy, such dizzying elation as he moved within her, taught her the ancient rhythm, that she was amazed by the utter, wild freedom it invoked in her. The pressure, the heat built until she felt as if she would explode internally. And then, as he tore his mouth from hers and suckled her nipple once more, an explosion of such magnitude and power occurred that Jessica arched, cried out and froze in his embrace. It felt as if lightning were dancing across her lower body, sending out forks of light and pleasure through every nerve ending within her.

She felt Dan move his hand beneath her hips and lift her slightly. The sensation, the volcanic molten feeling of pleasure, heightened and continued. He moved within her, danced with her rhythmically, sang in unison with her body, with her heart and soul as he thrust again and again to prolong the incredible feeling for her. Moments later, as the golden light burning within her began to ebb, she felt him stiffen and groan. He buried his head against her breast and held her hard against him and she knew it was her turn to love him, to cherish him as much as he'd cherished her. With a knowledge as old as woman, she moved her hips in a rolling, rhythmic motion and captured him tightly against her with her legs to prolong his release deep within her.

She saw his face tighten almost as if in pain, but with exquisite pleasure, too. With a groan, he suddenly collapsed against her, his hands tangled in her hair, his breathing harsh and shallow against her breasts. An incredible feeling of satiation, of completion, moved through her like soft moonlight caressing the earth. With a sigh of surrender, Jessica understood as never before about real love. What it was really all about. Her abdomen tingled beneath his weight as she slowly opened her eyes, moving her hands weakly through his dark, shining hair, and absorbed his gleaming profile as he lay against her. How fiercely she loved Dan!

In that moment, Jessica felt a breathtaking sensation move through her. Her heart was wide-open, receiving and giving. As she moved her hand languidly across his back and felt the strength of his spine, she smiled softly. To bear his children would be the ultimate gift. Yes, a child created out of love, born not of darkness, but of light, would be welcomed fully. Completely.

As she lay there, the sounds of the forest registering around her once again, Jessica realized that she and Dan would create a child from this first coming together. She didn't know how she knew it, but she did. Lying there in the cooling breeze, she gazed overhead as colorful leaves twirled and spiraled down around them, as if Mother Earth were celebrating their consummation of love with them. Smiling tenderly, Jessica slid her hands around Dan's face. She saw the dove gray of his eyes, the love shining in them for her alone. He eased up off her and leaned forward just enough to capture her smiling mouth. The kiss was tender. Filled with love. Her heart swelled even more and Jessica wondered if it was possible to die from happiness.

"You are my *shi shaa,*" he rasped, sliding his hand against her full lower lip, "the sunshine in my life. You're all I'll ever need or want, my woman of the earth."

His words were filled with passion and love for her. Dan eased out of her, pulling her into his arms so that she could rest her head against his shoulder. Savoring the way he brought her against him, she closed her eyes, content as never before.

"You are the lightning of Father Sky," she whispered. "You love me so fully, so beautifully. I thought I was going to die if you didn't complete me, darling."

He rose up on one elbow and kept her near as he looked down at her flushed face, her glistening blue eyes and well-kissed mouth. Smiling tenderly, Dan traced her cheek with his fingertip. "And you are the daughter of Mother Earth." His dark hand fell against her rounded abdomen and he caressed her gently. "Our children will be welcome here, between us."

"Oh, yes." Jessica sighed as she moved her hand over his own. She could feel the strength, the roughness of it against her feminine softness. "Children created out of our love for one another, Dan...."

"Marry me, Jessica?"

She opened her eyes and met his very serious ones.

"I'm poor," Dan rasped. "And I don't have a college education. I'll probably work myself into a grave someday, but it's good, honest work. I want you by my side every night, every day. We've come so far together. Let's go the rest of the way." He saw Jessica's expression change to one of tear-filled happiness. The luminous look in her eyes, Dan knew, was her way of saying yes. His heart soared in response like an unfettered eagle. Stilling his hand against her abdomen, he murmured, "I want you to be the mother of my children. They'll be so lucky to have you. I want to grow old seeing our children and grandchildren around us. I think they'll have a good life. Good growing-up years, not like what you had, but what we can give them with our love."

Tears choked her and she nodded once. "Y-yes, darling. Yes to all our dreams. And I don't care if you're a horse wrangler and you won't make that much money."

"I don't own any land. I'm poor," he said.

"In one way, maybe," Jessica whispered, "but in so many other ways, you're a treasure to me, Dan. You bring me love, respect and care. What's that worth compared to money?" She touched his cheek and watched his gray eyes narrow with hunger for her. It was a delicious feeling.

"When you put it that way, you're right," he admitted. A slight smile played at the corners of his mouth. "I'm going to love you forever and a day, Jessica. *Shi shaa,* my sunshine. My life and heart...."

Epilogue

"I can hardly wait until Rachel gets home," Jessica eagerly confided to Kate as they sat out on the porch swing in the warmth of late November. Everywhere else in the nation people were experiencing harsh temperatures and even snow, but not here in Arizona. No, on Thanksgiving Day, it was in the sixties and they were enjoying the pale blue sky and sunshine.

Jessica wore a pink angora sweater with a cowl neck, and a soft cream skirt that fell to her ankles. Her hair was caught back behind her head, a beautiful pink-and-white orchid in it. The fuchsia color of the orchid brought out the flushed quality of her cheeks. Dan had given her a gold heart locket shortly after he'd helped rescue her and it hung just above her collarbone as it always did. Inside the locket was a photo of him and her. Together. Like it should always be. He'd also given her a small pair of gold, heart-shaped earrings, which she adored.

Smoothing her fingers over the red velvet skirt she wore with a crisp white blouse, Kate said, "I can't wait to see Rachel, either. I just wish she could have made it home for Thanksgiving, that's all."

"She has to finish up her commitments," Jessica murmured. "Her teaching contract ends in early December. Just think, she'll be home soon." She smiled over at her older sister. Inside, Dan and Sam were finishing up the last of the dishes and cleaning up after the wonderful midday meal. Jessica was so happy to have been able to restart the tradition her mother had begun so many years before—of feeding the homeless of Sedona. A bus from the Sedona mission had just taken twenty homeless people back to town. Yes, Thanksgiving had been very special this year. In so many wonderful, joyous ways.

"December fifteenth, if everything goes according to plan." Kate sighed. "Rachel said she'd rent a car down in Phoenix and drive north to the ranch. I just hope we don't get any of those sudden, unexpected snowstorms."

Jessica nodded. Weather in November, particularly in Oak Creek Canyon, could be unpredictable. "She's probably used to driving in rain at least, having lived so long over in England."

"Probably," Kate agreed. She smiled a little. "I guess I'm just being big sister worrywart, is all."

Warmth touched Jessica's heart as she met and held Kate's gaze. "You love us, that's why." She watched as Kate wrestled with her obvious affection. Little by little, her sister had let down her guard, and over the months, Jessica had watched her begin to bloom in a way she'd never seen before. Kate was more vulnerable, more open emotionally, and Jessica relished those wonderful, unexpected gifts from her older sister.

Kate pointed to Jessica's left finger. "I think it was romantic of Dan to give you his grandmother's engagement ring this holiday morning. He's such a great guy."

Sighing, Jessica rocked in the swing with her sister.

"Isn't he though? Sometimes," she murmured, closing her eyes and fingering the gold-and-diamond ring, "I think I'm in this neverending dream. Sometimes I worry I'll wake up and Dan will be gone." Jessica opened her eyes and stole a look at Kate. "Do you know what I mean?"

Kate laughed. "I sure do." She looked back across her shoulder toward the screen door, through which she could hear the two men working noisily in the kitchen. "I feel the same about Sam. He loves me so much. I sometimes wake up at night in his arms and wonder what he saw in me in the first place. And then I go back to sleep and worry that I'm dreaming it all, and that I'm back in prison again." She frowned. "Boy, are we a jumpy lot or what?"

Giggling, Jessica shook her head, reaching out and gripping Kate's hand. "We have a right to be scared. Dan told me one time that we had such a rough childhood he's surprised any of us turned out so well. He's seen members of his own family who were abused. Some of those kids have scattered to the four winds, and most of them are in trouble in one way or another, lost forever."

Kate became serious. "We were all lost in our own way, Jessica. We all ran the minute we turned eighteen. You went to Canada. Rachel found sanctuary in England. My life went awry and I got involved with fanatical activists and ended up in prison."

"At least," Jessica replied softly, "with the love of two good men who helped us find our way home, we have a chance to change things for the better. Not only for ourselves, but for our children."

"*If* we can keep this ranch afloat for any children that might happen after marriage," Kate warned her grimly. She gestured toward the dried, yellow grass in the front yard. "No rain. Not an inch of it all autumn. I'm really worried about fire, Jessica. And if we don't get rain this winter, I don't know how we can survive. We're going to have to sell off the rest of the herd, the pregnant cows... If that happens, we're done for. Sam and I are counting on that spring crop of calves for—"

"Katie, let it go. Sometimes we just have to have blind faith about these things. Dan says it's the darkness before the dawn for all of us as a family. He sees it in symbolic terms. It's a test. He said all three sisters must come home and pour our lifeblood back into this ranch to get its heart beating again. And once we do that with our care, our love and commitment, he said the rain would come to nourish that seed we've all nurtured here by coming home again."

"Beautiful symbol. But everything still sucks."

Jessica laughed. She shook her head. "Oh, Katie, you're such a pessimist!"

"I have a right to be," Kate growled, though a grin crawled across her mouth. "I'm the one riding the range every day and checking on our cattle and horses, on the drought conditions, the loss of our alfalfa crop."

"Okay," Jessica said, matching her grin, "I'll hold

the faith. Rachel was always big on hope. We'll let you be the grouch of the three. I guess every family has to have a pessimist, right?"

Tousling Jessica's hair, Kate laughed. "Right, I've *always* been the grouch in this family. Not much has changed, has it?"

"A lot has changed," Jessica said, more serious now. "On Christmas Eve, we're having a double marriage. You're going to marry Sam and I'm going to marry Dan. Rachel will be our joint maid of honor. *That,* my older, grouchy sister, is *change.*"

Kate enjoyed her younger sister's prim look. "Confident little thing, aren't you?" And she laughed.

"Life is *good,* Katie. Okay, so the ranch is still hanging by a thread, and the bank is salivating over our shoulders, eager to snatch it away the moment we fail to make a monthly payment. On the other side of the ledger, the personal and emotional side, you and I have struck it rich. We've got gold in our hands."

Chuckling, Kate said, "How I wish some of that gold could be alchemically changed into money!"

"Quit!" Jessica playfully hit her sister on the shoulder. "You don't mean that and I know it."

"I guess I don't," Kate said, a little wearily. She lowered her voice so only Jessica could hear her. "What if we can't save the ranch? What will Sam and Dan do? None of us can afford to buy another spread. All we're good for is the open range, being part of this land as cowboys. They might as well shoot us in the head and put us out of our misery if this ranch goes under. I don't want to do anything else in my life except what I'm doing now. I'd like to die in the saddle."

"Ugh. How about in Sam's arms? That's a lot more preferable. I know you love horses, Katie, but geez...."

"You know what I'm trying to say," Kate muttered fiercely.

"I hear you, Katie. Maybe, with Rachel coming home to establish a wellness clinic in Sedona, it will help us with the bills and stave off the inevitable from this terrible drought."

"Rachel isn't exactly rich, you know. She gave us her whole life savings to pay off the bulk of what was owed to the bank so they wouldn't foreclose before. Sure, she's got talent, ideas and plenty of hope, but that's not going to convert into money right away." Kate shook her head worriedly. "No, we've got some long, hard months ahead of us. I just pray for a miracle. Any miracle to help us through, that's all."

"See," Jessica chided, "you're not so pessimistic after all. You believe in miracles."

Chuckling, Kate rose from the porch swing and smoothed out her skirt. "It's all we've got left between us with the bank ready to foreclose on us, you twit."

Giggling, Jessica followed her sister back into the house. The living room had been set up to feed the homeless earlier and the scent of roasting turkey still permeated the air. As Jessica sauntered into the small kitchen, she watched in amusement as Dan and Sam kept bumping unceremoniously into one another as one washed and the other dried dishes. Dan wore a deep cranberry red cowboy shirt, a bolo tie made from silver and a turquoise nugget, dark blue jeans and newly polished black cowboy boots. His sleeves were rolled up to his elbows.

"I should have a picture of this," Kate teased, laughing. She went to the pecan-colored cupboards, opened them and started to put away the plates that Sam had dried.

"I think," Sam grumbled, "we should get silver stars for action above and beyond the duty of males."

Dan grinned and winked at Jessica, who rested her elbows on the white tile counter near the stove. She colored fiercely and smiled that soft smile that was so much a part of her.

"Where I come from on the res," Dan said, up to his elbows in soapsuds, "men did their fair share of housework. About the only thing we didn't do was learn how to weave."

"I'll take dishwashing over that," Sam said, drying the plates furiously with a white towel.

"Thought you might," Dan murmured, grabbing a handful of silverware to wash.

While Kate and the men chatted amiably, Jessica busied herself cutting the last pumpkin pie into four large slabs. Placing the slices on the small oak table covered with a lacy, white linen tablecloth, she added big dollops of whipped cream. Dan had found some pyracantha bushes with bright orange berries against dark green leaves, and had put some cuttings in a small, cut glass vase in the center of the table. It looked Christmassy to Jessica.

Her heart expanded with joy as she saw Dan steal a look across his shoulder to check where she was. Her hands stilled on the last plate as she caught and held his smoldering gray gaze. Automatically, her body responded fully to his unspoken invitation. Surely today was a day of thanksgiving as no other she'd ever had. Her finger burned warmly where his grandmother's engagement ring rested on her hand. Dan had bestowed the gift on her in front of everyone. Jessica had been so humbled and surprised that she'd cried shamelessly. She'd seen tears in Dan's eyes, too. And everyone else's.

There was nothing she wanted more than to have Dan as her husband, her partner for life. Each morning she woke up with him at her side, and it was a miracle to her. A wonderful, unfolding miracle. Jessica realized she had never known love until Dan, the man wrapped in darkness, had walked quietly into her life.

"Is that for us?" Dan queried, raising his brows and eyeing the pumpkin pie.

Grinning, Jessica traded a look with Kate. "Well, we took pity on you cowboys and thought you deserved some kind of treat for doing all this kitchen duty. Right, Katie?"

"Oh, sure, right." Kate looked at them with mock sternness. "We cooked all day, so you boys can clean up the mess."

Dan crowed and shared a laugh with Sam. "Do we get whipped cream on our reward?"

Jessica colored fiercely at the innuendo. "On the pie, yes."

The foursome broke into ribald laughter. The kitchen rang with the sounds of love and joy. How much had changed since she was a child! Jessica realized. With Kelly around, they had always walked as if stepping on eggs, afraid they would break at any moment. Now there was teasing, good-natured competition between Dan and Sam, and obvious love for her and Katie. Enough to go around and then some.

There was a knock at the front door.

"I'll get it!" Jessica said, quickly putting the tub of whipped cream aside and fleeing through the kitchen.

"Who's comin'?" Sam asked, trading looks with Dan and Kate.

"I don't know," Kate said. "We're not expecting anyone else."

Dan chuckled. "By now I think you would have caught on. With Jessica around, surprises are the order of the day."

Jessica appeared at the doorway to the kitchen, breathless and flushed. "Look who's coming for a late dinner!"

All three of them turned in unison.

Jessica smiled and stepped aside. "I found out last week that Jim Cunningham and his crew had Thanksgiving duty at the fire department. None of them could go home and have turkey with their families, so..." She skipped to the refrigerator as Jim entered the kitchen, "I packed up ten meals, for all of his crew at the fire station."

Jim nodded shyly to everyone. "Hi," he said, a bit awkwardly.

Dan shook his head and laughed. "Come on in, Jim."

Sam stepped forward and extended his hand. "Glad you could drop by."

Kate nodded. "Yes," she said, her voice a bit strained.

Jessica knew that the old war between the Cunninghams and Donovans had gone on for a long, bitter time. But Jim Cunningham had reached out to her, Sam and Kate to try and make up for the many wrongs done to them by his cantankerous father. Dressed in his dark blue, serge trousers and light blue, long-sleeved shirt, the silver badge on his chest glinting in the lamplight, Jim gave her a look of thanks for the dinners.

"Can you at least have a cup of coffee with us?" Jessica pleaded as she brought out the foil-wrapped meals and set them on the table. Kate went to find paper bags to place them in.

"Uh, no.... With the permission of my captain, I faked a call to come up here to get the meals, so I'm living on borrowed time as it is," Jim said with a slight, hesitant smile. His dark blue gaze pinned Kate as she returned with the paper bags, her expression grim. "The crew down at the fire station is beholden. Donovan generosity is well known in these parts. I hear you served thirty needy families as well as the homeless at the mission earlier today."

Kate compressed her lips and put the meals into the paper bags. "I'm sorry you have to work today."

Jim shrugged. "Well, with the way things were going at home this last week, I'm kinda glad I have the duty, to tell you the truth."

Jessica gave him a compassionate look. She *liked* Jim Cunningham. He was quiet, clean-cut, terribly handsome in a rough kind of way and respectful toward everyone. "Maybe a meal made with lots and lots of love will help then," she whispered, bringing over both bags for him to carry. "There's pumpkin pie and whipped cream in there for dessert."

Jim brightened as he put the two bags beneath his arms and Sam moved by him to open the front door. "Thanks—all of you." He caught and held Kate's dark stare. "I mean it...."

Kate barely nodded and wrapped her arms defensively against her breasts.

Jessica placed her hand on Jim's upper arm and led him out of the kitchen, with Dan following. She could feel Jim's firm muscles beneath his shirt and noted how fit he was. "I just hope you don't have any calls. I hope you have a nice, quiet night."

"Thanks, Jessica," Jim murmured, smiling down at her.

Out on the front porch, they saw that the sun had set behind the thousand-foot lava wall that protected the ranch property. The sky was a light blue and gold as Jessica, Dan and Sam walked with Jim to the red-and-white ambulance with the Sedona crest on the front door. Dan opened the rear doors of the ambulance and helped Jim place the food where it wouldn't fall over during transit.

Jim hesitated as he opened the driver's door, then turned and extended his hand to Dan. "Congratulations. I hear you're going to marry this flower child at Christmas."

Jessica laughed and felt heat flow into her cheeks as Jim's eyes danced with gentle teasing. "Flower child! Oh, come on, Jim. Is that what the gossip going around in Sedona is calling me?"

Dan released Jim's hand and put his arm around Jessica. "Be happy they're calling you something nice, *shi shaa,*" he said with a grin. "Instead of a blooming idiot or something like that."

Jim laughed, got into the ambulance and shut the door. "No kidding. You don't want to know what they call me. I can guarantee you it ain't nice." He raised his hand in a mock salute to the three of them. "Thanks.

All of you. I know everyone at the station will want you to know how much your care means to them."

Her hands clasped to her breast, Jessica leaned warmly against Dan. "Just take care, Jim. I'll see you in town next week. I'll drop by and pick up the dishes and silverware, okay?"

"Okay, Jessica." He started the ambulance and slowly turned around on the gravel driveway.

Back on the porch, Sam rested his hands on his hips as the ambulance disappeared up the winding road out of the canyon. He turned his gaze on Jessica. "That was a good move, politically," he said in congratulations.

She looked at him in surprise. "What do you mean?"

"Hadn't you heard?" he rumbled. "Old Man Cunningham is fixin' to slap our ranch with a lawsuit later this month. Over water rights."

Groaning, Jessica raised her hands to her open mouth. "No! How can he? We've always shared that well between our properties—for nearly a hundred years."

Sam ran his fingers through his hair and looked grimly over at Dan. "Explain it to her, Dan?"

Dan rubbed his hand against Jessica's tense arm. "Yes... I will...."

Sam grunted before slowly walking back inside the house.

Jessica turned in Dan's arms, feeling secure as his hands moved gently down her back to capture her against him. "Dan, what's going on? Is there something you three know that I don't? Is Katie hiding things from me again?"

"Come on," he urged, leaning down and kissing

her lips tenderly, "let's go for a walk and let this dinner settle."

Petulantly, Jessica surrendered and fell into step with him as they walked toward the horse corrals near the red barn. "What's Sam talking about, Dan? What lawsuit?"

Dan settled his black Stetson on his head and drew her more surely against him. He wished he could protect Jessica from some of the harshness of life. He saw the consternation in her expression and the worry in her eyes. Everyone hid the truth from Jessica because they knew how easily she could become upset, and how much it distressed her. He tightened his fingers on her shoulder as they walked.

"About two weeks ago, Jim's father called Sam over there," Dan confided in a low tone. "The day before that, Jim had come to the ranch here and talked with Sam, to warn him that the call was coming in. Jim tried to talk his father out of it, but the old man refused to listen to him. The drought has dried up all the wells on Cunningham property and he told Sam he was going to court to get full rights to the well that both ranches have shared for the last hundred years."

"That's why Kate looked so unsettled, then," Jessica said. "She wasn't very happy to see Jim here. Now I know why."

"Kate doesn't trust Jim or his motivations. She thinks that he's in cahoots with his father and he's just bluffing us."

Jessica rolled her eyes. "That's silly! Jim Cunningham is the only good apple from that rotten barrel, and she knows it!"

"That's probably true," Dan conceded, "but Cunningham could destroy us if he goes to court. We don't have the money to fight that kind of a lawsuit. He's got money. And money talks."

"But we need that well, too!" Jessica protested, her voice high with indignation. "All our pasture wells have dried up with the exception of that one! What are we to do? Let our stock die of thirst?"

"Take it easy," Dan soothed, placing both hands on her tense shoulders as she faced him. He saw the anguish in her eyes. "It could be a bluff. Old Man Cunningham, from what Sam has said, often uses threat of a lawsuit to scare off someone who gets in his way."

Bitterly, Jessica gripped his upper arms. "But if he takes that well, our livestock will die, Dan."

"I know that...." Helplessly, he caressed her strained mouth with his fingertips. "We can always pump water from Oak Creek if it comes down to that, so stop worrying. At least the creek runs through our property and not Cunningham's. If their well goes dry, we have a second water source. They don't. I was hoping that today would be happy for you in all ways, Jessica."

She gazed down at the ring on her finger. The small diamond twinkled in the early evening light. "I'm sorry. I was happy, Dan. So very, very happy." She struggled to smile for his sake as she placed her arms around his neck.

"I wish," Dan said in a frustrated tone, "that I could make these problems at the ranch go away. This family doesn't deserve any more hard luck than it already has."

Anger, worry and concern warred within Jessica. "Jim isn't a two-heart like Kate thinks," she said fiercely. "I have a feeling he'll fight for us. He won't let his father get away with this. Jim is fair-minded."

Dan nodded. He didn't tell Jessica that Old Man Cunningham owned the ranch until he died, and that the property rights were not to be divided among the three sons. The ranch was going to Bo and Chet. Jim had absolutely no leverage at all, even if he wanted to try and help the Donovans in the lawsuit over water rights.

Gently, Dan stroked her warm, flushed cheek. Instantly, Jessica responded to his touch and he smiled inwardly. Little by little, as he caressed her cheek, her brow and soft, silky hair, she quieted. Much of the worry was replaced with that serene look in her eyes again. The effect she had on him was similar.

"I'm putting Gan out with his band of mares today," he told her as he led her toward the stallion's pen. "Sam agreed. The stallion is tame now and he isn't going to be attacking a man on foot or horseback, so it's safe to let him be with his ladies."

Jessica sighed and wrapped her arm around Dan's waist as they walked. Her heart was heavy with worry, but she knew he had worked hard to get the stallion trained to the point where such a gift could be bestowed upon the animal. It would be one more job they wouldn't have to do. Natural breeding could take place instead. "Yes, let's watch him race out of his pen for the pasture."

Gan was waiting at the corral gate, his head extended, his fine ears pricked forward. He nickered as Dan drew near. Jessica stood back and smiled softly. The stallion, over time, had grown to love Dan. It was obvious in the way the animal nudged his shoulder as he opened the gate. As Gan moved, the shining ripple of his muscles was something to behold. She watched the stallion lift his tail like a flag once Dan had opened the gate, and give a deep, bugling cry that echoed throughout the canyon.

Looking over at the south pasture, where all the broodmares were kept, Jessica saw a number of them lift their heads from grazing on the dry, withered grass, and whinny in return.

Gan dug his rear hooves into the dirt, the dust flying as he lunged out of his corral. His long black mane and tail flowed as he galloped full speed toward his mares, a little over a mile away. Jessica heard Dan chuckle as he closed the gate. She liked the smile on his handsome face, the warm look in his gray eyes as he watched the stallion fly across the hard clay floor of the pasture. Gan's joyous bugling sounded again and again.

Jessica felt her spirits lift unaccountably. With the coming lawsuit she should feel sad and afraid. Miraculously, she didn't, and she knew why. It was because of the man wrapped in darkness who was walking toward her. His eyes were banked with coals of hunger—for her. Reaching out, she touched his fingers.

"He's free," she whispered. "You helped free Gan—and me...."

Sliding his arms around Jessica, Dan nuzzled her cheek. The past few weeks had convinced him that he was worthy of Jessica in every way. Dan was going to let his past go—completely. His bout with alcohol wouldn't be forgotten, but now, thanks to Jessica, he had put it into perspective. She had helped him retrieve his dignity and reembrace who and what he was. He was a man with an incredible gift with horses, a gift that he would use here at the ranch. Over time, the money he'd save from his work would build toward their bright future—together. He no longer worried about his place in Jessica's life. Everything he was had helped to save Jessica. The power of that knowledge had given him back his shredded self-esteem.

Pressing his mouth against her soft cheek, he whispered, "We're free to love one another, like that stallion will love his mares." Gently framing Jessica's face, Dan whispered, "And I'm going to love you forever...."

* * * * *

After writing more than one hundred books for Harlequin, **Stella Bagwell** still finds it exciting to create new stories and bring her characters to life. She loves all things Western and has been married to her own real cowboy for forty-four years. Living on the south Texas coast, she also enjoys being outdoors and helping her husband care for the horses, cats and dog that call their small ranch home. The couple has one son, who teaches high school mathematics and is also an athletic director. Stella loves hearing from readers. They can contact her at stellabagwell@gmail.com.

Books by Stella Bagwell

Harlequin Special Edition

Men of the West

Her Kind of Doctor
The Arizona Lawman
Her Man on Three Rivers Ranch
A Ranger for Christmas
His Texas Runaway
Home to Blue Stallion Ranch
The Rancher's Best Gift
Her Man Behind the Badge
His Forever Texas Rose
The Baby That Binds Them
Sleigh Ride with the Rancher

Visit the Author Profile page
at Harlequin.com for more titles.

HOME TO
BLUE STALLION RANCH

Stella Bagwell

To all my horses,
for the love and happiness they've given me.

Chapter 1

Who the hell is that?

Holt Hollister pushed back the brim of his black cowboy hat and squinted at the feminine shape framed by the open barn door. He didn't have the time or energy to deal with a woman this morning. Especially one who was pouting because he'd forgotten to call or send flowers.

Damn it!

Jerking off his gloves, he jammed them into the back pocket of his jeans and strode toward the shapely figure shaded by the overhang. Behind him the loud whinny of a randy stallion drowned out the sounds of nearby voices, rattling feed buckets, the whir of fans, and the muffled music from a radio.

As soon as the woman spotted his approach, she stepped forward and into a beam of sunlight slanting down from a skylight. The sight very nearly caused Holt to stumble. This wasn't one of his girlfriends. This woman looked like she'd just stepped off an exotic beach and exchanged a bikini for some cowboy duds.

Petite, with white-blond hair that hung past her shoulders, she was dressed in a white shirt and tight blue jeans stuffed into a pair of black cowboy boots inlaid with turquoise and red thunderbirds. Everything about her said she didn't belong in his horse barn.

Frustration eating at him, he forced himself to march onward until the distance between them narrowed down to a mere arm's length and she was standing directly in front of him.

"Hello," she greeted. "Do you work here?"

Holt might forget where he'd placed his truck keys or whether he'd eaten in the past ten hours, but he didn't forget a woman. And he was quite certain he'd never laid eyes on this one before today. Even without a drop of makeup on her face, she was incredibly beautiful, with smooth, flawless skin, soft pink lips, and eyes that reminded him of blue velvet.

"It's the only place I've ever worked," he answered. "Are you looking for someone in particular?"

She flashed him a smile and at any other time or place, Holt would've been totally charmed. But not this morning. He'd spent a hellish night in the foaling barn and now another day had started without a chance for him to draw a good breath.

She said, "I am. I'm here to see Mr. Hollister. I was told by one of the ranch hands that I'd find him in this barn."

She was looking straight at him and for a brief second Holt was thrown off-kilter by her gaze. Not only direct, it was as cool as a mountain stream.

"Three Mr. Hollisters live on this ranch," he said bluntly. "You have a first name?"

"Holt. Mr. Holt Hollister."

He blew out a heavy breath. He might've guessed this greenhorn would be looking for him. Being the manager of the horse division of Three Rivers Ranch, he was often approached by horse-crazy women, who wanted permission to walk through the barn and pet the animals, as if he kept them around for entertainment.

"You're talking to him."

Those blue, blue eyes suddenly narrowed skeptically, as though she'd already decided he was nothing more than a stable hand. And he supposed he couldn't blame her. He'd not had time to shave this morning. Hell, he'd not even gone to bed at all last night. Added to that, the legs of his jeans were stained with afterbirth and smears of blood had dried to brown patches on his denim shirt.

"Oh. I'm Isabelle Townsend. Nice to meet you, Mr. Holt Hollister."

She extended her hand out to him and Holt wiped his palm against the hip of his jean before he wrapped it around hers.

"Is there something I can do for you, Ms. Townsend?" he asked, while wondering how such a soft little thing could have a grip like a vice.

She eased her hand from his. "I've been told you have nice breeding stock for sale. I'm looking to buy."

If Holt hadn't been so tired, he would've burst out laughing. She ought to be home painting her fingernails, or whatever it was that women like her did to amuse themselves, he thought. "Are you talking about cattle or horses? Or maybe you're looking for goats? If you are, I know a guy who has some beauties."

"Horses," she said flatly, while peering past his shoulder at the rows of stalls lining both sides of the barn. "This is a horse barn, isn't it? Or are you in the goat business now?"

The sarcasm in her voice was the same tone he'd used on her. And though he deserved it, her response irked him. Usually pretty women smiled at him. This one was sneering.

"I'm in the business of horses. And at this time, Three Rivers isn't interested in selling any. You should drive down to Phoenix and try the livestock auction. If you're careful with your bidding, you can purchase some fairly decent animals there. Now if you'll excuse me, I'm very busy."

Not waiting to hear her reply, he walked off and didn't stop until he was out the opposite end of the barn and out of Isabelle Townsend's sight.

Furious and humiliated, Isabelle turned on her heel and stalked out of the barn. So much for all she'd heard about Three Rivers Ranch and its warm hospitality. Apparently, those glowing recommendations didn't include Holt Hollister.

Outside in the bright Arizona sunlight, she crossed a piece of hard-packed ground to where her truck was parked next to a tall Joshua tree.

Jerking open the door, she was about to climb into the cab when a male voice called out to her.

Wondering if Holt Hollister had decided he'd behaved like an ass and had come to apologize, she turned to see it wasn't the arrogant horseman who'd followed her. This man was slightly taller and perhaps a bit older than Holt Hollister, but she could see a faint resemblance to the man she'd just crossed words with.

"Hello," he said. "I'm Blake Hollister, manager of the ranch."

He extended his hand in a friendly manner and Isabelle complied.

"I'm Isabelle Townsend," she introduced herself, then added dryly, "It's nice meeting you. I think."

His brows disappeared beneath the brim of his gray hat. "I happened to see you go in the horse barn five minutes ago. If you're looking for someone in particular, I might be able to help."

"I was looking for the man who manages your horse division. Instead I found a first-class jerk!" She practically blasted the words at him, then promptly hated herself for the outburst. This man couldn't be held responsible for his relative's boorish behavior. "Excuse me. I didn't mean to sound so cross."

"Isabelle Townsend," he thoughtfully repeated, then snapped his fingers. "You must be our new neighbor who purchased the old Landry Ranch."

Since she'd only moved here six weeks ago, she was surprised this man had heard of her. News in a small place must travel fast, she thought.

"That's right. I was interested in purchasing a few horses from Three Rivers. But unfortunately, your brother or cousin or whatever he is to you isn't interested in selling. Or showing a visitor good manners."

"I'm sorry about this, Ms. Townsend."

The ranch manager cast a rueful glance in the direction of the horse barn and Isabelle got the impression it wasn't the first time he'd had to apologize for his brother's behavior.

"Frankly, Mr. Hollister, I had heard this ranch was the epitome of hospitality. But after this morning, I have my doubts about that."

"Trust me. It won't happen again." His smile was apologetic. "You caught my brother at a bad time. You see, it's foaling season and he's working virtually 24/7 right now. I promise if you'll come back to the ranch tomorrow, I'll make sure Holt is on his best behavior."

Isabelle didn't give a damn about the horse manager. As far as she was concerned, the man could ride off into the sunset and never return.

"Honestly, Mr. Hollister, I have no desire to do business with your brother. Exhaustion isn't an excuse for bad manners."

"No. And I agree that Holt can be insensitive at times. But you'll find that when it comes to horses, he's the best."

He might be the best, but would dealing with the man be worth it? If it would help make her dream come true, she could surely put up with Mr. Arrogant for a few minutes, she decided.

Shrugging, she said, "All right, Mr. Hollister. I'll be back tomorrow."

He helped her into the truck, then shut the truck door and stepped back. And as Isabelle drove away, she wondered why she'd agreed to meet the good-looking horseman with a tart tongue for a second time. Solely for the chance to buy a few mares? Or did she simply want the pleasure of giving him a piece of her mind?

The answer to that was probably a toss-up, she decided.

* * *

"Holt? Are you in there?"

The sound of Blake's loud voice booming through the open doorway penetrated Holt's sleep-addled brain. Groggily, he lifted his head just in time to see his older brother step into the messy room he called his office.

"I'm right here. What's the matter? Is Cocoa having trouble?" He leaned back in the desk chair and wiped a hand over his face.

"As far as I know, nothing is wrong with Cocoa. I saw her five minutes ago. She was standing and the baby was nursing."

"Thank God. I had to call Chandler back to the ranch to deal with her afterbirth. I was afraid she might be having complications," he explained, then squinted a look at Blake's dour expression. "What's the matter with you? You look like you've been eating green persimmons."

"That task would probably be easier than trying to fix your mess-ups," Blake retorted.

This wiped the cobwebs from Holt's brain. "My mess-ups? What are you talking about?"

Blake shoved a stack of papers to one side and eased a hip onto the corner of the desk. "Don't feign ignorance. You know damned good and well I'm talking about Isabelle Townsend. The blonde who left the horse barn with smoke pouring out of her ears. What the hell did you say to her anyway?"

Holt used both hands to scrub his face again. "Not much. I basically made it clear that I didn't have time for her. Which is hardly a lie. You know that."

Blake blew out a heavy breath. "Yes, I know it. But

in this case, you should've made time. Or, at the very least, been polite to the woman."

Holt picked up a coffee cup and peered at the cold black liquid inside. He'd poured the drink about five hours earlier, but never found a chance to drink it. Now particles of dust were floating over the surface. "What is the big deal, Blake? It was very clear to me that the woman had no legitimate business here on the ranch. I seriously doubt she's ever straddled a horse in her entire life. We'll probably never see her again."

"Wrong. I invited her to return tomorrow. And I made a personal promise to her that you'd be behaving like a human being instead of a jackass."

Holt plunked the coffee cup back to the desktop. "Oh, hell, Blake, you have no idea how I behaved with Isabelle what's-her-name. You weren't there."

"I didn't have to be. I know how you are whenever you run out of patience. Like I said, a jackass."

"Okay, okay. I wasn't nice. I'll admit it. But I'm running on empty. And just looking at her rubbed me the wrong way."

Blake arched a brow at him. "Really? She was damned pretty. Since when has a pretty woman got your dander up? Unless—" His eyes narrowed with suspicion. "Dear Lord, I hope you didn't make a pass at her. Is that what really happened?"

"No! Not even close!" Holt rose from the chair and began to move restlessly around the jumbled room.

His mother often mentioned that he needed a nicer office, one that was fitting for a respected horse trainer, but Holt always balked at the idea. He liked the dust and the jumble. He liked having metal filing cabinets filled with papers instead of flash drives and computers with spreadsheets. If he wanted to throw a dirty saddle across the back of a chair, he did. If he wanted to toss a pile of headstalls and bridles into a corner of the room, he didn't worry about how it looked or smelled. He was in the business of horses. Not ostentatious surroundings. Or technical gadgets.

"Yeah, pretty women and I go hand in hand," he went on with a dose of sarcasm. "Except I don't like it when they pretend to be something they aren't."

"I don't get you, Holt. You don't know Isabelle Townsend. Why you've made this snap decision about her, I'll never understand. But I'm telling you, you've got it all wrong. She's purchased the old Landry Ranch and has intentions of turning it into a horse farm. And from what I hear about the woman, she has enough riding trophies to fill up this room."

Holt stopped in his tracks and stared at his brother. "Who says?"

"Emily-Ann for one. And working at Conchita's, you know she hears everything."

Holt sputtered. "Sure, Blake. Working at a coffee shop means she hears gossip."

"This is more than gossip," Blake countered. "Emily-Ann has become fairly good friends with the woman."

Holt looked away from his brother and down at the dusty planked floor. This part of the foaling barn had been built many years before Holt was born and the cypress boards, though durable, were a fire hazard. The floor actually needed to be ripped out and replaced with concrete, but like many parts of the century-and-a-half-old ranch, they remained as pieces of tradition.

"The old Landry Ranch, you say? That means she's our neighbor on the north boundary."

"Right," Blake replied. "And we don't need any kind of friction with a neighbor. So you think you can play nice in the morning?"

Holt grinned. "Sure. I'll be so sweet, she'll think she's covered in molasses."

Blake rolled his eyes. "I don't think you need to spread it on that thick, brother. Just be yourself. No. On second thought, that could be dangerous. Just be congenial."

Holt's weary chuckle was more like a groan. "Don't worry, Blake. I'll be on my best behavior."

By the time Isabelle reached the outskirts of Wickenburg, she'd managed to push her simmering frustration aside and set her thoughts on the breakfast she'd missed earlier this morning. Endless chores were waiting for her back at the ranch, and it would make more sense to go home and fix herself a plate of eggs and toast. But she was already close to town, and after that humiliating encounter with Holt Hollister, taking time for coffee and a pastry at Conchita's would be a treat she desperately needed.

After driving through the main part of Wickenburg, she turned onto a sleepy side street where the tiny coffee shop was located. Shaded by two old mesquite trees, the building's slab pine siding was weathered to a drab gray. Worn stepping stones led up to a small porch with a short overhang.

At the moment, the single wooden door stood open to the warm morning and Isabelle could hear the muted sounds of music. As she stepped inside the dim interior, she was met with the mouthwatering scents of fresh baked pastries and brewing coffee.

An elderly man with a cane was at the counter. Isabelle stood to one side and waited patiently while Emily-Ann sacked his order.

"Hi, Isabelle!" the waitress greeted. "I'll be right back as soon as I help Mr. Perez out with his things."

"Sure. Take your time. I'm in no hurry," Isabelle assured her.

The gentleman waved a dismissive hand at the young, auburn-haired woman and spoke something to her in rapid Spanish. Emily-Ann replied in the same language and made a shooing gesture toward the door.

"He insists he can carry his order out to the car on his own," she explained to Isabelle. "But I'm not going to let that happen."

While Emily-Ann assisted the customer, Isabelle stepped up to the glass cases holding a huge array of pastries and baked treats. She was still trying to decide between the brownies and the apple fritters when Emily-Ann returned and gave Isabelle a tight hug.

Laughing, Isabelle hugged her back. "You must have missed me!"

"I have!" Emily-Ann exclaimed, a wide smile lighting up her pretty freckled face. "You've not been in for a few days."

"I've been busy. So busy, in fact, that I missed breakfast this morning." Isabelle pointed to a top shelf. "Give me a brownie and an apple fritter. And a large regular coffee with cream."

Emily-Ann, who was the same age as Isabelle, looked at her in disbelief. "A brownie and an apple fritter? And you look like that? Do you know how frustrated that makes me? Just breathing the air in here makes me gain a pound!"

Isabelle shook her head. "You look lovely. I only wish I had your height. For the first fifteen years of my life, I was called shorty."

"That's better than being called freckles." Emily-Ann turned to a counter behind her and filled a cup with coffee. "Do you want this to go?"

"No. I don't want to gobble it down while I drive. I want to enjoy every bite."

"Great," she said. "The customers have let up for the moment so I'll join you. That is, if you'd like the company."

"C'mon. I'd love your company."

The two women walked outside and sat down at one of the small wrought iron tables and chairs sitting in the shade of the mesquites.

"So what's been going on with you since I was here?" Isabelle asked as she broke off a piece of the brownie and popped it into her mouth.

Emily-Ann tilted her head from side to side in a nonchalant expression. "Nothing new. At this time of year, lots of snowbirds come in for coffee. Most of them are friendly and want to chat and ask questions about things to see and do around here. Honestly, Isabelle, when you've lived in one little town all your life, you don't really see things as a tourist. For example, that saguaro over there across the street. The tourists ooh and aah over it. To me, it's just a saguaro."

"That's because you see it every day." Isabelle sipped her coffee, hoping the caffeine would revive her from the long morning she started before daylight.

"But think of it this way, one of those snowbirds that walk into the coffee shop might be your Mr. Right."

Emily-Ann grimaced. "I'm not sure I want to look for a Mr. Right anymore. The men I've dated have all turned out to be stinkers."

Isabelle shrugged. "At least you weren't like me and made the mistake of marrying the wrong man."

"From what you've told me, your ex would've been happy to stay married. And you did say that the two of you are still friends. Are you sure you don't regret getting a divorce?"

"Trevor was a good guy. A nice guy. But he—" He just hadn't loved her. Not with the deep, abiding love that Isabelle had craved. "Well, he was a great companion. Just not a husband."

Shaking her head, Emily-Ann sighed. "I'm not sure I get that. But as long as you think you're better off now, then that's all that really matters, I suppose."

Isabelle finished the brownie and unwrapped the square of wax paper from the fritter. "I am better off. I'm following my dreams."

Emily-Ann leaned back in her chair. "How is the ranch coming along? Have you found any horses to buy?"

Instead of blurting the curse word burning the tip of her tongue, Isabelle snorted. "Actually, I drove out to Three Rivers this morning to look at their horses, but I didn't get to first base."

"Oh, what happened? Out of all of the horses they have, surely you could find something that suited you."

"Ha! All I got to see was an arrogant cowboy and he promptly sent me on my way."

Emily-Ann's mouth fell open. "You mean Holt? *He* sent you packing?"

"He did. Emily-Ann, I thought you told me he was a charming guy and that he'd be easy to do business with. The guy is a first-class jerk!" Isabelle huffed out a breath and reached for her coffee.

Emily-Ann was perplexed. "I don't understand how that could've happened. But he's dreamy-looking. Right?"

Isabelle sipped the hot drink and tried not to think about the way Holt Hollister had looked standing there in front of her with his long legs parted and his arms folded against his broad chest. Dreamy? He'd looked rough around the edges and as tough as rawhide. "I'll admit he's sexy, but not the sort I dream about. I like manners and kindness in a man."

Emily-Ann batted a hand through the air. "Holt knows all about manners. Him sending you away— that's just not the man I know, and I've been friends with the whole family since I was a very little girl."

Isabelle shrugged, while trying not to take the man's behavior personally. "There must've been something about me that Holt didn't like. Or maybe something I said. Like hello," she added dryly. "No matter. Blake invited me to come back tomorrow and I'm going to take him up on the invitation."

Emily-Ann looked relieved. "Oh, so you met Blake. He's a real gentleman."

"I'll put it this way, he's nothing like his brother," Isabelle replied.

"So what did you think about Three Rivers? It's quite a place, isn't it?"

Nodding, Isabelle admitted, "Beautiful. But nothing

like I was expecting. I thought the main ranch house would be a hacienda-type mansion surrounded by a stone wall with an elaborate gated entrance. Instead, it was a homey three-story house with wood siding and a front porch for sitting."

Emily-Ann sighed. "The Hollisters are a homey bunch. Guess that's why the family is so well liked. They're just regular folks. Even though they have oodles of money."

Isabelle's ex had also had oodles of money. Perhaps not as much as the Hollisters, but he'd had enough to give her a tidy fortune in the divorce settlement. Money was necessary, and Isabelle would be lying if she said she didn't appreciate the life it was allowing her to lead. Particularly with her plans to build a horse farm. But money wasn't everything. In the end, Trevor's money hadn't made up for his inability to love her.

"Well, if I don't meet a different Holt tomorrow, I'm going to suggest he drive up to the Grand Canyon and take a flying leap off the South Rim."

"Ouch. He must have really rubbed you the wrong way."

Just the thought of Holt Hollister rubbing her in any way sent a shiver down Isabelle's spine. Maybe the women around here went for the barbarian type, but she didn't.

Purposely focusing her attention on the apple fritter, Isabelle said, "Let's talk about something else, shall we? I don't want to ruin the rest of my day."

For the first night in the past ten nights, no foals were born and Holt managed to sleep until four thirty in the morning without being disturbed. Even so, the moment he opened his eyes, he jerked to a sitting position and stared around the bedroom, disoriented.

What was he doing in bed and what the heck had happened while he'd been asleep? Swinging his legs over the side of the mattress, he reached for the phone on the nightstand and punched the button for the direct line to the foaling barn. It rang six times before someone finally picked it up and by then Holt was wide-awake.

"Yep."

"Matt, is that you?" Matthew Waggoner was the ranch foreman and had been for several years. His job was mostly handling the cowhands, the cattle, and everything that entailed. He usually stayed away from the mares and foals.

"Yep, it's me. What's wrong?"

"Why are you in the foaling barn?" Holt asked. "Has something happened?"

"No. Everything is quiet. I'm spelling Leo. He's dead on his feet. Sounds like you are, too."

Holt raked a hand through his tumbled hair, then reached for the jeans he'd left lying on the floor by the bed. "When I woke up and realized I'd been in bed all night, it scared me."

Matthew chuckled. "That's a hell of a thing to be scared about. Hang up and go back to sleep. The mares in the paddock are all happy and the hands and I won't be leaving out of the ranch yard until six anyway."

"Thanks, Matt. But my sleep is over. I'll be down as soon as I grab something from the kitchen."

In the bathroom, he sluiced cold water onto his face, then ran a comb through his dark hair. The rusty brown whiskers on his face hadn't seen a razor in three days, but he wasn't going to bother shaving this morning. He had more important worries.

After he'd thrown a denim shirt over his jeans and tugged on a pair of worn cowboy boots, he hurried down to the kitchen, where Reeva was already shoving an iron skillet filled with buttermilk biscuits into the oven. The scents of frying bacon and chorizo filled the warm room.

"Got any tortillas warm yet, old woman?" Holt asked as he sneaked up behind the cook and pecked a kiss on her cheek.

Without batting an eye, she pointed to a platter stacked with breakfast tacos wrapped in aluminum foil. "The tacos are already made. What do you think I do around here anyway? Sit reading gossip magazines or lie in bed? Like you?"

In her early seventies, Reeva was a tall, thin woman with straight, iron gray hair that was usually pulled into a ponytail or braid. She'd been working as the Hollister cook since before Holt had been born and now after all these years, she was a part of the family. Which was all for the best, he thought, since the little family she'd once had were all moved away and out of her life.

"Ha! I've seen you lounging around in the den reading gossip magazines and drinking coffee," Holt teased as he snatched up three of the tacos.

Reeva swatted the spatula at his hand. "Get out of here, you worthless saddle tramp."

"Don't worry, I'm going. As soon as I find my insulated cup."

"Right behind you. On the cabinet. And don't go out without your jacket. It's cold this morning."

"It's a good thing you're around to tell me what to do, Reeva. Otherwise, I'd be in a hell of a mess." He grabbed up the stainless steel cup and headed toward the door that led to the backyard.

"You stay in a mess even with my help," she said tartly, then added, "I'll send Jazelle down with some pastries later. And don't call me old woman."

Holt looked over his shoulder and winked at her. "Reeva, you look as fresh as a spring rose."

Reeva continued to flip the frying bacon. "You wouldn't know what a spring rose looked like. But I love you anyway."

"Right back at ya, old woman."

At the door, he levered on a gray Stetson and, to please Reeva, pulled on a Sherpa-lined jacket. After stuffing the tacos into one of the pockets to keep them warm on the long walk to the foaling barn, he stepped outside and was promptly slammed in the face with a cold north wind.

Ducking his head, he left the backyard and started toward the massive ranch yard in the distance. Along the way, he passed the bunkhouse where most of the single ranch hands lived. The scents of coffee and frying sausage drifted out from the log building and Holt figured the guys would be sitting down to breakfast any minute now, which was served at five on most mornings. Once in a while, he and Blake would join the group for the early meal, just to share a few casual minutes with the hardworking employees. But the bunkhouse cook was a crusty old fellow, who couldn't begin to match Reeva's kitchen skills.

At the cattle pens, there were already a half dozen cowboys spreading feed and hay. Dust billowed from the stirring hooves, a sign that so far the winter had been extremely dry. Grass on the range was getting as scarce as hen's teeth and Matthew had already warned Blake that the hay Three Rivers had baled back in the spring would soon be gone. As for the Timothy/alfalfa mix Holt fed the horses, he'd already been forced to get tons of it shipped in from northern Nevada.

At times like these, Holt figured Blake acquired a few more gray hairs at his temples. As manager of the ranch, his brother carried a load on his shoulders and he worried. But Holt didn't worry. Not about the solvency of the ranch. After a hundred and seventy-one years, he figured the place would keep on standing strong. No, the only thing he worried about was keeping the horses healthy. And his mother.

For the most part, Holt could control the well-being of the Three Rivers' remuda, but his mother was a different matter. Lately she was doing a good job of acting like she was happy. But Holt and his siblings weren't fooled. She was keeping something from the family.

Chandler wanted to think she'd fallen in love and was trying to hide it, but Holt didn't go along with his brother's idea. A woman in love had a look about her that was impossible to hide and his mother didn't have it.

When Holt reached the horse barn, the hands were already feeding the few mares that were stalled with their new foals. T.J., the barn manager, met Holt in the middle of the wide alleyway.

"Mornin', Holt," he greeted. "Everything is quiet. No problem with Ginger. She seems to have taken to her little boy. He's been standing and nursing and already looks stronger than he did two hours ago."

Holt wasn't surprised to hear T.J. had already been

at the barn for two or three hours. He was a dedicated young man with an affinity for horses. He'd come to work for the ranch six years ago and since then had proved his worth over and over.

"That's happy news. I was afraid we might have to put him on a nurse mare." Grinning now, Holt patted his jacket pocket. "I have breakfast tacos. If you're hungry, I'll share."

"Thanks, Holt, but I promised William I'd eat at the bunkhouse this morning. Now that you're here, I'll mosey on over there."

"Better do more than mosey or there won't be anything left."

"Right. I'll be back in a few minutes." The barn manager turned on his heel and hurried out of the barn.

On the way to his office, Holt made a short detour to Ginger's stall. As T.J. had informed him, the colt was looking remarkably stronger since his birth yesterday. The fact that the first-time mare was now bonding with her baby was a huge relief and he smiled as he watched her lick the white star on the colt's forehead.

"He's a good-looking boy. Big boned, bright eyed and straight legs. By the time he's a weanling, he'll be strong and sturdy."

The unexpected female voice had him whirling around to see Isabelle Townsend had walked up behind him. The sight of her at any time of the day would've surprised him, but he doubted it was daylight yet. Blake had told him she'd probably return to the ranch today, but he'd not mentioned she might show up at five in the morning!

"Ms. Townsend," he said in the way of greeting. "You're out early."

To his surprise, she must've forgiven his nasty behavior yesterday. There wasn't anything sarcastic in the smile on her face. On the contrary. It was warm enough to chase away the chill in the barn.

"Yesterday you were too busy to deal with me. This morning I came early in hopes I'd catch you before that happened."

He had a thousand and one things to do, including eating the meager breakfast he was carrying in his pocket. He didn't have time for Isabelle Townsend. Not this morning, or any morning. But he'd promised Blake he'd be a gentleman and one thing Holt never wanted to do was break his word to his big brother.

"I was headed to my office. If you'd like to join me, we can talk there." He turned away from Ginger's stall. "Have you had breakfast?"

"No. But I'm fine. Sometimes I don't bother with that meal."

From the looks of her, she didn't bother with eating much at all. Yesterday he'd noticed she was petite. This morning, he could see she was even smaller than he remembered. Even with the heels of her cowboy boots adding to her height, he doubted the top of her head would reach the middle of his chest. The notion struck him that he could pick her up with one arm and never feel the strain.

But he had no plans to get that close to their pretty neighbor, Holt decided. Not unless she wanted him to.

Chapter 2

Walking to his office, Isabelle was careful to keep a respectable distance from Holt Hollister. She had no idea if Emily-Ann's remarks about him being a ladies' man were true or just rumors. Either way, she didn't want to give him the impression that she was interested in anything more than his horses.

"You must have assumed I start the day early," he said.

"All horse trainers start the day long before daylight," she replied. "That is, the good ones do."

He let out a dry chuckle. "Does that mean you put me in the company of the good ones?"

His voice was raspy, like he'd just lifted his head from the pillow after a long sleep. The sound shivered right through her.

"I've heard a lot about you, Mr. Hollister, but I

don't go by hearsay. So I can't really answer your question—yet."

Her reply didn't appear to annoy him, rather he had an amused look on his face. "I've heard some things about you, too. But I don't rely on hearsay either."

Isabelle couldn't imagine what he might have heard about her. She doubted it could've been much, though. Since she'd moved here, she'd only made a few acquaintances around town.

At the end of the barn, he opened a door on the left and motioned for her to proceed him through it.

Isabelle stepped past him and into the small room that looked more like a tack room than an office. Jammed with a messy desk, two wooden chairs, and a row of file cabinets, it was also littered with bits and bridles, saddle blankets and pads, leather cinches and breast harnesses. In one corner, there was even a worn saddle thrown over a wooden sawhorse.

"Have a seat," he invited. "You might want to wipe the dust off first, though. We don't do much cleaning out here in the barn. It doesn't do much good."

"I'm used to dust." And mud. Rain and snow. Heat and cold. Early and late. In the horse business, a person had to get used to all those things and much, much more.

While she settled herself in one of the wooden chairs sitting in front of the desk, he placed the stainless steel vacuum cup he'd been carrying on the desktop, then walked over to a heater and adjusted the thermostat.

Back at the desk, he took a seat in a leather executive chair and picked up the receiver on a landline telephone. After punching a button, he promptly said,

"Reeva, as soon as Jazelle shows up—oh, she has—that's good. Send her on with the pastries, would you? And more coffee." He paused. "That's right. The horse barn. Not the foaling barn. Thanks."

He hung up the phone, then leveled his attention directly on Isabelle. "My brother Blake tells me you've bought the old Landry ranch. Are you living there now?"

Isabelle nodded. "I am. The Landry family had been out of the house for a long time and it needed some repairs. Fortunately, I've gotten most of them done. At least to where the place is comfortable now. The barns and utility sheds were in far better shape than the house. There are still areas of the ranch that need plenty of work and changes made, but it's good enough for me to start adding horses to the ones I already have."

He looked somewhat surprised. "You already have horses?"

"That's right. Ten in all. Two geldings for work purposes and eight broodmares that are currently in foal to a stallion back in Albuquerque, New Mexico. I don't have a stallion of my own yet. But like I said yesterday, I'm looking to buy. Preferably a blue roan that's proven to throw color and produce hearty babies."

He suddenly grinned and Isabelle felt her breath catch in her throat. She could definitely see why the rumors of being a ladies' man followed him around. He was charming without even trying. But she'd been around men of his caliber before. They weren't meant to be taken seriously.

"We'd all like one of those, Ms. Townsend."

She shook her head. "Please call me Isabelle. After

all, we're neighbors. Even if it is eighteen miles to my place."

"Okay, Isabelle. Since you seem determined to add to your workload, I'll show you a few mares I might be willing to part with. But I don't have a stallion I want to sell. Maybe in a year or two. But not now."

She shrugged one shoulder. "That's okay. I'll be happy to look at anything you have."

The room was getting nice and warm so Isabelle untied the fur-edged hood of her jacket and allowed it to slip to her back. As she shook her hair free, she noticed he was watching her as though he was trying to gauge what was beneath the surface. The idea was disturbing, but it didn't offend her. She was a complete stranger to the man. In his line of business, he had a right to wonder about her character and how she might care for the animals he sold her.

"You mentioned Albuquerque. Is that where you're from originally?"

She shook her head. "No. I was born in California and lived there all of my life until I, uh, married and moved with my husband to New Mexico."

Beneath the brim of his battered gray hat, she could see one of his dark brows quirk upward.

"Oh. You're married then?"

She felt like telling him that her marital status really had nothing to do with her buying horses. But she didn't want to irk him again. At least, not before she had a chance to do business with the man. Besides, her being a divorcée was hardly a secret, even if it was something that made her feel like a failure as a woman.

"No. I've been divorced for more than a year now. He still lives in New Mexico. I decided to move here."

She gave him a wide smile to let him know she was feeling no regrets about her ex or the move to Arizona. "And so far I love it. The Landry Ranch was just what I was looking for."

He reached in the pocket of his jacket and pulled out three long items wrapped in aluminum foil and placed them on the desk. From the scents drifting her way, Isabelle guessed he'd been carrying around his breakfast.

"I imagine you've changed the ranch's name by now," he said.

Her smile grew wider. "I have. To Blue Stallion Ranch. I might not own him now. But I will make my dream come true one day."

"I see. Sounds like you've put a lot of thought into this."

"When a woman dreams for her future, she does put a lot of thought into it. And the dream of Blue Stallion Ranch is something I've had for a long time."

He started to say something, but a knock on the open door of the office interrupted him. Isabelle looked over her shoulder to see a tall blond woman about her own age entering the room carrying a large lunch bucket and a tall metal thermos.

"Breakfast is here," she announced cheerfully. "The pastries are fresh and the coffee is hot, so you'd better dig in."

"Jazelle, you're an angel in blue jeans," he told the woman. "I'll dance at your wedding with cowbells on."

Jazelle pushed aside a stack of papers and placed the containers on the desktop. "Ha! You won't be wearing cowbells or anything else to my wedding. 'Cause that ain't going to happen. And yes, I said *ain't*—so there!"

He responded to the woman's caustic reply with a loud laugh. "Sure, Jazelle. You and Camille have sworn off men for the rest of your lives. I've heard it all before, but I don't believe a word of it."

She glared at him. "Well, you'd better believe it, buddy! And if you had any sense, you'd swear off women, too."

He coughed awkwardly and Jazelle turned an apologetic look on Isabelle. "Sorry," she said, then shaking her head, she laughed. "Uh—Holt and I like to tease. We really love each other. Don't we, Holt?"

He grinned. "Just like brother and sister," he said, then gestured to Isabelle. "Jazelle, meet Isabelle. She's our new neighbor to the north. She's a horsewoman."

Isabelle rose and extended her hand to the other woman. "Nice to meet you, Jazelle. And thank you for bringing the breakfast. It smells heavenly."

Jazelle's handshake was hearty and sincere and Isabelle liked her immediately.

"The cook and I bake pastries every other day. These just came out of the oven." She continued to eye Isabelle. "I'm sorry I'm staring. But you're just too darn pretty to be a horsewoman."

Isabelle laughed. "And you're too kind."

Jazelle left the office and Isabelle looked around to see Holt had opened the lunch bucket and was in the process of filling two foam cups with coffee.

"Let's eat," he said. "There's creamer and sugar for your coffee if you want it. And take what pastries you want. I have three chorizo and egg tacos. You're welcome to one of them, too."

"No, thanks. One of these cinnamon rolls will be

enough." She poured creamer into her coffee and with the cup and roll in hand, she sat back down in the chair.

Through the open doorway, Isabelle could hear the horses exchanging whinnies and the familiar clanking of gates as each stall door was opened and closed. Above those sounds was the faint hum of a radio and the noise of the workers as they called to each other.

Someday, she thought, her barn would sound like this. Look like this. With mares and foals everywhere and plenty of ranch hands taking care of the chores. As much as Trevor had tried to make her happy, he'd never shared Isabelle's dream of having a horse farm. He'd only tolerated her obsession with equines because he'd been smart enough to know if he'd given her an ultimatum, she would've chosen the horses over him.

"Is working with horses something you've done for a while?" he asked. "Or is this a new venture for you?"

Isabelle swallowed a bite of the roll before she answered. "I first started riding when I was five years old. That's when my mom introduced me to a little brown pony named Albert. And I fell in love. By the time I got to be a teenager, I wanted to be a jockey, but Mom steered me away from that and into reining and cutting competitions. She considered being a jockey too dangerous."

He grunted with amusement. "Walking through the mare's paddock at feeding time is dangerous."

"That's true. But anyway, I got into the reining thing in a big way and eventually started training for breeders in southern California. After I moved to New Mexico, I began to acquire the mares."

"I see. So until now, you've not actually had a horse ranch?"

She sipped the coffee, then shook her head. "Believe it or not, my ex-husband was overly generous in the divorce settlement just so I'd have plenty to purchase the property and the horses."

The taco in his hand paused halfway to his mouth. "That's hard to fathom."

No. She didn't expect him to understand. Something about Holt Hollister said he was the sort who'd love with all his heart, or not at all. And whatever he possessed, he'd fight to keep. Whether that be a wife, or material assets.

"I realize it sounds a bit crazy," she said. "But we're still good friends. And he wants me to be happy. Add to that, the man has more money than he knows what to do with. That's the way with some folks in the oil industry. Money flows and things are acquired so easily that after a while everything loses its luster." She cleared her throat, confused and embarrassed that she'd shared such personal things with this man. "Anyway, Trevor is a good and generous man. And he's made it possible to invest in my dreams."

"Lucky you."

His quipped reply rankled her, but she carefully hid her reaction. "There was nothing lucky about it. I didn't ask for the money. Or the divorce."

His gaze dropped to the cup he was holding. "Sorry. I shouldn't have said that."

Was he really sorry? She doubted it. But then his opinion of her personal life hardly mattered. After today, she wouldn't be rubbing shoulders with the man.

"Forget it," she told him. "I have."

* * *

She might've already forgotten, but Holt hadn't. Damn it!

He didn't know how their conversation had turned to such personal issues. One minute they'd been talking about her connection to horses and the next she was telling him about her divorce.

Hell! He didn't care if she was married with five kids or devotedly single. He didn't care if she had a good and generous ex-husband. And he sure didn't care that she was the sexiest woman he'd ever laid eyes on. To Holt, she was horse buyer. Nothing more. Nothing less.

"Has your family always owned Three Rivers Ranch?"

Her question jerked Holt out of his reverie and he looked at her as he swallowed down the last bite of taco.

"The Hollisters first built this ranch back in 1847. Since then it's always been a family thing."

"Wow! That must go back through several generations," she said, then shrugged. "I can't remember the house my parents and I lived in when I entered middle school, much less know what sort of place they had when I was born. They were nomads. Still are."

"So you think you want to root down." He wished she'd quit talking about homes and family. She didn't look the sort and he was as far from a family man as Earth was from Mars.

"More than anything," she said with conviction.

Jazelle had brought a few little pecan tortes along with the cinnamon rolls. He gobbled down two of them and was finishing his coffee as fast as he could when she said, "I realize you're in a hurry to get me out of your hair, but at the pace you're eating, you're going to have stomach issues."

Dear Lord, was there nothing she missed? "I always eat fast. Otherwise, I might not have the chance to eat at all. If you're finished with your coffee, we'll go have a look at the horses."

Smiling faintly, she leaned forward and gracefully placed her cup on the edge of his desk. "I'm ready any time you are."

Rising from the desk chair, he pulled on his jacket and buttoned it up to his throat. By then, she'd gotten to her feet and fastened the hood over all that white-blond hair and pulled on a pair of fuzzy black mittens. She looked as sweet as Christmas candy and as fragile as a sparrow's wing. How could this woman ever manage to work a horse ranch?

That's none of your concern, Holt. All you need to do is keep your mind on your job and off the way Isabelle Townsend looks or sounds or smells. She's not your type. She never will be.

Shoving away the mocking reminder in his head, he gestured toward the door. "You're welcome to look at the mares and babies here in the barn, but none of them are for sale. Anything I might be willing to part with is outside."

"I'd love to take a leisurely look. But you're just as busy as I am. Let's just head on outside."

Her response should have pleased him. The quicker he could get this meeting over with, the better. Yet he had to admit a part of him had wanted to show her some of the fine babies his mares had delivered in the past few days. Like a proud dad, he would've enjoyed sticking out his chest and preening just a little. But she wasn't going to give him the chance.

"Fine," he said. "We'll exit the barn on this end."

Outside the building, she followed him over to a ten-acre patch surrounded by a tall board fence.

"This is where I keep the mares that have two or three weeks before foaling," he told her. "When they start getting to that point in their gestation, I like to keep a closer eye on them."

"Do you have a resident vet here on the ranch?"

"My older brother Chandler is the vet," he told her. "If something comes up that I can't handle, he'll come running."

"I'm just now putting two and two together," she said thoughtfully. "He must run the Hollister Animal Hospital. Does he live here on the ranch, too?"

Her question reminded Holt that he and his baby sister, Camille, were the only Hollister siblings left who didn't have a spouse and children. As for Camille, he couldn't speak for her wants and wishes, but on most days Holt was happy he was still footloose and fancy-free. There were too many women in the world to waste his life on just one.

"Yes, with his wife, Roslyn, and baby daughter, Evelyn."

A bright smile suddenly lit her face. "Oh, so there's a baby in the house. How nice."

"It's nice and noisy. There are three babies in the house. Blake has twins." Curious, in spite of himself, he glanced at her. "Do you have children?"

To his surprise, a pink blush appeared on her cheeks. "No. Trevor wasn't the type for fatherhood.

But I'm hoping I'll be a mother someday. What about you—do you have children?"

He chuckled. "Not any that I know of."

She didn't reply, but the scornful expression on her face spoke volumes.

"I'm teasing," he felt inclined to say. "I don't have any children. And I don't plan on having any. I have plenty of four-legged babies to keep me happy."

She cut him another dry glance. "At least you know to stick to your calling."

If any other woman had said such a thing to him, he would've laughed. But hearing it from this blond beauty was altogether different. For some reason, it made him feel small and sleazy.

"At least I know my calling," he agreed. "Do you?"

"What is that supposed to mean?"

Suddenly Blake's voice was back in his head, reminding him to be nice to Isabelle. But damn it, Blake wasn't the one dealing with the woman. Holt was. And with each passing minute, she was getting deeper and deeper under his skin.

"I'm wondering if you've really thought about what you're taking on. Raising horses isn't an easy job."

"If it was easy, it wouldn't be rewarding, now would it?" she asked. "And I know all about hard work."

The sweetness in her voice was overlaid with conviction and Holt decided she was one of those stubborn females who'd rather die trying to prove a point than admit she might be wrong.

They reached the paddock and he opened a wide gate so the two of them could walk out to where the mares were munching hay from rows of mangers.

As they neared the horses, Holt pointed to one in

particular. "I have one mare in this bunch that I'd be willing to part with and that's Blossom, the little chestnut over there with the star on her forehead and snip on her nose. She's made perfectly, I'd just prefer her to be a tad bigger. She was bred late—in May to be exact, so she should have a late April or early May baby."

"I'll go take a look."

They walked over to the mare and as she approached the horse for a closer look, Holt opened his mouth to remind her to be cautious, but instantly decided to keep the warning to himself. If Isabelle knew so much about horses, he shouldn't have to tell her a thing. This might be a good way to find out if she was the real deal or a woman with money and her head in the clouds.

Five minutes later, Holt had his answer. Blossom had not only forgotten the hay in front of her, she was nosing up to Isabelle as if they'd been friends forever. On top of that, the young mare had always been skittish about her feet, but Blossom had allowed Isabelle to pick up all four like she was a diva waiting for a manicure. It was amazing.

"She has a really nice eye and her teeth look good," she said as she dropped the mare's lip back in place.

"Chandler floats their teeth on a regular basis," he said, his green eyes dropping away from her hands and down to her rounded bottom encased in faded denim. Yesterday he'd been too tired and annoyed to notice Isabelle's perfect figure. This morning he was having trouble keeping his attention away from it.

She turned to face him and Holt jerked up his gaze before she caught him staring at her cute little butt.

"What sort of sire is this mare bred to?"

"The ranch's foundation stud. He's black and big-boned. I'll show him to you after we look at the other mares."

She smiled and Holt's attention was drawn to the alluring sight of soft pink lips against white teeth. And suddenly he was wondering how she would look naked and lying next to him with her hair spilled over his shoulder.

"I look forward to seeing him," she said.

"So what do you think of Blossom?"

"She's nice. But I need to see the others before I make any kind of decision. Okay?"

Another smile softened her words and Holt felt his resistance crumbling like a shortbread cookie. Any man with half a brain could see she was a heartbreaker. But why should he let that put him off? He never made the mistake of letting a woman get near his heart. He enjoyed them for a while and then moved on. Isabelle was no different than the last beauty to warm his bed.

"Certainly," he answered. "Let's go find a truck and we'll drive out to the horse pasture."

Throughout the short trip to the pasture, Isabelle tried to ignore Holt's presence in the cab of the truck, but the more she tried to dismiss him, the more suffocated she felt. Back at the ranch yard, he'd wrapped a hand around her arm to assist her climb into the tall work truck, and even through the quilted thickness of her coat, the touch of his fingers had left a burning imprint.

But that was hardly a surprise. Everything about the man, from his sauntering walk to the growl in his voice, shouted sex. Or was he really no different than any other man she'd ever met? Could the long months of a cold, empty bed be causing her to see him in a different light?

Whatever the reason for her ridiculous reaction to the man, she needed to get over it and quick. There was no way she could make a smart business transaction when her mind was preoccupied with how he'd look with his shirt off, or wonder how it would feel to have those strong arms wrapped around her.

Damn it! She didn't need a man. Not now. And definitely not a Romeo in cowboy boots.

"I've not been here long enough to learn about your weather," she said, hoping to push her thoughts to a safer place. "Is it usually this cool in January? I was hoping that this part of the state was southern enough to miss the cold and snow."

"Other than a few rare flurries blowing in the wind, you won't see snow around here," he answered. "But it can get fairly cold. Especially at night. What little rain we do get comes in the winter months. I hope you have plenty of water sources on your ranch. Otherwise, when the dry months come, you're going to be in trouble."

Did the man think she'd gotten to Arizona on the back of a turnip truck? Or was he doubting her common sense because she was a woman? Either way, he seemed intent on insulting her intelligence.

But she was trying her best to ignore his remarks, the same way she was trying to dismiss the way his chin jutted slightly forward and the rusty stubble on his face had grown even longer since she'd seen him yesterday morning. Normally she had an aversion to men who didn't keep their faces clean-shaven. But there was something very earthy and sexy about the way the whiskers outlined his square jaw and firm lips.

She cleared her throat and said, "I made sure about the water supply before I purchased the property. And I've had enough firewood hauled in for the fireplace to last through the winter. I have fifty tons of Tifton/alfalfa in the hay barn and enough grain to last a month. In spite of what you might think of me, I do know how to make preparations."

He glanced at her and grinned. "I'm glad to hear you're prepared. And, by the way, how do you know what I'm thinking of you?"

She bit back a groan and decided the best way to deal with this man was to be forthright. Lifting her chin, she said, "It's fairly obvious you think I'm an idiot. I'm not sure why you've put me in that category, but you have. And I'm trying not to let it bother me. After all, I think you're a bit of an arrogant brute. So there—we're even."

Expecting him to be peeved with her, she was totally surprised when he let out a hearty laugh. "An arrogant brute, eh? I've been called plenty of things before, but never that one." He directed another lopsided grin in her direction. "And you have me all wrong, Isabelle. I hardly think you're an idiot. I merely think you might be biting off more than you can chew."

"Because I'm a woman?"

He shook his head. "No. Because you're clearly chasing a dream. Instead of facing the hard work in front of you."

She wanted to be angry with him. She wanted to tell him that a person without dreams wasn't really living. But she stifled both urges. There had already been too many personal exchanges between the two of them and it was beginning to make her feel uncomfortable. It was making her think of him as a man rather than a neighbor or horse trainer. And that was something that could only lead to trouble.

"I know all about hard work, Mr. Hollister," she said stiffly.

"Please call me Holt."

She rolled her eyes in his direction to see the grin on his face was still there. Five minutes with Holt Hollister was really too much for any woman to endure and hold on to her sanity, she decided.

He steered the truck off the beaten dirt track and braked it to a stop near a wide galvanized gate. Beyond the fence, Isabelle could see thirty or more head of horses milling around a cluster of long wooden feed troughs.

"Here we are," he announced. "And fortunately, the horses are still at their feed. I think there are thirty-five head in this herd."

Purposely keeping her gaze on the horses, she asked, "How many of these are for sale?"

"Four. I'll take a halter with me so you can take your time with each one."

"Thanks. I'd appreciate that."

They left the truck and after he collected a halter from the back, they walked over to the fence. While he slipped the latch on the gate, she said, "I thought you were in the business of selling horses. Why the limit of four or five?"

"This past year, we had to take several horses out of the working remuda for different reasons, such as lameness and age and so forth. And then Blake decided to add more cattle to our ranch down at Dragoon, so I've had to send more horses for the hands to use down there. Replacing them takes time and lots of training. So I'm actually running a bit short on older horses and somewhat short on the yearlings."

He followed her into the pasture and as Isabelle watched him carefully fasten the gate behind them, she realized that for once in her life, she was just as interested in looking at a man as she was a herd of horses.

"I see. I was thinking you might just limit the buyers who have their heads in the clouds."

He chuckled and Isabelle decided an arrogant brute who could laugh at himself couldn't be all bad.

"Not at all," he assured her. "I have special deals for those buyers."

Her laugh was shrewd. "I'll just bet you do."

Chapter 3

Over an hour later, Holt and Isabelle were back in the horse barn, where Holt had just finished showing her Hez A Rocket, the ranch's foundation stallion. She'd seemed very impressed with the animal, but Holt got the feeling she wasn't that enthralled with him.

And why would you want her to be, Holt? Right off the top of your head, you can probably think of four or five blond beauties who'd be happy to get a call from you. The last thing you need is a divorcée with a head full of dreams.

Holt purposely blocked out the voice of warning in his head as the two of them strolled in the general direction of his office. "Now that you've seen what I have to offer, are you ready to make a deal on one, or all?"

"Yes, I would. I—" She broke off as an ear-splitting

whinny reverberated through the barn. "Wow! Someone wants attention. That sounds like another stallion."

Holt silently groaned. She'd told him her dream was to find a blue roan stallion and build her herd around him. Blue Midnight definitely fit her wishes, but Holt was grooming the young stud to replace Hez A Rocket in a few years. He'd never put the young stallion up for sale.

"That's Blue Midnight, one of my other stallions," he reluctantly admitted. "He can be quite a talker at times."

Her brows piqued with interest. "Blue? Is he a roan?"

With a resigned nod of his head, he said, "That's right. I was hoping to spare you from seeing him."

Confused by that, she asked, "Really? Why?"

"Because you're going to want him. And I'm going to have to say no and then you're going to be peeved at me—again."

"I really doubt that would ruin your day." She smiled and shrugged. "I've been told no plenty of times. I won't burst into tears—unless you refuse to let me see this super stud."

He shook his head. "You get a kick out of looking at a piece of pie even though you can't eat it?"

"I can always dream."

He should've seen that coming, Holt thought. "Ah, that's right," he said wryly. "You are fond of dreaming."

Taking her by the arm, he led her across the wide alleyway and past three empty stalls until they were standing in front of Blue Midnight's roomy compartment. Always eager for company, the horse hung his head over the top of the mesh iron gate and nickered softly at the two of them.

"Oh! Oh, Holt, he's gorgeous! Absolutely gorgeous! His hair is so slick and shiny! You must be keeping him blanketed."

Holt glanced over to see an incredible glow had come over Isabelle's face. As though storm clouds had parted above her head and golden sunshine was pouring over her. He'd put some happy faces on a few women before, but none of those blissful looks compared to what he was seeing on Isabelle's lovely features.

"No blankets. Blue Midnight is naturally tight haired. He just turned four and I have to admit, he's my pride and joy."

"Most stallions bite. Does he?"

"Not this one. He's very sweet natured."

She stepped up to the gate and quickly made friends with the horse. As she gently stroked his nose, she glanced over her shoulder and gave Holt a beseeching smile.

"Are you sure you don't want to sell him?" she asked. "I'd give you top dollar. Just name your price. If I don't have enough money, I'll get the money."

From her rich ex-husband? The notion left a bitter taste in Holt's mouth and for one split second he wanted to tell her that if she'd keep smiling at him the way she was smiling right now, he'd give her the world and Blue Midnight with it. But thankfully, the urge only lasted a second before sanity stepped in and reminded him that pleasing a woman didn't require losing his mind and his best stallion with it.

"Sorry," he told her. "I have big plans for this guy and they're all right here on Three Rivers."

"Oh, I'm sorry, too." Disappointment chased all the lovely glow from her face and she turned back to Blue Midnight and rubbed her cheek against his. "You're such a pretty boy," she said to the horse. "I wish you could be mine. We'd be great buddies."

The interchange between her and the horse was something so palpable and real that Holt felt like an outsider listening in on a very private conversation.

Clearing his throat, he stepped forward until he was standing at her side. Immediately, the sweet scent of her drifted to his nostrils and pushed away the smells of alfalfa, dust, and manure.

"Blue Midnight has a few babies coming later this spring. If one of them turns out to be a colt, I'll sell him to you."

She looked over at him and Holt was stunned to see a sheen of tears in her blue eyes. He realized he was denying this woman her most fervent wish, but mixing sentimentality with business never worked. Neither did getting dopey over a woman he'd just met.

"Is that a promise?" she asked, her gaze searching his.

Aside from his mother or sisters, Holt didn't make promises to women. But something about Isabelle's blue eyes was dissolving that rule.

"I wouldn't have said it if I hadn't meant it," he answered.

Her gaze turned back to Blue Midnight, who was gently nudging her shoulder for more attention.

"Thank you, Holt. I'll hold on to that promise."

After a couple more minutes with Blue Midnight,

they returned to his office. A half hour later, she was using her phone to transfer money from her bank to a Three Rivers' account.

"You didn't have to take all five of them, Isabelle. Unless you really wanted to."

"I wanted to." She slipped the phone back into her handbag. "When will be a convenient time for me to come back with my trailer and pick them up?"

Holt wrote out a paper receipt, then went over to one of the many file cabinets lined against the wall. "No need for that," he told her. "Myself or some of the hands will deliver them. After what you paid for the five mares, it's the least I can do."

He flipped through several folders before he finally found what he was looking for. Back at his desk, he signed the transfers and placed them, the receipt, and the registration papers in a long envelope and handed it to Isabelle.

"Here's all the paperwork. If you have any problems changing the ownership into your name, just let me know. I hope you'll be happy with the mares, Isabelle."

She stood and reached across the desktop to shake his hand. "Thank you, Holt. It's been a pleasure."

Holt rose and clasped his hand around hers. "A pleasure?" he asked wryly. "Dealing with an arrogant brute?"

A pretty pink color touched her cheeks and Holt was charmed even more by her modesty. He couldn't remember making any of his old girlfriends blush, but then none of them could be labeled modest.

"You made up for it. Especially with letting me meet Blue Midnight."

"Good. Because I'd like for us to be friends."

She pulled her hand from his and reached for her handbag on the floor. "I thought we'd already become friends."

He moved around the desk and stood in front of her. "We have. I only meant, uh, that I want us to be closer friends. The kind that have dinner together. What do you say?"

Her eyes wide with disbelief, she looked up at him. "Are you inviting me on a date?"

She made it sound like he was suggesting the two of them make a lunar landing. "That's right. Nothing dangerous. Just a nice meal and some conversation."

Who are you trying to fool, Holt? For you, conversation with a woman is merely a means to an end. Just a step in the game of seduction. And once you do seduce Isabelle, then what? Is she the type you can brush aside like a pesky fly? You'd better think twice about this one, cowboy.

While he tried to ignore the taunting voice in his head, she said, "To be honest, I've not done any dating since my divorce. I'm not sure I'm ready to get back into that sort of thing."

That hardly sounded encouraging, Holt thought. But perhaps she meant dating in a serious way. If so, then the two of them would make a perfect couple. If there was one word in the dictionary that Holt tried his best to avoid in the presence of a woman, it was *serious*.

"Why?" he asked. "Is your heart too broken to enjoy an evening out with a man?"

She looked away from him and cleared her throat. "Do you think that's any of your business?"

She was his business. When and why he'd decided that, he didn't know. He only knew that at some point between eating pastries with her earlier this morning and making the final deal for the mares a few minutes ago, he'd become slightly infatuated with her.

"Probably not. But I'm a curious kind of guy. And I figured if I asked, you'd tell me."

She rolled her eyes and then her lips began to twitch as she fought off a smile. "Okay, since you asked, I'll tell you. I'm not carrying a torch for Trevor. My choice to stay away from dating is more about keeping myself on course with more important things."

"And having a man in your life isn't important?"

"No. And I'm not sure it will ever be important again. Not unless some incredible superman comes along. And I can't see that happening."

No. Holt couldn't see that happening either. The only superman he'd ever known was his father and he'd died several years ago.

"Sorry. Most of us guys do have faults," he said. "But I'll do my best to keep them to a minimum for one night. That is, if you're willing to spend an evening with me."

She laughed and Holt was surprised at how relieved he was to hear the sound. Normally, he didn't give a whit whether a woman turned him down. There was always another one waiting. But Isabelle was different.

"All right. I'll have dinner with you—sometime," she told him.

"Sometime? No. I'm talking about tomorrow night. I'll pick you up at six."

She placed the envelope filled with the horse papers into her handbag and pulled the strap onto her shoulder. "I might have something else to do tomorrow night."

He gave her a pointed grin. "Like feed the horses? You can let the hands do that."

She held up her hands. "These are the only hands I have."

"Oh. Then I'll come early and help you."

"Persistent, aren't you?"

"When something is important to me."

She looked at him for a long moment, then turned and started out of the office. Holt followed after her.

"Okay, I'll be ready. At six." At the door, she paused and looked back at him. "Goodbye, Holt. And thank you."

He clasped a hand around her elbow. "I'll walk you to your truck."

"That isn't necessary."

"I wasn't thinking it was a necessity. More like a pleasure."

Shaking her head, she said, "I have to say, when your older brother promised me you'd be in a better humor today, he wasn't kidding. What did he do? Give you some sort of nice pill this morning?"

Holt laughed as he ushered her through the doorway. "Isabelle, I have a feeling we're going to be more than just friends. We're going to be great friends."

The next morning Isabelle was out stretching barbed wire on a fence close to the barn when she heard the rattle of a livestock trailer.

Unfastening the stretcher from the wire, she allowed the heavy tool to fall to the ground, then turned and, shading her eyes, watched as a truck and trailer barreled up the dirt road that led to her ranch yard.

Was that Holt delivering her horses?

The mere thought that the driver of the big black ton truck might be the sexy horse trainer was enough to cause her pulse to quicken, but as she began walking in the direction of the barn, she determinedly kept her stride at a normal pace. If Holt was behind the wheel, she hardly wanted him to think she was eager to see him.

Still, she paused long enough to wipe her palms down the front of her jeans and smooth back the loose tendrils of hair that had escaped her ponytail. As for the long streak of grease on the front of her flannel shirt, there was nothing she could do about that.

However, by the time Isabelle reached the barn area, she realized all her preening had been for nothing. Instead of Holt climbing out of the truck, she spotted a pair of Three River Ranch hands. One was burly with red hair while his tall, lanky partner appeared to be much younger.

The older one of the pair was the first to introduce himself. "Hello, Ms. Townsend. I'm Pat," he said, then jerked a thumb toward the man standing next to him. "And this is Cott. We do day work for Three Rivers Ranch. Holt sent us over with your mares."

Disappointment rippled through her. Which was a totally silly reaction, she thought. He'd only suggested he might deliver the horses himself, he hadn't made it a promise. Still, it would've been kinda nice if he'd taken the time out of his busy morning to deliver the mares personally.

"Nice to meet you, Pat and Cott. Thanks for bringing the mares. If you'll follow me in the truck, I'll open the gates for you."

A few minutes later, the horses were bucking and

running around the wooden corral, sending a huge cloud of dust billowing into the air. The sight of their excited antics caused Isabelle to laugh out loud.

"They're feeling good, Ms. Townsend," Pat said as he and Cott joined her outside the corral gate.

"I'm very happy to get them," she said, then politely offered, "Would you guys like something to drink? A cold bottle of water or lemonade? Sorry, but I don't have any beer."

"Thanks, but we're fine. We have water in the truck," Pat told her. "If you'll just show us where you want the feed unloaded, we'll be on our way."

Isabelle stared at him. "Excuse me? Did you say feed?"

Cott answered, "That's right. Two tons of horse feed. It's Three Rivers' special mix. Or I guess I should say Holt's special mix. He's the one who originally concocted it."

She shook her head. "But I didn't purchase any feed from the ranch. Only the mares."

"No matter, Ms. Townsend," Cott replied. "Holt said to bring it to you and what he says goes."

Holt said. Holt said.

Just what was he trying to say to Isabelle? That much high-quality feed would be worth hundreds of dollars. Was he trying to butter her up?

She was being stupid. A man like him didn't need to score points with her, or any woman. She figured this was more about being concerned for the mares. Abruptly changing a horse's feed often caused serious health issues with their digestive track. Mixing the Three Rivers feed with hers would allow her to easily make the gradual change.

Realizing the men were waiting on her response, she gestured toward the far end of the big barn. "Okay. My feed room is around at the back of the barn. Follow me and I'll show you the way."

With the two men working in tandem, they had the stacks of fifty-pound sacks unloaded in no time. After Isabelle had thanked them and they'd driven away, she went straight to the house, where she'd left her cell phone on the kitchen counter.

A quick glance at the face told her she had two new text messages. One from her mother, who lived in San Diego, the other from Holt.

She punched Holt's open first and read: Sorry I couldn't make it with the mares. I'll see you tonight at six.

Tonight at six. The reminder caused her heart to thump hard in her chest.

What was the matter with her? Only two days before, she'd wanted Holt Hollister to jump off the rim of the Grand Canyon. How had she gone from that to agreeing to go on a date with the man? Sure, he'd been charming yesterday. But her failed marriage had left her emotionally drained. She had nothing to offer any man.

Deciding Holt's message didn't require a response, she opened the one from her mother.

I've managed to snag a showing at the Westside Gallery! Call me when you have a minute.

As far as Isabelle knew, Gabby Townsend had never had a one-minute conversation in her entire life. Especially when she got on the phone with her one and only child. But Isabelle hadn't talked with her mother in the past few days and now was just as good a time as later to call her.

Grabbing a bottle of water from the fridge, Isabelle downed a hefty drink, then sat down at the kitchen table with her phone.

"Issy, honey," her mother answered. "Can you believe my work is going to be shown at the Westside Gallery?"

The excitement in her mother's voice caused Isabelle to smile. "I absolutely can believe it. Your artwork is fabulous, Mom. It deserves to be shown to the public."

"That's what Carl said. Actually he was just as impressed with my charcoals as he was my oils, so both are going to be displayed. It's incredible!" Pausing, she let out a breathless little laugh. "I guess you can tell I'm walking on air."

"Just a bit," Isabelle said. "But you deserve to feel that way, Mom. Uh, who is this Carl? Do I know him?"

"I don't think so, dear. Carl Whitaker is the owner of the gallery. I met him a couple of weeks ago at the Green Garden Winery. Caprice has a few of my paintings on her walls there and Carl spotted them. You remember the Green Garden, don't you? That's where that suave Italian businessman tried to pick you up."

Isabelle remembered, all right. He'd been good-looking and wealthy to boot. But she'd been turned off by his constant boasting and sleazy looks.

"You mean that snake wearing alligator shoes? I try to forget those kinds of encounters."

"If you'd cozied up to him, you might be relaxing in a Mediterranean villa about now," Gabby suggested slyly.

"I'd rather jump into quicksand with concrete blocks tied to my feet."

Gabby groaned, then said, "I don't want you to get involved with a creep, but I do wish you'd take an interest in men again. It just isn't right for you to be alone."

For some odd reason, her mother's remark caused Holt's rugged face to appear in front of her vision and she promptly tried to blink it away.

"You're alone, Mom."

"That's different," Gabby said. "I'm sixty-three. I've already done the marriage-baby thing. You have your whole life ahead of you."

Isabelle grimaced. "You're not exactly over the hill, Mom. And I've already gone through the marriage thing, too. Remember?"

Her mother's short sigh was full of frustration. "Issy, your marriage—"

After a long pause, Isabelle wanted to butt in and change the subject, but she'd learned long ago that trying to steer her mother was like trying to make a cat obey commands. The task was pretty much impossible.

Finally, Gabby said, "Yours wasn't a real marriage."

Bemused by that remark, Isabelle pulled the phone away from her ear and stared at it for a brief second before she slapped it back to the side of her head. "Excuse me, Mom, but it was real to me."

"If it was so real, then why did you divorce?"

Isabelle let out a long, weary breath. She'd not planned to get into this sort of conversation with her mother today. In fact, it had been ages since Gabby had brought up anything about Isabelle's divorce.

"Okay, Mom, let me rephrase that. It was real on my part. For Trevor, I was just an enjoyable companion."

"Oh, honey—well, at least you didn't have a baby."

Isabelle pressed a hand to her forehead and closed her eyes. "Thanks, Mom. That reminder makes me feel great."

"Isabelle, you know what I mean. It's terrible when a child is passed back and forth between parents—just because the parents can't cohabitate. Just look at your own parents. Look what it did to you."

Isabelle's parents had divorced while she'd been in middle school. And back then, she would've been lying if she said it hadn't upended her life. She'd loved her father dearly and when he'd moved out of the house, she'd felt like he'd deserted her and her mother. She'd been too young to fully understand that her parents had divorced because they'd been two different souls, both wanting and needing different things in life.

"It hurt for a while. But I think I turned out fairly normal."

Gabby said gently, "You're better than normal. Especially with having a pair of hippies for parents."

Isabelle chuckled. "You and Dad aren't hippies. You're free spirits."

"Aww, that's a sweet way of putting it, honey. Most of our friends would describe us as harebrained or worse."

"Who cares? As long as you're both happy."

"I'm certainly happy. And I think your father is, too. The last I talked with him, he was in New Orleans playing nightly on Bourbon Street."

Her father, Nolan, was an accomplished pianist. Twenty years ago, he'd helped to form a small jazz band. Since then, the group had traveled all over the country playing small venues. He'd made a decent living at his profession, but like Gabby, his craft was really all he cared about. As long as he was making music, he was happy.

"Hmm. A dream gig for him," Isabelle replied. "I haven't talked with him in a while. I'll give him a call soon."

"He'd like that."

Once again, Holt's image swaggered across her mind's eye and the unexpected distraction caused her to pause long enough to cause her mother concern.

"Issy, is something wrong? Have you quarreled with your father?"

"No. Nothing is wrong. Actually, I was thinking about someone," she admitted. "Believe it or not, I'm going on a date tonight."

Gabby reacted with a long stretch of silence.

"Mom, are you still there? Or have you fallen over in a dead faint?"

Gabby laughed softly. "I'm still conscious. Just a bit surprised."

Isabelle said, "I'm surprised at myself. I'm having dinner with the rancher that sold horses to me. It's just sort of a thank-you date on both sides. Him for selling and me for buying."

"Oh. Sure, I see. It's really a business dinner or… something like that."

Business? Isabelle could hardly look across the table at Holt and think business. In fact, she doubted she'd be able to think about much at all. But her mother didn't need to know her daughter was looking at any man in such an intimate way.

"I'm very happy for you, Mom. Maybe you'll sell a few things and you can book that trip to Hawaii you've been wanting to take."

"I'm not really worried so much about selling right now. I'm just happy to have my work exhibited in such a notable gallery. The rest will take care of itself," she said, then asked, "Will you be able to come down on the opening day? I'll be there to meet and greet and the gallery is supplying refreshments."

"When is this happening?"

"Two weeks from this coming Saturday. Don't worry. I'll remind you."

"I'll try. But I can't make any promises. It all depends if I can hire a couple of hands between now and then. Until someone is here to care for the horses, I can't leave the ranch for more than a few hours at a time."

"Have you advertised for help?"

"I don't want to go that route. I'm afraid I'd have all sorts of creeps coming out here to the ranch. Before I hire anyone, I'm going to ask around and get some recommendations."

"I understand. Don't worry about the showing. You have your hands full right now. We'll get together later on."

"I'd love that, Mom. Now, I've got to hang up and get back to my fence repairs."

Gabby let out a good-natured groan. "My beautiful little girl out building fence instead of making use of her college degree."

"I'm happier now than I've ever been."

"You're just as much of a free spirit as your parents," she said gently. "And that's okay, too. Perhaps you can talk the rancher into helping you with the fence."

Holt Hollister stretching barbed wire? He was ranching royalty, a boss on one of the largest ranches in the state of Arizona. Isabelle seriously doubted he'd ever touched a posthole digger or a roll of wire.

"I can't talk that fast, Mom," Isabelle said with a laugh.

"Then add a little wink or two between words," Gabby suggested.

"Uh, if you knew what this guy looked like you wouldn't be giving me that kind of advice."

"Why? Ugly as sin?"

"No. Sinfully handsome."

"Oh," she drawled in a suggestive tone. "I need to hear more about this man."

Isabelle chuckled. "Bye, Mom. I'll call you soon."

"Isabelle—"

"Yes?"

"I'll keep my fingers crossed for you, honey."

Gabby ended the call and Isabelle put down the phone, but she didn't immediately leave the chair. Instead, she sat there thinking about Holt and their date tonight. She'd only agreed to go out with him so she could bend his ear about the horse breeding business, she told herself. And for no other reason.

Next time she talked to her mother, she'd explain the situation. For now it wouldn't hurt to let Gabby believe her daughter was interested in finding a man to love.

Chapter 4

Holt couldn't remember the last time he'd been anywhere near the old Landry Ranch. Not since the family had moved to Idaho several years ago and put the
property on the market. Holt had practically forgotten
all about the deserted ranch. Until Isabelle had shown
up on Three Rivers and Blake had informed him that
she'd purchased the place.

Located about eighteen miles north of Three Rivers
by way of a ten-mile stretch of narrow asphalt, plus
eight more miles of rough, graveled road, the land
butted up to only a half-mile section of Three Rivers'
land. But that was enough for the Hollisters to consider the owner a neighbor.

Before he'd left home this evening, Holt had been
about to step out the door when Blake had caught up to
him. Seeing his brother had been curious as to where

he was going on a weeknight, Holt had explained he was having dinner with Isabelle. In response, Blake had barely lifted an eyebrow.

I didn't figure you'd waste any time trying to get her into your bed, he'd said.

Ordinarily, Blake's coarse comment would've elicited a laugh from Holt. But Holt hadn't laughed. In fact, he'd felt strangely annoyed at his brother. Blake didn't really know Isabelle and to imply she was an easy girl had hardly been fair. But Holt figured his brother's remark had been more directed at him than at Isabelle.

The road he was traveling climbed a hill covered with agave and century plants, then curved abruptly to the right through spires of rock formation. After another curve in the opposite direction, the landscape opened up and far to his left he could see the house and the nearby cluster of barns and work sheds.

Holt remembered the ranch being in a beautiful area of Yavapai County, but until this moment he'd never really thought about how isolated the property was from neighbors or town. The idea of a tiny thing like Isabelle living out here alone left him uneasy. But then, she wasn't his responsibility. And how she chose to live was nobody's business but her own.

He'd barely had time to stop the truck in front of the hacienda-style house when he spotted Isabelle emerging from the front door. The sight of her jolted him and for a moment after he'd killed the motor, he sat there watching her walk to the edge of the porch.

She was wearing a black sweater dress that stopped just above her knees. The fabric clung to the curves of her body, while black dress boots outlined her shapely calves. Her blond hair was brushed to one side and waved against the side of her face. She looked sexy as hell and he wondered how he was supposed to eat a bite of food with that sort of temptation sitting across from him.

Collecting the flat box from the passenger seat, he left the truck and walked to the porch where she waited for him.

"Hello, Holt," she greeted. "I see you found the place."

The smile on her face was like sunshine on a spring day and it sent his spirit soaring.

"It wasn't hard. I've been here a few times. Back when the Landrys still lived here." He offered the box to her. "Here's a little something for you."

She took the fancy chocolates. "Thank you, Holt. This should keep up my energy."

He grinned. "I figured with all those extra horses you bought from me, you'd need it."

She gestured to the door behind her. "Would you like to come in and have a drink before we go?"

"That would be nice. We have plenty of time to make our dinner reservations."

She tossed him a wary glance before moving toward the front door. "You made reservations?"

"That's what I normally do when I go out to eat. Don't you?" he asked, as he followed her over the threshold and down a short, wide foyer decorated with potted succulents and a wooden parson's bench.

"No. I normally go to a fast-food joint. Or a café where you simply walk in and sit wherever you'd like."

They entered a long living area and Isabelle walked

over and placed the box of chocolates on a dark oak coffee table.

"Well, I do that sort of thing with my buddies or my brothers," he admitted, then grinned at her. "If I took you out for a hot dog, you might think I was cheap."

She walked back over to where he stood and Holt was once again staggered by the incredible smoothness of her skin, the vivid blue of her eyes. He'd heard the term *breathtaking* used many a time, but he'd never experienced it until he laid his eyes on Isabelle.

"As long as there's good conversation to go with the hot dog, I'd be happy."

Was she really that easy to please? She didn't look like a simple woman, he thought. But then, she didn't look like a hardworking horsewoman either. "I'll try to remember that."

An impish little smile played around her lips as she gestured to a long, moss green couch.

"Have a seat," she invited, "and I'll get the drinks. What would you like? Something alcoholic or a soft drink?"

Deciding he'd be able to breathe a bit better if he put some distance between them, he walked over and took a seat on the end of the couch, then crossed his boots out in front of him. "I'd really like a bourbon and Coke, but since I'm driving, a soft drink will do."

"I'll be right back," she told him.

She disappeared through an arched doorway and Holt glanced curiously around the long living room. He decided there was nothing frilly or overly feminine in Isabelle's taste. The furniture was solid and comfortable and all done in rich earth tones of greens and browns and yellows. Braided rugs added a splash of color to the dark hardwood floors. A TV filled one corner, while a tall bookshelf filled another, and though he was only guessing, Holt figured Isabelle reached for a book far more than she reached for the TV remote.

At the front of the room, a large picture window looked out at a distant cluster of hills dotted with cacti and rock formations. Since there were no curtains or blinds, Holt figured she either appreciated the view or enjoyed the sunshine streaming into the room or both.

The click of her high-heeled boots announced her return and he looked around to see her approaching with a glass of iced cola in each hand.

"Thank you," he said, taking the glass she offered.

"Would you like a chocolate to go with your soda?"

"No, thanks. I don't want to ruin my appetite."

She took a seat on the opposite end of the couch and carefully adjusted the hem of her dress toward her knees. The action drew Holt's attention to the shape of her legs and he found himself imagining what her thighs would feel like wrapped around his hips. Even though she was small, he had the feeling she'd be a strong lover. One that would look him boldly in the eye and dare him to thrill her.

"I'm glad I got this chance to talk with you before we left for dinner," she said.

Her voice jerked him out of the erotic daydreams and as he looked at her, he hoped to heck she couldn't read his mind.

"Pardon me, but what can we talk about here that we can't talk about later?"

"The feed you sent over with the mares. I need to pay you for it."

"The grain was a bonus that went with the mares. I won't accept pay for the feed."

She grimaced and looked away from him. "That makes me feel…very uncomfortable."

"Why? I've thrown in extras on other horse deals." Which was true, he thought. But he'd never given anyone else as much as he'd given her. The feed was something they mixed for their own use on Three Rivers. It wasn't sold or given to anyone. Until Holt had broken the rules this morning and sent her two tons of it. But she didn't need to know any of that. Nor did she need to know Blake had been a bit peeved at Holt's unusual generosity.

"I'm sorry you feel that way," he said. "It was meant to help you and the mares."

She leveled him with a pointed look. "And that's all?"

"What else?" he asked.

Through narrowed eyes, he watched her nervously lick her lips.

"Nothing, I suppose." She shrugged and glanced down at her drink. "I just don't like feeling beholden to anyone."

So she didn't want to owe him anything. Holt could understand her feelings. What he couldn't understand was how this woman affected him, how much he'd like for her to depend on him for advice and help and whatever else she needed. Which made no sense at all.

"That wasn't my intention," he said. "In case you hadn't noticed, I care deeply about my horses and even after they no longer belong to me, I want to know they're well taken care of. The feed was to help them make the transition from Three Rivers to here. It wasn't some sort of bribe for romantic favors. If that's what you were thinking."

The compression of her lips coupled with the bright pink color on her cheeks told Holt she was more than embarrassed; she was also annoyed.

"That wasn't what I was implying—well, not exactly," she said stiffly. "Anyway, I honestly doubt you need to play such silly games with the women you date."

Silly games? His sister Vivian had often accused him of playing women for fools. But that wasn't true. He never tried to manipulate a woman's feelings. That would be like trying to ride a horse without a bridle. It wasn't an impossible task, but it would take way more patience and time than he had.

He shook his head. "It's obvious you've already heard gossip about me. That I'm a playboy or worse."

The color on her face turned a deeper shade. "Believe me, Holt, whether you're a playboy or not means little to me. What you do with your private life is your business. You and I are just having dinner. That's all."

Just dinner. That's all he wanted, too, Holt thought. Having anything more to do with this woman would be inviting trouble. The kind he didn't need.

In spite of feeling oddly deflated, he smiled at her. "I'm glad we got all of that behind us. So if you're ready, I think we should be leaving. The drive to the restaurant takes a while."

Appearing relieved by his suggestion, she rose to her feet. "Certainly. Just let me get my bag and coat."

While she gathered her things from a nearby chair, Holt placed his empty glass on the coffee table and left the couch to join her. As he helped her slip into the coat, he was stuck by her flowery scent and small, vulnerable size. He could swing her into his arms without any effort at all. And with the silence of the house surrounding them, he could easily imagine himself carrying her to bed.

Dinner is what this evening is about, Holt. Remember? Not sex or drama or stifling strings or a broken heart.

And why the heck should his heart get involved if he took this woman to bed? He practically yelled the retort back at the negative voice going off in his head. He was thirty-three years old and he'd never made the mistake of falling in love. It wasn't going to happen to him. Not now. Not ever. He had nothing to worry about.

As Holt drove the two of them away from the ranch, Isabelle studied him from the corner of her eye. She couldn't deny he looked incredibly handsome tonight in a white shirt and dark Western-cut slacks. A bolo tie with a slide fashioned of onyx and silver was pushed almost to the top button, which had been left open. The black cowboy hat settled low on his forehead was made of incredibly smooth felt, the sort that cost a fortune. But the price of the hat was probably only a fraction of what he'd paid for the fish-skin boots.

The fact that Holt Hollister was rich should have been a total turnoff. Once her divorce to Trevor had become final, she'd made a silent vow to never waste her time or emotions on a rich man. From her experience, a man with stacks of money was rarely the homey sort.

He glanced in her direction. "Pat and Cott tell me you're looking to hire some day workers."

While the two men had been unloading the feed, she'd mentioned she needed to find a couple of dependable ranch hands. Apparently they'd relayed the information to Holt.

"That's right. I need help with the heavier chores. Right now I'm repairing fence and it's a rather hard job to do with only one pair of hands."

He shook his head. "Building fence without help is asking for trouble."

"The way I see it, working with a pair of creeps trying to take advantage of me is more dangerous than building fence alone."

"Hmm. You do have a point there."

She looked out at the passing landscape. "Trevor left me pretty well set financially. But not well enough for me to pay two hefty salaries every month. I can't manage that until the ranch starts making a profit. Which won't be for a long time yet. Right now I'd be happy to find a pair of trustworthy wranglers willing to work a few hours a day."

"My family and I have plenty of connections. Maybe we can help you with that."

"I'd appreciate your help, Holt."

He glanced at her and grinned, and Isabelle thought how different he seemed now from that first day she'd walked up to him in the horse barn. He'd been cold and abrupt and anything but charming. The guy sitting next to her tonight had to be the one that Emily-Ann had called dreamy.

He asked, "Have you always been so adventurous?"

"What do you mean?"

"Other than my mother, I can't think of one woman who'd be brave enough or ambitious enough to take on the huge task of starting a horse ranch. The idea of living alone in an isolated area would be enough to put most women off."

She didn't know whether he was giving her a compliment or questioning her wisdom. But then, it didn't really matter what this man thought of her. Did it?

"I've never been the timid sort. My parents always taught me to follow my dreams, no matter how big or daunting."

"What do your parents think about this new endeavor of yours?"

"They're very supportive. Honestly, the idea of me failing at anything never crosses my father's mind. He, uh, sort of lives in his own little world. He's a musician, you see, and has played piano in a jazz band for more than twenty years. My mother believes in me, too. Except that sometimes she worries about me. She's a very open-minded person, but she has this old-fashioned notion that I'd be happier with a man in my life. Thankfully she'd doesn't pester me too much about it, though. With her being single herself, there's not much she can say."

He glanced curiously at her. "Your parents aren't together?"

"No. Not since I was a small girl. But they're still good friends."

"Hmm. Must be something that runs in your family."

"Divorce, you mean?"

"No. Being divorced friends. Like you and—what's his name?"

"Oh, like me and Trevor." She shrugged. "I guess in that way I'm like my parents. Except that they had a child together. Trevor and I didn't. Which is a bless-ing—that's what Gabby thinks."

"Gabby?"

"That's my mother's name. Her real name is Gabri-elle, but no one ever calls her that."

His expression turned thoughtful. "So Gabby is re-lieved you didn't have a child with this Trevor guy. Are you?"

"Am I what?"

"Relieved that you don't share a child with your ex."

He was getting too personal, but then she'd prac-tically asked for it with all this chattering she'd been doing. Darn it, she'd been talking way too much. Be-cause she was nervous, she silently reasoned with her-self. Not because she found this man easy to talk to.

Shifting around in the seat, she tugged the hem of her dress closer to her knees. "*Relieved* is the wrong word, Holt. *Sad* is closer to it. I promised myself that whenever I had a child it would be with a man who loved me. Trevor didn't fall into that category."

A frown puckered his forehead. "You can tell me to mind my own business, but why did you marry him if you believed he didn't love you?"

He couldn't begin to know how many times she'd called herself a fool, or how often she'd questioned her hasty decision to marry. "We had a whirlwind court-ship and when Trevor whisked me off to a wedding chapel in Las Vegas, it was all so romantic. It felt like love. Later on I learned differently."

"I see."

How could he see? He'd never been married. And from the vibes she'd been getting from him, she seri-ously doubted he'd ever been in love.

"You do?" she asked quietly.

"Sure. Your ex mostly wanted a pretty woman on his arm and in his bed. Now you want a real husband and children. But you aren't interested in dating. How's that going to work out?"

Her short laugh was a cynical sound. "I'm only twenty-eight. I have a few years before my childbearing days are over."

His only reaction to her answer was the slight arch of one brow, and Isabelle figured he was probably thinking she was impulsive and silly and not the sort of woman he'd ever want to get involved with. Well, that was good, she told herself. Because he was the sort of man who would never fit into her future plans.

Twenty miles and just as many minutes later, darkness had settled across the desert landscape and Holt turned off the main highway and onto a narrow asphalt road. As the truck began to climb into a forested mountain, Isabelle grew increasingly curious.

"Excuse me, Holt, but are you sure we're going to dinner? This looks more like we're on the road to a hunting cabin. I'm getting the feeling that our food is hanging from a hook and you're going to cook it over an open fire."

He laughed. "What little I can cook, you wouldn't want to eat. Trust me. We're going to have a regular sit-down dinner with glass plates and silverware. No throwaway plastic."

"Do you always go this far out of town to eat? Or are you just driving this far to avoid being seen with me in Wickenburg?"

He laughed again and the sexy sound slid down her backbone like the warm tip of a finger.

"Now, why wouldn't I want to be seen with you?"

"You might have lady friends there who wouldn't appreciate seeing you with me," she said shrewdly.

"That would be their problem, not mine," he said, then added, "Actually, I'm driving this far because the place is unique and I thought you might enjoy it. Plus the food is delicious. Their specialty is Italian, but they have American dishes on the menu, too."

"I'm not hard to please," she told him. "I would probably even eat whatever you cooked over the fire."

He chuckled. "Maybe I'll practice up and put you to the test sometime."

Holt had been right when he'd said the restaurant was unique. The gray stone structure resembled an English manor and was perched high on the edge of a mountain. Footlights were strategically placed on the grounds to illuminate the planked board entrance and a beautiful lawn that was canopied with tall pines and spruce.

"This is like a forested fairyland, Holt. It's... completely enchanting!"

"I'm glad you approve."

He helped her out of the truck, then tossed the keys to a waiting valet. Then curving an arm against her back, he urged her toward the main entrance.

Once inside, they were greeted by a young hostess. She promptly ushered them to a small, square table near a wall of plate glass.

After they were seated and the hostess had disappeared, Isabelle looked around in fascination at the sea of linen-covered tables, tall beamed ceilings, and intricate tiled floor. As Holt had suggested, it was unique and very special.

"Beyond the glass wall, there's a balcony with tables. Usually in the winter, they keep a fire going in the firepit. It's a nice place to have after-dinner coffee—if you'd like," he suggested.

"Sounds wonderful," she agreed, then asked, "What do you usually eat when you come here?"

"Steak." Chuckling, he attempted to defend his mundane choice. "What can I say? I'm a rancher. But I do usually get ravioli or spaghetti with it. That gets me a bit out of the box, doesn't it?"

She laughed. "The spaghetti alone puts you way out of the box."

A young waiter arrived with menus and Holt ordered a bottle of sparkling red wine. While they sipped and waited for the first course of their meal to be served, Isabelle did her best to keep the conversation on the safest subject she could think of, which in their case was raising horses. But after a while, she found herself wanting to know more about Holt Hollister the man, rather than the successful horse breeder.

Throughout the delicious dinner, she managed to tamp down the personal questions, but after they moved to a table on the balcony, her guard began to relax and before she knew it, she was encouraging him to talk about himself and his family.

"So you got your love of horses from your father?" she asked, as they enjoyed cups of rich, dark coffee.

Behind her, the crackling heat from the firepit warmed her back and cast an orange gold glow over Holt's rugged features. Nearby, in a ballroom attached to the balcony, music had begun to play and the occasional sound of laughter drifted out to them. The atmosphere was decidedly romantic, Isabelle thought, but she was trying hard not to focus on that part of the evening.

He nodded. "The first time Dad put me on a horse I was too small to walk. Mom said I screamed to the top of my lungs when the ride ended. Dad was a great horseman and I always wanted to be just like him."

"You must have achieved your goal. From what people around Wickenburg have told me, you're a regular horse whisperer."

Smiling modestly, he shook his head. "I might be good with horses, but I'll never be the man that Dad was."

She frowned. "You keep saying was. Isn't your father still living?"

For the first time since she'd met Holt, she saw an unmistakable look of sadness on his face.

"Dad—his name was Joel—died over six years ago. An incident with a horse. He was found with his boot hung in the stirrup. He'd been dragged—for a long distance."

She gasped. "Oh, how tragic, Holt. To lose him that way—I mean, to have his death connected to a horse—something he dearly loved. Something you dearly love. It's horrible."

He cleared his throat, then took a sip of coffee before he finally replied, "A horse didn't kill Dad."

Totally confused by his remark, she stared at him. "What?"

His gaze left her face and settled on the shadows beyond the balcony. "I shouldn't have said that. We—

don't really know what happened to Dad. But we're pretty damned sure the horse didn't have anything to do with his death."

The tightness of his features told her there was much more to this story, more than he wanted to talk about. And it suddenly dawned on her that Holt Hollister might've been born into wealth, but his life hadn't been without heartache.

"Oh," she said. "Then you're thinking he must have had a heart attack or stroke or some sudden medical problem while he was out riding."

"That would be the logical deduction, but you're wrong. The autopsy showed no sign of any medical issue. Dad was in great health." He looked at her, his expression both bleak and frustrated. "At that time, the Yavapai County sheriff was a close friend of ours. He ruled Dad's death as an accident. Only because he didn't have enough evidence to prove otherwise. He passed away a few years ago from lung disease, or he would still be working on the case."

In spite of the fire behind her, she felt chilled. "Evidence? You mean—that someone—purposely harmed your father?"

He nodded. "That's what I'm saying. My brothers and I have been searching for answers all these years. We think we're getting close to finding out what really happened, but we need a few more pieces to put the whole puzzle together."

"I'm so sorry, Holt. I didn't realize your father was gone, much less that anything so—horrible had occurred. I'm sure it's not something you want to talk about."

He shrugged. "Sometimes it helps to talk about things that hurt."

Yes, like having a husband who hadn't loved her. Like desperately wanting children and not having any. Yes, she'd experienced things that hurt.

"What happened with the horse your father was riding?"

"Major Bob is still on the ranch," he said fondly. "Still being used in the working remuda. That's the way Dad would've wanted it. And once Major Bob grows old and dies, he'll be buried on the ranch next to Dad. They were great buddies."

"Like me and Albert." Tears suddenly filled her eyes and she blinked rapidly and reached for her coffee in an effort to hide them. "I'd like to see Major Bob and the rest of the remuda sometime. If that's possible." She gave him a wry smile. "I'm sure you've already come to the conclusion that I'm horse crazy. Or maybe just crazy in general."

"Not yet." He grinned and gestured toward her cup. "If you've had enough of coffee, let's walk over to the ballroom. It has a really nice dance floor."

Isabelle loved to dance. But she wasn't at all sure about taking a spin around the dance floor in Holt's arms. No. That wouldn't be smart, at all.

"I, uh, think I'd better pass on the dancing."

His eyes narrowed with speculation. "Why? Scared you might miss a step and crush my toes?"

She purposely straightened her shoulders. "No. I'm not scared of missing a step. Anyway, I'm not heavy enough to crush your toes."

Laughing, he rose to his feet and reached for her

hand. "Then I don't have a thing to worry about. And neither do you."

Deciding it would look silly to protest too much, she allowed him to pull her to her feet and lead her across the balcony.

As they entered the ballroom, the band began playing a slow ballad and Isabelle didn't have time to ready herself. He quickly pulled her into his arms and guided her among the group of dancers circling the floor.

Even if she'd had hours to brace herself, she wouldn't have been prepared for the onslaught of sensations rushing through her. Having his strong arm against her back and her hand clasped tightly in his was enough to cause her breathing to go haywire. But to have the front of his rock-hard body pressed to hers was totally shattering her senses.

"This is nice," he said. "Very nice."

His voice wasn't far from her ear and she knew if she turned her head slightly to the right, she'd be looking him square in the face. The thought of what that would do to her put a freeze on her neck muscles and kept her gaze fixed on a point of his shoulder.

"I've not danced in a long time," she admitted, hoping the sound of the music hid the husky tone of her voice. "I'm a little rusty."

He moved his hand ever so slightly against her back and she momentarily closed her eyes against the heat that was slowly and surely beginning to spread through her body.

"It's just like riding a horse," he murmured. "You get in rhythm and the rest comes naturally."

The man was undoubtedly a master at the art of seduction and if she didn't do something and fast, she was going to become his next victim.

"I'm beginning to think I should have worn my boots and spurs," she said.

His fingers tightened around hers and she wondered why the touch of his hand felt so good against hers.

"You know what I'm beginning to think?" he asked.

"I won't try to guess."

"You're scared of me."

That was all it took to repair the paralysis in her neck and she turned her head until her gaze was locked with his.

Lifting her chin to a challenging angle, she said, "I'm not scared of anyone."

The corners of his lips tilted ever so slightly. "You think that's wise?"

Nothing about being with this man was wise. But it was darned thrilling. And every woman needed to be thrilled once in a while, she decided.

She said, "I'd rather be brave than wise. Besides, I'm beginning to think you might just be a little afraid of me."

Amused by her remark, he grinned and Isabelle forced her gaze to remain boldly locked onto his.

"And why would I be afraid of you?" he asked.

She could feel her heart beating way too fast and hard. But with Holt's arms fastened around her, there was no way she could make her pulse settle back to a normal rhythm.

"You might get to liking me so much you'll decide to sell Blue Midnight to me," she answered.

Laughing, he pulled her even tighter against him.

"Oh, Isabelle, this evening is turning out to be better than I could've ever imagined."

Her resistance a crumbling mess, Isabelle rested her cheek against his shoulder and promised herself that she had nothing to worry about. This was just one dance, Holt was just like any other man, and tomorrow when she was back to stretching barbed wire, this magical night would be nothing more than a pleasant memory.

Chapter 5

The next morning Holt was up early enough to make his rounds at the barn and get back to the house for breakfast, which Reeva normally served at five thirty.

When he entered the dining room, the dishes of food were just starting to make their way around the long oak table. The scent of warm tortillas and chorizo made his stomach growl with hunger.

Blake, who always sat at the end of the table next to their father's empty chair, looked up as Holt sat down next to his sister-in-law Roslyn.

"Good morning, Holt," he said. "I thought you were probably sleeping in."

Evelyn, his baby niece, was sitting on her mother's lap and Holt leaned over and kissed the top of her little head before he glanced down the table at Blake.

Holt smirked at him. "You know I've never slept past six o'clock in my life. Even on my sick days."

Sitting on the opposite side of Roslyn, his brother Chandler let out an amused grunt. "What sick days? You've never so much as had a sore throat."

At that moment, Jazelle leaned over Holt's shoulder to fill his cup with steaming hot coffee. He gave the maid a wink before he replied to his brother's comment.

"It's all my clean living," Holt told him. "Keeps me healthy and fit."

Everyone at the table let out good-natured groans.

"Sure, Holt," Chandler said. "If only we could all be as straitlaced as you, we'd live to be a hundred or more."

"Where's Nick and the twins?" he directed the question to his sister-in-law Katherine while he filled his plate with eggs.

"Upstairs," she told him. "The twins are still asleep and Nick volunteered to watch them while his mom has breakfast with the rest of the family."

Holt nodded knowingly. "Nick is like me. Thoughtful."

Blake and Chandler groaned. Katherine said, "Nick is thoughtful. But he's also wise. He wants to go to the res this weekend and ride horses with Hannah."

"See, the boy is like me," Holt reiterated.

Blake rolled his eyes, then asked, "So how did your date with our new little neighbor go last night?"

Chandler glanced around the group at the table. "What new little neighbor?"

"She bought the old Landry Ranch," Blake explained. "And she's just Holt's type—young, beautiful, and single."

"What other type should I have?" Holt asked as he shook a heavy hand of black pepper over his food. "Homely and married?"

Holt had directed the question at Blake, but Chandler was the one to answer.

"I'm beginning to think you shouldn't be looking at any type," he said. "It's damned annoying to have your jilted girlfriends come into the clinic wanting me to give you nasty messages."

"Sorry," Holt told him. "The next time that happens just give her a worm pill and send her on her way."

"You're a worm all right," Blake retorted. "You worm right out of every relationship you've ever started."

Frowning, Holt picked up his coffee cup. Normally, he would simply laugh off his brothers' remarks, but this morning he wasn't feeling amused. True, after years of playing the field, he deserved a few negative comments from his family. But Blake and Chandler were already assuming that Isabelle would end up being just another jilted lover. They had no inkling that Isabelle was different. And that he had no intentions of treating her like a disposable toy.

Really, Holt? Last night when you took her home, you were practically panting for her to ask you in for a nightcap. All you could think about was creating a chance to make love to her. And if she'd given you one, you wouldn't have turned it down. So don't be thinking Isabelle is any different. That you want to be a different man with her. You can't change, Holt. You're a cheater, a user. You'd never be able to exist

*as a one-woman man. So get over these soft feelings
you're having toward the woman.*

Hating the taunting voice in his head, Holt sipped
his coffee and did his best to ignore it.

"What is this?" he asked. "Be mean to Holt morning?"

"I'm with Holt," Roslyn said. "You two are being
mean to your brother. Just because you both decided
to become married men doesn't mean that Holt wants
to go down that same path. He has a right to date who
and when he wants."

"Thank you, Ros," Holt told her. "I'm glad someone
around here is willing to stand up for me. And by the
way, where is Mom? She's never late to the breakfast
table. Has she already eaten?"

Katherine was the one to answer. "She gulped down
a cup of coffee and a doughnut. She's in a hurry to go
to Phoenix this morning."

Holt exchanged a concerned look with Chandler.
"Phoenix? Again?"

Chandler gave him a clueless shrug, while Blake
said, "She's going to some sort of meeting for Arizona
ranching women. Frankly, I think she just needs to get
away for a few hours. And God knows she deserves
some free time. We all know she works too hard."

A stretch of silence passed before Chandler said,
"Maybe she's going to see Uncle Gil, too."

Holt stabbed his fork into the mound of eggs on his
plate. For the past few months, everyone in the family had noticed a change in Maureen. At times she
appeared preoccupied and even depressed. They all
understood that she missed their late father. But this

was something different. It was almost like she was hiding something from the family.

"Yeah. I'd make a bet she meets with Gil," Holt said flatly.

Gil was Joel's younger brother. He'd worked on the Phoenix police force for more than thirty years and had never married. Everyone in the family had been expecting the man to soon retire, but so far he'd made no sign of giving up his career as a detective.

Holt could feel Blake's skeptical gaze boring into him.

"And what's wrong with her seeing Uncle Gil?" Blake asked. "They've always been close."

"Nothing is wrong." Holt wished he hadn't said anything. Now everyone was looking at him as though he had some sort of inside information. Which he didn't.

The group around the table suddenly went silent. Except for little Evelyn. The baby began to fuss and reach her arms out for Holt to take her.

Happy for the diversion, Holt gathered the girl from Roslyn and with his arm safely around her waist, stood her on his thigh. She immediately began to laugh and tug on his ear. He tickled her belly and as she giggled with delight, Isabelle drifted through his thoughts.

I've always wanted children.

Her revelation hadn't surprised Holt. At some point in their lives, most women did want to become mothers. And yet, hearing her voice her wishes had been a reminder that she was off-limits to him. That sometime soon, he'd have to step aside and allow her to find a man who'd give her children. A man who could give her that real love she'd talked about.

For some inexplicable reason, the idea saddened

him, but he wasn't going to allow himself to dwell on the situation. Isabelle was sweet and lovely and a joy to be around. It wouldn't hurt anything to date her a few more times before he told her goodbye. And by then, he was certain he'd be ready to move on to the next pretty face.

Later that afternoon, after riding fence line for more than two hours, Isabelle returned to the ranch yard and was unsaddling her horse when an old red Ford truck barreled up the long drive and pulled to a stop a few feet away from the barn.

The vehicle wasn't Holt's and Emily-Ann drove a car. Since those were the only two people she knew well enough to make the long drive out here, she couldn't imagine who this might be.

Swinging the saddle onto the top board of the corral, she walked toward the vehicle. She was halfway there when two men climbed to the ground, wearing stained straw hats, kerchiefs around their necks, and Sherpa-lined jean jackets that had seen better days.

The taller of the two lifted a hand in greeting. "Are you Ms. Townsend?"

She walked across the hard-packed dirt to join them. "I'm Isabelle Townsend," she said a bit cautiously. "This place is a far distance from town. Are you guys lost?"

"We probably look like we're lost, but we aren't. We know this whole county like the back of our hand," the shorter one said with a wide grin. "My name is Ollie and my partner here is Sol."

Ollie had a stocky build with mousy brown hair and a mouth full of crooked teeth. His partner was as thin as a reed and what little she could see of his hair beneath the bent hat was snow-white. Isabelle gauged both men to be somewhere in their early sixties, but since the Arizona climate was rough on a person, they could've been younger.

"Nice to meet you. Is there something I can do for you?"

Sol decided it was his turn to speak. "We heard you needed ranch hands. We're here for the job."

Isabelle studied both men as her mind whirled with questions. The only people she'd talked with about hiring help was Holt, and the men who'd delivered her mares. So how did this pair know she was thinking about hiring?

"I haven't advertised for help. Who sent you here?" she asked.

Ollie cast a cagey look at his partner. "Reckon we might as well tell her, Sol. She has to know."

"Tell me what?" Isabelle asked, then decided to voice her suspicions out loud. "Did Holt Hollister send you over here?"

"Well, he didn't exactly send us," Ollie said a bit sheepishly. "It was like this, we were in the Broken Spur having a cup of coffee and he just happened to stroll in. The subject of work was brought up and he told us about you needing an honest pair of men to help you."

"And that's us, Ms. Townsend," Sol added. "Honest as the day is long. Just ask the Hollisters. We've done day work at Three Rivers for close to thirty years now."

Ollie nodded. "That's right, Ms. Townsend. And we can do about anything you might need. Sol's a damned good farrier, too. He can save you lots of money."

Isabelle didn't know what to say, much less think. These two were just the sort she needed here on the ranch. Older, polite, and experienced with ranch work. She wouldn't have to waste time showing them every little thing that needed to be done.

"You men aren't working anywhere right now?"

The two cowboys glanced at each other again as though neither one of them knew how to answer her question.

"Uh—no," Ollie told her.

Sol shook his head. "Not steady. But we can be steady for you, Ms. Townsend. We're ready to go to work right now. Got our gear in the truck."

"Well, I'm going to have to think about this," she told them. "I do need help. But there's no way I can match the wages that Three Rivers pays you. And I can only afford to use you a few hours a day. You guys are probably looking for full-time work."

Again, the two men looked at each other and Isabelle decided the pair were like twins; one didn't make a move without the other.

"Oh, no. We aren't worried about wages, Ms. Townsend," Ollie assured her. "We're happy with whatever you can pay us."

Sol added, "We're all set to work every day. We don't have anything better to do. If you got some place we can bunk, we'll be as happy as a bear in a tree full of honey."

Isabelle stared at the two men in disbelief. "I must have missed something," she said. "You two are willing to bunk here and work full-time for part-time wages?"

Sol grinned. "Why sure. That way we can sorta be

your bodyguards. It's not safe for a woman like you to be living out here alone. Any kind of riffraff could wander up here at night."

Shaking her head, she said, "I don't know what to say about any of this."

"No need to say anything," Ollie told her. "Except you might show us where we can put our saddles and our horses. We have two mares and two geldings between us. They're in the trailer waiting to be unloaded. So you won't have to worry about mounting us on working horses."

Ever since Isabelle had moved onto the ranch, she'd been worrying and wondering how she was going to hire good, reliable help. The idea that it had practically fallen into her lap had left her a little dazed and a whole lot suspicious.

"I think—" Before she could go on, the cell phone in her shirt pocket began to ring. Annoyed with the interruption, she said, "Excuse me, guys."

"You go right ahead, Ms. Townsend," Sol said. "We'll go unload our horses."

The men walked away to tend to their horses and Isabelle tugged the phone from her shirt pocket. To her surprise, the caller was Holt.

"Hello, Holt. I wasn't expecting to hear from you today."

His raspy chuckle immediately took her back to last night when he'd held her in his arms on the dance floor. She still hadn't recovered her shattered senses.

"I couldn't wait to hear your voice again," he said.

He was teasing and she took his words in that manner. "Is that why you called me? Just to hear my voice?"

He chuckled again. "Partly. I also wanted to see if

Ollie and Sol have shown up yet. I thought you might be concerned and want a reference."

She looked toward the old red Ford and faded white trailer hooked behind it. The men had already unloaded one horse and Ollie was tying the bay to a hitching ring. The men were the real deal and would be a great help. But she couldn't afford them and, furthermore, Holt knew it.

"You sent them out here, didn't you?"

"They needed something to do. Presently, Three Rivers is a little crowded with help and I thought this would be a solution for all three of you."

Crowded with help? Maybe. But she had the feeling that he'd more than nudged them in her direction.

She said, "That's hard to believe. Calves start to drop in January. It's a busy time for cattle ranches."

He paused, then said, "I didn't know you knew about cattle."

"I'm hardly an expert," she admitted. "But I'm not green on the subject either. As for Ollie and Sol, they have the crazy idea that they're going to stay here on the ranch. I can't afford to pay them like round-the-clock ranch hands. I tried to make that clear to them, but they're not listening to me. I think I'd better put one of them on the phone and let you explain the situation before it gets out of hand."

"You really shouldn't concern yourself about that, Isabelle. Ollie and Sol are just happy to be helping out. They're not the type to worry about money. As long as they have a horse, a roof over their head, and something to eat, they're happy."

Isabelle was far from convinced. "What about their families? How do they support them?"

"Both men are widowers. No kids either."

The information tugged on her heartstrings. "That's sad. But it doesn't change the fact that I can only use them for three or four hours a day. Would you please make that clear to one of them?"

"Okay, put Sol on the phone. I'll set him straight."

"Thanks, Holt."

Isabelle walked over and handed the phone to Sol, then waited a few steps away while the man did more listening than talking.

Finally, Sol said, "Yeah. I understand, Holt… No. No problems here. We'll handle everything… Sure. You can count on us. I'm giving her back the phone right now."

The skinny, old cowboy handed her the phone, then without a word to her, went back to work unloading the last of the horses.

Shaking her head, Isabelle put the phone back to her ear. "Holt, I don't think you got the message across. Sol is unloading the last of the horses."

"Sol knows what he's doing. Don't argue, Isabelle. You needed good help and now you have it. Just quit asking questions and be happy."

"I am happy. But—"

"Good. Then maybe you'll invite me over soon and show me some of your cooking skills."

Totally caught off guard by the abrupt change of subject, she tried to assemble some sort of logical response. "You're asking me to cook for you?"

He chuckled. "When I say cook, I mean just give me something to eat. A sandwich will do. I'd like to come over and see the mares you shipped down from New Mexico."

Last night, when he'd brought her home, she'd very nearly made the mistake of asking him in for coffee. A part of her hadn't wanted the time with him to end. But thankfully, common sense had won over and instead of inviting him in, she'd given him a quick kiss on the cheek and rushed into the house.

"Isabelle, are you still there?"

She mentally shook herself. "Uh—yes, I was just thinking. It's foaling season. Aren't you terribly busy right now?"

"I figure I'll have a few days of peace until the next moon change. It comes on Monday. What are you doing tomorrow night?"

"Aren't you being a bit pushy? We just went out last night."

"And it was very nice, wasn't it?"

Too nice, Isabelle thought. Now every little nuance about the man seemed stuck in her head.

"Yes," she agreed. "It was enjoyable."

"Then why shouldn't we see each other again?"

Isabelle was smart enough to recognize that if she continued to see the man, she'd soon wind up in bed with him. And no matter how sexy or pleasant his company was, an affair with a playboy wouldn't be a smart choice. Now or ever.

And yet, she was starting a new life here in Yavapai County. It was nice and helpful to have a fellow horse trainer to talk with.

"No reason," she answered, then before she could change her mind added impishly, "I suppose I could manage to put some cold cuts between two slices of bread. Would that be enough cooking for you?"

He chuckled. "Sounds perfect. I'll be there before dark."

"I'll see you then."

Not giving him time to say more, she ended the call and dropped the phone back into her pocket. Tomorrow would be soon enough to worry about having Holt over for dinner. Right now she had to make two old ranch hands understand she couldn't use them on a full-time basis.

The next afternoon, after finishing several chores in Wickenburg, Isabelle decided to treat herself to a short break. When she dropped by Conchita's coffee shop for an espresso and frosted doughnut, Emily-Ann greeted her with a huge hug.

"If you hadn't shown up soon, I was going to file a missing person report," Emily-Ann said as the two women sat outside at one of the little wrought iron tables. "I haven't seen or heard from you since the morning you went to Three Rivers and had it out with Holt."

Isabelle carefully sipped the hot espresso, then lowered the cup back to the table. "The next day I went back to Three Rivers and things went far better with Holt. I ended up buying five mares from him."

Emily-Ann smiled brightly and Isabelle decided the young woman looked extra pretty today wearing a canary yellow sweater with her red hair braided over one shoulder.

"Now that's more like it," she said with approval. "I was going to be truly surprised if he didn't come through with a good deal for you."

"The mares are exceptional. Their babies should

fetch a good price," Isabelle told her. "I'm thrilled to get them."

Emily-Ann leaned eagerly toward her. "Forget the horses. I want to hear how you got on with Holt? You were mighty angry with him."

Isabelle could feel her cheeks growing warm. "We, uh, got on fine. Actually, we went on a date—to dinner."

Emily-Ann's mouth fell open. "You're kidding, right?"

"It was against my better judgment, but I did go," Isabelle admitted. "And frankly, I had a lovely time. It was nice to be out and away from all the work on the ranch for a few hours."

"Wowee!" Emily-Ann exclaimed. "You actually went on a date with Holt! I'm stunned. Not that Holt asked you out. But that you agreed to go!"

Isabelle shrugged. "I couldn't very well refuse. From what he told me, he had no intentions of selling any more mares this year. I was fortunate that he agreed to part with those five. The least I could do was show him my appreciation."

Emily-Ann giggled. "Sure, Isabelle."

Frowning, Isabelle picked up her espresso. "You act as though he's some sort of rock star in a cowboy hat."

Emily-Ann shrugged. "I admit I sound silly. But he's one of the most eligible bachelors around here. Doesn't it make you feel special that he's interested—in you? It would me. But then nobody of his caliber is ever going to take a second glance at me."

The frown on Isabelle's face deepened. "This isn't the first time I've heard you putting yourself down, Emily-Ann, and I want you to stop it. You're a bright, lovely woman. You're just as good as me or Holt or any person."

She smiled wanly. "If you say so."

"I do say so." Isabelle popped the last of the doughnut into her mouth and savored the taste before she swallowed it down. "I've got to be going. I have the truck loaded down with groceries. Oh, I almost forgot—I have two hired hands now. Ollie Sanders and Sol Reynolds. Do you know them?"

Emily-Ann shook her head. "I'm not familiar with either name, but I might recognize them if I saw them. Are they the sort to stop by here for coffee?"

Isabelle laughed at the image. "No. This pair is a little rough around the edges for Conchita's."

Bemused, Emily-Ann gestured to the small building behind them and the simple outdoor tables. "This place is hardly fancy. What kind of guys are they?"

"The sort that drink plain coffee at the Broken Spur. Ollie's sixty-one and Sol is sixty-three. Neither has a family and ranch work is the only job they've ever had."

Emily-Ann frowned. "Are you sure you can trust these guys? Where did you find them anyway?"

"Holt sent them over. They normally work at Three Rivers. Now they're staying on Blue Stallion with me. I'm helping them turn one of the feed rooms into a little bunkhouse so they'll have a comfortable place to stay. I already had a hot plate for them to use and today I bought a small fridge. Next I need to purchase a couple of single beds and some linen. Last night they slept on cots and sleeping bags."

Emily-Ann frowned thoughtfully. "Are you sure

these guys are going to be worth the extra money they're costing you?"

Isabelle nodded. "They've already done more in one day than I could do in ten. And don't get the idea that they're too old to be useful. Both of them could work circles around a man in his thirties."

"Sounds like you're happy with these guys," Emily-Ann remarked.

"I couldn't be more pleased," Isabelle told her. "But there is something nagging at me. When I told them the amount I'd be able to pay for a monthly wage, I expected them to turn tail and leave. Instead they seemed indifferent. It's weird."

Emily-Ann drummed her fingers thoughtfully against the tabletop. "Interesting that Holt sent them over. If I didn't know better, it sounds like he's trying to take care of you."

Isabelle reacted with a sound that was something between a grunt and a laugh. "That's ridiculous. Holt is only being a helpful neighbor."

The smirk on her Emily-Ann's lips said exactly what she thought about Isabelle's explanation. "None of my neighbors have ever been *that* helpful."

Isabelle didn't want to get annoyed with Emily-Ann. She was the closest friend she had here in Wickenburg and she genuinely liked her. Even though she did get these silly notions.

"Look, Emily-Ann, I'm sure you'd be the first person to advise me against getting serious about Holt Hollister," Isabelle told her. "So let me assure you. He's a friend and that's all he'll ever be to me."

Emily-Ann rolled her eyes. "How funny, Isabelle. Me giving you advice about a man. But I happen to think it would be fitting if you'd give Mr. Holt Hollister some of the same love 'em and leave 'em medicine he's dished out over the years."

Isabelle crumpled the wax paper that her doughnut had been wrapped in and dropped it in her empty cup. Thank goodness she hadn't mentioned to Emily-Ann that Holt was coming over to the ranch this evening. She'd really be having a field day with that tidbit of information.

"I thought he was an old family friend of yours," Isabelle remarked.

"He is. But it's past time he met his match." She smiled cleverly. "And I happen to think you're it."

"Oh, no. Not me." Isabelle rose to her feet just as a customer pulled into the parking area of the coffee shop. "Time for me to go. See you, Emily-Ann."

Emily-Ann waggled her fingers. "Drop by soon. I can't wait to hear what you'll have to tell me then."

Rolling her eyes, Isabelle pulled the strap of her purse onto her shoulder. "The next time I stop by for coffee, you're not going to hear one thing about Holt Hollister. And that's a promise."

Emily-Ann laughed. "You know what they say about promises. They're made to be broken."

Chapter 6

Sundown was still more than an hour away when Holt arrived on Blue Stallion Ranch. As he parked the truck a short distance from the house and climbed to the ground, he noticed a cloud of brown dust rising near the barn area.

Squinting against the lingering rays of sunlight, Holt spotted Isabelle in a large round pen riding a little bay mare with a white blaze down her face. Ollie and Sol were perched on a rail of the fence, watching their new boss in action.

As Holt approached the two men, Ollie threw up a hand in greeting. "Hey, Holt. Come have a seat and watch the show. Isabelle's got the little mare spinning on a dime."

Holt leaned a shoulder against the fence and peered

through the wooden rails as Isabelle continued to put the mare through a series of maneuvers.

Sol said, "I never thought I'd see anyone ride as well as you, Holt, but Isabelle comes pretty damned close."

Holt glanced up at the older man. "Aww, come on, now, Sol," he joked. "You think that just because she's a lot prettier than me."

Ollie chuckled. "Well, I wouldn't argue that point. But she sure knows how to handle horses. Surprised the heck out of me and Sol, that's for sure."

Holt turned his attention back to the pen just in time to see Isabelle rein the mare to a skidding stop. He couldn't argue that she sat the saddle in fine form. Loose and relaxed while being in total control, it was easy to see she was a very experienced rider. She was also the sexiest thing that Holt had ever laid eyes on.

Maybe that was why he couldn't stay away from the woman, he silently reasoned. It wasn't like him to take time away from the ranch when foals were coming right and left. But this evening when he'd made his rounds through the barns, the mares he'd put on foal watch had all seemed settled and happy. And if by chance one did decide to suddenly go into labor, Holt knew he could depend on T.J. and Chandler to handle the situation.

For the past few years, Holt's family had been urging him to ease his workload and spend more time away from the horse barn. Preferably finding himself a good wife and growing a family. Hell, why would he want to fence himself in like that? Even with a woman like Isabelle.

He was pushing the question aside when she suddenly spotted him and trotted the mare over to where he was standing near the fence.

"Hi, Holt. I wasn't expecting you this early," she said with an easy smile. "I haven't made those sandwiches I promised you yet."

He smiled back at her and wondered why seeing her made him feel like he was standing on a golden cloud with bright blue sky all around him.

"I'm not worried. I doubt you're going to let me starve."

Isabelle dismounted and led the mare out of a gate and around the fence to where Holt was standing.

Before she reached him, Ollie and Sol climbed to the ground and she handed the sweaty mare over to the two men.

"We'll take care of her," Ollie told Isabelle. "You go on with your visit."

"Thank you, guys."

The two men left with the horse in tow and Holt turned his attention to Isabelle. Her perfect little curves were covered with a pair of faded jeans and a yellow-and-brown-striped shirt. A dark brown cowboy hat covered her white-blond hair, while spurs jingled on the heels of her boots.

To him, she looked just as pretty in her work clothes as she had in the clingy black dress she'd worn to dinner, and Holt decided just looking at her made him feel happier than he'd felt in years.

"I noticed you didn't give the men any instructions about the mare," he said.

She shook her head. "I don't have to tell them anything. They know exactly what to do. But you knew that when you sent them over here."

So she'd figured that out. "Aren't you glad I did?"

She pondered his question for only a second. "I'm very glad. And if I haven't said thank you, I'm saying it now."

"No thanks needed," he replied, while telling himself there was no need for her to ever find out the whole deal about Ollie and Sol. Sure, he'd sent them over here, and that was all she needed to know.

She swiped the back of her sleeve against her cheeks and said, "Sorry I look such a mess. We've been repairing a bunch of feed troughs this afternoon and then I decided to give Pin-Up Girl a little exercise."

"No need to apologize. You look as pretty as Pin-Up Girl," he said.

She laughed and he realized he liked that about her, too. That she could laugh at him and herself.

"Thank you, Holt. Before we head to the house, would you like to walk on down to the barn and take a look at my horses?"

"I would like that," he told her. "And by the way, your little Pin-Up Girl looks great. Did you train her?"

She stepped up to his side and as they began to amble in the direction of the big weathered barn, Holt had to fight the urge to curl his arm around the back of her waist.

"Thank you. Yes, I did train her," she answered. "She's only three. She was born to one of my mares shortly after I moved to Albuquerque. It's only been these past few months that I've had a chance to work with her on a regular basis."

Albuquerque. He was beginning to hate the mention of that city. Not that he had anything against it. But he did resent the reminder of her ex and the married life she'd had with the man. Which was stupid of him, Holt realized. He'd dated divorced women before and nothing about their exes had bothered him in the least. He had no right or reason to be jealous or possessive of Isabelle.

"I'll be honest," he said, "When I saw you that first day you came to Three Rivers, I thought—"

Intrigued, she prodded, "You thought what?"

Right now he figured he looked as sheepish as the day Reeva had caught him digging into a pie she'd made especially for his sister Vivian's birthday party. Thankfully his sister had always forgiven him anything. He wasn't sure that Isabelle would be so forgiving, though.

He said, "That you looked like you spent most of your time on a tropical beach. That you were probably one of those women who wanted to try a new hobby every few months. And this month just happened to be horses."

Her laugh was deep and genuine. "What a wonderful impression you had of me. Is that why you gave me the cold shoulder?"

What was wrong with him? Nothing embarrassed him, or so he thought. But now that he was beginning to know Isabelle, he wanted her to think highly of him.

"I'm sorry about that, Isabelle. I was being a real ass that morning. But you see, I have a problem with women."

"Yes, I've heard that."

Her deadpan response had him laughing. "I'm sure you've heard plenty of things. What I meant was I have problems with women showing up at the barn as though it's a petting zoo. Most of them don't understand that horses can be very dangerous. Especially to a greenhorn. Then there's the loss of time and work it takes for one of the hands to escort the woman around the barn. It's worse than annoying. It's like I said— a problem."

"I see. You thought the only kind of horse I'd ever ridden was the kind where you drop a quarter in the slot." Her smile was playful. "I forgive you. After all, you'd never met me. But that should teach you not to make assumptions just by appearances."

"That's a lesson our mother tried to drive in all of us kids. I guess it didn't stick with me."

She chuckled. "Well, I wouldn't worry, Holt. You're still very young. You have plenty of time to learn."

Shadows were stretching across the ranch yard and the warmth of the springlike day had begun to cool when Isabelle and Holt finally walked to the house.

"I do hope you're hungry," Isabelle told him as they entered a door on the back porch. "I have a surprise for you."

He followed her into the kitchen. "Let me guess. You got more than one kind of lunch meat. Bologna, I hope. That's my favorite."

"I do have bologna. But I—"

She paused as she turned to see him sniffing the air.

"Something is cooking and it doesn't smell like sandwiches."

She walked over to a large gas range and switched off the oven. "No. I decided to take pity on you and give you something besides bread and cold cuts. But don't get too excited until you do a taste test. This dish is one of the few things I can cook and it doesn't always turn out right. If we dig in and it tastes awful, I'll drag out the bologna."

"With an offer like that, I can't lose." He held up his hands. "If you'll show me where I can wash up, I'll help you get things ready."

"Follow me. The bathroom is just down the hall," she told him.

They left the kitchen and started down a narrow hallway. Isabelle could feel his presence following close behind her and she wondered what would happen if she suddenly stopped and turned to face him? Would he want to kiss her? Had the thought of kissing her ever crossed his mind?

Stop it, Isabelle! You're a fool for thinking about such things! You just got out of a loveless marriage. Why would you want to enter into a loveless affair? Just so you could feel a man's strong arms around you? Forget it.

Shutting her mind off to the silent warning, she hurried ahead of him and opened the bathroom door. "Here it is," she said. "Help yourself and I'll, uh, see you back in the kitchen."

"Thanks."

As soon as he disappeared into the bathroom, Isabelle rushed to her bedroom and threw off her hat. After dashing a hairbrush through her hair, she swiped on pink lipstick, sighed helplessly at the dusty image in the mirror, and hurried back to the kitchen.

She'd barely had time to take the casserole out of the oven when Holt returned to the room and sidled up to her at the gas range.

"That really smells good, Isabelle," he said. "But

you've made me feel awful. I honestly didn't expect you to cook."

There were plenty of things about Holt that Isabelle hadn't expected, she thought. After their dinner date a couple of nights ago, she hadn't figured on seeing him again. At least, not this soon or in such an intimate setting. And from all she'd heard about his womanizing, she'd expected him to be making all kinds of sexual advances. So far she'd been all wrong about the man.

She cast him a droll look. "That is what you suggested on the phone."

"Yes, but I was only using that as an excuse to invite myself over."

She couldn't stop a playful smile from tugging at her lips. "I know that."

He grinned. "And you cooked for me anyway. That's sweet, Isabelle."

His eyes were twinkling as a grin spread slowly across his face. The tempting sight jumped her heart into overdrive and she knew if she didn't move away from him, she was going to say or do something stupid. Like rest her palm against his chest and tilt her lips toward his.

Drawing in a shaky breath, she turned and moved down the cabinets to where the dishes were stored.

"Just don't let it go to your head," she said. "And if you want to make yourself useful, you might fill some glasses with ice while I set the table."

"Ice? No wine?"

"Sorry. I'm out of wine. I have tea, soda, or water."

"I should've brought a bottle, but I thought we were having sandwiches. Water is plenty fine for me, though." He found the glasses and was filling them with crushed ice when he suddenly snapped his fingers. "Oh, I nearly forgot! I have something for us in the truck. I'll be right back."

He hurried out the back door of the kitchen and while he was gone, Isabelle set the table in the dining room, then added the food and drinks. She was lighting a tall yellow candle when he walked in carrying a round plastic container.

"This is nice, Isabelle." Standing next to her, he slowly surveyed the long room. "I love all the arched windows. You can see all the way to the barn from here."

"Yes and the mountains beyond. This is one of my favorite rooms in the house." She gestured behind them to the table and matching china hutch. "One of these days, I'm going to get more furniture. Like a longer dining table and a buffet to go with it. But since it's just me and I don't do any entertaining, there isn't much need for me to rush into furniture shopping. Actually, if you weren't here tonight, I'd be eating in the kitchen."

"Nothing wrong with that. I do it quite often because I'm usually late coming in from the barn. And sometimes I just want to have Reeva for company."

She pointed to the plastic container he was holding. "Is that something to eat?"

He grinned. "Pie. Blueberry with double crust. I asked Reeva to make it especially for us. I hope you like blueberries."

"I love them and what a treat to have a homemade pie." Isabelle took the container from him and set it on the table alongside the casserole, then motioned for him to take a seat. "Everything is ready. Let's eat."

"Not until the hostess is seated." He pulled out her chair and made a sweeping gesture with his arm. "For you, my lady."

She laughed softly. "What am I? Cinderella in dusty blue jeans?"

"Of course you are. And I'm the prince in cowboy boots. But I wasn't thinking. I should've brought you a glass slipper instead of a blueberry pie."

He pushed her and the chair forward and once she was comfortably positioned, she expected him to move on around to the other side of the table. Instead, he lingered there with his hands on the back of the chair and Isabelle held her breath, waiting and wondering if his hands were going to slide onto her shoulders.

But they didn't and when he finally stepped away, she expelled a breath of relief. Or was that disappointment she was feeling? Oh, Lord, the man shook her like nothing ever had. And he'd not so much as kissed her or even touched her in a romantic way. She must be losing her grip, she thought.

"No need to worry," she said. "I threw the other glass slipper away a long time ago."

He took the seat across from her, then leaned his forearms against the edge of the table and looked at her. "I think you meant that as a joke, but you didn't exactly sound like you were teasing."

"If I sounded cynical, I didn't mean to," she said. "It's just that sometimes I get to thinking about—" She paused and shook her head. "You don't want to hear this kind of stuff. Let's eat. You go first."

She picked up a large serving spoon and handed it to him.

He filled his plate with a large portion of the

Mexican-type casserole, then reached for a basket of tortilla chips. "I do want to hear. What is it that puts you in a pessimistic mood?"

She shrugged, while wishing she'd never said anything. "Okay, I get to thinking about all the time I wasted trying to make things be the way I wanted them to be."

He frowned. "You're very young, Isabelle. You have plenty of time to make your life's dreams come true."

Dreams. Yes, she'd always had those. But only one of them was coming true. Her dream of Blue Stallion Ranch. And that's the one she needed to focus on. Not on a man to hold her tight or put a ring on her finger or give her children.

She gave him the cheeriest smile she could muster and began to fill her plate. "You're right, Holt. I have my whole life ahead of me. I might just go buy myself a new pair of glass slippers and kick up my heels."

"Now that's more like it."

He reached across the table for her hand and as his fingers wrapped warmly around hers, she arched a questioning brow at him.

"What's wrong?" she asked impishly. "You think I'm going to run away from the table and leave you with all the mess?"

His thumb gently rubbed the back of her hand. The soft touch caused a layer of goose bumps to cover her arms. Thankfully, with her arms hidden by long sleeves, he couldn't see just how much he was affecting her.

"No. I was just thinking how pretty you look and how much I'm enjoying being here with you like this."

Her cheeks grew warm and she figured they had

turned a telltale pink. "You're flirting now," she murmured accusingly.

"A little," he admitted. "But I'm also telling the truth. You can't know what it's like being in a big family with three-fourths of us living under the same roof. It can get loud. And it takes work to find any sort of privacy."

Before she melted right there in her chair, she eased her hand from his and picked up her fork. "But it must be nice having brothers and sisters. I've always thought having siblings would be wonderful."

"It is. And I'm very close to all of them. It's just that sometimes I want to be alone and keep my thoughts to myself."

She nodded, then smiled. "Or perhaps just talk to the cook."

"Yes, thank God for Reeva. I can say what I really think to her. She gets me. How she does, I don't know. The woman is seventy-one. Nearly forty years older than me."

He took a bite of the food and Isabelle could tell from the look on his face that he liked it. The fact sent a ridiculous spurt of joy through her.

"Age isn't what makes two people click. It's being on the same plane and having the right chemistry mix and a lot of other things."

He looked up from his plate and Isabelle felt a jolt as his gaze met hers.

"You sound like my sister Viv. She's always telling me that one of these days I'll find a woman who I'll click with. One I'll want to be with the rest of my life."

"And what do you say to her?"

"I mostly laugh."

"Why? Because you want to change women like you change shirts?"

"Ouch! If that's how you think of me, then why did you invite me here tonight?"

That was a good question, Isabelle thought. Just why exactly was she spending time with Holt when she knew there was no future in it?

"You invited yourself, remember? And I agreed to it."

"Because?"

The smile she gave him came from deep inside her. "I like you, Holt. And I like your company. And I'm not expecting anything more from you than friendship. That's why I agreed to see you again."

He studied her face for long moments and Isabelle was struck by the look in his eyes. It was almost like she was seeing hurt or disappointment, yet that couldn't be right, she thought. Holt was a guy who was just out for a good time. He wasn't wanting anything from her, unless it was sex. And so far, he'd not given her any sign that he wanted even that.

"Hmm. That's fair enough. And being your friend would be special for me. I've never had a female friend before."

No, she thought dismally, he most likely considered them lovers rather than friends. "You have Reeva," she told him.

"She's like a second mom."

"What about Jazelle? The blond woman who brought the pastries to your office?"

He nodded. "Jazelle is like family, too. She's been with us for a long time."

"Really? She looks very young."

He ate a few bites of the casserole before he commented. "She is. But she came to work for us when she was only in her teens, so we've all known her for a long time. She's a single mother of a little boy. He's probably four or five now. Sometimes she brings him out to the ranch, but mostly her mother watches him while Jazelle works."

A single mother. Isabelle hadn't ended up being one of those, but sometimes she wished Trevor had given her a child. Even though he hadn't loved her, a child would've been something more than his money could buy. With a child, she wouldn't be so alone now. She'd have a real purpose and reason to build her ranch. And most of all, she'd have someone to give her love to. But he'd kept putting her desire to have a baby on the something-to-do-later list, like many years later.

Shoving those miserable thoughts aside, she asked, "What about your siblings? Do they have children?"

He laughed. "Lots of them. Blake and Kat have a son, Nick. He's getting close to thirteen. And then they have twin toddlers, Abagail and Andrew. Chandler and his wife, Roslyn, have a baby girl, Evelyn. Viv has a fourteen-year-old daughter, Hannah, and she recently learned the baby she's carrying is actually twins. Joseph, my youngest brother, has a three-year-old boy, Little Joe, and they're expecting again, too."

"Sounds like the Hollister family is growing fast. So you're the only one who isn't married with children?"

"No. My baby sister, Camille, is still single. She lives at our other ranch, Red Bluff. And before you ask," he added with a little laugh, "none of the horses down there are for sale."

She laughed with him. "Well, it never hurts to try."

* * *

When Holt finally pushed his plate to one side, the casserole dish was nearly empty and the corn chips were little more than a pile of crumbs in the bottom of the basket.

"You were telling a fib when you said you couldn't cook, Isabelle. That was delicious."

"Thanks, I'm glad you liked it." She stood and began to gather dishes. "Don't forget we have Reeva's pie for dessert. I'll carry these things to the kitchen and get some coffee going."

"I'll help you." Rising from the chair, he collected his dirty plate and silverware and followed her out of the dining room.

"Actually, there's something other than the dishes that you could help me with," she said. "Do you know how to build a fire?"

His gaze instinctively dropped to the sway of her shapely little butt. "What kind of fire are you talking about?"

Glancing over her shoulder, she pulled a playful face at him. "I'm not asking you to be an arsonist, if that's what you're thinking. I'm talking about the fireplace."

He'd forgotten she even had a fireplace. His mind was too preoccupied with the bedroom. Damn it! He must be developing some sort of personality disorder. What else would explain his uncharacteristic behavior? Where women were concerned, he'd always had one objective. Until the morning Isabelle sat in his office looking like a breath of spring. From that day on, something had tilted in his head. Now he wanted Isabelle more than any woman he'd ever known, but he was hesitant to even allow himself to touch her. What the heck was he doing here anyway?

Seeing that she'd paused to look at him, he mentally shook himself and tried to sound normal. "The fireplace," he repeated inanely. "Sure, I'm great at building fires."

The faint curve of her lips told Holt she'd also been thinking about another kind of fire. The notion not only surprised him, it rattled him right down to his boots. Making love to Isabelle might prove to be fatal to his common sense. That was something he needed to remember.

"I thought you would be."

Holt kept his mouth shut as he followed her into the kitchen and, after depositing the dishes in the sink, he went to deal with the fire.

In the living room, he found wood and kindling stacked on the left side of the fireplace and matches lying near a poker stand. In a few short minutes, he was standing with his back to the flames, soaking up the heat while he waited for Isabelle to appear.

When she finally entered the room, carrying a tray with the pie and coffee, she glanced appreciatively at the blazing fire.

"That's nice, Holt." She walked over and placed the tray on the coffee table in front of the couch. "I can feel the heat all the way over here."

So could he, Holt thought, and it had nothing to do with the burning mesquite logs.

"Come on over," she invited as she took a seat on the long green couch.

Holt left the fireplace to join her and took a seat more than two feet away from her, all the while his brothers' mocking laughter sounded in his ears. If they could see him now, they'd never believe it, he thought wryly.

"Help yourself, Holt," she said. "I brought the whole pie so that you could cut the size you want."

"I'll do yours first," he told her.

After he handed her a dish of the pie and cut a hefty portion for himself, she said, "If you like, I can turn on the TV. I have satellite so the reception is good and there's plenty of channels to choose from."

"I don't necessarily need it, unless you'd like to watch." He settled back with the dessert and tried to forget that the two of them were alone. That fire was warm and she'd be even warmer in his arms.

"It must be a horse trainer thing," she commented between bites of pie. "I don't watch either. After a day in the saddle, I don't have the time or desire to watch."

"Once I grew past cartoon age, I forgot all about TV."

She slanted an amused glance at him and he chuckled.

"What's wrong?" he asked. "You can't imagine me watching Looney Tunes?"

"I can see you rooting for that nasty coyote," she teased. "He's just your type. Fast and wily."

"I'll tell you one thing, I can't see you as the little helpless heroine tied to the railroad track yelling for help," he replied, then arched a questioning brow in her direction. "Do you ever yell for help?"

"Things have to get pretty desperate before I yell," she admitted. "But we all need a helping hand sometimes. And being too proud to accept it is really stupid."

And she was far from stupid, Holt thought. In fact, he'd never dated any woman who was ambitious and hardworking enough to build a ranch on her own. Was that why he was feeling so different about Isabelle? Because he admired and respected all those things about her? He wished he knew the answers. Maybe then he wouldn't be feeling like he'd lost all control of his faculties.

"I'm glad you accepted Ollie's and Sol's help," he said. "I won't be worrying about you so much."

She frowned and reached for her coffee. "Worrying about me? You shouldn't be doing that."

She was right. He had no right or reason to be fretting about her well-being. But something about Isabelle brought out the protector in him.

"Anything could happen to you out here. If a horse bucked you off and the fall broke your leg—" He paused and shook his head. "Well, it's just better that the men are here with you."

A gentle smile crossed her face and Holt noticed that even with her lipstick gone, her lips were still a soft pink. The color reminded him of cotton candy and he figured she'd taste just as sweet as the delicate treat.

"I'm glad the men are here, too," she said. "I like their company. I'm learning Ollie is the more talkative of the two and can be very funny at times. Sol is more solemn and serious, but just as nice."

She leaned forward to place her cup on the coffee table and Holt watched her silky hair slide forward to drape against her cheek. He didn't have to be told the color was natural. The texture was too smooth and the shades too varied to be anything but what she'd been born with. Which made the pale color even more amazing.

He was fighting the urge to reach out and touch the strands when she suddenly took away the opportunity by straightening from the coffee table and settling back in her seat.

A pent-up breath rushed out of him and he quickly decided he needed to leave before he lost control and allowed himself to do something that might ruin their relationship.

Relationship, hell! What are you thinking, Holt? You don't have any kind of connection to this woman! And even if you did, what good would it do? The Holt Hollister you once were is gone. He's turned into some sort of mushy cream puff. Since when did you ever worry about pulling a woman into your arms and kissing her?

Since he'd met Isabelle, that's when, he silently shouted back at the cynical voice revolving around in his head.

Suddenly feeling trapped, he started to rise and cross to the fireplace. At the same time she chose that moment to shift around on the couch so that she was facing him and Holt stayed where he was.

She asked, "Have you ever had any serious horse injuries?"

Grateful for the momentary distraction, he scooped up the last of his pie and placed the small dessert plate onto the coffee table.

"If I start listing all my injuries, you're going to think I'd be lucky to ride a tricycle."

She laughed. "Not hardly. I've taken plenty of spills and bites and kicks. It just goes with the job."

He nodded. "I've had black eyes and a lost tooth. A broken ankle that required surgery to repair. A cracked wrist and ribs. Oh, yeah, and a dislocated shoulder. I've had a few concussions, too. Which my siblings say I've never fully recovered from."

"That's mean of them."

"They like to tease me."

Her gaze dropped away from his. "I do, too," she murmured. "I like how you're such a good sport about it."

His mocking conscience had been wrong, Holt thought ruefully. He wasn't even a cream puff anymore. She'd just turned him into a melted marshmallow.

"Is that all you like—about me?" he asked.

She looked up at him and Holt was fascinated with the way the corners of her lips tilted upward.

"I like that you laugh about certain things instead of whine and complain."

There she went again, touching a spot in him that he'd thought was long dead. "Dad always taught his sons that real men don't whine, they fix."

"Sounds like your father was a wise and fair man," she said.

"He was all that and more. It's no wonder that Mom—" He broke off, surprised that he'd been about to share more personal details about his family with her. He didn't do that with other women. Why did it just automatically seem to come out when he was with Isabelle? "Right now she's going through a rough patch emotionally."

"We all go through those." Her gaze slid earnestly over his face. "Are you worried about her?"

She wasn't just mouthing a question. She really cared, he thought. The idea pierced something deep inside his chest.

"No," he said, then shrugged. "Well, perhaps a little. But she's a trouper. Eventually she'll get smoothed out. I'm sure of that."

She nodded and Holt told himself it was beyond time for him to go home. Even if the evening was still early, he was asking for trouble to keep staying.

He was about to push himself up from the couch and announce he was leaving, but then he heard her sigh. The sound prompted him to look at her and all at once his intentions of fleeing were forgotten.

"The fire is so lovely," she murmured. "It's especially nice when it's quiet like this and you can hear the logs crackling."

What he found lovely was the way the glow of the flames was turning her smooth skin to a pale gold and lit her blue eyes with soft yellow lights.

"Do you ever get lonely here, Isabelle?"

Her head turned toward his and his heart skipped a beat as he watched her lips slowly spread into a smile.

"I'm not lonely now. You're here," she said simply.

Something in him snapped and before he could stop himself, he was sliding over to her and wrapping his hands over the tops of shoulders.

"Isabelle, I—" He paused unsure of what he wanted or needed to say.

When he failed to go on, she shook her head. "I thought you didn't want me—like this. Do you?"

The doubt in her voice was so opposite of the yearning inside him that he groaned with frustration. "You can't imagine how much I want you, Isabelle. How much I want to do this."

He didn't give her, or himself, time to think about anything. He lowered his head until their foreheads were touching and his lips were lightly brushing against hers. She tasted soft and sweet and as tantalizing as a hot drink on a frigid night.

"I've thought too much about you," she whispered. "About how much I wanted this to happen."

Her last words tore away the safety he'd tried to erect between them and the next thing he knew, his lips were moving over hers like a thirsty man who'd finally found an oasis.

This wasn't a kiss, he thought. It was a wild collision. A wreck of his senses.

After a few seconds, he recognized he was in deep trouble. He needed to put on the brakes and lever some space between them before he lost all control. But how was he supposed to stop something that felt so incredibly good? Why would he ever want to end this delicious connection? He'd never felt so thrilled, or had so many emotions humming through his veins.

Her arms slipped around his neck and then the front of her body was pressing tightly against his. Desire exploded in his head and shot a burning arrow straight to his loins.

The assault on his senses very nearly paralyzed him and even though he was silently shouting at himself to pull back, he did just the opposite and deepened the kiss.

It wasn't until she broke the contact of their lips and began to press tiny kisses along his jaw that a scrap of sanity hit his brain.

"Isabelle, this isn't good," he whispered, then groaned. "I mean—it is good—so good, but not the, uh, right thing for us."

That was enough to snap her head back and she stared at him in dazed wonder. "Oh. I—thought. I don't understand, Holt."

"Neither do I," he said gruffly, then quickly jumped to his feet before he had the chance to change his mind and pull her back into his arms. "I really like you, Isabelle. I like you too much for this. So I—have to leave. Now."

He turned and hurried out to the kitchen to collect his hat from the end of the cabinet. By the time he'd skewered it onto his head and reached the back door, Isabelle had caught up to him.

"You're leaving now?"

The confusion in her voice intensified his determination to keep a space of sanity between them.

"Yes. I'm sorry, Isabelle. But I—don't want to ruin things with us."

She marched over to where he stood with his hand already clutching the doorknob.

"Ruin things? How do you mean? You kissed me and realized you didn't like it? Well, all you have to do is tell me so, Holt. You don't have to hightail it out of here to avoid being tortured again!"

Tortured? Yes, that was the perfect word for it, Holt thought. But not in the way she'd meant.

Spurred by her ridiculous remark, he snatched a hold on her upper arm and tugged her forward. She stumbled awkwardly against him and Holt was quick to take advantage by once again latching his lips over hers.

This time the kiss was just as deep, but he managed to end it before it turned into something neither of them was ready for.

"Good night, Isabelle. And thanks for the dinner."

She didn't reply. Or if she did, Holt didn't stay around to hear it. He left the house and hurried to his truck before he lost the last shred of decency he possessed. Before she had a chance to see the real Holt Hollister. The one who gobbled up sweet little things like her and moved on to the next one.

Chapter 7

Two days later, Holt entered Blake's office, located at the north end of the main cattle barn. A few years ago, his older brother had worked out of the study where their father had always dealt with all the ranch's official business. But as Three Rivers had continued to grow, Blake and the rest of the family had agreed it would be best to have the flow of ranch clients away from the house.

With Holt's office still a cubbyhole that had once been a tack room, he often teased his older brother about having the fancy digs to work in, while he had to deal with barn dust and pack rats. But in truth, Blake deserved the comfortable office, along with a devoted secretary, who helped him carry the heavy load of managing Three Rivers Ranch.

"Good morning, Flo," he said to the older woman sitting behind a large cherry wood desk.

She peered at him over the tops of her bifocals and as Holt took in her short red hair and matching lipstick, he figured in her younger years she'd been a raving beauty. Now, toward the end of her sixties, she was sporting some wrinkles. But there was still a shrewd gleam in her brown eyes that told Holt she'd dealt with men like him before and had always come out the winner.

"Morning, Holt. You have work for me today?"

There were times when he got behind on his paperwork and Flo was always charitable enough to do it for him.

"No. I'll need some registrations done on the new babies soon, but that can wait. I need to talk with Blake for a few minutes."

She jerked her thumb toward the closed door to Blake's portion of the office. "He's in there and your mother is with him."

"Good. I'll hit her up to give you a raise. You deserve one for putting up with Blake, don't you?"

"Ha!" She snorted. "I deserve a huge one for putting up with you."

Laughing, he patted the secretary's cheek before he crossed the room and entered Blake's office.

"What's going on in here? A family powwow?" He walked over to where his mother was standing at the window and smacked a kiss on her cheek. "Hi, Mom. You look beautiful this morning."

She wrapped her arm around his waist and gave him a little hug. "Okay, what are you wanting? Blake has already told you we're not getting an equine pool. At least, not yet."

"I'm not worried about a pool. But just think what a great tax write-off it would be," he said, slanting a pointed look at Blake, who was sitting casually at his desk. "Probably save the ranch a few thousand."

"We need another well drilled if we're going to turn that range over by Juniper Ridge into a hay meadow. And you know that isn't going to come cheap."

"Maybe we ought to just get more hay shipped in," Holt suggested. "The Timothy/alfalfa mix we get from Nevada is great."

"And very expensive." Maureen spoke up. "We have the climate and the machinery to grow and bale our own. All we need is water and it isn't going to fall from the sky, unfortunately."

"Sometimes it does. If you'd open those blinds and look outside right now, you might see otherwise," Holt told her.

She peeked through the slatted blinds and gasped. "It is raining! Oh, and I left my horse hitched in the arena and he's wearing my favorite saddle! I'd better run!"

Maureen raced out of the office and Holt walked over and sank into the chair in front of Blake's desk. "The rain started about ten minutes ago. Mom's saddle is probably already soaked."

"Some of the hands will oil it for her," Blake said, then leaning back in his chair, he crossed his arms over his chest and looked at Holt. "What are you up to this morning? I thought you needed to go into town for something."

Holt shook his head. "I decided that could wait. I

wanted to talk to you about the horse sale coming up this weekend at Tucson."

"I wasn't aware there was one. Why? Are you planning on going?"

"It's been on my mind. There's about six head in the catalog that interest me. And I'd like to replace those five mares I sold to Isabelle."

"Fine with me," Blake told him. "You know you don't have to ask me before you spend Three Rivers' money."

Holt chuckled. "Until it comes to an equine pool."

Blake groaned. "You're never going to hush about that, are you?"

"Probably not. I can always use it to irritate you."

A sly grin crossed Blake's face. "Speaking of Isabelle, I haven't had a chance to talk to you about this, but Matthew tells me that you sent Ollie and Sol over to Isabelle's ranch to work for her."

"That's right. I figured it would be easier for us to find day workers than it would be for Isabelle. She only knows a handful of people around here. And that ranch of hers is so isolated I didn't want riffraff out there with her."

Blake shrugged. "Well, I don't have any beef about them working for her. But they're still on the payroll here at Three Rivers and—"

"Uh, I'd like for you to keep it that way, Blake. I promised the men they'd keep getting their Three Rivers' paycheck—because Isabelle can only afford part-time help right now."

Blake leaned forward and stared at his brother. "I'm not sure I got this straight," he said. "Ollie and Sol are working for Isabelle, but we're paying them? And she went along with it?"

Grimacing, Holt shook his head. "Isabelle knows nothing about this setup, Blake. And I don't want her to know. She'd have a fit and send the men packing."

"I don't get this—or you, Holt! I—"

"Don't get all het up about this, Blake. Just take the amount of their pay out of my monthly salary. I'll never miss it."

Blake's mouth fell open and he studied Holt for long moments before he finally let out a heavy sigh of surrender. "Okay. Whatever you do with your money is none of my business. But—"

"But what? Go ahead and say it, brother," Holt muttered in a sardonic voice. "You think I've lost my mind or worse."

"What could be worse than losing your mind?" Blake shot the question at him.

Falling in love, Holt thought. But he wasn't doing that. No. Not by a long shot. He simply wanted Isabelle to be protected. He wanted someone there to help her. He wanted her to achieve her dreams and not be hurt along the way. That's all there was to it.

"Well, getting tangled up with a woman."

Blake's brows arched upward. "Are you getting tangled up with Isabelle?" he asked, then with a shake of his head, he rose to his feet and crossed the room to where a utility table was loaded with a coffee machine and all kinds of snacks. As he poured himself a cup of coffee, he went on, "Don't bother to answer that, Holt. You've already told me that you're more than tangled."

"I have? How so? Just because I sent Ollie and Sol over to help her?" Holt snorted. "Can't a man help a woman out without sex or love or anything like that being involved?"

"With you, Holt, we can safely rule out the love. But the sex is another matter and I—"

Annoyed that Blake was assuming he'd already been sleeping in Isabelle's bed, he barked back at him, "You what? I really don't have time for a lecture on women this morning, Blake. Besides, who are you to give me advice about women? You were lucky enough to literally run into your wife on the sidewalk. You didn't have to date dozens and dozens of women to find Katherine. You didn't have to wonder if she was marrying you for the Hollister money, or just because she liked having sex with you!"

Blake coughed loudly. "You're taking my concern all wrong, brother. I don't want you to get hurt, that's all."

"Since when has a woman ever hurt me?" Holt countered with the question. "Not once. And it's not going to happen this time. I'm just trying to help Isabelle. She's a fellow horse trainer and I admire her ambition and courage. I like her. That's all."

Blake rolled his eyes toward the ceiling, then looked at Holt and grunted with amusement. "You like her enough to pay her ranch hands' wages. I'd hate to see what you'd spend on her if you really loved her."

If he really loved her. Holt didn't know about love. Other than the kind he felt for his mother and siblings. He wasn't sure he'd recognize the emotion if it whammed him in the face.

"Don't worry, Blake, I'm not going to make the foolish mistake of falling in love with Isabelle. Be pretty hard to do anyway, for a man without a heart."

"Who says you don't have a heart?"

Holt wiped a hand over his face in an effort to swipe away the image of Isabelle's face when he'd left her house two nights ago. She'd looked angry, hurt, and shocked all at once. He figured right about now she'd be the first one to say he was a heartless man.

To answer Blake's question, he made a point of looking at his watch. "I'm not sure I have enough time to go down the list."

Blake shook his head and walked over to the window to peer out at the rain.

"So what was Mom doing in here?" Holt asked. "Didn't you talk to her at breakfast?"

"No. I missed breakfast. Kat needed help with the twins while she was getting ready for work." He pulled the cord to the blinds until the large window was uncovered. "Mom stopped by to discuss the cost of replacing a bull down at Red Bluff. He's getting too old to service the cows, but you know Mom. She doesn't want to sell him. He's going to be put out to pasture for the rest of his life."

"Oh. I thought she might've mentioned her trip to Phoenix the other day. Or Dad's case."

Blake glanced over his shoulder at Holt. "She didn't mention the trip. And you know good and well that she stopped talking about dad's case a long time ago. And I have no intention of bringing up the subject."

"I'm worried about her."

Blake shrugged, then walked over to his desk and eased a hip onto one corner. "I'm trying not to be. Whatever is going on in Mom's head will straighten itself out eventually. Our mother is a wise woman, Holt. We have to trust the choices she makes."

Holt wasn't too good at trusting. Especially when it involved women.

"What about Joe?" Holt asked. "Is he going out searching this week?"

At least one day a week, their brother Joseph came over to the ranch to ride the area where they believed their father had initially met his demise. Usually Blake rode with him, but sometimes Holt went instead. So far they'd found several pieces of evidence. Joel's spur rowel, a silver belt tip, and a small tattered piece of the shirt he'd been wearing that fateful day.

"He'll be over this afternoon. This rain won't last more than ten minutes anyway."

"Do you want me to ride with him this time?" Holt offered. "I can spare a few hours. And I only have about five two-year-olds to ride today."

Blake shook his head. "Thanks, Holt. But I'll go. Flo will take care of things here. And it gives me a chance to get on the back of a horse. I kinda get tired of being in an executive chair for most of the day."

Holt rose from the chair and started to the door. "I'd hate to think I had to trade that chair for a saddle."

Blake said, "Holt, about the sale, buy as many horses as you want. I trust your judgment completely."

Blake trusted his judgment with horses, just not with women, Holt thought wryly. Well, that hardly mattered. One of these days, his family was finally going to accept that he wasn't cut out to be a family man.

"Thanks, Blake. I'll keep the buying within reason. Good luck this afternoon on the search. Maybe this time you'll unearth something definitive."

"I pray you're right, little brother."

* * *

That afternoon on Blue Stallion Ranch, Isabelle picked up a lame gelding's front foot and used the handle of the hoof pick to gently peck on the sole. When the animal flinched on a certain spot, she examined it closer but failed to see anything out of the ordinary.

"This seems to be the area that's bothering her," she said as Ollie and Sol peered closely over her shoulder. "What does it look like to you guys?"

Ollie was the first to answer. "Don't see a thing, Isabelle."

"Could be a stone bruise," Sol added his thoughts on the matter.

"Can I be of help?"

The sound of Holt's voice momentarily stunned her. She'd not seen or heard from him since the other night when he'd hightailed it off the ranch like a demon was after him.

Slowly, she lowered the horse's foot back to the stall floor, while the men turned to greet their visitor.

"Hello, Holt," Ollie said. "You couldn't have shown up at a better time."

"Yeah, Isabelle's gelding is lame," Sol added. "Maybe you can figure out the problem."

Isabelle cleared her throat. "Holt isn't the vet at Three Rivers, his brother Chandler is. I'll load the horse in the trailer and take him to the Hollister Animal Hospital," she told the two men.

Holt entered the stall and shouldered his way between Ollie and Sol to stand next to Isabelle. She forced herself to look up at him and as soon as her gaze clashed with, her heart lurched into a rapid thud. Every moment of the past two days had been haunted by the memory of his kiss and how incredible it had felt to be in his arms. Now, she could only wonder how long he'd be here before the urge to run hit him again.

"Let me take a look first," Holt suggested. "I might be able to figure out the problem."

A part of her wanted to tell him to get lost, while the other part was jumping for joy at the sight of him. Dear Lord, the man had turned her into a bundle of contradictions.

"If you don't mind," she said. "Any help is appreciated."

She stepped to one side to give him room to work. Behind her, Ollie and Sol moved backward until they were both resting their shoulders against the wall of the stall.

"Did this come on the horse all of a sudden or did it start out barely noticeable and progress into a full-blown limp?" he asked.

"I'm not sure," she told him. "The last day I rode him, which was three days ago, he was fine. Then I turned him out to pasture with a few of the mares. When I got him up today to ride him, he could barely walk."

"Hmm. So you've not ridden him in the past few days?"

"No. And he's never had laminitis or arthritis or anything like that."

Holt picked up the gelding's foot and began to put pressure on the outside wall of the hoof. When he hit a certain spot, the horse tried to jerk away from Holt's tight grip.

"It's okay, boy. You're going to be all right." He lowered the animal's foot back to the floor and gently stroked his neck before he turned to Isabelle. "Like you said, I'm not a vet, but Chandler will tell you that I can doctor horses. This one is developing an abscess. Either a small foreign particle has entered his foot through the sole or it's been bruised or injured by striking it against something hard."

"So what happens now? Do I need to take him into your brother's clinic for treatment?"

"Maybe not. You might be able to treat him yourself. Do you have any soaking salts?"

"Yes."

"What about oral painkiller for horses?"

She nodded. "I always keep it on supply."

"Great," he said. "We'll start out by giving him a dose of painkiller and then his foot needs to be soaked for at least twenty minutes twice a day. Eventually, a spot near the hairline will burst open. But don't worry. That's a good thing. It relieves the pressure of the abscess and whatever is inside will run out."

Wanting to believe it was that simple of a problem, but still doubting, she asked, "You really think that's what it is?"

"I'd bet every dollar I own," he told her, then gave her a reassuring wink. "I have a supply of antibiotics in the truck you can give him to help with the infection. In a few days, he'll be fine."

"Don't worry, Isabelle." Ollie spoke up. "Holt knows what he's doing. He's an expert on horses."

"You stay here with Holt," Sol added. "We'll go fetch everything from the tack room."

The two men left to gather what was needed to treat the horse and Isabelle took a cautious step back from Holt.

"I think I'll go help Ollie and Sol," she said. "They might not be able to find the phenylbutazone."

She started to leave the stall, but he quickly reached out and caught her by the forearm. "Wait, Isabelle. I want to talk to you before the men return."

Her nostrils flared as she looked down at the strong fingers encircling her arm. "Look, I'm grateful for your help with my horse, Holt. But I'm not sure I want to talk with you about anything personal. That's over! Not that it ever started," she said in a brittle voice.

His fingers eased on her arm and Isabelle forced herself to lift her gaze up to his. The dark, bewildered look in his green eyes confused her.

He said, "I thought by now that you'd be wanting to thank me for leaving when I did."

"What is that supposed to mean?" she asked flatly.

He made a sound of frustration as he stepped closer. Isabelle told herself she really should pull away from him and run to the tack room and the safety of Ollie's and Sol's company. But something about Holt mesmerized her and chipped away the anger and hurt she'd been carrying around with her the past two days.

"It means that whatever was happening between us was getting out of hand—really fast. I wanted you to have time to take a breath and think about me and you. I wanted to give myself time to think about what was happening."

His voice was like the low, soft purr of a cat and the sound slowly and surely lured her to him. Closing her eyes, she rested her palms against his chest. "You're right. It was a quick explosion. But I—wished you had stayed long enough to explain. Running off like that was—not good."

His hands gently wrapped around her upper arms. "I'm sorry, Isabelle. I realize it probably made me look like a jackass. But if I'd stayed a second longer, I couldn't have stopped kissing you or—anything else. Don't you understand? For once in my life, I was trying to be a gentleman."

How could she stay annoyed with him when the simple touch of his hands was melting every cell inside of her? She couldn't. No more than she could resist the urge to be near him.

"I didn't know that, Holt. And why has it taken you this long to explain?"

His expression rueful, he shook his head. "Saying I'm sorry doesn't come easy for me, Isabelle. And when I do apologize, it never comes out sounding right. If you want the truth, I had to work up my courage to come over here."

Suddenly tears were stinging the backs of her eyes and she turned her back to him and swallowed hard. Something about his words and the way he'd said them had struck her in a deep, vulnerable spot.

She sniffed and said, "If you want the truth, I'm glad you're here. I just—"

"You felt like you needed to take me to task a bit," he finished for her. "I understand. I don't blame you."

Smiling now, she turned to face him. "It doesn't matter. I forgive you. And hopefully you've forgiven me."

Surprise arched his brows. "For what?"

Her cheeks felt as though they were flaming. "For acting like that kiss of ours was—something more than just a pleasant, physical connection."

His green gaze made a slow survey of her face. "Is that what you think it was? Just a physical reaction?"

Actually, Isabelle still wasn't sure what had happened between them or how they'd gone from a simple kiss to an explosion of passion. To her, it had been like nothing she'd ever experienced with any man. But she'd never admit such a thing to him.

Making love to a woman was second nature to Holt. He knew exactly how to make her feel special. Even loved. Isabelle wasn't going to be so stupid as to think Holt could ever have a serious thought about her. With him, everything was physical and that's all she was going to allow herself to feel about him.

"I'm positive it was," she answered.

He let out a long breath and Isabelle figured it was a sign of great relief.

"I see," he said. "Well, that's good. Because neither of us want strings between us."

Foolish pain squeezed the middle of her chest, but she smiled in spite of it. "No. No strings. I believe we can enjoy each other's company without any of those, don't you?"

Surprise, or something like it, flickered in his eyes and then he smiled back at her. "Absolutely."

There, she thought. She'd fixed everything. He believed that kiss had meant nothing more to her than a few moments of physical pleasure. Now, all she had to do was convince herself.

A half hour later, with the gelding treated and turned out to a small lot near the barn, Holt and Isabelle stood outside the fence observing the horse as he walked gingerly toward a hay manger.

The rain had cleared and bright sunshine was warming the muddy ground around the ranch yard. It was turning into a beautiful day, Holt thought. Especially now that Isabelle was smiling at him again.

She asked, "Would you like to walk to the house and have a cup of coffee? I'd offer you what was left of the blueberry pie, but I gave it to Ollie and Sol. I do have brownies, though. That's the least I can do for your vet services."

He put a finger to his lips and made a shushing noise. "Don't say that out loud. Chandler will have my hide for practicing without a license."

Isabelle laughed. "I'm sure," she said drolly. "He's probably grateful for the help."

"He does have too much to do," Holt agreed. "And I do, too. As much as I'd like the coffee, I'd better head on back to town. I actually need to stop by the clinic and pick up a few things we need at the ranch."

She rested her back against the board fence and jammed her hands in the pockets of her brown work jacket. In dress clothes, she looked like a glamour girl, yet she'd chosen a very unglamorous job for herself. She was such a paradox and he had to admit that everything about the woman fascinated him.

"You know, I do have a cell phone," she said. "You could've called to apologize."

There was an impish curve to her lips that made Holt want to snatch her into his arms and kiss her. But now was hardly the time when Ollie or Sol could walk up on them at any moment.

"I thought you said you were glad I came."

"I am," she replied. "I'm just wondering why you took the time to drive all the way out here."

He casually rested one shoulder next to hers. "It's always better to be face-to-face when you tell someone you're sorry for being a jerk. But I also have something else on my mind to talk to you about."

Her blue eyes widened a fraction, but she didn't bother to look at him. Instead she kept her gaze on the open land stretching away from the barn area. He wondered if that far-off look had anything to do with him or if she was simply thinking about this ranch and all that she wanted it to be.

Blue Stallion Ranch. She hadn't found her blue stallion yet, but she was already building her dream around him, he thought. Holt hadn't forgotten how she'd practically begged him to sell his roan colt, Blue Midnight, to her. Nor had he forgotten the instant bond she'd made with the stallion. If it had been any colt but that one, he would have been more than happy to sell to her. But his future was wrapped around that horse. He couldn't give him up just to make Isabelle happy.

"What is it you wanted to talk to me about?" she asked, breaking into his thoughts. "You want me to cook for you again?"

He laughed. "No. I wanted to invite you to take a trip with me. There's a horse sale going on at Tucson this coming Saturday. The horses are all registered and cataloged. I thought you might enjoy it. You might even want to purchase something."

That turned her head in his direction and she pondered his face for long moments before she finally replied, "I would enjoy it. Does it take very long to drive down there?"

"From Wickenburg, it takes about three hours or

a little over. But it's a nice drive and if you've never seen the Tucson area, it's very pretty."

"I've not been to that part of the state before. I'd love to see it. And I suppose I could take my checkbook. Just in case I saw a horse I like. Who knows, I might even find that blue stallion I want," she added with a clever smile.

"Did you ever see a horse you didn't like?" he teased.

She laughed. "I think you're beginning to know me, Holt."

And he was beginning to like her more and more, he thought. Asking her to join him on the trip to Tucson was like inviting trouble to walk right up and sock him in the jaw. But he'd never been one to take the safe route. Not even where a woman was concerned.

"So can I plan on you going?"

"Sure. How could I possibly refuse a day of horses and—you?"

Holt wasn't sure whether she was being serious or sardonic. Either way, it didn't matter. The playful twinkle in her blue eyes was enough for him.

"Great. The sale starts at ten so I thought we might meet at Chandler's clinic around six and leave from there. That way we'll have about an hour to look over the horses before the auction begins."

She pushed away from the fence. "I'll be there."

"See you then." Smiling, he bent and placed a swift kiss on her cheek.

"Saturday. Six o'clock. Don't leave without me," she said.

Feeling like he'd just stepped onto a cloud, Holt laughed and started the short walk to his truck. "Not a chance," he called back to her.

Chapter 8

That night, after a long shower and a plate of leftovers, Isabelle carried her phone and a cup of coffee to the couch in the living room and punched her mother's number.

Gabby didn't answer and Isabelle hung up, thinking she'd probably already gone to bed for the night. But after a couple of minutes, the phone rang with her mother's returning call.

"Did I wake you?" Isabelle asked. "I didn't realize it was getting so late."

"You didn't wake me. I just got back in the apartment. I was over at the Green Garden going over some things with Carl about the showing."

"How's that working out? Is everything still on go?"

"Yes! I'm really getting revved up about this, Issy. I'm thinking this might give me a giant step forward."

Isabelle felt a pang of guilt, but only a small one. "Well, the showing is what I'm calling about. I was planning on flying down this weekend, but I've had something else come up."

Her mother paused, then groaned. "All at once, you've managed to make me happy and sad. I'm thrilled that you were coming and sad that you aren't. I hope that whatever has come up is important."

Isabelle had to be honest. "I don't know about being important, but it's something I want to do. I'm going to a horse sale down at Tucson—with a friend."

"A friend? Male or female?"

Isabelle drew her legs up beneath her while wondering what her mother would think about Holt if she actually met him. That her daughter was playing with fire? She wouldn't be wrong, Isabelle thought.

"A man. The rancher I went to dinner with. The one who sold the mares to me. Remember?"

"Yes. I remember. I think you said his name was Holt something or other."

"Hollister. They own half this county and more."

Gabby was slow to reply and when she did Isabelle noticed a thread of concern in her voice. "Issy, I've been praying you'd find someone else. But I honestly can't say I'm getting good vibes about you seeing this man. Trevor had too much money and it sounds like this one does, too. Don't you think you'd be happier if you found a poor ole Joe? One that would focus on you instead of padding his bank account?"

"I don't think Holt's that way about making money. Yes, when it comes to his horses, he's a workaholic. But I don't think wealth is all that important to him.

And anyway, I'm not getting serious about him, Mom. He's just a man that I enjoy being with."

"That's the worst kind. You get to enjoying it so much you never want to be without him."

Isabelle wasn't going to let herself get that attached to Holt Hollister. When she did finally open her heart and allow a man to step inside, it was going to be one who was yearning for the same things that she was longing for. A home and children together. Their old age spent together.

"That isn't going to happen, Mom. He's not the serious type. And after what I went through with Trevor, that's just the kind I need right now."

There was another long pause from her mother and then she said, "Okay, you're a grown woman and I'm not going to try to run your love life. I am curious about one thing, though. You said you were planning on flying down—what about the horses? Have you finally hired some ranch hands?"

Isabelle told her all about Ollie and Sol and what a great help they'd been to her, then ended with describing the bunkroom she'd helped them construct in the barn.

"Oh, so the men are staying on the ranch full time. That's great, honey. I can stop worrying about you living out there alone now."

I won't be worrying about you so much.

Holt's comment had taken Isabelle by complete surprise. It had almost made him sound like he cared about her.

Don't start going there, Isabelle. Holt only cares about himself and his family. And you're not a part of the Hollister family. You never will be.

"Isabelle? Are you still there?"

Her mother's question pushed away the warring voices in Isabelle's head. "Yes, Mom. I'm here. I was just thinking—you never mentioned that you worried about me."

"You've had enough to deal with these past few months without listening to a whiny mother. But sometimes I—wish you would've decided to stay here with me in San Diego. It would've been a cinch for you to have gotten your old job back with the energy company. You made a humongous salary there. And the stables where you boarded your horses weren't all that expensive. You had a nice life here until—"

For some reason, Isabelle looked over at the cushion where Holt had sat next to her. Just having him here with her in front of the warm fire, listening to his voice, and watching the subtle expressions play across his face had been so nice and special. Then when he'd reached for her, she'd been shocked and thrilled. In a matter of moments, she'd wanted to take him by the hand and lead him straight to her bed.

Shaking her head, she tried to focus on her mother's remarks. "Until I met Trevor. Isn't that what you were going to say?"

"Yes, but—forget I said any of that. It's just that I miss you."

"I made a foolish choice when I married Trevor. But as for me ever moving back to San Diego—that isn't going to happen. I love my ranch, my land. Someday it's going to be the home I always wanted."

"Complete with horses and children," Gabby said, her voice tender. "That's really all I want for you, honey, to be happy and loved by a man. God knows your father never really loved me. Not as much as he did his piano. But that's okay. He gave me you. And that's a priceless gift."

A lump of emotion was suddenly burning Isabelle's throat. "Oh, Mom, you're making me cry. I'm hanging up—I'll call you later."

"Good night, Issy. And have a nice time with your rancher."

Isabelle ended the call, then left the couch and walked over to the picture window. From this angle, she could see a portion of the main barn and a light burning in the small window of Ollie and Sol's bunkroom.

Knowing the men were there was a comfort to her. Yet they couldn't fill up the emptiness in the house or in her heart.

To be happy and loved by a man, that's what her mother wished for her. And that was all Isabelle had ever really wanted. Not money or travels or a glamorous social life. Just a loving, caring man at her side. But would she ever find that man?

Not with Holt, she thought sadly.

But that didn't mean she couldn't enjoy his company. And that was exactly what she intended to do.

At half past eleven that night, Holt was still in the foaling barn, carefully watching the newly born filly wobble to her feet and begin to nose her mother's flank. Eventually, she found one of the warm teats and he smiled with satisfaction as the baby latched on and began to nurse hungrily.

He was still watching the pair when Chandler's voice suddenly broke the quietness of the barn. "I ran into T.J. heading to the bunkhouse. He told me you were in here."

Holt glanced over his shoulder to see his brother entering the large stall. "What the hell are you doing down here at this hour? You should be in bed with Roslyn," he scolded.

Shaking his head, Chandler came to stand next to him. "I couldn't sleep. I didn't want my tossing to disturb Roslyn and I was a little concerned that you might need me to help with the mare. You've been out here at the barn too long."

"The mare seemed to make it okay. But from my records, I think she's delivered a bit early. Maybe that's a good thing, though. Look how big the foal is. Mama might have had real trouble if she'd carried it any longer."

Chandler carefully moved closer to the bay mare and matching filly. "The baby looks good and strong, Holt. No matter about the due dates. Mother Nature always knows best. Since I'm here anyway, do you want me to check them over? Just to make sure?"

"I'd feel better if you would," Holt told him.

Chandler approached the new mother and daughter and went to work examining both. Once he was satisfied with his findings, he folded the stethoscope he'd carried with him and jammed it back into the pocket on his jacket.

"Both of them are fit as fiddles," he pronounced.

Holt slapped a hand on Chandler's broad shoulder. "Thanks, brother. Now get back to the house and go to bed."

"I'm not ready for bed."

"Hell, it's almost midnight. And you have a busy

day tomorrow." Holt took a second look at his brother's taut features and decided there had to be more to his showing up here at the foaling barn at such a late hour. "Okay, what's wrong?"

Chandler patted the mare's neck, then moved to the opposite side of the stall. "Nothing is wrong. Well, not exactly," he mumbled. "Hell, I'm not sure what I'm feeling right now."

"There's a crease in the middle of your forehead as a big as the Grand Canyon." Holt gestured to the stall door. "Let's go to my office. I think there's some coffee still on the hot plate. You can tell me what's on your mind."

Chandler nodded. "I'll pass on your syrupy coffee, but there is something we need to talk about."

The two brothers left the foaling barn and entered the end of the main horse barn where Holt's office was located. After both men were seated and Holt was nursing a cup of the strong coffee, Chandler closed his eyes and passed a hand over his forehead.

"Man, you must really be down about something," Holt commented as he carefully studied his brother's miserable expression. "Are you and Roslyn having problems? Has her father been making waves?"

"No. It's nothing about Roslyn. And miracle of miracles, Martin seems to be getting softer as time goes by. He's already talking about coming out for another visit this spring."

Holt let out a humorous snort. "Maybe you'd better prescribe yourself some horse calmer before he arrives."

Chandler grunted. "My father-in-law won't give me any problems. Anyway, it's the Hollister family that's worrying me now. Joseph just left the house a few minutes ago."

Totally puzzled, Holt leaned forward. "Joe went home earlier this afternoon—after he and Blake got back from their ride. I heard Joe say they didn't find anything. He came back over here tonight? For what?"

Chandler pulled off his hat and raked both hands through his hair. Since he rarely showed signs of stress, his unusual behavior was making Holt uneasy.

"When Joe got back to the Bar X, he found Tessa in one of her cleaning moods and asked him to carry some boxes down from the attic. She's slowly been trying to sift through all the things that Ray had stored up there before he died."

"So what happened?"

Chandler clapped his hat back on his head. "The two of them were digging through some old papers and correspondence and happened to run into a note-book filled with logs about Dad's case."

Holt's jaw dropped. "Seriously? This sounds too far out to be real, Chandler."

"I can assure you it is real. Joe brought the notebook over and showed it to me and Blake."

"Hell, I leave the house for three hours and all of this happens," Holt muttered. "So what did it say? We've been hoping and praying for a break in uncovering the truth. Is there anything in there that's going to help?"

Chandler shook his head again. "We don't know. Maybe. One thing is for sure, if the evidence gets out, it's going to cause a hell of a storm."

Stunned, Holt stared at him. As sheriff of Yavapai County, Ray Maddox had ruled, for lack of evidence,

Joel's death an accident. But their old friend had never actually quit investigating the incident.

"Evidence? I thought we had everything Ray had gathered."

"I shouldn't have called it evidence. It's not that exactly," Chandler told him. "It's more like a break that might lead to solving the case. Ray kept some things to himself."

"Why would he do such a thing? Ray and Dad were like brothers. He wanted to expose the truth about Dad's death just as much as we do."

Chandler heaved out a long breath. "We suppose he hid the info because he couldn't connect it with anything. And given the nature of it, he probably figured it would cause more harm than good. But damn it, he should have told us. Mom didn't have to know then. And she sure as hell isn't going to know now. Not unless we put two and two together and come up with a feasible explanation."

"I'm in the dark here, Chandler. Maybe you'd better tell me exactly what you found in these notes of Ray's."

Chandler glanced away from Holt and swallowed as though he was trying to get down a handful of roofing nails. "From Ray's notes, he believed that Dad was meeting a woman on a regular basis at the stockyards in Phoenix."

Holt couldn't have felt more dazed if the ceiling of the barn had crashed in on his head. "What?"

"That's right. The same finding was entered several times in the notebook. More than once, Joel had been observed in the company of a blond woman. Petite in build and about the same age as him. Whoever gave Ray this information must not have known the status of their relationship, because Ray didn't mention any of that. Ray scribbled down a list of dates with the word *Phoenix* written out to the side. One of the dates was a day after Dad's death."

Holt's mind was racing with a thousand questions and just as many possible answers. "The stockyards. A day after Dad's death," he mused out loud. "Chandler, a year or so ago, Mom found that old agenda book of Dad's. There's a note in it, saying he was to meet a man at the stockyards on that day. Joe researched the man's name and learned the name was phony. Maybe it wasn't a man Dad was planning on meeting that day, but rather the blond woman?"

"It's possible. But why would Dad have been so deceitful about it? Why would he put down a man's name if it had been a woman he was meeting? Mother never was the jealous kind. If he'd been meeting a woman for a business lunch or something of that sort, she wouldn't have cared."

Holt felt sick inside, then immediately felt guilty for even doubting his father's fidelity for one minute. "I don't know what you and Joe and Blake think. But as far as I'm concerned, I don't believe there was any sort of romantic involvement between Dad and this woman. Yes, he probably was seeing her and what that reason might have been is a big question mark. But he wasn't cheating on Mom. Dad wasn't made like that. He was an honorable man. A family man. And he loved Mom more than anything on this earth. Even more than Three Rivers and that's saying a lot."

Chandler blew out another heavy breath. "Yeah, that's what I think, too. I'm not sure what Blake thinks. You know how he is, he keeps most of his thoughts to himself. The important ones, at least. Joe is different, he sees things as a lawman. He weighs the evidence in an analytical way. And during his tenure as a deputy, Joe has witnessed some shocking things. I don't think he'd be that surprised to discover our father had been having an affair. After all, think how stunned everyone was when we learned that Ray was really Tessa's father."

Holt swigged down a mouthful of the gritty coffee. "That's true. But Ray's wife was wheelchair bound. They had no children. That was no excuse for him having an affair, but I can kind of see why it happened. But Dad had a beautiful, vibrant wife with six children. He had no reason to have an affair."

Chandler eyed him for several pointed moments. "I'm surprised to hear you say that. You love women. I thought you didn't have to have a reason to have an affair. Other than lust."

"Damn it, Chandler, that's a low, low blow."

"Oh, come off it, Holt. Righteousness doesn't fit you."

"Thanks. Being noble was never my goal in life," he said sarcastically. "Just give me faster horses and more women and I'll die a happy man."

He tossed the remainder of his coffee into a trash basket and replaced the glass cup next to the coffee maker.

Behind him, Chandler groaned. "Okay, that was a low blow. I'm sorry."

"Forget it. I can admit that I'll never be like my brothers. I'm not cut out for it, Chandler. But that doesn't mean I'm a tomcat with no feelings or discretion." He wiped a hand over his face as Isabelle's image tried to push itself to the front of his brain. "Oh, God, brother, what if we're wrong about Dad? What if he was cheating on our mother and an enraged husband or boyfriend killed him? Mom would be—well, I don't want to think of what that might do to her."

Chandler looked resolute. "Listen, none of us are going to breathe a word of this to Mom. She's already been having too many melancholy moods. This might send her into a tailspin."

"What does Joe intend to do with this bit of information?" Holt asked. "You suggested it might be a break in the case. But how? It's been years since Dad died. It would be miraculous if anyone remembers anything."

"Joe is going to keep asking questions. He believes he'll eventually find a cattle buyer or worker at the stockyards who might remember something about Dad and the woman."

Holt's stomach gave another sickening lurch. "I understand now why Mom doesn't want to search for the cause or reason of Dad's death. The truth might make everything worse."

His expression grim, Chandler rose to his feet. "If we find that Dad was living a secret life, we're going to bury the facts. No one will know except us four brothers."

Holt couldn't believe Chandler was even considering the possibility that Ray's speculations could be true, much less that they should hide the truth from their sisters. "And not tell Viv and Camille? Chandler, your thinking is all mixed up!"

"If I'm confused, then so are Blake and Joe, because they think the same thing. Viv and Camille adored

Dad. He was their hero. Nothing good would come from crushing their ideals and memories."

Their father had been Holt's hero, too. He'd gotten his love of horses from Joel and his ability to laugh at the challenges that training them presented. Had he also inherited a straying eye for the ladies from his father?

No! Until Holt's dying day, he'd always believe Joel Hollister was a true husband and father.

Isabelle gazed out the passenger window of Holt's truck at the desert hills covered with tall saguaros and areas of thick chaparral and slab rock. In the past few minutes, the sun had dipped behind a ridge of mountains to the west and shadows were painting the rugged landscape. It was a lovely sight, she thought. A fitting close to the beautiful day she'd spent in Holt's company.

"Are you sure you didn't mind leaving the auction early?"

Holt's question broke into her pleasant thoughts and she glanced over to where he sat behind the steering wheel, driving them toward Wickenburg. Throughout the day, he'd never left her side and during all that time, their hands had brushed, their shoulders rubbed. The touches had been incidental, but to Isabelle they'd felt like the sizzling contact of a branding iron.

Now, with each passing minute, she felt a connection growing between them. Whether the link was emotional, sexual, or something in between, she couldn't determine. And she wasn't going to ruin the remainder of their trip trying to figure it out.

"I didn't mind at all. Each of us already purchased

two mares," she said pointedly, then chuckled. "And leaving when we did probably saved me a few thousand dollars. I would've probably gotten into a bidding war for that buckskin colt that caught my eye."

"Just about every horse at the auction caught your eye," he said.

"I'm guilty. I confess. Mom always said I never saw a horse I didn't love."

"I'm curious about your mother," he replied. "Where did she get her knowledge about horses?"

"From her parents—my grandparents. They owned a small ranch near Bishop and Granddad was an excellent horseman."

"Are your grandparents still living?"

"No. Granddad died from complications of diabetes. When he passed, Grandmother was still in fairly good shape, but losing him took a toll on her. They'd been married for more than fifty-five years and she wasn't the same with Granddad gone. She died about a year after he did." She glanced at him. "What about your grandparents, Holt? I don't think I've heard you mention them."

He shook his head. "Both sets are gone now. My Hollister grandparents lived and worked on the ranch all their lives. They both died of different ailments when I was in elementary school. My mom's parents lived in another state and we didn't see them very often. Her father passed away from a stroke and her mother died from a car accident. It was just a little fender bender, but she wasn't wearing her seat belt and her head hit the windshield." He reached over and slipped a forefinger beneath her belt and gave it a tug.

"That's why I want you to promise me that you'll always buckle up."

Did he really care about her safety that much? No. She couldn't let herself go down that path. No serious strings. No thinking about love or the future, she scolded herself.

She forced a little laugh past her throat. "I promise. But we don't have safety belts on our saddles."

"No, we just have to hang on tighter." The grin on his face disappeared as he slanted her another glance. "I'm sorry you didn't find a blue stallion for your ranch, Isabelle. I was hoping you would."

He honestly seemed to care about her dreams and wishes. Something that Trevor never bothered to do. Oh, he'd wanted her to be happy, but he was never interested in the things that were most important to her. He'd thought handing her a check to a limitless bank account was enough to make up for his indifference. Maybe that should have been enough for her, but it hadn't been. She'd felt like an afterthought, something to be petted and admired and placed back on a shelf.

"That's okay," she told him. "Blue roans are not that plentiful. That's one of the reasons why they're so sought after and expensive. The two that we watched go through the ring weren't that great. I'll find my stallion someday."

"There's always a chance Blue Midnight will throw some nice colts. I won't forget I promised you a shot to buy one."

She smiled at him. "That's a long time off, but I'll hold you to your promise."

He didn't reply and for the next few miles Isabelle could see he was deep in thought about something.

Was it her, the horses, or something too personal to share with her? Was he thinking about some other woman he'd rather be with? No. If he wanted to be with some other woman, he wouldn't have invited Isabelle to join him today. At least she could take comfort in that.

Minutes later, the lights of Wickenburg appeared on the dark horizon and Isabelle realized she was dreading telling Holt good-night. She didn't want this special day to end, or her time with him to be over.

They had passed through the small town and were nearing Hollister Animal Hospital when Isabelle questioned an earlier plan they'd made to deal with getting the two horses she'd purchased home to Blue Stallion Ranch.

"Now that I think about it, Holt, leaving my horses overnight at the clinic barn isn't such a good idea. They haven't been quarantined. They could pass shipping fever to Chandler's patients and I'd feel very guilty if that happened. Not to mention how angry it would make him. I can drive home, pick up my trailer, and be back in an hour or so to collect them."

His attention remained focused on the highway. "Don't fret about it, Isabelle. We're not leaving your horses or mine at the clinic. I'm going to take all four of them out to your ranch."

She sat straight up and stared at him. "Oh. But I thought—"

He arched a questioning brow in her direction. "The four of them have been trailered together for the past three and half hours. Penning them together tonight won't hurt. I'll leave mine at your place and haul them home to Three Rivers in a few days. That is, if you don't mind."

"Um—no. I don't mind."

That meant Holt would be following her home to Blue Stallion Ranch. After they tended the horses, would he want to stay? Or was he worried that if he let her get too close, she might try to throw a lariat on him?

The notion of any woman trying to tie Holt down was ridiculous. He was a maverick. But even mavericks needed love sometimes, she mentally argued. And tonight he just might decide he needed her.

Chapter 9

During the twenty-minute drive to Isabelle's ranch, Holt tried not to think past getting the mares comfortably settled, but he knew the smart thing to do would be to kiss her and tell her goodbye. But the kiss would have to be on the cheek, not her lips. Otherwise, he'd be totally and completely lost to her.

And what would be wrong with that, Holt? This day with Isabelle has been more than special for you. It's been a game changer. She's no longer just a sexy female you want to bed. You want much more from her. Like her company and friendship and—

Muttering a curse, he reached over and turned up the volume on the radio in an effort to drown out the voice in his head. Tonight wasn't the time to let his heart do his thinking for him. If Isabelle was ready to invite him into her bed, he'd be a fool to turn her down. It was that simple.

When he braked the truck to a stop near Isabelle's barn, she, along with Ollie and Sol, were waiting to help. With the four of them working together, it took only a few short minutes to have the mares settled into a sheltered pen with plenty of alfalfa and water.

As Ollie and Sol headed back to the bunkhouse, Holt turned to Isabelle. "Now that we've finished that chore, how about you and me having coffee?"

Her smile flashed in the darkness. "I can probably come up with a cup of coffee."

"Only one cup?"

Her laugh was suggestive and Holt couldn't stop his thoughts from heading straight to her bedroom. But what kind of consequences would that produce? After learning his father might have been involved with another woman, Holt had been pondering on his own past. Before, he'd never really wondered if his playing the field had ever caused anyone to suffer. Now it bothered him to think that what he'd considered fun and games might have actually hurt another person.

He was getting soft, he thought sickly. He was getting all messed up in the head, and why? Because he thought his father might have been an adulterer, or because Isabelle was transforming him into a different man? Either way, Holt felt like everything around him was rapidly changing. And he was helpless to stop any of it.

"If you mind your manners, you might get two cups," Isabelle said, breaking into his thoughts. "I might even give you a brownie to go with the coffee."

"I can't wait." He curled his arm around her waist

and kept it there as they walked the remaining distance to the house.

Inside the mudroom, they both shed their jackets and hung them on a hall tree. Holt added his black hat to one of the wooden arms, then followed Isabelle into the warm kitchen.

While she went to work putting the coffee makings together, Holt stood to one side, watching her graceful movements. All day long, he'd had to fight with himself to keep his eyes off the way the soft pink sweater outlined the shape of her breasts and the way her jeans cupped her pert little bottom.

Now that the two of them were completely alone, the urge to stare was turning into a need to touch. By the time she handed him a steaming cup of coffee and a brownie wrapped in a piece of wax paper, he didn't want either one. All Holt wanted was her in his arms.

"Do you want to go out to the living room?" she asked. "There's no crackling fire waiting for us, but the furniture is more comfortable."

"I can build a fire—if you'd like," he suggested.

She paused for a second, then reached for her cup. "No. That's too much trouble. And you'll be leaving soon."

Her gaze lifted to meet his and the flicker of yearning Holt spotted in the soft blue of her eyes caused his heart to do a crazy flip.

"I will?" he asked softly.

Her rose-colored lips formed a surprised O. "Uh—I thought that's what you wanted," she said, huskily. "You said you needed time to think about you and me and—"

Holt couldn't stand anymore. He placed the brownie

and the cup onto the cabinet counter and reached for her. As he circled his arms around her, he murmured, "These past few days I've done a hell of a lot of thinking, Isabelle. About that kiss that blew me away—about those strings that neither of us want. And the more I think, the more everything comes down to this."

He lowered his head and covered her lips with a kiss that was just long enough to fill his loins with heat, yet short enough to keep him from losing his breath.

"Holt, I—"

"You want me. I can hear it in your voice. Taste it in your lips."

There was no indecision in her eyes as her hands came up to curl over the tops of his shoulders.

"Yes," she murmured huskily. "I do—want you—very much."

He brought his lips back to hers and she groaned as his lips moved over hers in a rough, consuming kiss. She matched the hungry movements of his mouth and in a matter of a few short seconds, Holt was out of his mind with need to have her closer.

When he finally found enough willpower to tear his mouth from hers, he could see a dazed cloud in her eyes. He was equally stunned by the passion exploding between them, and his rattled state must have flickered in his eyes.

"You're not thinking about leaving, are you?"

Tightening the circle of his arms, he said, "I couldn't leave you now even if Ollie and Sol started yelling the barn was on fire."

Her laugh was low and sexy and the erotic sound was like fingertips walking across his skin.

"I think the coffee can wait." She took his hand and led him out of the kitchen and down a long hallway to her bedroom.

There was no light on inside, but like the rest of the house, the windows were bare of curtains and the silver glow from a crescent moon was enough to illuminate a path to a queen-size bed covered with a patchwork quilt.

As soon as they reached the side of the mattress, she released her hold on his hand and slid her arms around his waist. Holt dropped his head and found her lips once again. This time he tried to keep the kiss slow and controlled, but that plan was waylaid the moment her lips began to respond to his. Like a flash fire, their embrace turned hot and out of control.

"This is going too fast, Isabelle. But I—"

Frantically, she whispered, "I don't want you to slow down." She planted quick little kisses against his jaw and throat. "I can't bear the waiting. We'll go slower the next time."

The next time. Just the idea of a second time with this woman was enough to lift the hair off his scalp.

"I can't bear the waiting either." His voice sounded like he'd been eating gravel and his hands were shaking as they skimmed down her back and onto her hips.

Having sex with Isabelle. That's all he was doing, Holt silently shouted at himself. This wasn't anything to fear. It wasn't going to change him. All it was going to do was give him pleasure. Hot, delicious pleasure.

He recognized her hands were on the front of his shirt, jerking at the pearl snaps. When the fabric parted and her palms flattened against the bare skin of his chest, he was already hard, his body aching for release.

"I, uh, better do this, Isabelle—or—we might never make it onto the bed."

With the smile of a tempting siren, she stepped aside and began to undress. Next to her, Holt hastily jerked off his boots and jeans, then added his shirt to the pile. From the corner of his eye, he saw a circle of denim pool around her bare feet. Before she could step out of it, he planted his hands on either side of her waist and lifted her backward and onto the bed.

The jeans dangled from her toes and she laughingly kicked them off as she waited for him to join her.

"You're still dressed," Holt said.

She glanced down at the black scraps of lace covering her breasts and the V between her thighs. "You should be able to handle these little ole things."

He joined her on the bed and allowed his gaze to take in the glorious sight of her nearly naked body.

"It'll be my pleasure." Propping his head up on one elbow, he used his other hand to slip over the mound of one breast, then onto the concave of her belly. "The moonlight makes you look like a silver goddess. I'm not sure that you're real. I should kiss you just to make sure."

She rolled eagerly toward him. "I'm real, Holt, and at this moment I wouldn't want to be anywhere else, except here with you."

Holt wasn't expecting her little confession to smack him in the chest, but then nothing about this time with her was how he'd thought it might be. She was making him feel vulnerable and insecure. It was crazy. Even laughable. Yet he couldn't laugh. He was too busy worrying that he was going to disappoint her.

"Isabelle." Her name came out on a whisper as he

thrust his hand into her hair and allowed the white-blond strands to slide through his fingers. "I've imagined you—us—like this so many times. But I—wasn't sure it would ever happen."

"I wasn't sure I wanted it to happen."

"And now?"

Sighing, she echoed his earlier words. "I couldn't leave you if Ollie and Sol yelled the barn was on fire."

He leaned over and kissed the lids of her eyes, then moved his lips down her nose and finally onto her mouth. Her arm slipped around his waist and she tugged herself forward, until the front of her body was pressed tightly against his. The sensation of having her warm skin and soft curves next to his bare body very nearly shattered the fragile grip he held on his self-control.

He broke the kiss and scattered a trail of kisses beneath her ear and down the side of her neck until he reached the spot where her pulse thumped against the soft skin. His lips lingered there, savoring the taste, before he finally claimed her mouth in another hungry search.

After that, his brain became too fuzzy to clearly perceive what the rest of his body was doing. He remembered slipping away her lingerie and his boxers, recalled her reassuring him that she was on birth control. Then the next thing he knew, his hands were cupped around her breasts and he was entering her with one urgent thrust.

Her soft cry of pleasure jolted his rattled senses and he looked down to see her face bathed in moonlight. The delicate features were almost ethereal, making him wonder if he was going to suddenly wake and discover this was an incredible dream.

But then her hips suddenly arched toward his and the reality of the moment hit him. Slowly and surely he began to move inside her and as he did, he realized his greatest fear about making love to Isabelle had happened. After this night, he'd never be the same.

This was not what Isabelle had imagined. Making love to Holt wasn't supposed to be turning the room upside down. His kisses, his touches weren't supposed to be slinging her senses to some far-off galaxy. But that was exactly what was happening.

His hands were racing over her bare skin, lighting a fire wherever his fingers dared to touch. His lips were consuming hers, while his tongue probed the sensitive area beyond her teeth. She welcomed his dominating kiss and reveled in the fact that it was melting every bone in her body.

Over and over, he thrust into her and the feeling was all so glorious, so incredible, that the pleasure was almost too intense for her to bear. And when she began to writhe frantically beneath him, he must have recognized her agony.

He tore his mouth from hers and buried his face in her tumbled hair. "Hold on, my sweet," he whispered urgently. "Just a—moment longer. A moment more—so I can give you—everything. Everything!"

With her legs wrapped around his hips, she gripped his shoulders and tried to hang on, but it was impossible to stop the white-hot tide of pleasure from washing her away.

Through the whirling haze, she heard him cry her

name and felt his final thrust. She tried to breathe, but her lungs had ceased to function. And then breathing suddenly seemed superfluous as the room turned to velvety space and the both of them were drifting through an endless universe.

When Isabelle finally regained awareness, her cheek was pinned between the mattress and Holt's shoulder. With most of his weight draped over her, the pressure on her lungs made breathing even more difficult. Even so, she didn't want him to move. She wanted to hold him close for as long as he would stay.

"Sorry, Isabelle. I'm squashing you." He rolled to one side and pulled her into the curve of his warm body.

Sighing, Isabelle pillowed her head on his shoulder and closed her eyes. Neither of them spoke, but the silence was far from awkward. She was enjoying the precious sound of his breathing, the night wind blowing against the window and the faint whinnies of the mares as they accustomed themselves to their new home.

This was everything she'd ever wanted, Isabelle thought drowsily. Her ranch and a man who filled her heart to the very brim.

"I hear the mares," Holt murmured. "They've been through some changes today. They're not sure what's going to happen to them now."

Isabelle could empathize with the horses. Her life had taken a drastic change tonight, too. And she had no idea what it might do to her future or her happiness. She wanted to think that Holt might want them to remain together. Not just for a few weeks or months, but for always. And yet, she recognized that wasn't likely to happen.

Resting her palm upon his chest, she said, "They'll soon realize that they're safe."

His fingers absently played with her hair. "I've been thinking about those two mares I bought today. Do you like them?"

She slid her hand across his warm muscles until she felt the quick thump of his heart. "I love them. Next to blue roan, my favorite color is plain brown with no markings. They're almost as hard to find as the blues and today you happened to latch onto two of them. You're a lucky man, Holt."

"Yeah, like latching onto you." He pressed a kiss to the top of her head. "Now, about the mares—what would you say about keeping them here at Blue Stallion for a while? Since they're already bred, there's no need for me to put my stud on them. Maybe we could go partners on them?"

She snatched the sheet against her naked breasts and sat straight up. "Partners? Really?"

A lopsided grin spread over his face. "Yes. Really."

The grin coupled with the dark hair tousled across his forehead, along with the five o'clock shadow on his jaw, was enough to shred her focus. The subject of the mares completely left her mind as she leaned down and kissed him softly on the lips.

"Mmm. That's so nice," she said.

His hand came to rest against the back of her head and he held her there, kissing her again, until desire began to flicker and glow deep within her.

"My suggestion about the mares? Or the kiss?" he wanted to know.

She smiled against his lips. "The kiss. And the mares. I'd love to keep them here with me."

And keep you here, too, she wanted to add. But bit back the words before they could slip out. For tonight it was enough to be in his arms.

He said, "That's what I wanted to hear."

She cupped her hands around his face. "I thought you wanted to hear it was time to finally eat those brownies we left on the counter."

A chuckle fanned her lips, and he pressed her shoulders backward until she was lying on the mattress and he was hovering over her.

"What brownies?"

Her soft laugh was instantly blotted out with a kiss.

"Wake up, sleepyhead. You're burning daylight."

The sound of Isabelle's voice caused Holt's eyes to pop open and he blinked several times before he managed to focus on her image standing at the side of the bed.

She was already dressed in jeans and boots and a blue shirt that matched her eyes. One hand was holding a cup of steaming coffee.

"Is that coffee for me?"

The smile on her face was as bright as the morning sunlight streaming through the windows.

"It is. How do you want your eggs? Fried, scrambled, or in an omelet?"

He didn't have time for eggs! He shouldn't even be here! What had he been thinking last night?

He hadn't been thinking, that's what. Making love to Isabelle and lying next to her warm body had lulled him into a quiet sense of contentment. Instead of getting up and going home, he'd fallen asleep.

He took the cup from her and swallowed several

hurried gulps before he swung his legs over the side of the bed.

"I really shouldn't take time to eat, Isabelle. If I don't get home, I—my family is going to send the law out looking for me."

Her brows shot up. "Really? Aren't they used to you being out all night?"

His face hot, he purposely set the coffee aside and reached for his clothing. "Not like this. Not overnight."

"Oh."

He pulled on his boxers and jeans before he glanced at her. She looked confused and skeptical, which made him even more frustrated with himself. Holt had always made special rules for himself regarding women. And he'd always followed them. Until now.

Standing, he zipped and buttoned his jeans. "That doesn't ring true with you, does it?"

"I didn't say that." She moved close enough to rest her hand on his forearm. "And frankly, it doesn't matter. That was then, this is now. Anyway, we agreed there'd be no strings. Remember?"

Hell, was she going to keep bringing that up? He was getting tired of hearing it.

That's the way it has to be, Holt. Keeping things casual is the best way for both of you. She won't get hurt when your eye starts to stray elsewhere. And you won't give it a second thought when she finds herself another man.

The mocking voice in his ears made his head throb and he reached for the coffee cup. Caffeine was all he needed right now, he assured himself. That and a plate of food. The rest would fix itself once he got home to Three Rivers.

After several more sips of the hot liquid, the bitter taste in his mouth eased enough for him to speak. "Yeah, I remember."

She studied his face for a long moment, then stepped closer. "Holt, are you regretting last night?"

The confusion on her face suddenly wiped away the turmoil going on inside him. He placed the coffee back on the nightstand and wrapped his arms around her. "Oh, no, Isabelle. Last night was incredible."

She tilted her face upward until their gazes locked. "It was that way for me, too," she said softly.

Everything about her was warming him, touching him in ways that tilted his common sense and went straight to his heart.

You don't have a heart, Holt. You have lust and pride and a man's ego, but when it comes to women, you're lacking a heart.

Shoving aside the brittle voice in his head, he smiled and rested his forehead against hers. "You know, those eggs sound mighty good."

"What about your family calling out the law to search for you?" she teased.

He pressed a tiny kiss between her brows. "My family might as well get used to me being gone. 'Cause the two of us are just getting started."

Chapter 10

February arrived with a wallop. Only this morning, Isabelle had spotted a few bits of snow flying on the north wind. After living in Albuquerque for two and half years, she'd gotten used to the cold winters and the heavy snowfall. But that didn't mean she liked it any more than Ollie and Sol did. Both men had shown up at feeding time dressed in heavy coveralls. Now, as Isabelle entered the cozy, warm interior of Conchita's coffee shop, she was grateful to be out of the bitter wind.

The clang of the cowbell over the door brought Emily-Ann up from behind the counter, where she'd been placing a tray of fresh pastries in the glass case. The moment she spotted Isabelle, her face creased into a smile.

"Well, I finally get a customer on this freezing

morning and it happens to be one of my favorites," she said. "Hello, Isabelle. What are you doing out in this weather?"

Isabelle yanked off her mittens as she walked up to the glass counter. "A rancher's work never takes a holiday, even during bad weather. I had to come to town for a load of feed."

"I thought you had two ranch hands to do all that stuff for you."

"I still have them," Isabelle told her. "But I had a few more personal errands to run."

She pointed to a cake doughnut covered with white icing and chopped peanuts. "Give me one of those and a regular coffee with cream."

Emily-Ann looked surprised. "That's all? No apple fritter, or maple long john?"

Isabelle laughed. "Okay. Give me a cinnamon roll, too. The one with the raisins. That will be my attempt at a healthy diet today."

While Emily-Ann gathered her order, Isabelle walked over to one of the two small tables in the room and hung her puffy red coat on the back of one of the chairs.

"Good thing you're not busy," Isabelle commented as she took a seat. "I'd hate to have to eat outside in this weather."

Emily-Ann carried the coffee and pastries over to Isabelle and sat down across from her.

"I'm hoping this cold will blow out before Thursday. The Gold Rush Days celebration will be kicking off then."

Isabelle munched on the doughnut. "When I first

drove into town, I noticed the banners crossing the street. Just what is this celebration?"

Emily-Ann's eyes sparkled. "Oh, it's such fun. There's a carnival, plus all kinds of street vendors and entertainment. And then, of course, there's a big rodeo, too. This one will be the seventy-first annual celebration. It's been going on for a long time."

"Exactly what is being celebrated?" Isabelle asked.

Emily-Ann made a palms-up gesture. "I'm not much of a town historian, but it's to celebrate how the ranchers and miners first got the town going. Which was back in 1863—even a few years before the big city of Phoenix came into existence."

"That's interesting. So do very many people show up for Gold Rush Days?"

"Thousands and that is no exaggeration. It's always a busy time for everyone in town. Even with this street being off the beaten path, I get lots of extra customers. You should come join the fun. There's even a gold panning event. Who knows, you might get lucky and find a nugget." She cast Isabelle a clever look. "But from what I'm hearing, you've already found your nugget."

The doughnut in Isabelle's hand paused halfway to her mouth. "Me? I haven't been panning for gold. Even though Ollie and Sol tell me there might be some on my property. From what they say, one of the richest gold mines ever was somewhere in this area." She shrugged. "But I don't have time to chase after a fortune in yellow mineral. My dream is pastures filled with horses."

"Hmm. I thought since you started seeing Holt, your dreams might include a husband and children."

Isabelle stared at her. "Where did you hear that Holt and I were—seeing each other?"

Emily-Ann giggled. "Holt's sister Camille told me. We've been best friends since kindergarten. Her mother and sister keep her caught up on family happenings. Have you met all the Hollisters yet?"

Holt had been coming over to Blue Stallion Ranch to be with her almost every night, but so far he'd not invited her to Three Rivers or suggested she meet his family. Isabelle had been telling herself that none of that was important. The two of them hadn't been together for that long. They needed to focus on each other first before his family or her mother were involved.

Isabelle said, "The subject of meeting his family hasn't come up."

"Well, I figure it will. From what Camille says, the whole family believes he's besotted with you."

Isabelle made a scoffing noise. "Then they're over-blowing the whole situation. Holt isn't falling for me. We're just—enjoying each other's company—for now."

Emily-Ann shook her head. "It's exciting to think of you and Holt together, but I'm kinda glad you're saying it's not serious with you two. Holt is gorgeous and sexy, but it would be heartbreaking to end up being just a notch on his belt. I'd rather have a simple man who loves me for real. Wouldn't you?"

Real love. That's what Isabelle wanted more than anything. And sometimes when she was in Holt's arms, when he was kissing her, touching her, she thought she felt love in the touch of his fingers, the taste of his lips. But she was afraid to believe or hope his feelings were the real thing.

"You couldn't have said it better." Isabelle reached across the table and patted her friend's hand. "What about you? Have you found anything close to that 'simple man'?"

"Me?" Her short laugh was scornful. "I've quit looking. There's something about me that turns men off. My red hair and freckles, I guess. Or I'm too big and gawky, or maybe I talk too much, I don't know. Anyway, most of the guys around here I've been acquainted with all my life. And they know about—"

Isabelle noted the somber expression on her friend's face. "About what? Or would you rather not tell me?"

Emily-Ann's gaze dropped to the tabletop. "It's hardly a secret. I'm from the wrong side of the track, I guess you'd say. My real father left town right after I was born. He never married my mother. She was from a poor background and his folks would've never stood for their son to marry a girl like my mom. Even though she was pretty and hardworking and honest— that wasn't enough. You know the kind."

Isabelle nodded. "Unfortunately those kind of snobbish people are very easy to find."

"Well, anyway, my grandparents kicked my mom out of the house. They never could forgive her for having a child out of wedlock. And just between you and me, I don't think they wanted to spend any money to help support us. But somehow Mom managed on her own to care for the both of us. Until she finally married a salesman who showed up one day in Wickenburg. He filled my mother's head with all sorts of big dreams. But he was nothing but a blowhard. None of the promises he made ever materialized. But the old saying about love being blind must be true. Mom believed every word he said. When she died, she was still waiting for the nice house and all the things that would've made her life easier."

"I'm sorry your mother is gone. And sorry that her dreams didn't come true," Isabelle said gently. "Does your stepfather still live here in Wickenburg?"

"No. Shortly after Mom died, he left and no one has seen or heard from him since. That's been ten or more years ago." She let out a long sigh. "So you see, I'm not exactly the sort of gal a guy takes home to meet Mama."

Isabelle grimaced. "That's ridiculous. You had nothing to do with your mother's decisions, or the way her family treated her."

"Isabelle, it's just like spilling something. The stain keeps spreading and spreading. That's how it is with me. The past spilled over and I can't outrun it or wash it off."

"Well, you shouldn't be trying to outrun or wash anything," Isabelle gently scolded. "And you know what I think? Some really nice guy is going to show up in your life and he's going to make you see just how special you are."

Emily-Ann's eyes grew misty as she gave Isabelle a grateful smile. "I'm so happy you came to live here, Isabelle."

"You know what, I'm pretty happy about it, too."

Blue Stallion Ranch was a beautiful piece of Arizona. The rugged hills and desert floors that made up the property were everything she'd been looking for. Given time and work and money, it would be thriving again. And the prospect was exciting.

But this past week and a half since she'd welcomed

Holt into her bed, she'd come to realize that her dream of a horse ranch wasn't enough to give her complete happiness. Nothing would mean anything without him at her side.

She'd tried to gloss it all over with Emily-Ann and pretend that what she felt for Holt wasn't serious. But she couldn't delude herself. She was falling for the cowboy in the worst kind of way. Now she could only pray she wouldn't end up being just another name in his little black book.

When Holt unsaddled the two-year-old and started toward the ranch house, it was already dark. Any other time, he would've been feeling the fatigue of being in the saddle for the past five hours, but this evening he actually had a spring in his step. He was going to see Isabelle. He was going to talk to her and listen to her talk to him. He was going to eat with her, sleep with her, and make slow, delicious love with her. In short, being with Isabelle was like stepping into paradise. Just the thought was enough to push the tiredness from his body.

As soon as he entered the back of the house and let himself into the kitchen, he knew something out of the ordinary was going on. The room was full of womenfolk scurrying from one task to the next, including his sister Vivian.

She was standing at the cabinet counter, placing tiny appetizers on a silver tray. Wearing a vivid green dress that flowed over her pregnant waistline, she looked like she was dressed for a party.

"Sis, what are you doing here?"

She looked up and, with a huge smile, walked

straight into his arms. "Hello, my naughty little brother!" Considering the girth of her belly, she gave him the best bear hug she could manage. "I thought I was going to have to go drag you out of the saddle to get you up here to the house!"

He dropped a kiss on the top of her red head. "If I'd known you were here, I would've shown up sooner. What's going on anyway? Is it someone's birthday?"

She laughed and not for the first time Holt thought how beautiful she looked now that she was carrying her and Sawyer's twins. Her face glowed and there was a shine in her eyes that mirrored her happiness.

"Have you been hiding under a rock? Gold Rush Days are starting Thursday and Mom always throws a little party beforehand."

Oh, Lord, none of that had entered his mind. "Uh—yeah. It—just slipped my mind." He glanced quickly around the room. "Is Sawyer here? And Savannah?"

"They wouldn't have missed it for anything. Onida came, too." She winked slyly. "I think she didn't want to miss the opportunity of seeing Sam. She thinks he's a real gentleman."

Sam was the crusty old cowboy who worked as foreman for Tessa and Joseph's ranch, the Bar X. So if Sam was here, that meant Tessa and Joseph and Little Joe were here, also. Everyone would expect Holt to join in on the fun. Especially his mother, he thought with a pang of guilt.

"I've never been able to figure out what that old man has, but whatever it is, the women seem to like it. I think he's an older version of Holt Hollister," Vivian added with a cunning laugh.

Holt grunted with amusement. "I always did want to be like Sam."

She tapped a forefinger against his unshaven chin. "There's only one Sam and only one you. Thank God."

Holt patted the front of her protruding belly. "How're my little nephews? Isn't it about time for them to show their faces?"

"Not yet. And the boys or girls are doing fine. Just because you guessed the gender of baby Evelyn correctly doesn't mean you'll get lucky this time."

"It's a pair of boys. They'll probably look just like Sawyer and grow up to break dozens of hearts."

She laughed. "Possibly. But your son, whenever you finally have one, will be the real heartbreaker."

Holt noticed Vivian said when, not if, he had a son. Marriage had really messed with her mind, he thought.

"You're dreaming, sis."

Vivian was about to reply when Reeva practically yelled from across the room. "Holt! What are you doing in my kitchen with those dirty chaps and spurs on? I don't want horsehair flying all over my food! Get out of here!"

"Excuse me, sis, I've got to go charm the cook."

He sauntered over to where Reeva was taking a pan of crescent rolls from the oven. "Reeva, why do you want to be mean to a hardworking man like me? All I want is a little love."

"Ha! Just like you don't get enough of that already." The cook playfully swatted a hand against his arm, which caused a puff of dust to billow out from his shirtsleeve. "Get out of here and see if you can find some soap and water. We'll be eating in twenty minutes."

"Can't eat," he told her. "I have a date tonight."

She was stabbing him with a stern look when Maureen walked up behind him.

"Holt, did I hear you say you have a date tonight?"

He turned from Reeva's reprimanding frown to his mother's unsmiling face.

"You heard right," he told her. "I do have a date with Isabelle. Sorry, Mom. I didn't know about the party."

She rolled her eyes. "I've been having a Gold Rush Days party since before you were born. Every year at this same time. Where the heck have you been living, Holt, besides the horse barn?"

Normally he would've laughed at Maureen's scolding sarcasm, but not tonight. He worked his butt off and then some for Three Rivers and there were times, like this one, when he felt his mother took him for granted.

"In case you haven't noticed, Mom, someone has to keep the ranch's remuda going," he retorted.

"Holt! You don't have to be so snippy," Vivian chided as she came to stand at his side. "This party is important to her and so is your being here. That's all she's trying to say."

"I have a life outside of this ranch and this family! And it's important to me!" He reached to the back of his leg and started unhooking the latches on his chaps. "I'll go have a drink with the men and then I'll be leaving."

He started out of the kitchen with the three women staring after him. He was almost into the hallway, when his mother's hand came down on his arm.

"Holt, just a minute," she ordered.

He turned to her and for an instant, as he took in

her troubled face, he wanted to grab her into a tight hug. He wanted to rest his face against her shoulder as he had as a boy, feel her comforting hand stroke the top of his head, and hear her say that everything was going to be all right. But those days of his childhood were over and though he hated to admit it, his life, and the whole Hollister family, were changing.

"Mom, I apologize. I didn't mean to sound so short."

"I'm sorry, too," she said ruefully. "Nothing I said came out right. That's been happening too much with me here lately."

He shook his head, while feeling guiltier by the minute. His mother had an enormous workload on her shoulders. She didn't need any of her sons adding to her stress.

"I wasn't exactly Mr. Charming either," he admitted. "Look, Mom, if you want me to hang around for the party that badly, I can call Isabelle and cancel our date for tonight."

"No! That isn't what I want at all. You deserve time for yourself. I only—" She grimaced as she seemed to search for the right words. "You've been seeing Isabelle for a while now. I wish that you cared enough to have her over here to Three Rivers."

Did he care about Isabelle? Yes, he could admit that he cared for her. A lot. But he couldn't go so far as to say he loved her. No. That was for men like Blake and Chandler and Joseph. Not him. His mother should know that.

"I'll have her over," he promised. "Sometime. Whenever it's right."

Maureen knew he was hedging. Just like Holt knew

it. But thankfully, she wasn't going to hound him about it tonight.

"I'll look forward to that day, son." She motioned on down the hallway to where his bedroom was located. "You go on and clean up. I'll tell Jazelle to make you a bourbon and cola. The good stuff that Sam gets," she added with a wink.

"Thanks, Mom."

She patted his check, then turned and headed back to the kitchen. Holt trotted on to his bedroom and after texting Isabelle a quick message to let her know he'd be running late, he jumped into the shower.

Short minutes later, he was buttoning his shirt when a light knock sounded on the door. Figuring it was Jazelle with his drink, he went over and opened it. But instead of Jazelle, it was Vivian.

"Here's your bourbon." She handed him a short tumbler. "Everyone else is going in for dinner. May I come in?"

"Sure. I'm just about finished here anyway." He tucked the tails of his shirt into his jeans, then walked over to the dresser and picked up a hairbrush. "But you should go on to dinner. You don't want to be late to join the others."

"It's okay. Sawyer is going to fill my plate for me. Double everything. To feed two babies. Or so he says. I think he just wants me plump." She eased onto the edge of his bed and looked at him. "I wanted to talk to you for a minute. We don't get to do much of that since I moved to the reservation. I miss you."

His throat tightened. Even though she was his sister, Vivian had been his best buddy since he was old enough to have a memory. Through good and bad, they'd stuck together. And even now, with her living some ninety miles away, he didn't have to wonder if she still loved him, or if she'd run to his side if he needed her. She'd be there in a heartbeat.

"I miss you, too, sissy. But you're happy with Sawyer and that's what counts."

"Happiness, I want that for you, too, Holt."

He cast a droll look at her. "Listen, I apologized to Mom for that outburst in the kitchen. And she apologized to me. We grate on each other's nerves sometimes. That's all. See, I'm so happy I can hardly stand myself."

She left her seat on the mattress and came to stand in front of him. "Right now, I'm finding it very hard to stand you myself."

Seeing that she really meant it, he was taken aback. "What is that supposed to mean? You just said you missed me."

"I do miss you. In more ways than one. Because of the miles between us, yes. But I miss the old Holt, the adorable Holt, the one who wasn't trying to hide his feelings."

He tossed the hairbrush back onto the dresser top. "Carrying twins is affecting your eyesight, sis. I'm not trying to hide anything." Except that their father might've been an adulterer. And he was getting far more attached to Isabelle than he'd ever planned to be.

"Liar, liar, pants on fire. You know better than to try to fool me, Holt. You're getting in deep with this Isabelle, aren't you?"

He rubbed a hand against his forehead, then glanced at his watch. "As much as I love spending time with you, sis, I've got to run."

She threw up her hands. "Okay. Go ahead and run off. You just answered my question anyway. You've fallen for Isabelle Townsend."

"And what if I have?" He tossed the question at her. "What's the problem? You and everybody else in this family has always wanted me to find *the* woman."

"I'll tell you the problem. If you ˙an't even admit to me that your feelings are serious, then how do you expect things to work with her?"

Holt grabbed his jacket from the closet and shouldered it on. "I don't expect it to work forever. Not like you and Sawyer will. I'm not built that way. But I love you for caring about me." He kissed her forehead. "Now go join everybody for dinner. And I'll talk to you soon."

Over on Blue Stallion Ranch, Isabelle glanced at the small clock on the end table. Nearly two hours ago, she'd gotten Holt's text explaining he'd be a little late. Just how late did he consider a little? At this rate, they'd be eating supper at midnight.

That first day Isabelle had walked up on Holt in the horse barn, she'd been struck by his rugged good looks, but she'd not missed the fact that he'd looked like he'd been running on empty for too many miles. After that initial meeting, she'd quickly learned that in a day's time he usually accomplished the work of two men.

Only yesterday he'd told her that the bulk of his mares had already foaled, so he'd been spending his time in the training pen, breaking two-year-old colts. It was a slow, painstaking job, along with being extremely dangerous. Holt's text message earlier this evening hadn't explained why he would be late. Now as time ticked on, without him showing up, she was beginning to worry that something had happened with one of his horses or, God forbid, to him.

The fire in the fireplace had turned to little more than a pile of burning coals, so she got up from the couch to add another log. She was finishing the chore when a sweep of headlights passed in front of the living room windows.

Relieved, she put away the poker and hurried out to meet him. As soon as he stepped down from the truck, she hugged him tight.

"I was beginning to think you weren't going to show," she said.

He kissed her cheek. "You got my text, didn't you?"

"Yes, but it's getting so late I was afraid there might've been some sort of accident."

"No. Just lots of company at the house." He wrapped his arm around the back of her shoulders. "Let's go in and I'll tell you about it. Got anything to eat?"

"Peanut butter and jelly sandwiches," she said, loving the warmth of his arm around her. "The pork chops and scalloped potatoes are ruined. Oh, but if you don't want the peanut butter and jelly, you can have bologna. I know you like that."

"Are you serious?"

The deflated look on his face had her laughing. "Yes. I'm kidding. I have the chops and everything to go with them in the warmer."

He playfully pinched the end of her nose. "You little teaser. I'm going to get you for that."

She let out a sultry laugh. "I'll just bet you will."

They entered the house and the first thing he noticed was the fire. "Wow, you built a fire for me? I feel special."

"That was my intention," she said, then tugged his head down so that she could kiss his lips.

"Mmm. You keep that up and those chops will have to stay in the warmer a little longer," he murmured, then kissed her twice more before she grabbed both his hands and tugged him into the kitchen.

"We'd better eat," she said. "You look famished and I'm starving. Let's fill our plates off the stove and carry them to the dining room. It'll be quicker."

"Sounds good to me."

Minutes later, they were eating at the long table, where Isabelle had lit a pair of candles and poured blackberry wine. Beyond the row of arched windows in front of them, the starlit sky shone down on the quiet ranch yard. The view was always beautiful to Isabelle but having Holt sitting across from her made it perfect.

As their conversation naturally turned to work, he asked, "How's the fence building coming along?"

"Good. We're making progress. And since we've moved farther away from the ranch yard, I'm finding more good grazing land. There's one little valley where Mr. Landry used to grow hay. I'm thinking I might like to try my hand at that. Ollie and Sol seemed to know a bit about it. And they believe they can get the irrigation system going again."

He said, "Sounds like you've turned Ollie and Sol into big dreamers, too."

She pulled a face at him. "Ollie and Sol believe in themselves and me. The three of us plan to get all sorts of things accomplished—together. And to grow my own hay would be a big savings. Especially when my herd gets a lot larger."

He smiled. "You really love this place, don't you?"

"I do love it. Very much. It makes me feel—well, like I'm home. Really home. Do you understand what I mean?" she asked, then shook her head. "That's a stupid question. Of course, you understand. Three Rivers is undoubtedly in your blood the way Blue Stallion is in mine."

His fork hovered above his plate, while his green eyes made a slow survey of her face. "Is there anything that could make you move away from here?"

The question surprised her. Not only because he'd asked it, but because it was so easy to answer.

"No. I'm here to stay. Like I told you before, my parents were free spirits. While they were together, we moved around. Mostly to follow Dad's gigs, but sometimes just because my parents wanted something different. As a kid, I didn't know what it was like to put down roots. Later, Mom and I settled in San Diego, but city life wasn't for me. Then I thought I'd found a home in Albuquerque with Trevor. But that place was never really where I was meant to be." She gestured toward the window. "This is my land, my home. It's where I want my children to be raised. Where I want to live out my life."

"I figured that's what you'd say."

She wasn't going to ask him to explain what had prompted his question. She didn't know why, but she had the uneasy feeling she might not like his answer.

Picking up her fork, she began to tackle the mound of scalloped potatoes on her plate. "You haven't told me about the company at Three Rivers tonight."

"Every year my mother throws a little family party in honor of Gold Rush Days. My whole family was there. Plus Matthew, our foreman, and Sam, the Bar X foreman. I think they were all a little peeved at me because I didn't stay."

A family party. Isabelle supposed she should feel honored that Holt had chosen to spend the evening with her. And yet, a part of her felt dejected because he'd not invited her to attend the party. With everyone there, it would have been the perfect time for him to introduce his new girlfriend.

But Holt might not think of her as his girlfriend, Isabelle pondered. In his eyes, she might just be a woman he had sex with and that's all she'd ever be.

Stop it, Isabelle! Quit feeling wronged or sorry for yourself! You went into this thing with Holt knowing who he was and what he was. You even told him there'd be no strings, so don't go thinking he's going to change.

Shutting out the taunting voice, she said, "I'm sorry you're missing the party, Holt. You should've told me. I wouldn't have been annoyed if you'd canceled your time with me."

The frown on his face slowly turned into a wan smile. "That's nice of you, Isabelle. But to be honest, I didn't want to stay for the party. I wanted to be here with you."

His words wrapped around her heart and she reached across the table and folded her fingers over his. "I'm happy you are here with me."

"So am I."

Chapter 11

In the past, Holt had never been bothered very much by his conscious. The only time he'd ever regretted his behavior was when he'd believed he'd disappointed his father or mother. Other than that, he was usually the to-hell-with-it sort. He tried to be a decent person, but he wasn't going to break his back trying to please everyone. If he offended or disappointed someone, it was their problem to get over it. Not his.

But tonight as he sat across the table from Isabelle, he suddenly realized he was a bastard. He didn't deserve her, or her sweet, understanding nature. If he had any decency about him at all, he'd put an end to this thing between them. He'd step away and let her find a good man, one who'd love her with all his heart.

Yeah, if he was a decent man, he could do that. But he was selfish and for most of his adult life he'd taken what he wanted and not worried about the consequences. And he wanted Isabelle. Wanted her more than he'd ever wanted anything in his life.

"Are you going to attend any of the Gold Rush Days celebration in town?"

Her question broke into his troubled thoughts and he looked over to see she'd finished the food on her plate.

"I used to go to the rodeo," he said. "But not these days. I have too much work at the ranch."

"I do, too. But it sounds like fun. Emily-Ann tells me Valentine Street is filled with a carnival and all sorts of interesting vendors. She thinks I should try my hand at gold panning." She paused and laughed. "I told her I could do that right here on the ranch."

He swallowed the last bite on his plate and pushed it aside. "You might find a nugget or two. The ranch hands on Three Rivers sometimes find rocks with streaks of gold. And Blake and Joe found a couple of nuggets in the same gulch where they believe, uh, where they found the scraps of Dad's shirt."

A thoughtful look suddenly came over her face. "Holt, did you ever think someone might have been digging around on your property for gold? I know it sounds far-fetched, but think about it. With gold prices what they are nowadays, one nugget would be worth a lot of money. Your father could've run across a trespasser and a fight ensued."

"That's a very logical deduction. But that's not what happened," he said resolutely.

Her brows arched. "How can you say that? You told me that you don't know what actually happened concerning your father's death."

Unable to look her in the eye, he rose to his feet and

gathered up his glass and plate. "Trust me. It didn't happen that way!"

He carried his dirty dishes to the kitchen with Isabelle following directly behind him.

As she began to put the leftover food in plastic containers, she said, "I'm sorry I theorized about your father's death, Holt. I realize it's not something you want to talk about."

Holt watched her place the containers in the refrigerator and walk over to the coffee machine. He should've already told her that she looked extra beautiful tonight in a long, blue and green skirt that swished around the tops of her cowboy boots and a matching green sweater tucked in at her tiny waist. It amazed him how she could go from a rough and tumble ranching woman to a soft, feminine siren. But then everything about Isabelle amazed him. That was the problem.

"Would you like coffee and dessert? I have ice cream. Or candy bars. The kind with caramel and nuts."

He walked over to where she stood and wrapped his arms around her. The feel of her soft body next to his was like a sweet balm that filled him with goodness. "I don't want anything—except to hold you. Make love to you."

She tilted her face up to his and he kissed her for long moments before he bent and picked her up in his arms.

With her hands locked at the back of his neck, he carried her to the bedroom and carefully placed her in the middle of the mattress. Then without bothering to remove his clothing or hers, he lay down beside her and gathered her into his arms.

His lips hovering near hers, he said, "I think about you all day. About you. About being inside you. You're making me crazy, Isabelle."

She slipped her arm around his neck. "That's the way it's supposed to be. Crazy good."

With a groan that came from deep within him, he completed the connection of their lips and kissed her deeply, urgently. Her desperate response caused desire to erupt in him, arousing him to an unbearable ache.

Mindlessly, he rolled her onto her back and pushed the hem of her skirt up to her waist. She moaned as he hooked his thumbs beneath her lace panties and peeled the scrap of fabric down around her ankles and over her boots.

The urge to be inside her was pounding in his brain, gripping every cell in his body. There could be no holding back. No waiting.

His hands shaking, he managed to unzip his jeans and release his arousal, but that was as far as he got before she grabbed his hips and pulled him into her.

The hot, frantic connection wiped all thought from his brain, except that Isabelle was beneath him. Her arms were around him and her lips and breaths were merged with his. His thrusts were rapid and each time she rose up to meet him, she took more and more of him. And each time he felt his control slipping.

He was going to die right here in her arms. And he was going to die a happy man. The fateful thought was flashing through his mind just as she cried out.

"Oooh—Holt! Hold me—hold me tight!"

He tried to answer her pleas, but his body wouldn't

cooperate. In the next instant he felt everything pouring into her until there was nothing left of him, except a beating heart. And even it wanted to belong to her.

When Holt eventually returned to earth, he felt as if he'd been on a long, long journey and his body was too spent to take another step. As to what had just occurred between them, he couldn't define it, much less understand why this woman made him lose all control. But he did realize one thing: the whole thing scared him more than anything he'd ever encountered.

He rolled away from her and with a forearm resting against his forehead, fought to regain his breath.

Next to him, Isabelle stirred, then draped her upper body over his.

"That was pretty darned incredible, cowboy," she whispered against his cheek. "Just think how good we might be if we ever get our clothes off."

He chuckled, then silently groaned, as her lips came down on his and the fire in his loins started all over again.

Three days later, on Friday night, Isabelle had been expecting Holt to show up for supper and she'd taken the time out of her busy day to put a roast and vegetables in the oven. But shortly after dark he'd called to inform her that one of his young mares was about to foal and he didn't want to leave Chandler with the job of watching over her.

She'd understood his dilemma, but for the past three nights, he'd called with a reason he couldn't see her. True, they'd all been legitimate reasons. But she was getting the impression there was something else going on with Holt.

Was he getting ready to end things with her? He'd not said anything that hinted at those types of feelings. But then he'd definitely not spoken about how much he needed or loved her. No. Holt would probably never say the *L* word to her. Because, whatever he was, he wasn't a liar. He'd be blunt and painfully honest before he'd lead her on with words he didn't mean.

Oh, well, she thought, as she bit back her disappointment. Tomorrow was another day. And the food wouldn't go to waste. Ollie and Sol would be more than happy to eat it.

With that thought in mind, she donned a coat, placed the roast pan into a cardboard box, and carried it out to the barn.

The door to Ollie and Sol's bunkroom was closed to shut out the cold night air. Isabelle stepped up on the wooden step and started to knock when she caught the sound of the men talking and one of them said her name.

She'd never been one to eavesdrop. A person rarely heard good things said behind his or her back.

With that old adage in mind, she raised her knuckles to the door, then let them drop a second time as Holt's name was spoken by Ollie.

"Have you noticed Holt hasn't been over here in the past few days?"

"Yep, I've noticed," Sol said. "I'd be blind not to."

"Yeah," Ollie said after a moment. "As much as I like the guy, I hope he stays away."

There was a long pause and during the intermission, one of the female barn cats began to weave around Isabelle's legs and meow up at her. No doubt, the cat smelled the roast. Isabelle just hoped the men didn't hear her loud cries and open the door.

Finally, Sol said, "That's bad for you to talk that way about Holt. After all the man has done for us. Why, even now he's paying our way."

Paying their way? What did that mean?

She held her breath and refrained from placing her ear against the wooden panel. If one of them suddenly opened the door, she didn't know how she'd explain herself. She wouldn't be able to. She'd simply have to confess that she'd been listening in on their private conversation.

"That's all well and good," Ollie retorted. "But that doesn't mean we're blind to his ways. We both know if this keeps up, he's going to hurt Isabelle. And I don't mean just hurt her pride. He's gonna break her heart wide-open. I can see it coming."

There was another long stretch of silence and then Sol said, "Well, I'm thinking that she loves him, Ollie. We can't just come out and tell her she needs to stop seeing Holt. We're just a pair of old widowers. Neither one of us have had a wife in years. We don't know anything about the way young folks feel and think nowadays. Besides, she'd probably tell us it's none of our business."

"Don't guess it is," Ollie remarked. "But being her ranch hands sorta makes us her caretakers in a way. And I sure hate to see her heart broken. We both know Holt will never settle down with just one woman. And he'd sooner jump off a cliff before he'd get married."

"Yeah," Sol soberly agreed. "Isabelle's too good for that. She needs a man who'll marry her and help her run this place. Holt is a Hollister through and through.

He wouldn't leave Three Rivers for any reason. And sure not for a woman."

After a moment, Ollie said. "Let's talk about something else. Something happier. Are we going to the parade in the morning?"

"We haven't ridden in the Gold Rush Days parade in years. Why would we go now?"

"I don't know. Might be fun if we dug out our fancy chaps and spurs. We might catch the eye of some widow women."

"Hell." Sol snorted. "What would we do with widow women? Invite them out here for a cup of tea?"

"Well, what would be wrong with that? Isabelle drinks coffee with us. She likes it."

"Yeah, but Isabelle is different."

Isabelle had heard more than enough. She blinked back the foolish tears in her eyes and knocked on the door.

Sol opened the door and looked at her with dismay. Hopefully he didn't have a clue she'd been standing on the step for the past five minutes.

"Hey, guys, would you two like some supper?"

"Why, Isabelle," he said. "What are you doing out in the cold and dark?"

She did her best to put on a cheery smile. "I cooked a roast and vegetables for Holt, but he can't come tonight. I thought you two might want to share it."

Ollie's face suddenly appeared over Sol's shoulder. "That's nice of you to think of us, Isabelle. And it sure smells good. You want to come in and eat with us?"

Handing the box to Sol, she said, "Thanks, but I've already eaten and I have some chores in the house to finish before bedtime. You two enjoy it." She started to leave, then on second thought turned back before the men had a chance to shut the door. "Uh, I forgot to mention it earlier this evening, but if you two would like the day off tomorrow to go to Gold Rush Days, it's okay with me."

Sol's solemn face brightened considerably. "Thanks, Isabelle. Are you going to go? Me and Ollie might get in the parade. You could watch us ride down the street."

Ollie elbowed him in the ribs. "Goofy, she sees us on horseback every day. She might want do something else. Like go to the carnival."

Any other time, Isabelle would be laughing at the two men. But tonight she could hardly keep her voice from wobbling. "No. I won't be going to town. I have something else to do," she told them. Something she should have done from the very first day she'd met Holt Hollister.

Back in the house, she sat down at the kitchen table and picked up her phone. Gabby had been ringing her earlier, but she'd been outside helping finish the evening chores. After that, she'd gotten busy with supper, until she'd gotten Holt's inauspicious call.

Now, as she punched her mother's number, Isabelle wondered what she was going to tell her. What could she tell her? That she was happy? That everything was wonderful? Three days ago, she'd thought everything was great. In fact, the intensity with which Holt had made love to her had almost made her believe he was really beginning to care for her. Perhaps even falling in love with her.

But now her eyes were wide-open. And they were filled with stupid, useless tears.

"Hello, Issy! I gave up on you calling back. I was about to step into the shower."

"Sorry, Mom. Go ahead with your shower. I'll catch you later."

"No! I'm already wrapped up in my bathrobe and taken a comfy seat on the end of the bed. I just wanted to see how things are going and if you'd taken time to call your father."

Isabelle tried to swallow the lump around her throat. Her mother had lived without a loving husband for more than twenty years and she was happy. Isabelle could be happy, too. Just as soon as she got Holt out of her system.

"I called Dad yesterday. He sounded good, but like he was on another planet, as usual. He's been working on some new arrangements," Isabelle explained. "You know how preoccupied he gets."

Gabby laughed knowingly. "Why do you think I'm living alone? Bless his heart, he can't help himself."

Just like Holt couldn't help his fascination for horses and women, she thought sadly. In the very plural sense.

"So how are you and your rancher friend getting on? Holt? Isn't that his name?"

"Forget his name, Mom." Isabelle's throat was so tight she could scarcely speak. "Because I'm definitely going to forget him!"

Gabby went silent for a long stretch. Then she said, "Okay. What's wrong?"

Isabelle explained how she and Holt had been seeing each other on a regular basis until the past three days. Then she went on to relate everything she'd over-head Ollie and Sol discussing.

"Oh, Issy, you're being unreasonable and unfair. You can't make that sort of snap judgment just because your ranch hands think Holt is the wrong man for you. That's crazy thinking!"

"Yes, it would be. But Ollie and Sol know Holt just as well as anyone. They've worked around him for years."

"Yes, but people change, darling. Now that Holt has been dating you, he might be thinking differently."

"When I first mentioned Holt you didn't approve of me seeing another wealthy man, Remember?" Isabelle asked pointedly.

"That's because I spoke before I thought," Gabby said. "Having money or several girlfriends in his past doesn't make him a bad person. Nor does it mean he's the wrong man for you."

Her mother had always had a Pollyanna sort of view on everyone and everything. Isabelle sometimes wished she could be more like Gabby. But where Holt was concerned, she had too much of a realistic streak in her to believe he was a changed man.

"Oh, Mom," she said in a choked voice. "This misery is all self-inflicted. I knew all about Holt before I ever agreed to date him. I kept warning myself, but I couldn't resist him. And now I have to own up to the fact that I've made another mistake with a man."

"You've fallen in love with him, haven't you? I can hear it in your voice. I can hear the tears. Oh, Issy, I think—well, I can step away from the art exhibit for a weekend. I'm going to catch a flight up there!"

"No! No! And no! You've been waiting years for a

break like this. You're not going to mess up the exhibit because of me. I'll be fine, Mom. Really."

Gabby was slow about replying and when she finally did, Isabelle was relieved that she sounded reassured.

"All right, honey, if that's the way you want it."

"I do. Now I need to get off the phone. I have laundry to do."

She told her mother goodbye, then hung up and promptly burst into tears.

Early the next morning, Holt was sitting at his desk, trying to sift through a list of hay suppliers, but Isabelle's voice kept drifting through his mind and getting in the way.

To grow my own hay would be a big savings. Especially when my herd gets a lot larger.

She was always so animated when she talked about Blue Stallion. She loved the land and the horses with equal passion. But what about Holt? In lots of ways, she'd showed him that she cared about him. But she'd never said the word *love* to him, or even hinted that she might be falling in love with him.

But you've felt it in her kiss, Holt. You've felt it every time she puts her arms around you. Each time she welcomes you into her bed. That's why you've been finding excuse after excuse to avoid seeing her. You're afraid that you're falling for her, too. And you don't know how to stop it. Other than stop seeing her completely.

To hell with that, he silently shouted back at the arguing voice in his head. He wasn't going to stop seeing Isabelle. She was the only thing that made his life seem worthwhile.

Shaking his head, he tried to refocus his attention on the list in front of him. Burl Iverson, Kern County, California; Walter Williamson, Churchill County, Nevada; Renaldo Ruis, Fresno County, California. The list continued, but Holt's attention was drawn away once again as he caught the sound of a woman's voice just outside the door.

Dear God, he was beginning to hear Isabelle's voice everywhere.

"Thank you, Matthew. You're very kind."

That was her voice! She hadn't said anything about coming here to see him. And at this early hour!

He jumped to his feet just as she was stepping through the open doorway. Her usual smile was nowhere to be seen. In fact, she looked drawn and peaked.

"Isabelle! What are you doing here?"

She carefully shut the door behind her, then walked over and took a seat in one of the chairs in front of his desk.

Not bothering with a greeting, she said, "Don't worry. I'm not here to ask you to introduce me to your family. I'll be gone before they ever know I'm here."

The bitter tone in her voice knocked him off-kilter for a moment. "I'm not sure what that is supposed to mean. But you meeting my family isn't worrying me."

"I'm sure it isn't. Why would it?"

"I don't know. Why would it?" he repeated inanely.

She crossed her legs and tapped the air with the toe of her cowboy boot. This morning she was wearing a pair the color of butterscotch. Tiny metal studs covered the tops and the slanted heels, and he didn't have to be told they cost a fortune. Clearly she wasn't here to walk through the horse paddock, he thought wryly.

"Why would you worry about something you never intended to do in the first place?" she asked, then shook her head. "Sorry, Holt, I'm going at this all wrong. I didn't come here this morning to be curt or tacky. I wanted to be nice about all this. That's the way two people who've shared the same bed should be to each other, wouldn't you say?"

"Nice. Naturally, I would." He walked around the desk and looked down at her. "I'm not yet sure what this visit is about, but I'm glad to see you."

She swallowed hard and as he watched her features tighten, he realized something was very off with her. This wasn't the Isabelle he knew, the Isabelle he'd spent hours with, the one who made him feel as if he was the only man in the world.

"Are you?" she countered.

"Look, Isabelle, if you're angry because I've not been over—" He broke off as she began to shake her head.

"I'm not angry," she said. "I understand you have more work on your shoulders than any one man should have."

Folding his arms across his chest, he said in a slow, inviting voice, "Okay, so if you're not angry, then why aren't you kissing me? Why aren't you telling me how much you've missed seeing me?"

Her sigh was weary. "Because I'm not going to kiss you anymore. I'm not going to see you anymore. Period."

Her words were like a punch in the jaw and he reached backward to clamp a steadying hand around the edge of the desk. "Isabelle, I'm well aware that you like to tease, but this isn't amusing. Frankly, I don't like it."

Her head dropped and Holt was faced with the shiny crown of her blond hair. The other night when she'd talked about finding gold nuggets, he could have told her he'd found his treasure when she'd come into his life. But he'd kept the thought to himself. He didn't dare utter anything she might take to heart. That was the way a man like him had to be.

"I'm not teasing, Holt. Whatever we had between us is over."

"Who says? You? Isn't that a one-sided decision?"

She looked up at him and Holt was shaken by the emptiness he saw in her blue eyes.

"Probably," she answered. "But I'm sure you've made more than your share of those one-sided decisions before. You understand the drill."

He frowned with confusion. "I'll tell you one thing I don't understand—this—you! Do you think I've been seeing another woman? Is that what this is about?"

"I don't think you're seeing other women. Not now, but you will soon." Shaking her head, she stood up and stepped close enough to place her hand on his arm. "Holt, it's become clear to me that the two of us are headed nowhere. At first I told myself that didn't matter. But I can't keep fooling myself. It does matter. All those evenings I waited and watched for you to come to Blue Stallion, I asked myself why I was devoting so much time and emotion. Just to have you in my bed? That's not enough, Holt. And it's my fault for ever thinking it could be."

The anger that poured through him was far more

potent than a double shot of Sam's bourbon. He wanted to ram his fist into the wall. At least he could think about the pain in his hand, instead of the one that was boring a hole in the middle of his chest.

"Oh, this is perfect, Isabelle. This coming from a woman who insisted she didn't want strings between us. Now you're whining because there are no strings."

Her nostrils flared as two red spots appeared on her cheeks. Dear God, she was so beautiful, he thought, so perfect. What was he doing? Had he lost his mind?

No. He was hanging by his fingernails, he thought. He was desperately trying to hold on to his life the way he'd always lived it. The only way he could live it. Without fences or restraints.

"I'm not whining, Holt. I'm walking out. Because I can see the future that I'm dreaming of is nothing like the one in your mind."

He sneered. "Oh, that's right. I keep forgetting you were born to a couple of dreamers. And you have to be just like them—always carrying around a fantasy. What is it now? Rainbows and unicorns? A fairy tale where some prince appears and makes everything perfect for you? Well, I don't want a dreamer. I want a real flesh-and-blood woman!"

Her teeth snapped together. "Good! Because I don't want a man like you! You're just like Trevor—incapable of giving your heart—your love. And as far as I'm concerned, you can go find yourself a real flesh-and-blood woman. Gold Rush Days has Wickenburg brimming over with people. Today would be the perfect time for you to start looking for one!"

She turned to walk away and he instinctively

reached out and caught her forearm. "You're wrong, Isabelle."

Her blue eyes darkened with shadows. "I only wish I were," she said soberly, then quickly added, "Don't worry about your brown mares. I'll have Ollie and Sol bring them to you."

The brown mares. The mares he'd wanted for her and only her. He felt sick to his stomach.

"I don't want the mares! Keep them!"

She pulled her arm from his grasp. "I don't want anything that doesn't belong to me."

There was nothing for him to do now but to watch her walk out the door. But even after she was gone, her soft scent lingered about him, her cutting words continued to wound him.

Holt was still standing in the same spot, trying to compose his fractured emotions, when Blake knocked on the door frame and stepped into the room.

"Was that Isabelle I just saw driving off?"

Holt shoved out a heavy breath and managed to walk around to the back of the desk. As he sank limply into the executive chair, he said, "Yeah. That was her."

Blake poured himself a cup of coffee and took a seat. "Why didn't she hang around? You know how much Mom has been wanting to meet her."

Avoiding the truth would be pointless now, Holt thought miserably. He cleared his throat, but his voice still sounded like he'd been eating chicken scratch. "Mom might as well know that meeting Isabelle isn't going to happen. She just dumped me."

Blake's jaw dropped. "Is this one of your jokes?"

Holt was suddenly furious at himself and the waste of it all. He'd been stupid to attempt to have anything remotely close to a long-term relationship with a woman. Or to think he could ever have what his brothers had with their wives. "No! It isn't anything to joke about, Blake."

Over the rim of his coffee cup, Blake carefully studied Holt's mutinous face. "Well, well. A woman has finally dumped my little brother. How does it feel?" he asked, then barked out a short laugh. "Forget I asked. Whether you did the dumping or she did, you must be feeling damned relieved."

Holt wasn't relieved. He was angry and sick and crushed. Most of all, he was afraid. Scared to even think of the coming days without Isabelle.

Rising from the chair, Holt tugged on his jacket and plopped his hat onto his head. "As much as I appreciate this brotherly visit, I have things to do," he muttered.

Blake frowned at him. "Go ahead. Run off. But before you do, I'll tell you straight out, I'm glad Isabelle put an end to this."

Holt pierced him with a steely look. "Can you explain that?"

"Easily. You're not equipped to handle a woman like her. And I don't want to see you unhappy."

Blood was suddenly boiling beneath Holt's skull. "You do manage Three Rivers, Blake, but that doesn't mean you manage my life," he practically shouted. "And while we're at it, I'll tell you something. If it turns out that our father was a cheating bastard, then our sisters are going to know about it! You and Chandler and Joe might think you know what's best for everybody else, but I have a say in this, too!"

"Holt! What—"

Holt didn't stay around to hear more. He stalked

out of the office and didn't stop until he reached the mares' paddock. But even though he was a quarter mile away from Blake's know-it-all advice, he found no relief from the anger and pain inside him. The sight of the mares milling around in the small pasture only made it worse.

If Ollie and Sol showed up with the brown mares, he'd send the men right back to Blue Stallion Ranch with their load. The mares were a symbol of the day he'd spent with Isabelle in Tucson and the night they'd first made love. The horses were meant to be on Blue Stallion—with Isabelle.

And him? Well, he was going to get out his little black book and find a woman who'd make him forget.

Nearly two weeks later, on Friday evening, Holt was sitting in the den, having a drink with Chandler. A half hour from now, he needed to head to town, where he was meeting his tenth different date in as many nights. He wasn't looking forward to it. Hell, he'd rather pull out his back molars with a pair of fencing plyers than to go pretend he was having a good time. Pretending that the woman sitting across from him was piquing his interest mentally, or sexually.

So why are you doing this, Holt? Why do you keep going through this long list of ladies, when you know none of them are going to wipe Isabelle from your mind? She's burned into your brain and no matter what you do, she's going to remain there.

The mimicking voice in his head was like a propaganda message being shouted repeatedly over a megaphone. And if it didn't stop soon, he was going to go crazy, Holt thought.

"Well, look who's here! Our beautiful sister," Chandler said, suddenly breaking into Holt's miserable ponderings.

Holt looked around to see Vivian strolling into the den. Since she was still wearing her ranger uniform, it was obvious she'd driven straight here to Three Rivers from her job at Lake Pleasant. He couldn't imagine what she was doing here, but he was more than pleased to see her.

Rising to his feet, Holt said, "Hi, sis. This is a nice surprise."

Chandler rose, too, and both brothers kissed their sister's cheek.

"Did you forget and think you still lived here at Three Rivers?" Chandler teased.

Vivian chuckled. "No. Pregnancy hasn't confused the navigation system in my head. I do still remember east from west."

"Sit down and I'll make you something to drink," Holt told her. "Take the chair by the fire. It's cold out this evening."

"Just a bit of sparkling water or juice," she told him as she sank into the wingback chair. "I can't stay long."

While Holt went to a small bar in the corner of the room to get the drink, Chandler's phone began to buzz.

"You two are going to have to excuse me," he said as he scanned the message. "Roslyn needs me upstairs. Evelyn is throwing one of her fits. The little diva never wants to get out of the bathtub."

"Tell me about it," Vivian said with a laugh. "I have a fourteen-year-old diva."

"Bah!" Holt said as he handed her a small glass of orange juice. "Hannah has never been spoiled. Well, there might've been a few occasions when I spoiled her a little."

"You certainly did—letting her ride those wild two-year-olds when I wasn't looking. It's a wonder she didn't break every bone in her body!"

He eased down in the matching chair across from her and took a long sip of his drink. It was the second one he'd had this evening, and since he'd not eaten anything but a few bites of gooseberry pie early this morning, his stomach was more than empty. Now the bourbon was going straight to his head. Thank God. He didn't want to have to think. Not about anything.

Vivian watched Chandler leave the room, then glanced over at Holt. She didn't appear to be in a happy mood, but he smiled at her anyway.

"That belly of yours is getting enormous," he told her. "Makes you look real pretty."

She eyed his half-full glass. "How much of that bourbon have you had this evening?"

"Not enough," he muttered.

She grimaced. "Aren't you wondering why I'm here?"

He shrugged. "I figured you came to see Mom. She's not made it in yet. She and Blake went up to check out some of the Prescott ranges."

She took a sip of the juice. "I know. She texted me."

"Oh." He darted a glance at her. "Then why are you here?"

"Because Mom and Chandler told me you looked like hell and I wanted to see if they were right."

His jaw tight, he stared into the fire. "Were they?"

"No. They were wrong. You look worse. What are you doing? Trying to commit a slow suicide?"

"I'm not trying to do anything," he lied. "I've just gone back to being good ole Holt. You know, the one that changes women as often as he changes wet saddle blankets."

"Don't try to play cool with me. I may not live in this house anymore, but I hear what goes on. And I hear you've been staying out late every night, dating one woman after another. Are you actually enjoying this marathon you're putting yourself through?"

He rose from the chair and stood on the hearth with his back to the fire. After swigging down a good portion of his drink, he said, "It's nice that you've always thought of yourself as my little mother, Viv. But in this case, I don't need your mothering. There's nothing wrong."

She snorted. "Don't try to give me any of your bologna. It won't work. And you might as well down the rest of that drink. Because you're going to need it after you hear what I have to say!"

He frowned at her. "I have a date tonight. In fact, I should be getting ready to leave right now. I don't have time for a lecture from my big sister."

"Cancel the date. You're not going anywhere."

The stern resolution on her pretty face got to him more than anything she'd said and he suddenly bent his head and closed his eyes against the onslaught of pain hitting him from every direction. Of the whole Hollister family, Vivian had always loved him the most. Just as Isabelle had loved him.

Oh, yes, he could admit that to himself now. Even if she hadn't so much as spoken the words to him, he'd known it and felt it in his heart. He'd just not wanted to acknowledge her feelings or think about what any of it meant to him. Now he could only wonder if he'd thrown away the most precious gift he could've ever been given.

Vivian's hand suddenly rested on his arm and he looked up to see she'd joined him on the hearth.

"Why did you let this breakup with Isabelle happen? And don't try to tell me your relationship with her was nothing. I can see how much you're hurting."

He groaned. "I didn't let it happen, Viv. She's the one who ended things."

"No. You did. Because you couldn't be honest with her. You couldn't tell her that you loved her or wanted to be with her for the rest of your life. No, that would have taken some guts. Courage that you don't seem to have."

He scowled at her. "What do you know about it?"

"Ha! You ask me that after all I've been through? Think about it, Holt. Before I met Sawyer, he was a known ladies' man. I didn't trust him any farther than I could throw him. Plus, he was just like you. He didn't believe he could ever be a husband or father."

Holt looked at her as he remembered back to those days when Vivian had been agonizing over falling in love with the wrong man, or so she'd believed. "I called you a 'fraidy cat back then," he recalled. "I told you that if you really loved Sawyer you needed to hold on to him and never let go."

She smiled. "That's right. Imagine me taking love advice from my tomcat brother. But I did. And because I did, I learned real love has a way of taking away all those doubts and fears we have. If you let yourself grab hold of Isabelle and never let go, you'll learn that, too."

He scrubbed a hand over his haggard face. He had

to find the guts to face Isabelle again, to tell her exactly how he felt about her. Otherwise, his life was going to be a big black hole. "She doesn't want me in her life. Not now."

"Since when would you let something like that stop you? Don't you think you can change her mind?"

"I don't know," he mumbled. "Maybe Holt Hollister has lost his mojo."

Laughing now, Vivian leaned over and kissed his cheek. "You'll never lose that, little brother."

The next morning, Isabelle tethered the brown mares beneath the tin overhang of the barn and began the chore of grooming them. Since there'd been a sprinkle of rain sometime during the night, the horses had enjoyed a roll in the damp dirt. Now dust flew as Isabelle moved the brush over the mare's back.

She'd never intended to keep the pair. She'd even loaded them in the trailer and had Ollie and Sol drive them over to Three Rivers Ranch. But they'd come back with the two mares and told her that Holt had refused to take them. After that, Isabelle had decided not to worry about the matter. If he wanted the mares, he knew where they were. He could send some of his hands to collect them.

"Need some help?"

Isabelle looked around to see Ollie walking up near the mare's hip. Sol was a step behind him.

"No. I got this." She continued to brush down the horse's shoulder. "It's Saturday. Aren't you guys going into town for coffee at the Broken Spur? There might be some single women hanging around just waiting to join you."

"We're going." Sol spoke up. "But we don't expect to see any women."

"Don't ever say never, Sol," Ollie told his buddy. "We might get lucky one of these days."

Isabelle glanced up just in time to see Sol frowning at Ollie and making a motion toward her. From the sheepish looks on their faces, she decided they wanted to discuss something with her but felt awkward about it.

"What's up, you two? Is there something you want to talk to me about? Are you needing a raise in salary?"

"Oh, no, Isabelle. We're making more than enough money," Sol was quick to answer.

"We don't need money," Ollie added. "You just forget about that, Isabelle."

She didn't see how the men could consider the meager amount of salary she paid them as plenty, but for now it was the best she could do. Later, when the ranch began to actually take in money, she'd do her best to give them a substantial raise. "Okay. Then what's on your mind?"

"We're wondering about Holt," Ollie answered. "He hasn't been here for a while. And when we hauled the mares over to Three Rivers, he wasn't exactly a happy camper. Did you two have a falling-out or something?"

Isabelle bit down on her bottom lip to stem the tears that burned her eyes. "Uh—I guess you could put it that way. I'm not seeing Holt anymore. I decided he— wasn't the right guy for me."

Sol exchanged a guarded look with Ollie. "We thought— To be honest, we didn't much think Holt was the right guy for you. But you were happy when he was coming around. You're not happy now."

It was all Isabelle could do to keep from bursting into tears. These past two weeks since she'd parted ways with Holt, she'd never hurt so badly or felt so empty inside.

"For a while there I was mixed up. I thought Holt was the right guy for me. But you two know Holt. He's not the marrying kind. And I want—well, I want more than just a boyfriend."

Ollie said, "Isabelle, if you're letting gossip about Holt sway your thinking, then you're messing up. Sure, he's been a bachelor for a long time, but he's a good man. Better than you probably even know."

Sol cleared his throat and frowned at Ollie. "It might take some doing, but me and Ollie figure if anybody can settle his roaming ways, it'd be you."

"That's right," Ollie added with a nod of his head. "If you care anything about him, you ought to go after him. You don't want some undeserving gal to snatch him up."

Isabelle pulled a tissue from the pocket on her jacket and dabbed her misty eyes. "Oh, guys, this doesn't have anything to do with gossip. I've been married once and that man didn't love me. I, uh, don't want to get into that again."

Ollie gave her a kindly smile while Sol patted her shoulder.

"We just want you to be happy," Ollie said.

"Yeah, that's what we want," Sol added. "So you think about what we said, Isabelle."

The two men must have decided they'd talked enough. Sol mumbled that they'd see her later and the two of them walked off. Moments later, she heard them climb into their truck and drive away.

Isabelle thoughtfully went back to grooming the mares, but all the while she brushed and curried, her mind was replaying everything she'd said to Holt and everything he'd said to her that last day she'd seen him at Three Rivers. The whole scene was like watching the world crumble around her.

He'd accused her of living with her head in the clouds, of fantasizing of a prince coming to make her life perfect. Was Holt right? Was she guilty of wanting too much from him? Expecting too much from the brief time they'd been together?

With Trevor, she'd waited for more than two years, hoping his feelings for her would turn into real love. It hadn't happened. She'd accused Holt of being just like her ex, incapable of giving his heart. But she'd flung those words at him out of hurt and frustration.

Holt wasn't like Trevor. He wasn't like any man she'd ever known. He was incredibly special. He was everything she'd ever wanted and she loved him. Now that she'd found him, she couldn't give up and let him slip away.

But would he be willing to try again? She wouldn't know the answer to that until she faced him and laid her heart out for him to see.

Determination fueling her, Isabelle quickly finished the grooming chore, then released the mares into a nearby paddock. As she hurried to the house, she decided not to text or call him. No. Better to catch him off guard, she thought, than to give him a chance to run from her.

Inside the house, she went straight to her bedroom

closet and began searching through the hangered clothes for something suitable to wear. She needed something feminine. Something that would make her look irresistible to him.

No, she thought suddenly. She shut the closet door and walked over to the dresser mirror. The image staring back at her was a woman dressed for the job she loved. This Isabelle, in her jeans, yellow shirt, and dusty boots, was the essence of who she was and what she wanted. If Holt couldn't love her like this, then she truly needed to put him behind her once and for all.

With that decision made, she went back to the kitchen to collect her handbag and truck keys.

And then she heard it. The rattling sound of a stock trailer coming down the long driveway.

Who on earth could that be? Ollie and Sol hadn't taken a trailer with them. And it couldn't be a horse buyer. It would be a year or more before she began advertising Blue Stallion Ranch.

Deciding someone had taken the wrong backroad and was lost, she exited the front of the house and from the edge of the porch, peered out at the vehicle that was rolling to a gentle stop.

Oh! Oh, my! It was Holt's truck and an expensive-looking horse van hooked to it.

Her heart racing wildly, she watched him climb down from the cab and start toward the house. The moment he spotted her, he paused briefly, then continued striding toward her.

Fearful and hopeful at the same time, Isabelle stepped off the porch and began walking toward him, until the two of them met just inside the yard gate.

"Hello, Holt," she said, relieved that she'd managed

to squeeze the words past her tight throat. "Are you here to collect your brown mares?"

The expression on his face was unlike anything she'd seen on him before. It was rueful and pleading and so raw that it made her ache just to look at him.

"Those aren't my mares," he said huskily. "Those are yours and ours—together. Remember? We're partners."

Tears filled her eyes and spilled onto her cheeks. "Are we?"

Groaning, he reached for her and Isabelle fell willingly into his arms. His face buried itself in the curve of her neck and she wrapped her arms tightly around him.

"Isabelle. My darling, Isabelle," he said hoarsely. "Will you forgive me for being a blind, stubborn fool?"

She let out a sob of joy. "I'm the one who should be asking for forgiveness. I'm the one who broke us apart. But only because—"

He eased his head back and looked deeply into her eyes. "We both know that everything you said that day in my office was true. That's why it made me so angry. For years, my family warned me that one day I'd find my match and fall in love. I didn't believe them. Until you forced me to see how empty my life would be without you. I love you, Isabelle. More than you can ever know."

Holt didn't just want her. He loved her! The knowledge caused something to burst inside her and send sweet, warm contentment flowing into her heart.

"Oh, Holt, I love you so much. But I was afraid to tell you. Afraid you didn't want to hear it."

"I didn't want to hear it," he admitted, "because

it would've forced me to examine my own feelings." Smiling, he pressed his cheek against hers. "But I want to hear it now, Isabelle. Every day. For the rest of our lives."

She was trying to take in the wonder of those words when, a few feet behind them, a loud whinny sounded from inside the horse trailer. Across the way, the freshly groomed brown mares answered the call.

Isabelle eased out of his arms and looked at the horse van. The side windows were closed, blocking any view of the interior, but the subtle rocking movements told her a horse was inside.

Her gaze slipped back to Holt. "You brought a horse with you?"

Grinning, he caught her by the hand and led her out to the truck and trailer. "Not just any horse," he said, then with a hand on her arm, carefully guided her to a safe spot. "Let me show you."

A minute later, Isabelle stared in stunned disbelief as he backed the blue roan stallion down the loading ramp and onto the ground. "That's Blue Midnight! What is he doing here?"

His expression full of love and tenderness, Holt handed the horse's lead rope over to Isabelle. "He's yours now. He's going to make Blue Stallion Ranch more than just your dream, Isabelle. He's going to help turn this place into a prosperous horse farm for you—for us. That is, if you want me here with you."

"As my partner?" she asked.

"Your partner, lover, husband, and father of your children. Anything you want me to be," he told her, then with a big grin, added, "As long as I don't have to sleep in the bunkroom with Ollie and Sol."

"You want us to be married? But what about those strings you never wanted? What about your job at Three Rivers?"

She barely got the question out when Blue Midnight nudged her in the back and propelled her right into Holt's loving arms.

His hands cupped her face. "You can throw a lariat on me if you want—just as long as we're together. As for my managing the horse division at Three Rivers, I can still do that and help you, too. My family has been telling me to hire more trainers to ease my workload. The time has come for me to follow their advice." He brought his lips next to hers. "I want Blue Stallion Ranch to be my home—our home. Together."

"Oh, Holt, I'm so glad you've come home to Blue Stallion Ranch."

He closed the tiny distance between their lips and as he gave her a kiss full of promises, Blue Midnight looked over at the brown mares and whinnied a promise of his own.

Epilogue

"You know, roses are delicate and romantic. Most women like having a garden of roses in their backyard," Holt said as he peered down at Isabelle who was on her hands and knees, carefully planting a large barrel cactus. "But no, you want a garden of tough, thorny cacti."

Tilting her head back, she pulled a playful face at him. "That's right. How long do you think a rose would last in this blistering heat? Besides, cacti have beautiful blooms," she argued.

"They grow at glacier speed and you're lucky if they bloom once a year," he pointed out.

She stood up and brushed her gloved hands on the seat of her jeans. "You want instant gratification. That's your problem," she joked and poked a finger into his hard abs. "I honestly don't know how you bear to wait eleven months and twenty days for a foal to be born."

"Patience, my beautiful Isabelle. I'm brimming over with it. That's why I waited until I was thirty-three to find the perfect wife for me."

"Ha! You mean you waited until I chased you down. Or did you chase me?" She laughed and curled an arm around his lean waist. "It doesn't matter, does it? We caught each other."

A little more than six months ago, she and Holt had been married in a simple ceremony here on Blue Stallion Ranch. All of the Hollister family and a few of their close friends had attended, along with Isabelle's mother and father. Emily-Ann had acted as Isabelle's maid of honor, while Chandler had stood next to Holt as his best man.

Isabelle's dreams had come true that day as she and Holt had spoken their vows of love to each other. And since then, she could truthfully say she was happier than she could have ever imagined.

Holt nudged her toward the back door of the house. "The sun is going down. We'd better go in and get ready. If I know Reeva, she'll have Jazelle passing out drinks and appetizers two hours before dinner."

Tonight they were going to Three Rivers Ranch to attend Blake's fortieth birthday party. From past visits to the big ranch house, Isabelle knew there would be piles of delicious foods and all sorts of drinks, along with plenty of conversation and laughter.

"I'm going to miss seeing your mother tonight," Isabelle remarked. "Do you have any idea when she might be coming home?"

A little more than two weeks ago, Maureen had

packed up and driven down to Red Bluff to visit her youngest daughter, Camille. Her decision to make the trip had been rather sudden and Isabelle knew the rest of the family didn't quite know what to make of Maureen's unexpected departure. All of them wondered if she'd gone down there with intentions of bringing Camille back to Three Rivers, or if she'd made the trip just as a way to escape whatever was gnawing at her.

"Blake heard from her last night. He said she sounded cheerful enough, but he couldn't pin her down as to when she might be coming home." He shook his head. "This isn't like her at all, Isabelle. Normally, she's content to be working around the branding fire or herding cattle."

"Well, you do you have a few cowboys working the ranch down there. Could be she's keeping busy helping them," Isabelle reasoned. "Or it could be that she simply wants to be with her daughter."

Holt nodded. "That's true. Camille has been gone for a couple of years now. I know Mom misses her." He wrapped an arm against her back and urged her into the house. "Come on, we can't let any of this dampen the party."

Inside the house, they walked through the kitchen and started down the long hallway to the bedroom. As they passed the open door to the guest bedroom, Holt said, "Speaking of mothers, where is yours? Isn't she going to the party with us?"

A month ago, Gabby had flown up from San Diego for an extended visit. So far, her mother had been having a blast getting to know the Hollisters and exploring Wickenburg and the surrounding areas. Isabelle loved having her mother's company and Holt seemed to enjoy her offbeat personality. Thankfully she made it a point not to intrude on their privacy.

"Yes. Mom's going to the party. But not from here. She's over at the Bar X with Sam. They'll be leaving for the party from there."

Holt paused to shoot her a comical look. "Gabby is with Sam?"

Isabelle laughed. "I know. It's hard to figure. She took one look at the old cowboy and flipped. Now she's talked him into sitting still long enough to let her paint his portrait."

Chuckling, Holt shook his head in amazement. "Do you really think she's attracted to him? In a romantic way?"

Isabelle made a palms-up gesture. "Who knows? I thought she was falling for the guy who exhibited her artwork. But she's obviously forgotten all about him."

They entered the bedroom and while Holt showered, Isabelle began to lay out the clothing she was planning to wear for the party.

"Isabelle? Are you sure you don't mind going tonight?" Holt called to her over the sound of the running shower. "I know it must feel like we go over to Three Rivers for some reason all the time."

She walked over to the open doorway of the bathroom to answer. "I love visiting with your family. Gives me a chance to see all the new babies. Vivian and Sawyer's twin boys, Jacob and Johnny, and Tessa and Joe's new daughter, Spring. And just think, it won't be long before Chandler and Roslyn have their second baby to go with little Evelyn. I think her due date is sometime before Halloween."

The shower turned off and Holt stepped out of the

glass enclosure and wrapped a towel around his waist. The sight of his hard, muscled body never failed to excite her and just for a moment she considered stepping into the bathroom and pulling the towel away.

Grinning slyly, his wet hair tousled around his head, he walked over to her. "Are you sure you don't have something to tell me? Like the smell of breakfast is making you sick?"

She tried not to smile. "Actually breakfast has been tasting better than ever."

"Damn."

Her smile grew coy. "Could be I'm eating for two."

His eyes grew wide. "Is that what I think it means?"

The eager hope in his voice told her how very much he wanted to be a father.

She nodded. "I made a doctor's appointment today. We'll find out for certain tomorrow."

"Oh, Isabelle, honey!" He pulled her into his arms and she laughed as she wrapped her arms around his wet torso. "This is fantastic! I'm going to be a father! Let's tell the family tonight. While everybody is there."

She leaned back far enough to look at him. "But, Holt, we don't know for certain yet."

He gently touched his fingertips to her cheek. "I'm certain. You have a glow in your eyes."

"That's because I'm looking at the man I love." She kissed him, then added slyly, "By the way, I thought you might want to know that Ollie and Sol made a confession today."

His brows arched. "That's good to hear. I'll bet the priest was exhausted before they ever finished."

She pinched his arm. "Not that kind of confession! They ratted on you. About how you paid them an extra salary long before we got married. Why did you do that?"

Pulling her close, he rested his cheek against hers. "Can't you guess? That was just my way of saying I love you, darling."

* * * * *

Get 4 FREE REWARDS!

We'll send you 2 FREE Books plus 2 FREE Mystery Gifts.

FREE Value Over **$20**

Both the **Romance** and **Suspense** collections feature compelling novels written by many of today's bestselling authors.

YES! Please send me 2 FREE novels from the Essential Romance or Essential Suspense Collection and my 2 FREE gifts (gifts are worth about $10 retail). After receiving them, if I don't wish to receive any more books, I can return the shipping statement marked "cancel." If I don't cancel, I will receive 4 brand-new novels every month and be billed just $7.49 each in the U.S. or $7.74 each in Canada. That's a savings of at least 17% off the cover price. It's quite a bargain! Shipping and handling is just 50¢ per book in the U.S. and $1.25 per book in Canada.* I understand that accepting the 2 free books and gifts places me under no obligation to buy anything. I can always return a shipment and cancel at any time by calling the number below. The free books and gifts are mine to keep no matter what I decide.

Choose one: ☐ **Essential Romance**
(194/394 MDN GRHV)

☐ **Essential Suspense**
(191/391 MDN GRHV)

Name (please print)

Address   Apt. #

City   State/Province   Zip/Postal Code

Email: Please check this box ☐ if you would like to receive newsletters and promotional emails from Harlequin Enterprises ULC and its affiliates. You can unsubscribe anytime.

Mail to the Harlequin Reader Service:
IN U.S.A.: P.O. Box 1341, Buffalo, NY 14240-8531
IN CANADA: P.O. Box 603, Fort Erie, Ontario L2A 5X3

Want to try 2 free books from another series? Call 1-800-873-8635 or visit www.ReaderService.com

STRS22R3

Get 4 FREE REWARDS!

We'll send you 2 FREE Books plus 2 FREE Mystery Gifts.

FREE
Value Over
$20

Both the **Harlequin® Special Edition** and **Harlequin® Heartwarming™** series feature compelling novels filled with stories of love and strength where the bonds of friendship, family and community unite.

YES! Please send me 2 FREE novels from the Harlequin Special Edition or Harlequin Heartwarming series and my 2 FREE gifts (gifts are worth about $10 retail). After receiving them, if I don't wish to receive any more books, I can return the shipping statement marked "cancel." If I don't cancel, I will receive 6 brand-new Harlequin Special Edition books every month and be billed just $5.49 each in the U.S. or $6.24 each in Canada, a savings of at least 12% off the cover price, or 4 brand-new Harlequin Heartwarming Larger-Print books every month and be billed just $6.24 each in the U.S. or $6.74 each in Canada, a savings of at least 19% off the cover price. It's quite a bargain! Shipping and handling is just 50¢ per book in the U.S. and $1.25 per book in Canada.* I understand that accepting the 2 free books and gifts places me under no obligation to buy anything. I can always return a shipment and cancel at any time by calling the number below. The free books and gifts are mine to keep no matter what I decide.

Choose one: ☐ **Harlequin Special Edition**
(235/335 HDN GRJV)
☐ **Harlequin Heartwarming**
Larger-Print
(161/361 HDN GRJV)

Name (please print)

Address   Apt. #

City   State/Province   Zip/Postal Code

Email: Please check this box ☐ if you would like to receive newsletters and promotional emails from Harlequin Enterprises ULC and its affiliates. You can unsubscribe anytime.

Mail to the **Harlequin Reader Service:**
IN U.S.A.: P.O. Box 1341, Buffalo, NY 14240-8531
IN CANADA: P.O. Box 603, Fort Erie, Ontario L2A 5X3

Want to try 2 free books from another series! Call 1-800-873-8635 or visit www.ReaderService.com.

*Terms and prices subject to change without notice. Prices do not include sales taxes, which will be charged (if applicable) based on your state or country of residence. Canadian residents will be charged applicable taxes. Offer not valid in Quebec. This offer is limited to one order per household. Books received may not be as shown. Not valid for current subscribers to the Harlequin Special Edition or Harlequin Heartwarming series. All orders subject to approval. Credit or debit balances in a customer's account(s) may be offset by any other outstanding balance owed by or to the customer. Please allow 4 to 6 weeks for delivery. Offer available while quantities last.

Your Privacy—Your information is being collected by Harlequin Enterprises ULC, operating as Harlequin Reader Service. For a complete summary of the information we collect, how we use this information and to whom it is disclosed, please visit our privacy notice located at corporate.harlequin.com/privacy-notice. From time to time we may also exchange your personal information with reputable third parties. If you wish to opt out of this sharing of your personal information, please visit readerservice.com/consumerschoice or call 1-800-873-8635. **Notice to California Residents**—Under California law, you have specific rights to control and access your data. For more information on these rights and how to exercise them, visit corporate.harlequin.com/california-privacy.

HSEHW22R3